I0602393

Black Stones of Ter Chadain

C. S. Yelle

Dedication

This book is dedicated to my wife Jenny, my sons Karsen, Baxter, and Kasey, and daughter Amy for their constant support. To my "Beta" Mike, his patient wife Kathy, and Editor Dick Sackett, for their guidance and polish. To my friends Steve and Yvonne for their encouragement. To my proofers, Wendy, Kathy, Mary, and Jan who found what I didn't. To Devan Michaels at Nimbi Design for the incredible cover. Most of all, to my family, my friends, my high school classmates of Grand Rapids Senior High, and the fans who have supported me in this endeavor.

Protector of Ter Chadain Characters

Name	Title or Position
Logan Lassain	Protector of Ter Chadain
Saliday Talis	Tarken/Tracker
Sasha	Betra/Seeker
Teah Lassain	Queen/Protector of Ter Chadain
Lizzy Bridon	Zele Magus Student
Rachel Craddick	Zele Magus Student
Galena	Zele Magus/Mistress of Power
Caldora	Zele Magus/King's Magical Advisor
Ordestan	Captain
Redrick	Governor
Morgan Task	Captain of the Morning Breeze/Tarken
DukeBanderkin	Duke of Fareband
Talesaur	Captain of the Queen's Guard
Mr. Gentry	First Mate of the Caltoria Star/slave
Zeva	Governor Redrick's slave
Niles	Viri Magus
Bastion	First Protector of Ter Chadain
Falcone	Protector betrayed by Zele Magus
Stalwart	Protector betrayed by Viri Magus
Galiven	Protector killed by the Betra
Benton	First Mate of Morning Breeze
Quinty	First Mate of Morning Breeze
Raven Gassler	Scalded Island magical leader of revolution
Massa Blane	Seer of magical revolution on Scalded
Caslor	Son of Empress Shakata
Shakata	Empress of Caltoria
RowanAnthony	General of Caltoria/Lover of Empress
Governor Stone	Governor of Scalded Island
Berza	Female personal slave of Empress Shakata
Tanlor	Male personal slave of Empress Shakata
Brock	Stone Town revolution supporter who
Dee	Brock's wife
Grinwald	Viri Magus

CALTORIA
Bellatora
Palace
Stone Town
Governor's Residence
Marshlad Valley
Spire of Pamania
Scalded Island

Prologue

The old woman strolled across the bridge separating the two houses of magic of Ter Chadain, her breath plainly visible from her mouth and nose as a light mist on this cold night. The large buildings dwarfed her small frame, towering over her in proclamation of their dominance in this world.

She could have been any woman at that moment. A homeless woman, a traveler, a beggar, but she was none of these. She strode with confidence that exuded from her even at this waning hour and alone and seemingly vulnerable. But if anyone thought her vulnerable, they would be mistaken. For here walked the Magus Matris, the leader of the Zele Magus, the order of female magicals in Ter Chadain.

She moved closer to the looming brown castle which housed the Viri Magus, the order of male magicals in Ter Chadain. She didn't come here often, even though her Citadel stood just across the bridge, but this night she came to discuss happenings and plan strategies with the Magus Patris, leader of the Viri Magus. Jelisia approached the gate. The two guards on either side of the entrance looked her way, but did not straighten from their relaxed posture leaning against the columns flanking the portal.

A wave of her hand and the guards froze in place as she passed, not able to move or see her any longer. She smiled as she entered the courtyard, the thought of the guard's lack of recollection of her passing pleasing her. This visit needed to be as unnoticed as possible.

She continued through the deserted corridors, weaving her way higher and deeper into the stone castle, her footsteps echoed faintly as she went, until she stopped at the large oak doors. She reached up and tapped the darkened wood with her hand and the doors opened as the hinges creaked in protest. Jelisia stepped through and the doors closed behind her with a resonating thud.

The room welcomed her with warmth and she removed her cloak and let her hazy blue eyes take in the outer chambers of the Magus Patris. A fire crackled in the fireplace lighting the small area in the dark room where two high-backed chairs sat with a small round table set between them. On the table a golden pitcher and two golden goblets glistened in the firelight.

Jelisia walked around and sat in the only vacant chair, nodding at the shadowed figure occupying the other.

"Welcome," the deep voice said as a large hand reached over, grasped the pitcher and poured wine in first one, then the other goblet. The hand set the pitcher down and lifted a goblet, handing it to the Magus Matris.

Jelisia took the goblet with a nod and drank.

The occupant of the other chair grasped the remaining goblet and drank deeply.

"Things have taken a turn away from our desired path," he said.

"Indeed." The Magus Matris nodded.

"I blame the guidance of the boy for the wayward direction he has taken. . . but his mission was still accomplished as we'd hoped."

"You had no way of foreseeing that your most powerful Viri Magus would be killed so early in Logan's quest, Jonathan."

"Grinwald's loss has cut deeply."

Jelisia took another drink." I never expected Zele Caldora to turn to King Englewood's path so easily. She turned out to be our largest obstacle to placing Logan's sister, Teah on the throne."

"I agree."

"It is regrettable that Grinwald was lost to her before he had the chance to council the boy on his Viri Magus abilities," she added.

"And yet you allowed him to leave the Citadel without notifying us of his presence," the Magus Matris growled.

"We needed expediency and you would have held him up for training, a delay we couldn't afford."

He stared at her hard, his anger glowing in his eyes with the reflection of the fire.

"We shouldn't have to worry about that any longer now that the boy has killed King Englewood and cleared the way for his sister to claim the throne. He can come and train with us as soon as she takes her rightful place."

"That is good news, but there is a problem still, I fear." "And what is that?"

"Teah, along with Galena and two other Zele Magus Students, have been taken by the Caltorians," the Magus Matris said the sorrow heavy in her voice.

"So Logan must take the throne and activate the spell barring the Caltorians from entering Ter Chadain himself," the Magus Patris rationalized.

The Magus Matris took another drink and sighed.

"The spell only works with the female heir to the throne. Logan cannot do this, it must be Teah."

"Where have the Caltorians taken the queen?"

"They appear to be headed for the port city of Stalwart," the Magus Matris said.

The comment straightened the shadowed figure in his chair and he leaned forward revealing the man's massive, muscular build. His long dark brown hair pulled back in a tail showed the years of experience as silver at his temple. He glared at her with anger and fear raging beneath the surface of his deep brown eyes.

"We cannot let this happen," he said, the anger shaking his voice, betraying his control." Logan is headed to Stalwart as well and if the Caltorians leave with Teah, he will be sure to follow. We could lose them both to the Empress."

"That would be the end of Ter Chadain," the Magus Matris said gravely.

"The spirits help us," the Magus Patris whispered.

Chapter 1

The rain whipped at Logan's face as he leaned into his horse, urging the mount on not only with his legs, but his growing sense of urgency. His dark green, rain-soaked clothing weighed him down, only deepening the feeling of impending doom.

He pushed his thoughts out from his mind, reaching for any sign, any glimmer of Teah. Shaking his head in frustration, he wiped the rain from his eyes only to have fresh rain fill them again.

When will this incessant rain end?

We have no better insight into the weather than you, Bastion said.

I didn't mean. . . never mind.

Ever since Logan and Teah became protectors, they made contact mentally and spoke every day. Every day until Captain Ordestan reached Teah and her party. From that moment on, nothing.

Saliday Talis rode hard behind him, pushing to keep her horse close to his. Her forest green cloak clung to her small, shapely body as her auburn hair stuck to her face. The last of the Tarken people, she homed in on Teah and led them to her.

Sasha crouched in her saddle struggling to keep the vicious pace. Her people, the Betra, exiled for hundreds of years by the Queen of Ter Chadain, now sought restitution for their past crimes by protecting Logan and aiding his cause. Her lanky, but muscular, body jostled and slipped in the wet saddle. She kept a watchful eye on Logan's back, fighting through her fatigue and embracing her duty as the, "Seeker of the Protector."

The three had outdistanced the regiment of cavalry about a day before as the path became more treacherous with the continuing rain. Logan and his companions pressed on, not willing to wait, needing to reach Stalwart on the northwestern most tip of Ter Chadain. Scouts followed Ordestan and his party to Stalwart and discovered he awaited a ship to take his prisoners to Caltoria.

They named this after you? Logan directed his thought to Stalwart.

One cannot control what is done in your name after he is dead, Stalwart said and Logan nodded.

Saliday explained that Ordestan collected magicals to take back to Caltoria to infuse their slave population with stronger magic. Her own village fell prey to this type of collecting, leaving her the last of her kind in Ter Chadain.

The three riders pulled up on a ridge overlooking the port city of Stalwart. Ships of various sizes sat in the slips. A flurry of activity bustled on and around the ships as dock workers loaded and unloaded cargo.

The rain slowed to a light drizzle and Logan pushed back his cloak's hood from his long, wet hair that was tied back in a tail. He studied the port, looking for the ship bearing the symbols he sought. He straightened in his saddle and pointed into the distance at a ship with a star emblem painted on the stern.

"The Caltoria Star, sitting in the third slip from the right."

Saliday and Sasha struggled to see the ship Logan pointed to through the waning light. They looked at each other with sadness. Armed soldiers lined the deck as well as the docks around the largest ship in port.

"All right," Logan said, taking the reins from the saddle horn and pulling his mount's head up." Let's go get her."

Saliday reached over, grasped hold of the horse's harness, and stopped it with a jerk.

Logan looked confused and frowned.

"What are we going to do, walk into the midst of the enemy and proclaim, 'The Protector of Ter Chadain has arrived', and they will fall to their knees in fear?" Saliday asked.

"Either that or they can die by my blades," Logan said without emotion.

"Don't be a fool, you aren't invincible," Saliday said and then grimaced as Logan glared.

He leaned across his saddle, getting close to her face, his breath brushing her cheeks and eyes. His eyes held such intensity Saliday struggled to hold her ground.

"I know I'm not invincible, but what would you have me do?" He said in a hiss.

"Uh, wait for the cavalry to arrive and then go and get her," Saliday said putting as much conviction in her uncertain words as she could.

"I agree with Saliday, Master," Sasha added, drawing Logan's unwanted attention from Saliday, who sighed with relief when he turned to the Betra.

"They are at least a day out and it appears the Caltoria Star is nearly ready to depart. I can't take that chance." He held Sasha's gaze until she nodded. He turned back to Saliday who jumped with a start at his stare and also agreed with a shrug." Then we go now," he said with a nod and pulled the reins free from Saliday's hand.

As they turned to descend the ridge, a horn's call rose up from the harbor and men scurried from around the Caltoria Star up the gang planks and the lines fastening the ship to the pier loosed. The large ship began to ease from the slip, water already showing in the space to her stern.

"No," Logan cried and kicked his mount into motion.

Sasha and Saliday rushed after as Logan barreled down the ridge at a breakneck pace, crashing through brush and anything else in his path. He reached the main road and raced through the town's gates without slowing, even as the guards commanded him to halt. They bounced off his horse's chest and into the entrance walls, dazed by the sudden aggression.

Saliday and Sasha followed, staring at the stunned men in surprise. By the time they reached the slip where the Caltoria Star docked, Logan battled with more than twenty Caltorian soldiers.

Logan's anger raged unchecked as he hewed down anyone in his path. He took one soldier's arm off and spun smoothly to decapitate another standing too close behind. The soldiers, now aware of their peril, widened the once close circle around the protector.

Sasha and Saliday rode into the circle and slid from their horses before they stopped. Saliday raced to the front of the fight, a short sword in each hand.

"Surrender now to 'The Protector of Ter Chadain', or die," she said, her tone leaving no room for doubt.

A flurry of steel hitting the dock followed. Sasha collected the weapons and herded the prisoners to one side. Logan and Saliday stood on the dock, staring out at the Caltoria Star two hundred or more yards out, easing through the mouth of the harbor.

Logan spun and strode over to one of the prisoners leaning against the wall of a nearby warehouse. Lifting him off his feet by the front of his shirt, Logan stared down at the terrified man. "Did they have magicals on board?" Logan asked.

"Uh, uh, yes," the man stammered.

"Women magicals?" Logan pressed.

"Yes, my lord, all the magicals on board were women."

Logan let out a roar and threw the man against the wall where he slid down and crumbled into a heap. The protectors inside Logan's head broke free of the barrier in his mind and erupted into exclamations of dismay and plans of action. Logan closed his eyes and fought the voices back." Stop it, quiet, all of you. I need to think. Please, when you talk at once, I hear nothing. Stop!" Logan said, his words building to a scream.

Sasha and Saliday looked at Logan in horror, their only hope in this revolution going crazy before their very eyes.

****

Logan's voice echoed in Teah's head as she strained to hear him. It felt so feeble and distant. She eased her eyes open as her surroundings blurred in the dim lighting. She could feel others around her, the heaviness of the air and the closeness of the bodies giving her a trapped feeling. The scent of salt mixed with the sour smell of sweat filled her nose.

A face leaned in close, familiar, yet unsettling to her. She blinked rapidly to clear her vision as Caldora stared down at her, concern creasing her forehead.

Teah flinched and scrambled away as much as she could against the unforgiving wall.

"I told you to stay back," Galena said as she wrapped a comforting arm around Teah's shoulders." It will be all right, dear. We are here with you."

Galena's voice lacked confidence and Teah sat up to discover why.

Teah stared around the wooden room, the walls curving up to the ceiling plank by plank. The damp smell of salt permeated everything. But the salt didn't come from the people in the room, but the air itself. Teah sat up straight with realization. A ship.

They were in the hold of a ship. She had never seen a ship before, much less on one, but heard stories around the fire at home about them.

Teah eased her head into her hands, her thoughts spinning. The home she remembered became that, a memory, after Caldora destroyed it.

Teah lunged for Caldora as she leaned over her, taking the woman's throat in her hands and squeezing with all her might. Caldora toppled backwards, Teah on top of her. The two landed on other people as they lay about the ship's hold and tried to scurry out of the way.

"Teah," Galena cried." No, stop, you don't understand."

Arms wrestled Teah from her victim with surprising ease, Teah realized, as they pulled her to her feet. Teah looked right and then left to see her friends, Lizzy and Rachel restraining her. Her protector powers seemed to have abandoned her.

Teah frowned with confusion and then glared at Caldora as she stood rubbing her neck.

"Why did you stop me? She is the reason for all of this. Why did you stop me?" Teah said, turning to Galena.

"She is as much a victim here as we are," Galena explained.

"Victim? How are we victims? A Zele Magus is no one's victim," Teah said firmly, flailing her arms so Lizzy and Rachel released her.

"We are the prisoners of the Caltorians," Caldora said, walking around to stand beside Galena as she came to her feet.

"We will see," Teah said as she reached inside to take hold of the magic she knew to be there. But instead of embracing the wonderful power and feeling of the magic, she felt a muffled, subdued presence that didn't respond to her command, but simply lay there.

She looked at Galena in shock as the Zele Magus took a step closer and placed her arm around her again." I've been trying to explain, but you have to rush off in a flurry all the time. We've been drugged so our powers can't be used. We are prisoners of the Caltorians and on our way to Caltoria."

"Why would the Caltorians take us to Caltoria instead of killing us here?" Teah asked.

"Because," Caldora said stepping forward with her hands before her in a calming gesture." We are to become magical slaves for the empire."

Teah stared at Caldora in blank as a thought came to her." Why are you here? Aren't you the prize Zele Magus of the King?"

Caldora nodded." True. But Logan killed King Englewood and the empress has decided I should become her personal Zele Magus pet. I am, in fact, no better off than you, in this."

"You're getting off easy, if you ask me," Teah shot back as Galena, Rachel, and Lizzy groaned." You should be dead for what you've done to me, Logan, and Ter Chadain."

Caldora lowered her eyes and hung her head." I couldn't agree with you more, my queen."

"Quiet," Galena hissed." Do you want to doom us all?"

"I'm sorry, that is not my wish," Caldora whispered looking around nervously.

"The Caltorians don't realize what a prize they now have. We must never let them know who Teah really is."

Galena looked around the small circle of Zele Magus. Rachel, Lizzy, Teah, and Caldora all nodded their understanding.

"Good."

"What could possibly be good for you right now, witch?" The deep voice echoed from the stairs leading to the deck. A man stood at the top of the stairs with his hands on his hips.

He waited, his long black hair hanging past his shoulders and his handsome face marred by a long pink scar running from his right temple to his chin. His beard and mustache parted reluctantly around the battle wound and it turned redder as he smiled down at them.

"Ordestan," Teah hissed with hatred.

"I ask again. What do you have to feel good about? Unless you have come to realize that magic needs to be controlled by those of noble blood and not allowed to run around unrestrained."

"Not likely," Teah said and then spun away.

Ordestan clumped down the remaining steps and strode through the scurrying bodies of magicals trying to get out of his way. One woman proved too slow and Ordestan kicked her back, sending her tumbling into the others.

He stopped in front of Teah as she kept her back to him. Grabbing her by the shoulder, Ordestan roughly spun her to face him, but what he saw made him take a step back and release her. Teah glared defiantly up at Ordestan, the anger and hatred so powerful in her eyes, they seemed to glow red in the dimness. Ordestan gathered himself, stepped close to Teah, and leaned down so his face stopped a fraction from hers.

"Why is it, a girl, seems to lead this group of magicals?" he said, his spittle landing on Teah's face.

Teah didn't lift a hand to wipe the spit away, but met the captain's stare evenly.

"You don't know much about our customs if you don't know that," Caldora spoke up.

Rachel, Lizzy, and Galena turned to Caldora with alarm, but Ordestan and Teah still locked glares.

"What custom would that be?" Ordestan asked, only briefly glancing at Caldora and then turning back to Teah.

"The most promising students are allowed to take up leadership roles to help them develop the confidence required to wield their magic."

"Humph, silly," Ordestan scoffed. He turned away from Teah and headed back towards the stairs.

"The troops who were with us?" Teah asked before Ordestan got to the stairs.

Galena and Caldora gasped, but went silent as Ordestan slowly turned back to Teah.

"What about them?" Ordestan asked." What did you do with them?" "The ones who survived were left at Stalwart to be executed for treason." Ordestan smiled at the pain in Teah's eyes. He turned, laughing, as he walked up the stairs and slammed the hatch shut.

Chapter 2

Logan sat in the small inn's common room, his back against the wall in the corner along the staircase; the seat he always chose when in a common room. He glanced at the passed-out drunk in the far corner, lifted the mug of mead, and took a long drink. The mead helped hold the protectors at bay in his head, but only if he didn't drink too much.

Sasha and Saliday entered the room and walked over to the table, sitting down in chairs opposite each other, being sure to leave Logan a clear view of the door. They also knew his ritual.

The inn keeper came over and deposited a mug of mead in front of each woman and hurried away, glancing once over his shoulder at the strangers, his eyes showing his fear.

Saliday took a deep drink and wiped her mouth with the back of her hand, giving a loud sigh." That took a lot of convincing. You could have killed fewer and done so with a lot less gore," she said shaking her head. Logan looked at her, unmoved, as he took another drink.

"The Duchess Heniton has agreed to wait for the arrival of the cavalry to verify we are who we claim," Sasha added, eyeing Logan cautiously.

"She should be thankful I don't kill her for treason myself and then wait for the cavalry to clean up the mess," Logan growled.

"I think she is afraid of that," Saliday whispered." She has sent for her general and Zele Magus and there is a platoon of soldiers outside assuring we stay here until they arrive."

"What happened with the Caltorians we captured?" Logan asked.

"Most of them are outside guarding the inn," Sasha said, bringing Logan's glare to her. She leaned back in her chair with her hands raised in front of her." I tried to tell her. . ."
Saliday leaned in and placed a calming hand on Logan's forearm above his clenched fist. He turned and she forced herself not to flinch under his demanding eyes." I told her as well, but she

claimed there are no Caltorians here, just immigrants faithful to Ter Chadain."

Logan's mood eased as he looked into Saliday's green eyes. Her auburn hair hung over her shoulders, framing her pale face. He reached over, took Saliday's hand in his, and nodded. Inhaling deeply, he slowly let it out." All right, we can't expect everyone to fall in with us after thirteen years of betrayal from the throne and the systematic infiltration of our troops and society by the Caltorians." Logan lifted his mug and drank deeply.

The women took the opportunity to drink as well." What about a ship? The sailors on the docks said there isn't any ship in port able to cross the ocean or catch the Caltoria Star before it reaches Caltoria."

Sasha nodded as she swallowed the mead and gasped to catch her breath to speak." They say there are some ocean-going vessels due in any day and they might be willing to take on some passengers for a price."

"What kind of price?" Logan asked, raising an eyebrow.

"A gold piece per passenger per day of travel," Sasha said and quickly took another drink.

"It's at least two weeks to Caltoria," Logan sputtered.

"If the wind holds," Saliday added." Sometimes it's closer to three."

"Sixty-three gold pieces?" Logan exclaimed." I could build a ship twice the size of the Caltoria Star for that."

"We know," Saliday said nodding, "but do we have the time?"

Logan looked at her hard and then his features softened and he gave a sad shake of his head." No, we need to reach them before the empress figures out she has the queen. . . if she doesn't know already."

"The soldiers we spoke to on the dock said the cargo was typical magicals. I doubt having the Queen of Ter Chadain prisoner could be kept quiet, not likely." She shook her head with reassurance.

"She's right. Sailors on the docks gossip as much as the barber shop or the knitting club. There isn't anything that happens on the docks that the dock hands and sailors don't know about. That secret is just too big to keep," Saliday added.

The conversation came to a halt when a large man entered the inn. His bald head showed many scars and wounds. His full beard, braided into a neat tail, came down to the middle of his chest. His clothing announced his importance before any titles could be exchanged. The General of Los Clostern needed no introduction. His elaborately embroidered shirt and overcoat shone with silver and gold and each finger bore a large ring adorned with jewels.

Spotting Logan and his companions he strode over, confidently, exuding an air of importance.

Logan glanced to the woman on either side of him with amusement in his eyes.

Sasha gave Logan a warning look and Saliday shook her head in the attempt to dissuade Logan from acting foolishly.

Ignoring their warnings, Logan sprung to his feet, pouncing upon the much larger man before the general could react. The general toppled over backwards, one of the protector's swords pressed firmly against his neck and Logan's knee planted squarely on his chest.

Sasha and Saliday rushed to them, each grabbing an arm and trying to pull Logan off the man. Logan lowered his shoulders and held firm, his blade drawing a thin line of blood against the general's neck.

"I should kill you now for allowing the Caltorians free access to Stalwart," Logan said, his voice low and threatening.

"I had no, choice. . ." the general panted, very aware of the pressure of the sword against his neck.

"There is always a choice. You now have another one to make," Logan said, his eyes burning with rage.

"That would be a poor decision, mate," a melodic male voice said from behind them.

Logan's head spun as he looked back over his shoulder and the women twirled, drawing their blades.

The man they thought to be sleeping off a night of drinking stood with his hands on his hips, his clothing not exhibiting wealth, but station, with tailored clothing that hugged his body from his pants to his well-fitted suit coat, embroidered in gold. His neatly trimmed hair and clean shaven face framed his mouth filled with white teeth, something rare except for the most privileged. The only blemish to his perfect appearance was a slight scar in his right eyebrow, showing a thin line of white against the black hair.

"Killing the general would only turn the people against you and slow you from what you really need waiting just around the point," the man said as he smiled broadly.

"I can't believe it," Saliday whispered.

"What?" Sasha asked. The general groaned as Logan's sword slipped against his neck, lengthening the thin wound the blade inflicted. Logan gave a quick glance at the general and turned back to the man, looking from him to the stunned Saliday.

"Morgan Task," Saliday said.

The man gave a deep bow, the long sword strapped to his hip rising up behind him." At your service, Saliday," he said, straightening with a broad smile on his face.

"You know him?" Sasha asked.

Logan eased his blade from the general's neck, but didn't move his knee from the man's chest. His eyes fixed on Saliday.

Saliday stared at Morgan Task and nodded in response to the Betra's question." He is a Tarken."

"With a ship that can get you where you need to go," Morgan added with a nod.

"I thought you said you were the last Tarken in Ter Chadain," Logan accused, coming to his feet.

The general rolled to his stomach and began to get to his knees.

Logan spun quickly and shoved the man back to the floor under the weight of his foot.

The general took the warning and lay still upon his stomach, the dirt stirring around his mouth and nose as his breathing remained labored.

"Uh, I thought I was the last Tarken," Saliday said, meeting Logan's questioning eyes.

"If I may, mate?" Morgan questioned. Logan nodded." For all technical purposes that statement is correct. I've been
out harassing the Caltorian ships at sea."

"And why have you returned?" Logan's eyes narrowed.

"Why? To carry you to Caltoria and recover our queen, of course," Morgan smiled.

"Tarken, remember, they can sense the need," Sasha answered Logan's questioning stare.

"She's right," Morgan said." I knew I needed to be here today and lucky for me I am. It will be a mistake to take out your rage on the general here," he motioned at the man on the floor, "when you really want to get at the empress."

"And you have a ship that can get us there. . . fast?" Logan asked, his hopes rising.

"It is at your disposal, mate," Morgan bowed again.

Logan looked at Saliday as her eyes fixed on the other Tarken, unable to look away.

A soldier barged into the common room, stopping awkwardly at the sight of his general laying on his belly on the floor. The soldier's hand reflexively went to his sword on his hip, but stopped as his eyes met Logan's now fixed on him.

"What is it?" Logan ordered." Your tr... tr... troops have arrived," the man forced out. Duke Banderkin marched in behind the soldier as the man turned and scurried past without a word.

The duke stopped before the general under Logan's foot and stared with shock at Logan.

The duke bowed to Logan." Nice to see you again, Protector Logan."

"Duke Banderkin," Logan nodded." Take control of the city and see that the duchess and her general don't leave until I return."

"Yes, Protector, but where are you going?"

Logan glanced at Saliday who still stared at Morgan, and then to Sasha who shrugged at his raised eyebrow. He gave Morgan a curt nod.

"We travel to Caltoria, to take back the Queen of Ter Chadain," Logan said as he sheathed his sword and strode past the stunned Duke, leaving Morgan, Sasha, and Saliday staring after him.

Logan burst out into the street, the tears welling in his eyes as he fought to control them. The rain came down again, pelting his face as he stared out over the harbor. He spun and hurried down the dock until he reached a small alley leading back into the town away from the water. He took two strides into the alley and stopped, leaning against the building wall. He allowed himself to slide down into a sitting position with his head hanging low. *How could she lie to me like that. . .?*

Maybe she didn't do it intentionally, Galiven comforted as the mental barrier Logan put up came down with his overwhelming emotions.

She had to know there were more Tarkens alive. But it's the way she looked at him. . .

With all the passion built up over many years of yearning, Falcone pointed out.

There is no need for that, Stalwart protested.

What? All I speak is the truth. We all saw her desire and wanting in her eyes, Falcone insisted. Logan listened in silence.

That's enough. You're all correct, Bastion said. Saliday's feelings for Morgan are obvious, but there is no need to speak of it when it only hurts Logan. She may not have known Morgan still lived, meaning she never intentionally misled Logan when she insisted she was the last Tarken in Ter Chadain.

All the voices inside Logan's head went silent and Logan felt their agreement.

But why does it hurt so much? Why does it feel like she betrayed me?

Because you have given that one thing which has no logic. . . love, Falcone said.

Logan sensed they all felt the same. For someone with four others inside his mind, he felt very alone and empty. He placed his head in his hands and closed his eyes as the protectors became mercifully silent.

The clattering of garbage at the other end of the alley brought Logan's head up, his cheeks wet with tears. A large man staggered at the end of the alley towards him, falling first into one wall for support before standing and staggering a short distance and falling into the other wall.

As the man came nearer, recognition crossed Logan's face. Something about the man's build, his stature, Logan recalled, but his physique didn't seem quite right. Logan eased to his feet as the man grew closer. Their eyes met and surprise mixed with recognition flashed on the man's face just before his eyes rolled back in his head and he fell into Logan's arms, unconscious. "Talesaur," Logan whispered as he bore the man's weight and lowered him to the ground.

Chapter 3

Teah sat with her back to the other Zele Magus, trying to concentrate on Logan's muffled thoughts. She stared at the wooden walls of the ship's hold, trying to break through the hazy effects of whatever she'd been given. While she thought, she ran her hand over the spot where her tattoo marked her as a protector. She frowned as her hand passed over her breast. It didn't feel right. Pulling her shirt out at the collar, she stared down to where the tattoo should be. Her eyes shot wide as the silver swords and crown weren't there.

She sprang to her feet, rushing to Galena, panicking. Galena glanced up at her as she approached and stared with a frown.

"What is it?" Galena asked.

"My protector mark is gone," she said, panic in her voice.

"Quiet," Galena said, pulling her down next to her." Calm down. I needed to cover the mark in order to hide your identity. The weave is permanent until it is untied. It needs to remain hidden until we get out of this. Do you understand?"

Teah stared hard at the Zele Magus and then her features softened and she nodded.

"Good, now go get some rest."

Teah stood without a word and went back to her spot across the hold.

Teah refused to eat the rest of that day, trying to lessen the drug in her system and allow her to break free of the effects, but it wasn't working. She still couldn't touch the magic and her protector's senses and reflexes responded as if she had consumed too much ale.

A pair of feet marched up next to her, just inside her vision as she stared at the wall, and waited. Teah let the person wait a while longer before looking up. When she finally tilted her head to see Galena glaring down at her, the Zele Magus stood with her arms crossed and a scowl on her face.

"Did it work?" Galena said.

"No," Teah shook her head.

"Exactly. When will you learn to listen to those who have experience with these things?"

"When you can do the things I can do," Teah said getting to her feet. She leaned closer, stopping only inches from Galena's face.

Galena staggered back a step before regaining her composure and leaning forward defiantly again." The drug shields us from our magic. They use enough to keep us drugged until we either eat the food containing it, or die from starvation."

"But if I could just break through. . ." Teah began, but Caldora stepped up beside Galena with her hands on her hips.

"This isn't their first slave ship," Caldora said through clenched teeth." They do this all the time and have learned how much drug they need to keep control. In the state we are in now, they could easily walk down those stairs," she pointed to the stairs leading to the hatch, "and slit each of our throats without much resistance from us."

"You maybe, but I will fight for every last breath in this body," Teah said stepping threateningly towards Caldora.

"This isn't the time or the place to settle past differences," Galena said moving between the two women, each determined not to back down." We all have the same goal now."

"That I doubt," Teah said turning and striding to the far side of the hold.

Lizzy and Rachel hurried to her side, exchanged worried looks, and then moved closer.

"We know what you're trying to do, but maybe Galena and Caldora are right. Maybe you can't beat it like that," Lizzy said.

"Yeah, maybe we can just wait for the right time and take advantage of it," Rachel agreed.

Lizzy held out a hand with a biscuit and some meat on it." Here, you have to eat to keep up your strength."

Rachel's eyes went wide on seeing the food.

Teah quickly took the food from Lizzy and hid it inside her clothing.

"What are you thinking? You heard what they said. They will whip us if we take more food than we can eat in the allotted time," Rachel said in an intense whisper.

Teah looked around nervously." She needed to eat something," Lizzy argued.

"But it is too dangerous," Rachel said.

Teah froze as she made eye contact with an older woman close to the stairs. The woman raced up the steps and pounded on the hatch, shouting for the guard.

"Now you've done it," Rachel said, looking over at the stairs.

Teah began to stuff the food into her mouth, having a difficult time chewing the dried out biscuit without any water. She only had half the biscuit consumed when the hatch opened and Captain Ordestan clumped down the stairs.

Rachel broke off a chunk of the biscuit, stuffing it into her mouth.

Lizzy tried to do the same, but Teah pushed her hand away and shoved the remaining food into her mouth, expanding her cheeks to their limits.

The old woman stood at the bottom of the stairs and pointed to Teah and her friends as the captain stopped beside her.

Ordestan listened with a disgusted look on his face as the woman sold them out. A smile spread across the captain's lips as he lifted his eyes to look at Teah with satisfaction. He took several large strides and stopped before Teah.

Teah chewed feverishly until Ordestan stood before her. Teah stopped chewing and looked at her feet, refusing to make eye contact with the man.

Ordestan reached a hand and took hold of Teah's chin, forcing her face up to his, her cheeks still stretched by the food in them. With his fingers on her cheeks, he squeezed his hand together, oozing the food from Teah's mouth and onto the back of his hand. He reared back and backhanded Teah smearing the food across her face and sending her sprawling.

Teah slid across the floor, shaking her head to clear her blurred vision as she came to a stop.

Ordestan closed the distance between them in an instant, pulling her to her feet by the front of her shirt and proceeding to lift her off the floor, her feet dangling helplessly." You were told about the food. Now you will pay," Ordestan said, his face inches from hers.

"It wasn't her," Lizzy said.

Ordestan turned to Lizzy, still holding Teah off the floor." What do you mean, it wasn't her?"

"You said it was against the rules to take more food than you can eat. You never said anything about eating the food someone else took and gave you." Lizzy began to tremble as she spoke the words.

Ordestan thought for a moment, set Teah down, and strode over in front of Lizzy." No, I guess the person who took the food is the guilty party. You're saying she didn't take the food, but was given the food to eat by someone else?"

Lizzy could only nod as the captain's eyes stared into hers. Her body now visibly shook with fear.

"Well, then, who took the food?" Ordestan licked his lips in anticipation of the beating sure to follow the confession.

Lizzy gathered her courage and opened her mouth.

"I did," a voice came from behind Ordestan. The man spun to see Rachel, her hands on her hips, trying to look brave in spite of her terrified eyes.

"You?" Ordestan asked uncertain.

"Yeah, me," Rachel said as she crossed her arms and her fear waned a bit.

"Guards," Ordestan shouted and two men raced down the stairs to snap to attention behind the captain." Take these two on deck and prepare them for lashing," Ordestan said motioning to Teah and Rachel.

"What?" Rachel shouted." You said. . ."

Ordestan spun and crouched down so his nose touched Rachel's." I lied," he said with a wink." And you," he turned to Lizzy," be thankful you have friends who watch out for you. But maybe they won't after today. The old woman told me you did it, but I got two for the price of one and this one," he motioned to

Teah, "I'm going to really enjoy knocking her down a notch or two."

Ordestan nodded to the guards who grabbed hold of Teah and Rachel and towed them to the stairs. They pulled the two girls after them as they climbed the stairs, the girls flailing like rag dolls as they clumped on every step along the way.

Ordestan turned to follow, but caught the eye of Caldora as she stood glaring at him. He moved over to her as she stood her ground.

"I would watch who you stare at, witch. You aren't the king's pet and under his protection anymore," he sneered.

"Just pray I never encounter you when I have control of my powers, Captain. It will be very unpleasant for you," Caldora said as her eyes narrowed to slits.

Ordestan punched her full in the face, sending the woman careening off the wall and onto the floor, her nose bleeding profusely.

"Witch," he spat on her, strode to the stairs, and marched up to the deck. The hatch slammed back into place and the hold went quiet except for Caldora's moans of pain.

Captain Ordestan walked up on deck as the two guards finished tying each girl with their hands above their heads facing the main mast.

Teah tried to keep her fear in check and she looked over at Rachel who bit her lip so hard to stay in control that a drop of blood hung on her chin from the hole in her lip.

"Well, well, the little witch will finally get what she deserves," Captain Ordestan growled." Shirts."

A guard stepped up to Teah, took hold of her shirt and ripped it open, exposing her back. Teah gasped in shock.

Teah locked eyes with Rachel, willing her to stay strong as the man moved over and tore Rachel's shirt as well. Rachel flinched, but kept quiet.

"What do you say, men?" Ordestan shouted.

"Twenty, Captain," a man close to the girls spoke up.

"Twenty-five, Captain," another cheered.

"We need to be fair about this. We give thirty for taking the food. How about double for eating it and allowing another to do your dirty work?" Ordestan said unable to contain his excitement.

The crew went wild, cheering madly.

"Thirty for the taker and sixty for the eater it is," Ordestan laughed. He turned to a large man brandishing a long whip. The whip split at the end forming several tips, each containing a small piece of metal.

"Mr. Gentry, if you would be so kind."

The man nodded and reared back his arm as the whip coiled and slid smoothly behind him on deck. He started forward before the whip stopped moving behind him and sent it snaking towards Rachel. Just as it reached her, Gentry flicked his wrist and the whip stopped. . . all but the tips which kept moving and then recoiled as they touched Rachel's skin.

Rachel cried out in pain as each tip dug a hole into her flesh, sending a spray of blood out behind her.

The men cheered.

Teah braced herself as the man turned at the waist and coiled the whip towards her. As the tips touched her flesh, Teah braced for the pain, but as the whip snapped back, the pain didn't come. Neither did the blood nor the cheers from the men. The deck went silent as the sound of the metal tips of the whip sliding across the wood stopped.

Teah looked stunned at Rachel and then it dawned on her. The chain mail shirt. They couldn't take it from her since they couldn't see it.

"What form of magic is this?" Captain Ordestan cried." Gentry, again."

The whip arched into motion before Ordestan finished and it snapped across Teah's back again, once more with no effect on her skin.

That simple snap of the whip did something she'd been trying to do since she awoke on this ship. . . cleared her mind. Logan's thoughts mixed with the thoughts of the protectors inside his head rushed to her. Betrayal and surprise washed into her from her brother. And then shock.

Come and get me, my brother. I am waiting.

"Hit the other one again. If one doesn't take it, the other will take them all," Ordestan ordered.

Gentry hit Rachel again and she cried out in agony.

Rage surged through Teah. Rage she tried to control, but the strength of the protector would not heed her plea, but rushed to her hands pulling her bonds free. She spun around and caught the whip in mid-flight, ripping it from Mr. Gentry's hands. Teah spun away and sent the whip into the men who finally shook off their shock and began to advance on her. The men went sprawling in every direction to avoid the whip's slashing tips.

Ordestan reacted too slowly and received a gash on his other cheek to match his first scar. He pulled his sword with a snarl and rushed in, chopping the whip into pieces as he hurtled himself at Teah.

Teah threw the handle of the useless whip at him as he came, slowing him for a second and then took his assault head on. Ordestan swung to take off her hand that had held the whip and missed terribly as Teah leapt above the strike and came down nimbly behind him.

He spun, outraged at missing his prey and charged again. Teah sidestepped his sword and grasped his wrist, twisting it forcefully until the hand released the blade. She dropped to a knee as she took hold of the sword, flipping Ordestan over her shoulder onto the deck on his back with a loud crash.

She loomed over him before he could draw air back into his vacated lungs. He gasped as his own sword pressed against his neck and the men on deck stood in shock at the sight. Teah didn't look away from Ordestan's terrified eyes, but glared back, unwavering.

Ordestan's fear turned to determination as he stared back at Teah.

"You know something, little witch?" he hissed.

"What?" Teah growled." At least I won't die begging like your cowardly captain did." Teah's eyes narrowed and she leaned close so only Ordestan could hear." I'm a protector and

Queen of Ter Chadain, and I will go to Caltoria and rip your precious empress's heart out. And you are dead."

Teah ran the blade across Ordestan's throat in one smooth motion, nearly severing his head. His blood sprayed everywhere, covering Teah in a deluge of warm, red, gore and then slowed to a gurgle from the wound.

The men circled Teah and Rachel moving in cautiously, planning on overpowering them with their numbers. Teah reached over and cut Rachel free with the sword.

Rachel winced as she lowered her arm, the blood oozing in spots on her back instantly. She turned and stared in shock at Ordestan's body in front of them.

The men moved in, uncertain of what to do next, until Mr. Gentry took a cautious step forward. He raised his hands to Teah.

"You know you can't come out victorious in this. We are too many for you and we will have you subdued eventually."

"That doesn't give me much reason to surrender, does it?" Teah asked.

Gentry frowned, shaking his head." No, no it doesn't. But it is the truth."

"The truth in this is that I will kill some, if not many, of you on this deck today. The choice you need to make is who is willing to take the risk they will be one of the dead?" Teah held Gen- try's gaze, feeling the uncertain eyes of the other men upon her.

"What do you propose, little witch?" Gentry said.

"First, I'm not a witch. Second, I will tell you that I now have total control of my magic as well as my ability to fight." She stared hard at the man, hoping she wasn't bluffing, because she didn't know for certain, but she followed her hunch.

"And, if that is the case, why would you need to negotiate anything? Why wouldn't you kill us all and be done with it?" Gentry looked skeptical.

"I wouldn't want to needlessly kill men who might have families back home and are only following orders. Are you one such man, Mr. Gentry?" Teah tilted her head with the question.

"Yes madam," Gentry said nodding." I guess I am. So what will it be?"

"Aside from unarmed men to sail the ship, I want all the prisoners on deck and the rest of the men. . ."

Before she finished, Teah's body lifted off the deck and slammed into the mast. She looked down as a red weave held her ten feet up the mast. Scanning the deck furiously, she searched for the attacker, but found only Rachel.

Then a cabin door squeaked open and a tiny woman, no larger than a small girl, her straight black hair cut short, walked for- ward followed by a large man. Greasy black hair hung down to his shoulders and folds of fat flowed down over his belt. His silken clothes and many golden rings shone in the light as his hand rested on the woman protectively. No, not protectively, but proudly.

Teah? Teah, are you all right? Logan spoke in her head.

No, brother, Teah stared at the woman with a bright red jewel on her forehead. I'm afraid not.

Teah fought to free herself, touch her magic and lash back at the woman, but she could accomplish neither.

"Bring her," the man said in a deep gravel voice.

Men approached and Teah descended the mast, her arms still pressed to her sides. They took hold of her, carrying her to the stairs leading to the man and the woman on the platform before the cabin.

The woman looked over her shoulder at the man who nodded. She then descended the stairs to stand before Teah. The woman looked up at Teah standing nearly a head taller than her and then down at something in her hands.

Teah stared at the tiny hands holding a clear, faceted gemstone. Fear gripped Teah, but she couldn't understand why. The stone and woman were so small, how could they possibly harm. . .

"I'm sorry," the woman said and reached up quickly, placing the stone against Teah's forehead.

Any thoughts Teah held exploded in a display of light and pain in her mind. Teah cried out, her body going rigid as every muscle in her body convulsed at once.

Teah. . . no! Logan cried out in her thoughts and then his words burst into shards of glass as they cut into her brain.

Teah's vision blurred as something thick and warm ran down her face, filling her eyes and causing them to sting.

The men let her drop to the deck and she fell to her side writhing in pain as the stone burned deeper and deeper into her head. But it wasn't her flesh it wanted, it sought. It pushed deeper and deeper, reaching far inside Teah's mind until it found what it needed, what it desired. It stretched around the prize, encircling it and claiming it, taking it and making it its own.

Teah lay panting on the hard wood decking; the pain that assaulted her disappeared in an instant. She moved her arm tentatively and discovered her bonds were gone. She sat up wiping the blood mixed with tears from her eyes and then stared down at her bloody hands. She ran her hand across her forehead feeling the protruding stone under the congealing blood. It extended only slightly further than her own flesh, but she couldn't mistake its presence.

She reached for her magic, but touched the hard cover the stone placed around it. Teah looked at the woman who stared without emotion back at her.

The woman stepped away with a nod to the man still standing at the top of the stairs so Teah and the man made eye contact.

The man raised his hand, holding an enormous ring between his thumb and first finger, showing it to Teah. The gold ring held a large clear stone in it. . . the same as the stone the woman placed on her head.

With a smile the man looked from Teah's forehead to the stone in the ring.

Teah's eyes locked on the stone in the ring, somehow knowing the importance of this moment. The stone began to cloud over and a light pink color slowly eased into existence. The man nodded his approval as the color became darker and darker, from the pink to a light red, then to a darker red. The man's eyes widened as the color continued to darken to crimson and then a deep red. His mouth opened wide as the color became black, a black darker than the darkest night.

The men on deck gasped, understanding the significance of this where Teah could not.

Teah looked to the woman who stared back in horror, terror distorting her features, a dark red gem nestled in her forehead. The woman ran up the stairs to the man, ripped the ring from his fingers as they held it before his paralyzed eyes. She roughly took his hand and shoved the ring onto his only vacant digit. Fear gripped Teah as she felt a piece of herself tear from her being. She looked with horror to the man staring down at her, his smile so vile, so evil, it made Teah shudder.

"The empress will reward me well for giving her the strongest magical slave as a gift. . . but for now. . . you are mine." The man began to laugh as the crew cheered.

Chapter 4

Logan burst into the common room carrying the unconscious Talesaur over his shoulder causing Banderkin, Saliday, Sasha, and Morgan to spin in surprise. He moved to a table, pushed the plates and mugs crashing to the floor, and eased the man down. The others rushed over, pulling the smelly, bloody cloak from the man, revealing Logan's confusion over Talesaur's stature. They gasped at the sight of Talesaur's missing right arm. From shoulder to hand, the entire arm. A large scab covered the wound, but green puss oozed from cracks in the dark red mass.

"Who?" Saliday asked.

"Talesaur, Captain of the Queen's Guard," Logan explained as he pulled the rest of the cloak free and tossed it to the floor." He was with Teah."

"He's burning up," Banderkin said, placing the back of his hand against the man's sweaty head." We need to heal him."

"We have no powers to heal him," Logan shouted.

"Yes we do," Banderkin corrected." My Viri Magus is in camp just outside the city's gates. He'll be able to heal this if the infection hasn't gotten too far." The duke didn't wait for a response but ran out of the room.

Logan glanced over his shoulder and then returned to the task of disrobing the man dying on the table before him.

"If this is what happened to Talesaur," Sasha said, "what happened to the rest?"

"I don't know, but I intend to save Talesaur so he can tell us," Logan said, looking determinedly at the Betra.

He is too far gone," Bastion said, slipping past the meager defense Logan now ignored.

I won't let him die. I need to know what happened to Teah and why she can't hear me anymore, Logan argued.

His mind may be nothing but mush now that the infection has taken hold, Stalwart pointed out.

Logan pushed the barrier in his mind back up and pulled the man's shirt off, tossing it onto the pile of sweaty, bloody clothing stacking up on the floor.

The inn's door slammed open against the wall as Banderkin rushed in and then eased Logan aside as Viri Magus Niles stepped up to Talesaur. The man placed his hands upon the stub of the severed limb. The slender man cloaked in black with long black hair and black goatee bent low, causing his hair to drape down along his cheeks and his closed eyes. He straightened and looked at Logan, the futility heavy in his eyes, and then turned to Duke Banderkin, stroking his black goatee.

"I'm not sure there is anything I can do. The infection is very extensive," he said.

"Do what you can," Logan shouted, causing everyone in the room to jump, except for the unconscious Talesaur.

They stared at Logan, their eyes wide.

"Please," Logan sighed and lowered his eyes. The protestors shouted their council in muffled voices." I need him to live to learn all I can of Teah's situation." Logan lifted his pleading eyes to Niles and then turned to Duke Banderkin.

Niles looked to the duke who gave him a nod and the Viri Magus stepped to Talesaur once more. He placed a hand on the wound and another on the man's head.

Talesaur's back arched off the table and he screamed in agony that echoed through the room.

Logan swayed on his feet, staggered a step, and then dropped to a knee next to the table where Talesaur lay. He cried out as pain burned into his brain, the flames of magic scouring his mind, sending him into a convulsion. He knelt for a moment and then fell over, shaking uncontrollably on the floor, his eyes rolled back in his head revealing only the whites through his eyelids.

Saliday and Sasha rushed to him, pulled him between them, and cradled him in their laps trying to calm the tremors taking hold of him.

"What's happening to him?" Saliday cried, beseeching the Viri Magus as he stared down at her, his hands still on Talesaur.

Niles released Talesaur from his magical grip halting his cries, but it didn't diminish the echoing cries of agony bouncing off the walls as Logan continued to scream.

Niles dropped to his knees next to Logan and the women, placed a hand on Logan's head and instantly catapulted across the room, slamming against the stone wall, his head impacting with a sickening thud. The Viri Magus's lifeless body slid down the wall leaving a streak of red blood. He crumpled on the floor, a pool of blood spreading out from beneath him.

"By the gods," Banderkin shouted and rushed to Niles. He knelt next to him and checked for any signs of life. Banderkin straightened, shaking his head at the inquiring gaze from the others.

Logan continued to scream as a small bloody circle formed on his forehead and a stream of blood ran down his face and blood oozed from his clenched eyes.

Inside Logan's mind the protectors panicked, trying to avoid the shards of magic bursting through his mind. The pain kept Logan from controlling his own thoughts, much less the protectors, so they all shouted at once, causing a chaotic chatter making it impossible for Logan to focus.

The pain built to a crescendo along with the panicking protectors, reaching a fevered pitch, threatening to turn Logan's mind into jelly. It stopped all at once. The pain and the chattering protectors came to a sudden halt.

Logan opened his eyes, the sticky mat of blood clinging to his lashes, making it difficult. He wiped a hand across his eyes and saw the worried looks from Banderkin, Sasha, and Saliday. Morgan stood off to one side, his expression a mix of shock and horror.

"What happened?" Logan asked his voice hoarse from his screams of pain.

Banderkin glanced over his shoulder at the motionless body of Niles as Logan followed his gaze.

"I did that?" Logan asked. The shame and disgust hung heavy in his voice.

"Not intentionally," Saliday spoke up as Banderkin nodded.

"How?" Logan started, but his memory jolted back at the sight of the Viri Magus leaning over him and then disappearing from his view.

"What is that upon your forehead?" Sasha asked.

"What is it?" Logan asked, wiping a hand across his head, flinching when he contacted a bloody wound. He held his hand before him, staring at the blood glistening on his fingertips.

"I've seen this magic before. . . many times."

All heads turned to Morgan as he stood off to one side, his brow furrowed in thought and concern. He lifted his chin slightly with a twist of his neck and tightened his arms crossed over his chest.

"It is the mark of the soul stone, but it is not. . ." Morgan hesitated as he took a step towards Logan lying in Sasha's and Saliday's arms and then retreated next to the fireplace.

"It is not what?" Saliday pressed.

"It is not possible without a soul stone," Morgan said, motioning to Logan's wound." He has no soul stone placed on his forehead, yet the wound is there as if it is."

Banderkin strode to the middle of the room between Morgan and Logan." What are you talking about? Soul stones? The Caltorians use those on magicals to control their powers. Logan isn't a magical and none of us are Caltorians except. . . possibly you."

Banderkin drew his sword and advanced on Morgan before the Tarken could react. The duke pinned Morgan against the fireplace mantle, his sword pressed against the Tarken's neck.

"Banderkin, stop," Saliday shouted, sliding Logan onto Sasha's lap and scrambling to her feet. She rushed to the men and pressed herself against the duke's back, her hands firmly gripping the man's shoulders.

"I can vouch Morgan is no Caltorian. Lower your weapon," Saliday said in the duke's ear.

The duke looked at Saliday over his shoulder with a raised eyebrow and then released Morgan with a nod of acceptance.

"If what Morgan says is true, then Logan should have a soul stone placed on his forehead, instead of. . ." The duke paused as he turned to Logan resting in Sasha's lap, shock spreading across his face.

Morgan and Saliday stared at the duke, waiting for him to continue, but when Banderkin stood staring at Logan, they also turned their attention to the protector. Their expressions soon mirrored the duke's.

"What is it?" Sasha asked, trying to turn Logan so she could see his face.

Logan rolled to his knees and got to his feet, pressing a hand to his forehead as the wound no longer throbbed. The skin felt smooth against his fingers and when he pulled his hand down and glanced at his fingertips, he found no blood.

Logan walked to a window shuttered from the outside and stared at his reflection in the glass. He ran a hand across his head showing no sign of injury.

"How did that happen?" he asked turning to the others. They didn't answer and Logan turned his question inward.

What happened?

He waited, surprised by the lack of response the protectors always eagerly gave, but none came.

Logan stared with disbelief at his reflection in the glass, his eyes wide as the reality grew sharper.

Sasha walked over next to him, staring at him through the reflection.

Logan turned to look at the Betra, the concern evident on her face as she stared into his terrified eyes.

"They're gone. . . I'm alone," he whispered as his voice seemed echoed in what now seemed like a very lonely mind.

Chapter 5

Teah knelt at the base of the stairs wiping the blood from her eyes as it ran from her forehead. The flow began to slow and she drew the back of her hand across her eyes a final time and then stared up at the man she now suspected to be in control of her magic.

She reached for the magic, but a barrier held it tight, out of her reach.

What am I to do?

What are you to do? Hell, what are we doing here? A male voice said.

Teah flinched in surprise at the voice inside her head. She lifted her chin to look closer at the man standing at the top of the stairs.

"Why would you taunt me like that?" she said.

"You will not speak to me in that manner," the man sneered and pain erupted inside Teah's mind.

Teah fell backwards writhing in pain and then the pain stopped as suddenly as it began, but the voice didn't. In fact, it cried out in protest.

Foolish girl, stop playing and keep your mouth shut until I can figure this out. The voice commanded her with poise, something lacking in the man on the stairs.

Who are you?

The damned soul stone. . . must have pulled me from Logan's mind here. But where is here?

Teah froze in disbelief. Did he say Logan's mind? Logan confided in her who shared his mind with him. Could it be?

A protector?

Bastion at your service your Majesty, Bastion said pulling out of his train of thought.

How?

Still trying to figure that out. Bastion said. I'll get back to you on that.

Bastion went silent.

Teah, being so caught up with this sudden development, didn't see the man descend the stairs to stand before her prone body.

He leaned over her, a curious look on his large face as his dirty, stringy hair hung down to touch her cheek.

"Has the stone rendered you mentally defective now?" Teah made eye contact with the man and he gave a nod." Get up, little witch, and take your punishment," the man said, giving Teah a kick in the side.

Teah let out a grunt and eased herself from the deck, Bastion mumbling something incoherent. The man reached down and took hold of Teah's chin, forcing her face up towards his." You have taken one of my men and now I will take one of your kind as payment," the man said his tone hard and cruel. He glanced over the top of Teah's head and gave a nod.

Two men shuffled around Teah pulling Rachel between them, stopping in front of the man.

Rachel's eyes spread wide with terror beseeching Teah for help as the men pushed her to her knees before the large man.

The man stared at Rachel for a moment, but then shook his head.

"Not this one. This one needs to get her lashes and be put back in the hold," the man said with a wave of his hand.

"Yes, Governor Redrick," one of the guards said as they pulled Rachel to her feet and back to the mast, fastening her hands above her head again.

Teah groped for her magic. It felt so close, yet remained beyond her grasp. She needed it now more than ever. She needed to help Rachel. She couldn't stand by and let this happen.
Just when her hope failed, she brushed something hard in her mind, but behind it, the sweet essence of her magic sat just a touch away. She reached for it, but the barrier remained hard, not giving, but seeming to thicken at her touch.

She retreated in despair, but as she turned back to the outside world, Bastion let her know to have hope.

I will look further at this problem. Concern yourself with staying alive long enough for it to do some good. Bastion said flatly, and then added, My Queen.

Teah's eyes focused as Gentry stepped forward with another whip. He lifted the leather strap high above his head with a thick, hairy arm, giving Rachel a vicious lash, opening her skin to expose muscle beneath. He raised his arm again and down came another blow, and then another, one after another.

Teah turned away from them, staring straight ahead, flinching at every crack of the whip and cry from Rachel.

Redrick stood watching, a smile of satisfaction on his lips. He turned to the nearest men, "Get the other girl who came in with these two," Redrick instructed.

Two guards hurried to the hold and disappeared below, soon reappearing with Lizzy between them, the girl looking horrified. Seeing Rachel being whipped, she pulled against the men, but they easily dragged her with them. The men pushed Lizzy to kneel in front of Redrick.

Lizzy met Teah's frightened stare, her body shaking uncontrollably.

"This is not a game, witch," Redrick told Lizzy as she pulled her eyes from Teah and gawked up at the man.

"You were told the rules and the punishment, but you chose not to obey."

Rachel's cries of pain echoed on the ship's deck, each stroke bringing a scream and then the sobs of her suffering.

"I... I... I'm sorry, I didn't mean to disobey," Lizzy pleaded.

"I'll take her lashes, give them to me. She took the food for me, it's my fault," Teah said taking a step forward.

Pain erupted in Teah's brain dropping Teah to her knees and filling her mind with a frenzied rush of emotions and thoughts.

"Oh, lashes are no longer the punishment," Redrick said to Lizzy, ignoring Teah as she fought the pain, her hands upon her head.

"No, your actions have caused one of my men to die and now the punishment is death."

"No!" Teah shouted, fighting through the pain and standing.

The pain increased and dropped her down to one knee once more.

She gritted her teeth and refused to fall to the deck, using every ounce of strength she had to push herself back to her feet.

Redrick turned from Lizzy's terrified quivering form to stare at Teah in shock. He clenched his fists and furrowed his eyebrows.

Let him believe he is in control or he will continue to increase the pain, Bastion warned.

Teah held her ground, ignoring Bastion's advice and the pain increased, but still Teah stood.

Teah, girl, listen to me. You need to let him believe he is winning. Your stubbornness will do nothing but anger him. Bastion shouted at her.

Teah dropped to a knee again, but she refused to drop further. The pain eased and then stopped.

Redrick nodded and looked back to Lizzy." You are the cause for a loss of my man and your punishment is death to atone for his." He turned with a flick of the wrist to the guards and walked up the stairs. Once at the top, he paused, looking first at Teah and then at the little woman with the dark jewel in her forehead. The small woman scurried after him as he strode into the cabin, slamming the door behind them.

The guards took hold of Lizzy and then two more grabbed Teah before she could react. They marched over to where Rachel hung unconscious by her wrists by the mast and stopped. Gentry purposefully set down the bloodied whip and pulled a long broadsword from its scabbard. The steel rang eerily across the deck as everyone fell silent.

"What are you doing?" Teah shouted." You can't do this. I killed Ordestan, kill me. . . kill me." Teah pleaded, pulling at the guard's restraining hands. Tears rolled down her cheeks as Lizzy turned to her.

Lizzy's face showed nothing but calm. The girl no longer cried, but the remnants of tears streaked her face. She caught and held Teah's gaze, her demeanor at peace with her fate.

"Make your brother's Betra find my sister like you promised. . . okay?" Lizzy said.

"I will, I promise," Teah nodded.

"It has been an honor to be your friend, Teah. Thank you for allowing me to know the real Teah, the person inside, the real you," Lizzy said, her eyes watering again.

"You have been the best friend anyone could have and I will make sure everyone in Ter Chadain knows of the brave Lizzy Bridon and what you sacrificed for me," Teah said, her voice filled with conviction.

"Remember. . . my sister," Lizzy repeated and then bowed her head.

Gentry reached over and slid Lizzy's long blond hair to one side and stepped back. He placed the blade against the back of Lizzy's neck and the girl gave an involuntary shudder.

Teah wanted to look away, was just about to, but Lizzy turned to stare at her, the determination radiating from her blue eyes.

Gentry drew the sword back and stopped it at the top of his arch.

Lizzy mouthed the words "Long live the Queen."

The sword rushed down and cleanly severed Lizzy's head, dropping it to the deck with a sickening thud.

Teah turned away, refusing to remember Lizzy this way, wanting to keep the vision of her strength at the forefront of her mind.

The protectors didn't speak, but Teah felt remorse and sorrow coming from him.

Teah hung limp as the guards dragged her to the hatch, opened it, and tossed her down the stairs, sending her tumbling to the bottom.

Rachel's limp body soon rolled down the stairs to land on top of Teah and Teah rolled out from underneath her and held the bloodied, unconscious girl in her arms.

"Every last man on this ship will die. . . this I swear," Teah whispered in Rachel's ear.

Amen, echoed in her mind.

Chapter 6

"Who's gone?" Sasha asked, confusion evident on her face.

"Uh, nothing. . . no one. . . I mean Niles is gone. How could I do that?"

Logan looked over Sasha's shoulder where Niles lay motionless;

Banderkin crouched over him, looking as if he would be sick. Banderkin shook his head with dismay." He touched you. . . and then he flew across the room into the wall." The duke kept his eyes lowered, staring at Niles." He only tried to help you and you. . ." Banderkin's eyes lifted and locked on Logan's eyes.

"It wasn't Logan," Saliday said, walking between Logan and the duke, breaking their connection." It was magic. It gripped Logan and when Niles touched him, it repelled him."

"I know of no such magic," Banderkin argued." That doesn't mean it doesn't exist," Sasha said.

"The Betra is right," Morgan stepped forward from the mantel." It appeared a soul stone was placed upon Logan's head and now it is gone, but I know what a soul stone does and it is powerful magic."

"Fine," the duke stood and marched up to Morgan." Let's say it was soul stone magic. Where is the stone now and if there is none, how did it come to be inside of Logan?"

Logan took this all in, but kept asking questions inside his mind that remained unanswered. As he listened about the magic of the soul stone, dread spread through him. What if Teah's and his connection provided a passage for the magic of the soul stone to travel between them?

Can that happen?

He waited, ignoring the ongoing argument between Morgan and Banderkin, hoping for Bastion, Stalwart, Falcone, or Galiven to explain, but in his mind he remained alone.

Moaning came from behind Logan and he turned to see Talesaur struggling to sit up. He looked much better, the color beginning to return to his face, and his eyes, once cloudy, shone sharp and bright.

Logan got up and rushed over, followed by Sasha, to help the man slide off the table and ease into a chair. The stub remains of his right arm shone pink and red, much better than the oozing pus of green.

"What happened?" Talesaur asked, bewildered. He recognized Logan and began to drop to the floor to kneel, but Logan caught his arm and Sasha his shoulder, lifting the man back into the chair.

"Easy, you are too weak for that," Logan said.

"But Master Protector, I have failed in my duty to protect the queen and now she is the slave to the empress. I beg for your forgiveness." Talesaur tried to pull free of their hands, but couldn't in his weakened state.

"So Ordestan took Teah to be a slave to the empress?" Logan asked, knowing the answer wouldn't change even though he prayed it would.

Talesaur nodded, lowering his eyes from Logan's as the boy searched for the slightest glimmer of hope.

Logan released Talesaur and spun back towards the shuttered window.

Sasha caught Talesaur from falling forward, easing him back further into the chair.

"I'm so sorry, Master," Talesaur reiterated.

"No," Logan shook his head, not looking back at him." You defended her with honor, but the odds proved too great. There is no shame. You gave your arm and very near your life to protect her. Now I need to get her back." Logan turned to Morgan." Ready to catch up to the Caltoria Star?"

"Uh, of course," Morgan smiled." When do we leave?"

"As soon as you're ready," Logan said nodding.

"Give me an hour to get to my ship and another hour to have her here in port," Morgan told him." I will get a platoon ready for departure," Banderkin said, striding for the door.

"Not likely," Morgan said, stopping the man in his tracks.

"What do you mean?" Banderkin retreated to stand before the Tarken.

"My ship can only carry about eight passengers, the rest are my crew," Morgan said.

"That is not acceptable," Banderkin shouted, turning to Logan for support.

"It is what it is," Logan shrugged.

"But. . . but. . ." Banderkin looked to Sasha and Saliday, but both women mirrored Logan's reaction." How do you expect to save the queen and remain safe with only eight men?"

"That would be five men, since Logan, the Betra, and Saliday count for three of our passenger allotment," Morgan pointed out.

"Ah," the duke moaned, threw up his hands in disgust, and stormed from the room.

"I wish to accompany you as well, Master Logan," Talesaur said.

They turned to the man in surprise.

"I think we will be better served by someone who is fit for battle," Morgan said.

Logan shot the Tarken a hard glare, silencing him and causing him to turn red with embarrassment. Logan turned back to Talesaur, his anger softening as he looked at the injured Captain of the Queen's Guard.

"Talesaur," Logan began with compassion, but then stopped as their eyes met. Logan stared silently into Talesaur's eyes and then slowly nodded." Okay."

Saliday, Sasha, and Morgan shot Logan shocked looks, but Logan ignored them and continued to look deep into Talesaur's eyes. He gave one final nod to the man.

"Get him something to eat, some supplies, and clean clothes. Have a tailor brought in to fit him so he doesn't have to carry around an extra sleeve." Logan grinned and strode from the inn. Logan stopped just outside the door, closed his eyes, and took a deep cleansing breath. He opened his eyes and jumped with a start. Sasha and Saliday stood on either side.

"Why would you bring him along. . . he is not able to fight, not without his sword arm?" Sasha asked.

"She's right, sympathy won't help us in a fight," Saliday agreed." Banderkin isn't going to like having one less man to protect you."

"Did you see his eyes?" Logan asked. The women shook their heads." What I would give for an ounce of his courage and determination in each of the other men coming with us. Talesaur will learn to fight with his left arm and he will be the most dangerous man in any battle because of what he doesn't have."

"His arm?" Sasha and Saliday said in unison.

"No... anything to lose," Logan said. He walked away leaving the women behind contemplating the truth of his words.

Chapter 7

Teah held Rachel's bloody, unconscious body in her arms, rocking back and forth as the horror of it all overwhelmed her. Galena and Caldora rushed to her, trying to pry Rachel from Teah's arms, but she gripped the girl's limp body defiantly, staring straight ahead, the shock drowning her in sorrow.

"Let her go, child," Galena urged, pulling at Teah's arm." We need to tend to her."

Let her go, they need to help her, a voice said compassionately.

"Teah," Caldora said." Let her go. We need to help her."

Teah frowned, not because she heard a voice in her mind, no, she understood Protector Bastion now inhabited her head instead of Logan's, but because this didn't sound like Bastion.

The thought pulled Teah back to her surroundings and she stared up at the Zele Magus, her confused expression falling from her face as she looked down at Rachel. Teah pulled her arms free of the girl and the two women took Rachel and gently carried her to a spot away from the stairs and began to examine her.

Teah watched as the women examined her wounds, tore strips of cloth from their clothing and began to cover the open gashes on Rachel's back.

Bastion? Is that you? It didn't sound like you. Even as she thought this, she questioned if she knew the sound of Bastion's spirit well enough to tell it apart from another's.

A long silence followed as she stared at the activity before her and waited for a response from inside her head.

As she waited, the ghastly scene on deck played out in her mind. Lizzy's pleading eyes and the sickening thud of her head landing on the deck.

Teah turned to one side and emptied her stomach, surprised she had held it down this long. She wiped the spit from her mouth with the back of her hand and recalled where that food came from and what it cost.

She lowered her face into her hands and began to sob. A comforting hand touched her shoulder and she looked up expecting to see Galena or even Caldora, but instead she stared up at the old woman who betrayed them.

Rage erupted from Teah as she sprung to her feet and lunged at the woman. The woman's scraggly hair flew around her scarred face as Teah drove her to the floor, sitting on top of her, hands clasped around her neck.

The woman didn't cry out, but her face began to turn red as Teah denied her air.

Hands pulled at Teah, trying to pry her off, but she held fast, Lizzy's beseeching eyes burning at her memory.

Let her go. She is a victim like you. Let her go before this gets worse. Bastion's thoughts pounded at her. She recognized this voice, not like the one before, but more the refined and composed.

Teah looked up to see the other prisoners surrounding her, many reaching and pulling at her. She turned to the woman beneath her, her face turning blue and her eyes filled with panic. Teah released her and stood up, pushing through the mass of bodies pressing in around them until she stepped clear of them.

She dropped to her knees, her body shaking uncontrollably as the horror played through in her mind again, and again, and again. She eased into an isolated spot away from anyone else, or maybe they all gave her a wide berth now they knew her to be crazy. It didn't matter either way. She wanted to be alone, to be left alone, to keep from hurting anyone else she cared for.

First Grinwald, the Viri Magus who guided and protected her and Logan after Caldora and King Englewood's troops destroyed their farmstead, died trying to keep them away from Caldora. Then Galena nearly died when Caldora attacked at the inn. Talesaur, the Captain of the Queen's Guard died when Ordestan took her and the other magicals captive. Now Lizzy executed for saving food for her and Rachel whipped within inches of her life for trying to protect both her and Lizzy.

Teah pulled her knees close to her chest and wrapped her arms tightly around them, pulling them even closer. She closed her eyes, the tears running down her cheeks.

How is all this worth it? How can hurting or killing good people be worth putting me on the throne?

Because if we don't, better people will die at the hands of the Caltorians.

The voice inside her head made Teah gasp. It most certainly did not belong to Bastion. It lacked the refined nature of the oldest and first Protector of Ter Chadain. It almost sounded youthful except for the sadness woven through it.

Bastion? That was not you. Is there someone else in there with you?

A long silence followed, but Teah couldn't bring herself to ask again. She wasn't sure she wanted to know the truth.

No, My Queen, it was not me. Bastion finally said, his voice ringing with confidence. It is Galiven. . . who was not supposed to speak to you.

Teah gasped, but then buried her head between her knees and chest, not wanting to draw any attention from the other prisoners. She opened an eye and peered across the hold to where Galena and Caldora tended Rachel. The women's slower movements showed that urgency had passed as they tried to soothe the injured girl.

Teah turned her thoughts inward, searching for Galiven's presence. When she sensed him, it surprised her. How did she miss him being there before?

There you are Protector Galiven. Teah greeted, a bit uncertain.

Your Majesty, Galiven said. How did you come to be inside my mind? Has something happened to Logan?

Teah panicked. When we left him, he was well, but we left so abruptly, it is uncertain the toll our sudden exit may have caused, Bastion said.

Don't frighten her for no reason, Galiven said. We do not know of any harm that may have come to him after our departure, but he was well when we left.

You two never did have a way with words, a third voice said.

Teah froze, not sure she liked where this protector spirit thing led. Logan had four protector spirits in his mind. Is that you Stalwart?

Yes, My Lady, Teah could almost feel Stalwart bow. I apologize for their babbling, but it seems the soul stone has drawn us from Logan's mind, across the connection you two have, into your mind. Definitely something new for all of us. Being inside a female is. . . awkward to say the least.

The three protectors burst into argument over who babbled the most.

Bastion, Stalwart, Galiven, Teah named each protector and then paused trying to remember the last name. Falcone? Teah thought.

The protectors went silent. Falcone are you in here? Teah asked. Still nothing. Teah searched, touching the spirit of Bastion, Stalwart, Galiven, each with an amount of respect radiating from their presence. But then she brushed up against something that made her recoil at the hostility pushing forward towards her spirit. Anger radiated from this presence wishing her harm.

No, this can't be. She rationalized. Why would Falcone have such anger, such hatred for me? What have I ever done to harm him?

Teah waited for any of the spirits to enlighten her as to why Falcone's spirit withdrew to a corner of her mind and possessed such vile thoughts towards her.

It is not you, Galiven finally told her. He hates and distrusts all Zele Magus.

Teah sensed Falcone again, shocked at the hatred for her. Is this true, Falcone? She pressed. Do you hate me because I am a Zele Magus? Surely being a protector and Logan's sister should count for something with you.

It does, Falcone admitted flatly. It means you are the most dangerous woman who has ever existed and that is why I despise you more than all the rest. You are a monstrosity which should never be. Something that can destroy us all. I am only sorry that you are Logan's sister. I do not wish to bring the boy any pain when I destroy you.

The other protectors pressed in against Falcone and shielded any further communication with Teah. His hostility, once very evident in her mind, faded to a dull throb behind the others' power.

Please understand, Galiven pleaded, he lost everything he cared about at the hands of a Zele Magus and now he can feel your immense power and it scares him to know what you are capable of.

May the gods save us, Falcone shouted through the barrier and went silent again.

Teah opened her eyes, her tears gone, but the fear and horror ever present. Was she really the monster Falcone believed her to be? Was her destiny to destroy all the good people around her and the world if given the opportunity?

Logan, help me. . . please help me.

Chapter 8

Logan watched Stalwart shrink on the horizon as the large schooner, The Morning Breeze, raced out to sea. The thought of the protectors tugged at his insides. He never believed having them out of his head would be something he could miss, but he did. The comfort that came with their chaos, he now longed for.

How could his life change so much so quickly? He remembered the devastation at their homestead on the edge of the Treebridge Forest that day he raced back to the house after witnessing his father's death. His mother lay on the kitchen floor with her own kitchen knives sticking from her stomach.

He swallowed hard, taking a stuttered deep breath as Stalwart blurred in his vision and he fought back the tears.

The vision of finding his older sister lying against the well, already gone, came to him and he cried in earnest, his tears rolling down his cheeks.

A smile fought through his sorrow as he recalled finding Teah alive. They ran for their lives, not knowing where they would go or who they could look to for help.

He wiped the tears from his eyes and a soft chuckle escaped his throat as he remembered first seeing Grinwald, the skinny healer with his glasses hanging on the end of his nose always threatening to fall off. His memory flashed ahead to the forest where Grinwald sacrificed himself to ensure that he and Teah escaped Caldora. The rage and anger he once thought reserved for Englewood surged through him as he saw Caldora standing over Grinwald releasing a burst of magic into his chest, killing the Viri Magus.

His hands gripped the rail, crushing the wood under his grasp as his anger took on new targets. When he found Caldora, she would answer for what she did to his family and friends. The Protector of Ter Chadain would seal her fate. Ordestan already assured his death by the protector's hands.

He looked down at the crumpled railing and then at Stalwart now only a speck on the diminishing horizon. He once believed the protectors' spirits fueled his anger, stoked his rage, but perhaps they only fanned it. With the protectors gone, his rage smoldered strong under the surface waiting to be unleashed on Caldora, Ordestan, or anyone else who stood between him and Teah.

And not only rage. . . he felt his passion wavering and failing to find solid footing on the path to his heart. Now more than ever, he needed Falcone to share his insight on women. To explain to him the distance he felt growing between Saliday and him.

Ever since Morgan entered their lives, she gravitated towards him, another of her own kind, a Tarken. Saliday told him she thought herself the last of her kind, but discovering Morgan in Stalwart, she rarely left the man's side.

Morgan didn't seem to mind, but included Saliday in all his functioning as the captain of the ship. Morgan raced from one side of the ship to the other, encouraging his crew and pointing out areas to be wary of and shouting orders. Saliday trailed after him like an entranced child.

At least that's how Logan forced himself to see it. He knew if Falcone still resided inside his head, the protector would explain it differently. Logan urged himself to deny it. The obvious attraction between the two Tarken and the lack of interest Saliday now showed him, he willingly denied.

"We will reach her and bring her back," Sasha said, pulling Logan from his daydream.

"Huh?" Logan looked up, confused.

"Teah, we will catch up to them and bring her back."

"Uh, yeah, I know we will." Logan nodded and glanced at Sasha, the Betra woman betrothed to him.

"Then what is troubling you if it isn't your sister?"

Logan inadvertently glanced past Sasha to where Saliday stood beside Morgan as the captain manned the wheel.

Sasha followed Logan's gaze and turned back to him with a knowing grin." I'm sorry she has feelings for another," Sasha began.

"He's just another of her kind, someone she thought didn't

exist anymore. That's all," Logan grumbled, turning back to the rail and staring at Stalwart, now a speck in the distance.

"All right, but it makes sense. You have to agree it makes sense."

"I don't have to agree to anything. She loves me. How can she change in an instant?"

"You are young and inexperienced in these things." Sasha looked at him with sympathy.

Logan stared at her and his anger rose.

"Don't look at me like that. If she wants him, she can have him," Logan snarled.

He turned and walked across the deck, nodding at the four soldiers Banderkin insisted accompany them.

The men leaned against the rail nodding back.

Logan paused a moment, looking at Morgan and Saliday again, and then ducked into the door leading to the cabins.

****

Saliday stared after him, the hurricane of emotions visible in her eyes. She met Sasha's indifferent, almost sympathetic, stare, but even that made her turn away and lower her eyes.

****

Logan slunk through the narrow passageway leading to his small cabin. He pushed open the wooden door, the creaking of the hinges sounding right at home for the old boat. He stepped into the room and shut the door behind him, leaning against it as he closed his eyes, fighting the feelings of betrayal springing up in his mind.

How could she do this to me? How could she toss me aside like rubbish, into the street?

He opened his eyes and Talesaur stared at him from his bunk. Logan turned away, trying to hide the hurt that must be obvious on his face.

"What troubles you, Master Logan?" Talesaur asked.
"Nothing," Logan lied.

"Even a one-armed, washed-up failure of a soldier can see that isn't true," Talesaur said, his voice filled with sorrow, but laced with a touch of compassion.

Logan looked over his shoulder at Talesaur. The man lost an arm and nearly his life to protect his sister and even in failing to do so, he refused to give up and pushed on.

Logan walked over to Talesaur's bed and pulled up a stool to sit down. Dropping onto the stool, Logan nodded." I'm being silly," Logan admitted.

"One cannot minimize the effects affairs of the heart have on us," Talesaur shook his head." Being able to accomplish incredible feats is near impossible without our hearts behind it."

"I have bigger things to do than to worry about affairs of the heart," Logan grumbled." My sister and a country are counting on me. I can't fail. I need to return Teah to Ter Chadain."

"Aye, I agree, but who says you need to be miserable, or ignore your feelings in order to accomplish this?"

Logan stared at the man, trying to see where his insight and optimism came from.

"I failed Teah and you, and I ask your forgiveness," Talesaur said.

Logan leaned back on his stool, nearly falling off." You fought valiantly and pushed on where others would have given up. I hardly feel you need to ask for my forgiveness and I know Teah feels the same."

"I should have fought on. . . even after he took my arm, I should have picked myself up and stopped him," Talesaur lamented.

Logan stood, the sudden force sending the stool skittering across the cabin floor.

Talesaur looked up at him in surprise.

"Damn you and men like you," Logan shouted." A man once gave his life to assure that Teah and I could escape Caldora and King Englewood's troops. He wouldn't allow me to help him, but sacrificed himself to save us."

Logan played back the moment when Caldora unleashed a burst of magic into Grinwald's chest, ending the man's life. He could never forget the feelings he had at that moment or the look in Grinwald's eyes as the magic surged through his body. The surprise on Grinwald's face remained with him to this day.

"You are only a man. You need to quit holding yourself up to a standard that is unattainable."

"I swore to protect her. . ." Talesaur shouted.

"You did, until they took your arm and left you for dead."

"But. . ." Talesaur stammered.

"You're alive today only because you refused to die where ordinary men would have. You pushed yourself through blood loss and fever of infection to find me and continue your service to my sister. That is enough. You can't expect more of yourself. Neither Teah nor I would."

Talesaur turned away, the sheen of tears on his cheeks glistening for a second before he wiped his hand across his cheek, removing the evidence.

Logan walked over, recovered his stool, and placed it next to Talesaur's bed again and sat down. Talesaur continued to face the wall.

"Look at me," Logan said, leaning towards Talesaur.

Talesaur turned to look at Logan, the protector's gaze, intense.

"I forgive you. . . now you must forgive yourself." Logan held the man's stare for a moment, stood, and walked to the door.

"It's perfectly natural," Talesaur said. Logan stopped and looked over his shoulder at the man." You love her, Saliday, and I believe she loves you too, but it has become bigger than just you and her. She is torn between your love and the future of her kind. That is weighing heavily on her."

Logan nodded and walked out.

He's right. This is bigger than all of us now.

Chapter 9

Teah lay curled in a ball facing the wall where it intersected with a support beam. She didn't sleep, but closed her eyes to the outside world and tried to block out the protectors and their bickering.

They bickered constantly.

Except for Falcone. He remained silent even when the other protectors asked him a direct question. His negative vibes seemed to penetrate Teah with their hatred and resentment. He loathed being inside her more than she hated him there.

Why do you hate me, Falcone? She finally asked.

The other protectors went silent, the inside of her head echoed with their silence, but Falcone didn't respond.

How can you put the sins of others onto me? Teah pressed, her anger building and taking over her self-pity.

Still the protector remained quiet.

Don't be a coward, speak your mind. Teah shouted in her thoughts. Be a man, tell me why you think you know me so well when you don't have the slightest knowledge of me.

Teah felt the other protectors gasp and pull back from her thoughts. She had touched a nerve, she knew. She understood how all men hated being called cowards or have their manhood questioned.

It is your kind I know, not you specifically, but you are all the same. Falcone's thoughts came to her as a hiss more than words.

Don't give me your all-encompassing answer. What do you have against me, Teah Lassain, Queen of Ter Chadain, Zele Magus, and Protector? As she said her titles for the first time, Teah felt their weight press heavy against her shoulders, heightening her guilt over the fate of Lizzy.

One of your kind betrayed me, betrayed her queen, and took from me something more precious than life. . . my love of a woman. She erased my love for the only one I ever loved.

Teah knew this story. She and Logan read about it in the library of the Protector's Fortress. A Zele Magus wove a spell around Falcone, making him forget his true love, Queen Caderal.

The Zele Magus then used Falcone to start a revolution against the queen. With the help of a Viri Magus, Falcone regained his memory and eliminated the Zele Magus using him, foiling their plot to take over Ter Chadain.

How can you lump me into a group with someone like that? I would never do anything like that. Teah argued.

You may not be capable of that now, but as your power grows, you will see things differently. They all do.

Teah pulled out of her thought with Falcone, frustrated at the stubbornness of the protector. She sat up and looked around the hold. Nighttime hung over the ship as the hold stood black and still, most everyone sleeping.

Light shone down the steps from the gated hold opening, leaving a checkered effect on the wooden floor. She made out shapes here and there, mostly people lying by themselves, distancing from any affiliation with another magical.

Three shapes stood out from the rest of the solitary figures and Teah crept on her hands and knees towards them. They nestled in the middle of the room against the main support beam, the main mast, Teah rationalized.

Teah eased up next to them in the blackness, unable to see their faces. She preferred this. The judgmental expressions that should be on their faces more preferred than the sympathetic ones that more than likely would greet her.

The figures moved as she slid up to them.

"Teah, is that you?" Galena asked.

"Yes," Teah whispered. A searching hand found her own, giving a gentle, but firm, squeeze. It then slid up her arm to her shoulder, along her cheek and to her forehead. As it brushed the stone, it recoiled.

"Oh," Galena gasped.

"What?" Caldora asked." What is it?"

"She's been stoned," Galena forced out the words.

Now Caldora gasped." How. . .?"

"You know perfectly well, how," Galena scolded.

"Of course I know how, but they usually wait to get the

magicals back to Caltoria. It usually takes another magical to place a stone," Caldora shot back.

"They have a magical," Teah said. She felt the eyes of the two Zele Magus upon her.

"Redrick has control of another magical. She placed the stone," Teah explained.

"Governor Redrick?" Caldora whispered.

"You know him?" Galena asked.

"Yes," Caldora said." He is the only noble who travels to Ter Chadain to collect. All the others see it as too dangerous, but Redrick loves to get the first pick of magicals before the others."

"He said I am for the empress," Teah told them.

"Why would he say that?" Caldora questioned." He wouldn't know the empress's preference for a slave. . . unless. . ."

"Unless what?" Galena pressed.

"What color did the stone turn?" Caldora asked.

"I didn't see it," Teah said.

"Did you see the jewel he put on after they placed the stone?" Caldora continued.

"He put on a large ring with a black jewel," Teah said.

"Oh, to the spirits," Caldora moaned.

"What?" Galena asked.

"The stone turns red for a woman and blue for a man. The stronger the magic, the darker the color," Caldora explained.

"So black would mean. . .?" Teah asked.

"There has only been one black stone in the history of their use and that was by none other than your ancestor, Tera, the first Queen of Ter Chadain." Caldora leaned back against the pillar, her head drooping.

Galena's head hung low as well as the hope to keep Teah from being noticed by the empress waned.

Nobody said the stone turned black, Stalwart complained about the lack of information.

We are all going to be presented to the empress as a gift, Galiven lamented.

I remember the stone on Tera's forehead. Black as night, signifying the dire situation she was in. I fear your situation is no less dire, Bastion said sadly.

Teah expected to hear Falcone laughing, but he remained silent. She sensed his spirit and frowned at what she felt. Remorse.

Why? Teah asked, directing the question at Falcone.

 With the empress in control of you, our goal is pressed beyond our reach. I can only pray that our lad, Logan, can overcome this enormous obstacle.

Teah nodded at Falcone's logic. So do I.

Chapter 10

Logan stood at the bow of the ship, letting the sea spray wash over him until his hair and clothes dripped with the salty water. His conversation with Talesaur renewed his determination to stick to his goal and let the rest of the feelings bounce off him like arrows bouncing off his chain mail.

He turned, resting his back against the rail and then jumped at the sight of Sasha standing a step away.

"What are you doing here?" Logan asked.

"You haven't been yourself lately. I didn't want you to do anything foolish."

Logan frowned at her, confused, and then looked back at the bow and the water rushing past as the ship cut through the waves.

"Oh. . ." he said as he considered." Oh, no, no, no," he turned back to her, his eyes wide with shock." I would never do that," he said holding his hands up defensively in front of him.

"If you say so," Sasha nodded, unconvinced.

"Really, I would never do that. I have to get Teah back. I can't worry about anything else until then."

Sasha raised a doubtful eyebrow." If you say so."

"I do." Sasha looked over her shoulder at Morgan and Saliday laughing at the wheel.

Logan followed Sasha's gaze and his face noticeably drooped as Sasha turned back to him.

"Whatever you say, but I will always be close if you need me." She gave him a nod.

"Thank you," he said and pressed his lips tightly together." I will get over this."

"Do, or don't, I will still be here."

A member of the crew stepped up behind Sasha and Logan looked to him past her shoulder.

"What can I do for you?" Logan grinned in spite of himself; fairly certain he knew the answer.

The man, tall and lean, fidgeted as Sasha turned and frowned at him." I, I . . . well, we, we were wondering. . ." the man struggled to get the words out.

"If you could see the swords of the protector?" Logan smirked.

The man nodded, relief washing over his strained features.

"And who else wants to see them?" Logan laughed.

"The entire crew, sir," the man blurted out.

"Then let's go show them, shall we?" Logan walked up beside the man, draped his arm across his shoulders and moved with him to the stairs leading from the bow. Logan glanced back at Sasha and nodded as she shook her head and chuckled.

Logan and the sailor walked to a group of men waiting for them and watching the exchange eagerly.

Sasha didn't follow, but made eye contact with one of the soldiers on the rail nearby. He nodded and poked his men, bringing their attention to Logan and the sailors.

Under the watchful eyes of the soldiers, Logan pulled his swords and twirled them in front of him. The sailors backed away in awe.

"So ye really him?" A large sailor said as Logan stopped twirling the swords, sheathed one, and then held the other in his open hands before him.

"That's what I've been told," Logan said.

The man reached out, uncertain, but his curiosity proved too much for him not to, and he touched the blade with his fingers.

His face split in two with a grin." It's like ice," the man laughed.

The other sailors crowded in, each taking a turn to touch the magical blade.

The soldiers slid closer to the group, but held when the sailors backed away from Logan again.

Logan twirled the sword one last time and slid it into the sheath with a metallic ring.

The first man to touch the sword stepped forward and extended a hand." Benton," he said, "First Mate of the Mornen' Breeze."

Logan clasped the man's hand in his and shook it." Logan."

The men held their hand shake for a moment, measuring each other, and then gave a nod and backed away.

"Been t' sea before, Master Logan?" Benton asked.

"No, first time," Logan said.

"You seem t'be takin' tuh it. Takes most dry-landers a while tuh get ther sea legs."

"I'm a fast learner." Logan smiled.

"Enough play time with the protector," Morgan shouted from the wheel." The wind is picking up and we need to furl all the canvas to take advantage of it while at our heels."

The men burst into motion, rushing for the canvas lines and mast.

Logan watched for a moment and then hurried next to Benton as he pulled at a line.

Logan took hold and pulled, causing Benton to nearly stumble to the deck.

Benton looked back and after the shock washed from his face, he laughed and began to pull the line in earnest once more.

Logan followed Benton around the deck, taking only a few moments to watch the man begin some new task before joining in. Before long, the ship sailed with full canvas and raced across the choppy waves of the sea.

A crew member walked along the royal yard of the main mast, trying to free some tangled rigging. The ship struck a large wave, bucking the ship hard to port and causing the man to fall from the yard. His foot became tangled in the rigging and held him precariously above the deck some eighty feet below. The man cried out and the crew rushed to his aid.

Logan stared up from the deck for a second and then burst into motion, leaping to the first yard ahead of the sailors and then running along it to the mast. Reaching the mast, he scaled it hand over hand, until reaching the top yard and the dangling sailor. Logan leaned down, pulled the man free with one hand, and set him on the yard.

The crew cheered, staring up from different parts of the mast as they stopped their climb.

Logan helped the shaken man descend the mast where the crew welcomed them with slaps on the back and smiles. Benton slapped Logan hard upon his back nearly sending Logan face-first onto the deck. Logan regained his balance and turned to the man. Logan's eyes met Benton's who gave him a nod and walked away.

Logan beamed as he let the men recount his heroics and share their amazement with him.

Morgan stood watching, his look not happy.

Saliday smiled proudly, but upon seeing Morgan's face, she went stoic.

"I'll be below," Saliday said as she walked to the stairs, gave one last glance to Logan, and went below.

Logan walked to the rail where Sasha stood smiling. He turned to look out to sea, seeing it in a new way.

Sasha slid over without a word, pressing her side against his.

Neither looked to the other, but continued to stare at the fading light without a word.

****

Saliday walked into her cabin lit by a single candle, exhausted from the events of the day. She slid between the covers of her bunk and closed her eyes as Sasha came in.

The Betra deposited her weapons near her bunk and blew out the candle as she climbed in her bed. Sasha exhaled with a slight moan and rolled over.

"I didn't plan on him being here. . . or alive," Saliday said. The dark cabin remained silent." I mean, I thought Morgan was dead. I thought they all were dead. I didn't lie to you and Logan about me being the last Tarken. I thought I was the last."

Sasha didn't respond.

"I don't want to hurt him, but the chance to keep my race alive is important to me."

Still nothing.

"Sasha?"

"What do you want me to say?"

"I want you to understand," Saliday pleaded.

"I do."

"I want you to forgive me," Saliday continued when Sasha didn't.

"You have done nothing I need to forgive," Sasha answered.

"But I hurt Logan," Saliday argued.

"And that is between you and Master Logan."

"I know it bothers you that I've hurt him," Saliday continued.

"Tarken, the only thing bothering me is that your behavior is a distraction to the protector and if he is distracted, he can get himself killed. That is why this is dangerous. We need him to be in top form and focused if we are to leave Caltoria with the queen."

"But I still love him," Saliday said.

"As do I, but your love can do nothing but hurt him while mine is what will keep him alive. Make your choices for your own reason, but remember that their consequences may determine all our fate."

Saliday stared at the blackness on the other side of the room. She wanted to protest, to argue that her race was more important than her feelings for Logan. But Sasha spoke the truth. If she caused Logan to be distracted and get killed, all their futures could be over.

Saliday rolled her back to the Betra and closed her eyes. Why does this have to be so hard?

****

Morgan sat in his cabin behind the large wooden desk set before long windows at the stern of the ship. He looked over the maps and charts as his lantern above his desk swayed with the movement of the ship casting shadows back and forth across the map.

A tap at the door and the captain didn't look up but gave the order to enter.

"Come." Benton hurried in, closing the door behind him. His long hair hung greasily down his back, tied in a tail and his scraggly beard sat matted and dirty against his sweaty face. He stood so tall he needed to stoop in the spacious cabin and his shoulders were a tight squeeze for the doorway. His shirt and pants bore patches, tatters, spots of oil and dirt spread across them.

He waited picking his teeth with his knife and leaned against a support beam.

"What is it, Benton?" Morgan asked, not taking his eyes from the maps.

"The 'findin stone' says a Viri Magus is on board," the man said without emotion.

Morgan looked up, confusion across his face as he stared at the man. He shook his head.

Benton nodded as Morgan disagreed with the man's statement." Really Capt'n, the stone is glowin like the sun, in the hold."

"Those damn Viri Magus swore that thing worked. Why would they give me a bad stone?"

"Don't know, but who do you s 'pose it is?" Benton asked.

"It might be targeting Saliday. The soldiers can't be Viri Magus. It's possible the Betra has some sort of magic about her. I guess it could be her."

"What 'bout the protector?" Benton blurted out.

"That kind of magic shouldn't set off the stone. His magic is a spell cast upon him. He doesn't have magic of his own. That is what the stone seeks."

Morgan put a hand to his chin in thought as he spun in his chair and looked out at the black night.

"So we ignore it?" Benton asked.

"What else can we do? The Magus Patris only pays for those with the male gift."

"What does he do with 'em anyway? Why does he need us to capture 'em? Don't they jus' talk 'em boys with the gift into joinin'?" Benton babbled on.

Morgan turned back in his chair and frowned at Benton." Sure full of questions, aren't you, Mr. Benton?"

"Sorry, Capt'n," Benton said backing towards the shadows of the door.

"Don't be," Morgan chuckled and motioned Benton back into the glow of the lantern.

The man moved closer and took a chair in front of the desk as Morgan motioned him to sit. Morgan stood and began to pace behind his desk.

"You see, the Viri Magus have been asking us to gather the boys with magical potential so they can sell them and fill their diminishing coffers," Morgan explained.

"I thought the king supported them," Benton said.

"You are smart, aren't you Benton," Morgan smiled." That was true until Englewood came along and decided the Viri house was on its own. Now they need to gather funding any way they can, forcing them into partnerships with people they normally wouldn't consider."

Benton nodded, but his frown deepened as he thought.

Morgan moved around the end of the desk and continued to pace behind Benton in his chair.

"So, you see, it is very beneficial to us, being the middle men, to agree to use the stone and gather these recruits so the Viri Magus can sell them and stay viable. Understand?"

Benton nodded, but as he did, he looked up at Morgan with confusion." So we sell 'em to the Magus and they sell em to. . . the Caltorians? That's messed up, eh Capt'n?"

"Messed up, but profitable, Benton."

"So if the stone ain't actin' up, then you think it could be the protector?"

"I guess anything is possible," Morgan conceded.

Benton looked up over his shoulder at Morgan, a twinkle in his eye." I got in good with the boy. I can make it easy and keep my mouth shut for a cut of the take. . ."

A knife across Benton's throat stopped his statement with a gurgle of blood as Morgan held the man's head by the hair and pulled it back to expose the throat so the blade ran deep and true.

Benton's shock and terror showed in his eyes as he struggled against Morgan's restraint. His eyes lost their focus staring off at a different world.

Morgan held Benton until his struggling stopped and then leaned his head forward until the man's chin rested on his bloody shirt. The blood seeped down the man's lap and legs, pooling under his chair and spread out across the wooden floor. The blood found the cracks in the flooring and seeped into the hold below.

Morgan strode to the door, opened it, and peered down the hallway to the deck.

"Quinty," Morgan called and a short, stout man came rushing up to him.

"Aye Capt'n?" The man stopped in front of him.

"I need you to clean up a mess for me," Morgan ordered and stepped to one side so Quinty could see Benton in the room.

"Aye Capt'n," the man nodded and pushed past Morgan and began to gather the dead man. Ignoring the blood, he threw the body over his shoulder.

Quinty came back to the door, Benton's blood drenching his own clothes and Morgan stopped him. Quinty looked at the captain expectantly.

"Tell the crew he must have gone overboard. They should buy that, right?" Morgan nodded.

"Aye Capt'n. Benton stuck to 'imself, no one knew 'im too well. They should agree with that," Quinty smiled.

"And if they don't?" Morgan pressed.

"I'll convince 'em, eh Capt'n?" Quinty laughed.

"That's a good man, First Mate Quinty," Morgan smiled, slapping the man on the back as he stepped out the door and shuffled down the hall." Get back here with a bucket and mop and finish this up."

"Aye Capt'n," the man said beaming as he stepped out the door leading to the deck.

The sound of Benton's body hitting the water echoed down the hall just before the deck door swung shut.

"Too smart and greedy for his own good," Morgan smiled as he stepped back into his cabin and closed the door.

****

Talesaur sat on deck just to the side of the mast, the shadows hiding him from view. He watched as the deckhand slipped inside the cabin area and paid no notice until he reemerged carrying a body.

The soldier slid to his feet with his back against the mast as the sailor lifted the lifeless body to the rail and pushed it over the side. A resounding splash drifted to Talesaur's ears. The deck lanterns glistened off the fresh blood covering the deckhand as the man turned, scooped up a bucket and mop, and headed back into the cabin area.

Talesaur's eyes narrowed and he slipped over to the hatch leading down to the hold with the crew's hammocks. Easing the hatch open, he stepped silently down the stairs, crouching to see his surroundings before he got too far.

The crew slept soundly in their hammocks suspended three high, swaying with the waves, most snoring loudly.

Talesaur slipped by them and moved further to the stern, under the cabins. He took a lantern hanging by the stern hold door and stepped inside.

Cargo lined each side of the ship hold, leaving a narrow path down the center. He moved further to the stern, lifting the lantern as high as possible with his left hand, staring at the ceiling. He moved along, searching, until he reached the stern of the ship.

He looked around, but saw nothing. He turned to leave and a drip of water splashed down from the floor above.

The mop and bucket. He suspected.

Moving to the area where the water landed, he searched on top of the cargo, the crates, and the barrels. Setting the lantern on a crate, he made out a shiny puddle on top of a barrel. Dipping his finger into it, he brought the liquid to his nose.

Even diluted with water, he knew that smell too well. . . blood.

Morgan killed someone in his cabin tonight. . . but who and why?

Footsteps outside the hold drew Talesaur's attention and he doused the lantern, plunging him into darkness.

He needed to tell Master Logan about this, but he needed to get out of this hold first and the crew couldn't be trusted to support him.

The door to the hold flew open and a figure holding a lantern stood in the doorway looking in.

"Who's in here?" a voice shouted." Who's down here?"

Talesaur slid down between a barrel and a crate, gripping his only weapon in his left hand. . . the lantern.

Chapter 11

"You," the guard said, kicking Teah in the ribs as she lay sleeping curled next to Galena, Rachel, and Caldora.

"Ouch," Teah groaned and looked up, rubbing her ribs.

"On your feet," the man ordered." Redrick wants to see you."

Teah rolled to her hands and knees and pushed herself up, using the column for support as she stood, arching her back to pull out the kink.

She noted two more men standing at the bottom of the stairs eyeing the other prisoners suspiciously.

"Hurry up. Redrick doesn't like to be kept waiting," the man said, giving her a shove.

Teah staggered a few steps but caught her balance instantly. A slight smile crossed her lips.

Seems I still have some protector agility left in me.

Don't get any crazy ideas, Bastion warned. There are too many of them to overpower and the stone can drop you in an instant.

Don't worry. I will only strike when the time is right. She assured them.

Fool, Falcone growled. You are too inexperienced to know when the time is right.

Teah's foot caught on a raised board in the floor, surprised by Falcone's comment and she tumbled to her hands and knees.

She doesn't need you distracting her, Galiven spoke up. The fate of Ter Chadain lies with her. You need to support her or keep quiet.

The tension between the two protector spirits thickened in Teah's mind as she picked herself off the floor and followed the guard up the stairs as the other two followed.

They reached the deck and Teah followed the guard as the other two stopped, secured the hold door, and stood watch. She glanced back over her shoulder a few paces and then turned her attention to where they headed as they climbed the stairs to the main cabin.

Reaching the door, the guard motioned for her to stay there and lightly knocked on the door.

"Enter," Redrick grunted.

The guard opened the door and stuck his head inside." The girl," the guard said.

"Send her in," Redrick grumbled.

The guard stepped back opening the door wide and motioned for Teah to go in. Teah nodded and stepped into the cabin as the guard closed the door behind her.

The room wasn't at all what she expected. Contrary to the damp and musty hold, light streamed in through windows and the light breeze wafted salty air to Teah's nose. The scent of salt felt familiar, but it lacked the sweet, sour smell of sweat and stink that infused everything and everyone in the hold.
She bent to sniff her shirt at the shoulder and crinkled up her nose in distaste at the disgusting odor.

Windows lined the cabin walls on three sides, showing the blue sky and white fluffy clouds all around. The sunlight lit the room highlighting the brilliant colored fabric on the furniture and drapery. Fine rugs covered the wooden floor, giving the room a

stately look and statues sat on shelves along the walls and on pedestals placed around the room.

Several of the art pieces bore the image of a young woman, not much older than she, in various poses and all elaborately decorated and detailed with jewels, silver, and gold. Teah stared at the image on a nearby statue curiously. Teah felt she knew the girl from somewhere, but how could she?

"You have never seen the empress before. . . have you?" Redrick said.

Teah jumped at his voice as it broke the silence of the room. She looked at him as he sat on a raised dais on a large couch covered in pillows. The vibrant red of the fabric hurt her eyes to look at and the pillows represented nearly every color she knew and some she didn't.

"She will be your mistress when we reach Caltoria, you can be sure, but for now, I am your master," Redrick lifted his right hand to show the gold ring with the large black stone setting.

Teah looked at the statue again and then back to him without responding. She wanted to say plenty, but forced her jaw tight and followed the example of the protectors who remained silent.

"Come here and let me get a look at you," Redrick said, motioning her to come closer.

Teah walked with her head held high the few paces between them and stood a step from him, only then noticing the small magical who placed the stone on her, kneeling to one side of the couch.

The girl did not look up, but kept her gaze on the floor and her head bowed.

Teah stared at Redrick closely, analyzing him from top to bottom in an instant. Heavy and slow, flabby arms and legs unable to get near her unless she allowed him. His opulent stomach hung over itself and rested on the tops of his legs.

"That will not be acceptable to the empress," he scolded." You must never look directly at her unless she orders it."

Teah smirked at the thought of such arrogance, but paid the price for her outward expression as pain erupted in her head,

dropping her to a knee. The pain came like blinding light, piercing her skull with sharp, biting magic.

My magic. She fought for control.

The pain vanished and she looked up, panting from her exertion.

"What was that?" Redrick asked his magical.

"Master?" The girl looked at him, confused.

"She reacted instantly. How could her magic weave so quickly?" Redrick questioned.

"I did not see, Master." The girl shook her head.

"Watch then," Redrick said.

"Wait, don. . ." Teah raised her arm in protest, but the pain hit her again and she fell on her side, convulsing in agony. The magic stopped and Teah's screams echoed off the walls of the room and then fell silent. The protectors' voices trailed off in her mind as their screams also faded away. She lay catching her breath, not sure she wanted to draw Redrick's attention as he questioned his magical." How can the magic act instantly? Doesn't it need to form the weave first, and then cast it upon her?"

"Yes Master, but. . ." the girl stopped, afraid to continue.

"But what?" Redrick pressed.

"The magic didn't weave."

"Are you stupid," he shouted at the girl." Of course it wove. How could it affect her if it didn't weave?"

Teah lifted her head as they looked down at her in amazement.

"I could not see the magic weave." The girl said." Oh, it can't

be."

"What can't be?" Redrick said frowning down at the diminutive girl.

"She must be a caster," the girl said in a whisper.

Redrick stared at the girl in shock and then turned his wide eyes upon Teah as she lifted herself onto an elbow and stared at them flatly.

"There has been no spell caster since. . ." Redrick said airily.

"Tera Lassain," Teah said, looking him straight in the eye.

"No, no, no, no," the girl shouted, over and over again, hiding her eyes and wailing.

"Don't say that name," Redrick shouted over the magical's cries." That name is never to be spoken in Caltoria again."

"But we aren't in Caltoria," Teah said.

This sent the magical into a new round of wailing and Redrick sent a shot of magic from the ring into Teah's head again.

The pain took hold, but not quite as much. It hurt, but she wasn't blinded by it this time. She still had the ability to function if she concentrated on what she wanted to do.

With the magic still raging in her head, trying to force her into submission, Teah lifted herself from the floor and stood before Redrick's terrified eyes.

She saw him push more effort into the ring, but the pain only increased a small amount and she stood her ground.

"Guards, guards," Redrick screamed in horror.

Guards burst through the door and swarmed the room. Confused expressions looked from the magical wailing in panic, Redrick shrieking for them uncontrollably, and Teah standing before both as calm and poised as a girl attending a tea party in a garden.

"What is it governor?" the man who escorted Teah into the room asked.

"Uh, uh, take her back to the hold," Redrick said out of breath, trying to regain his control." I am done with her for now."

The girl now huddled in a corner, curled as small as she could, her head covered with her hands and her face pressed to the floor.

Teah looked at the two Caltorians going crazy and only then realized the pain still echoed in her head.

"Could you stop please," Teah said.

"What?" Redrick asked and then realized what she referred to.

"Yes, yes, of course. Sorry, so sorry."

The pain stopped and Teah nodded to him.

The guards stood, mouths open, shocked to hear Redrick speak to a prisoner so respectfully.

"Take her, now," he ordered again in a panic.

A guard close to Teah took her arm and pulled her after him.

"Wait," Redrick said, stopping the man before he reached the door with Teah in tow.

Teah and the entire group of guards turned to Redrick, waiting.

"Put her down there, but do not disrespect her in any way. . . is that understood?"

The guard holding Teah's arm frowned at Redrick at such a

thought." Do you understand?" Redrick repeated more forcefully.

"Uh, yeah, but. . .?" The guard questioned.

"The empress will not want this one harmed or marred in any way when we arrive. Her wrath will be on you if you or anyone else disobeys. Are we clear?" Redrick looked to each guard as they nodded." Good, now take her."

The guard released Teah's arm, opened the door, and motioned her out.

Teah walked out and waited for the man to exit and then walked a step behind him as they moved back to the hold.

The man kept turning to look Teah up and down, not certain what to make of her and of Redrick's behavior. They reached the hold and the two guards on duty opened it and stepped back as the guard escorting Teah offered her his hand as she took the first step.

Teah looked at it curiously and walked down without his assistance. One of the guards went to swat Teah on the back of her head, but the first guard stopped the blow. The gate slammed down as the two burst into a heated argument.

"If you touch her, it is the empress's anger you will feel," the guard shouted.

Teah pulled her eyes from the strange scene and walked down the stairs into the damp and odiferous hold. The smell of

urine and feces, ripe in her nostrils, she stopped, turned, and marched up the stairs to the gate.

"Guard," she said in her most persuasive voice.

"Get down there," one of the hold sentries said, moving to poke a stick through the bars at her.

The guard who escorted her stopped the man and moved closer to Teah, crouching down.

"What is it?" he asked.

"If we can get this filth cleaned up down here, I'm sure I will be more likely to survive the trip and not anger the empress." Teah held the man's gaze for a moment.

The man nodded, straightened, and walked out of her sight.

The two sentries studied her as they waited until the guard returned.

"We can give you mops and buckets and open the side ports for you to dump the slop out. . . if that would suffice?"

"That will suffice," Teah nodded and proceeded down the stairs.

When Teah reached the bottom of the stairs, all the occupants of the hold crowded around her, amazed at what they witnessed. Smiles and pats on the back greeted Teah as she walked back to where Rachel now sat up gingerly against the mast support with Caldora and Galena standing next to her, taking in the activity. Caldora and Galena looked curiously at Teah as she ignored them and crouched to greet Rachel.

"How are you feeling?" Teah asked.

"Been worse, but been better too," Rachel shrugged and then grimaced at her forgetfulness.

"Should be getting better very soon," Teah said, forcing a smile." At least until we reach Caltoria."

"What have you done, child?" Galena asked.

"Nothing," Teah shrugged." They discovered I am a spell caster when they used the stone to control my magic."

"What did they say?" Caldora asked.

"They say I'm the first spell caster since Tera Lassain."

"And how did they respond to that knowledge?"

"I think I scared the spirits out of them." Teah grinned.

You are scaring us as well, Stalwart told her.

Why is that? Teah asked.

Now we realize you have the power to do what Falcone fears you will, Bastion said.

But you have to know that I would never do anything like that, Teah argued.

The protectors answered her with silence.

Come on. You must know I love Ter Chadain too much to ever harm it. Teah shouted.

Still silence.

What we hope to do sometimes becomes secondary to what we must do at the time, Galiven said. I, for one, can attest to that.

Teah felt Galiven's sorrow as he went silent.

Chapter 12

Talesaur held his breath and tried squeezing farther into the opening between the two crates he wedged in when the door flung open. He kept his eye on the lantern light shining on the floor, easing closer with each step of the lantern's carrier.

Talesaur exhaled the last of his air from his lungs and slipped the last bit to the wall of the hold and out of imminent discovery along the isle of cargo. The light lit the area he just vacated and two boots stopped outside Talesaur's hiding place.

"Hmm," the person moaned as a dry finger rubbed against the wooden crate like sandpaper." Captain wouldn't like me to leave this for someone to see."

The boots turned and walked out, leaving the lit lantern sitting on the crate.

Talesaur listened to the footsteps echo across the hold and up the stairs. He pried himself from his hiding place and hurried to the doorway of the rear hold. He listened and then took a peek outside in the main hold.

The only light illuminating the dark hold came from the rear hold, sending a large shadow of Talesaur across the hammocks of sleeping men.

Footsteps sounded on the stairs. Talesaur shuffled through the doorway and crawled under some hammocks as they swayed with the roll of the ship.

Talesaur saw the boots and the bottom of a bucket followed by a dragging mop go past and he eased over to the stairs. As the footsteps stopped and the slosh of the mop hit the bucket, he hurried to the stairs and climbed without hesitation. He reached the top of the stairs, still looking over his shoulder to assure his escape remained unnoticed.

He turned and sighed with relief just as he ran right into Captain Morgan on deck. The two stumbled and fell into a heap of jumbled arms and legs.

The men scrambled to their feet, both taking up defensive postures, only then realizing who they collided into.

"What are you doing below?" Morgan asked. His hand eased to the hilt of his sword.

"I had some things stowed and decided to go and take a look at them," Talesaur said. His hand eased for his sword but came up empty. His blade still leaned against the wall in his cabin. He tensed as his hand opened and closed nervously.

Morgan eyed the Captain of the Queen's Guard and a smile spread across his lips. He eased the sword from the scabbard as the tinny sound echoed on deck and became lost to the sea and the waves beyond.

Another sound of steel sliding from the scabbard rang across the deck much deeper and more commanding. Talesaur and Morgan looked around to find Logan standing with his blades drawn and crossed in front of him as he stared down Morgan.

"Protector," Morgan stammered.

"Why did you draw on one of my men?" Logan asked.

"Uh, I didn't know who tackled me as I came to the hold and I drew to defend myself," Morgan said.

Talesaur shook his head at the lie but said nothing, waiting for Logan to continue.

"Not the way it happened in my observation." Logan shook his head." I believe you drew on Talesaur once you recognized him."

"Why would I do that?" Morgan protested.

"Exactly," Logan said.

"What's going on?" Saliday said as she and Sasha walked up to the three men." Put those away," she told Logan, giving him a shove as she walked past.

Sasha stopped beside Logan, but Saliday walked past both Logan and Talesaur to stand in front of Morgan.

"What are you three doing?" she asked Morgan.

"I am merely defending myself. Talesaur attacked me," Morgan said.

"We ran into each other," Talesaur protested." I didn't see him."

"That doesn't explain why Morgan and Logan are standing here drawing swords on each other," Sasha interjected.

"When I observed Morgan drawing on Talesaur, I drew as well," Logan said.

"What I want to know is why Talesaur was down below?" Morgan changed the subject.

"I told you, I was looking for something I stowed below," Talesaur said.

Logan caught Talesaur's eye and gave a knowing nod." An honest misunderstanding," Logan said, sheathing his swords.

Morgan stood his ground. His eyes danced between Logan, Saliday, and Talesaur.

"It's fine. Put that away," Saliday told him. She placed a hand on his arm and he jumped, turning to her defensively.

"What are you doing?" Saliday questioned." Put that away." She gestured at his sword.

Morgan hesitated for a moment and then slid the sword into the scabbard.

"Uh, sorry, I haven't slept much, I just need to get some rest," Morgan said. He turned, walked across the deck, and through the door leading to his cabin.

The others watched after him in awkward silence.

"That was strange," Sasha broke the silence.

"He needs some rest, that's all," Saliday said.

They turned to her in disbelief.

"What? Can't a person overreact because they're stressed and tired?" Saliday argued.

The others didn't say anything, but their eyes showed their doubt.

"Fine, be that way. I'm glad you're all so perfect," she said and stormed across the deck into the cabin entrance without looking back.

Sasha, Talesaur, and Logan watched after her.

"What's going on?" Logan asked Talesaur.

"Not sure," Talesaur shrugged.

"Tell me what you suspect." Logan held Talesaur's gaze.

Talesaur nodded." I think Morgan killed someone tonight in his cabin and then had the body tossed overboard."

Sasha and Logan stared at him in shock.

"I saw a member of the crew toss a body over the side and then went below to see if there were any signs of what happened. I found blood in the aft hold, right below the captain's cabin."

"Who?" Sasha asked.

"Not sure, but the same crew member came down to clean up the evidence when I was in the hold and I sneaked out. That's when I ran into Morgan. I think he suspects I know something and that's why he drew on me." Talesaur looked around as he explained, making sure no one overheard.

"I noticed all the soldiers in their cabin before I came topside," Logan reasoned." It must have been a member of the crew."

"But why?" Sasha posed.

"Don't know, but we need to keep an eye out for anything unusual," Talesaur said.

Sasha and Logan nodded their agreement.

****

Morgan walked into his cabin, slamming the door after him and leaning against it.

"Damn," he said, slamming his fist against the door.

A tap at the door caused him to jump. He turned and opened the door to peer through the crack.

"Morgan, it's me," Saliday said.

Morgan ran a hand through his hair and stepped back letting her in. He closed the door behind her and turned to find Saliday with her hands on her hips and her expression not happy.

"What was that?"

"I don't know," Morgan said throwing his hands up in exasperation." Talesaur rammed into me and I reacted. You don't stay alive as long as I have by not being quick to react."

"But who would attack you on your own ship? Why would you be so on edge?"

Morgan paced away from her, pushing his hand through his hair again, trying to find the words. He turned back to Saliday and shrugged.

"There are many who would wish me dead. I must always be on edge. It keeps me alive. And now that you are with me, I have even more to stay alive for."

Saliday softened and moved over to wrap her arms around his waist and rest her head on his chest.

"That is sweet, but I can take care of myself and you need to only worry about you."

"I didn't mean you, but our children. The seed for the next generation of Tarkens who will bring our race out of the valley of extinction and put it into a place of respect among the races."

"I thought I was the only one who hoped for that," Saliday said, not looking up.

"Don't get me wrong, you have always been in my heart and I will always find you attractive, but being the last female Tarken in this world means we need to proceed for purely selfless reasons. We need to assure our race will live on, pure in blood and breed."

Saliday nodded against his chest, her tears ran down her cheeks. She couldn't be sure if the tears she cried were tears of joy for knowing her people would live on, or tears of sorrow for giving up a life she wanted with Logan. She pressed her face against Morgan's shirt, crying for all the things she felt.

****

Logan and Talesaur stared at each other as they sat on the edge of their beds. They didn't speak for a long time, digesting all the details and information about Morgan.

Logan nodded as he came to a decision and looked over at Talesaur." You need to begin your training tomorrow. We need you battle ready by the time we reach Caltoria, before if possible."

Talesaur nodded his agreement as he stared at Logan." Do you think she's okay?"

"She has to be," Logan said, knowing of whom he spoke.

"I can't live with myself knowing I failed to protect her."

"So did I," Logan said." I should have been better prepared

for someone like Ordestan."

"How long has it been since you spoke. . . the way you can?"

"She contacted me for a short instance when we were at the Inn, but nothing since then."

"Is that strange to go so long between contacts?"

"Very," Logan said. He stopped as he listened for any voice other than his own in his mind. He began to chuckle at the thought.

"What?" Talesaur asked.

"I never thought I would miss having another's voice in my head, but I do." Logan lowered his eyes as he remembered the first time the protectors entered his thoughts and made them known to him. He missed Galiven's compassion and insight into empathy for others. He longed for Bastion's strength and confidence. He wished he could draw upon Stalwart's caution when dealing with magicals, especially Viri Magus, but most of all he missed Falcone, who always knew how to read a woman. Logan needed Falcone's insight right now to assure he read Saliday's intentions with Morgan correctly. Falcone loved a woman without condition and without remorse. Logan wished he had half the admiration Falcone did for women.

"I feel like I'm missing a part of me and it leaves me empty inside," Logan said.

"I understand," Talesaur nodded." Teah gave my life purpose and pleasure at the same time."

Both men fell silent, deep in their own thoughts of what it would mean to lose Teah for purely selfish reasons, not even considering what it would mean for Ter Chadain.

Chapter 13

Your kind has no understanding of what it means to do for others without strings attached, Falcone said. Everything you do has a plot or a motive that serves your larger goal or plan.

Teah listened and said nothing to the protector. She sensed the other protector's lack of desire to enter into this conversation. Possibly they slept now, if they slept, she reasoned.

So what is your motive? What do you wish to control or rule over by your actions? Falcone pressed.

Teah lay against the mast in the hold, her eyes closed and the sounds of sleeping prisoners around her.

Ter Chadain, Teah answered, for the protection and unification of all the people of Ter Chadain.

Falcone laughed. A little at first, but it built until he laughed uncontrollably. Noble cause, that has to be a first for your kind.

Stop it, Teah lashed out. What do you know about our nobility? I can't say I understand or condone the actions of the Zele Magus who harmed you, but it is wrong to judge all with the power of a Zele Magus as bad or corrupt.

Who are you to judge me? Falcone shouted.

His words bounced off the inside of her head as her hands pressed against her temples, trying to control the pain.

How could Logan stand you in his mind without going insane? Teah cried.

Falcone, that is enough, Galiven said.

You are the last one of us who should be giving me orders, Falcone countered.

Then let me, Bastion said.

They are right, Falcone, you need to stop this. It has no purpose and it harms us all, Stalwart added.

Teah felt the pain and sorrow from all the spirits, but the most came from Falcone as he went silent.

She lay awake, staring at the darkness of the hold, the only light shining down from the deck through the gated opening. She fought her urge to think, knowing her thoughts would not be private but fodder for Falcone to hear and use later. She instead cleared her mind of all thoughts.

As she hovered between the waking and sleeping worlds, the image of Lizzy kneeling before her, her pleading eyes searching for some kind of hope, some kind of salvation, but finding none. In that moment right before her death, Lizzy realized something that Teah refused to accept. . . they might fail. Lizzy's eyes, in the split second before her life in this world ended, filled with acceptance and calm.

"No," Teah screamed, jerking upright and holding her hands over her ears, blocking out the violent cry she herself emitted.

The hold burst into a flurry of complaints and shouts of anguish as she continued to cry out uncontrollably.

"Teah, you're all right. You will be all right," Galena said as she held Teah in her arms and rocked her, trying to comfort her.

Teah sat up wiping the tears away and looking around the dim hold. Natural light shone down the stairs and spread out as far as possible, but more light shone in openings in the side of the hold. A light breeze filtered through the stench of their prison, but the stench seemed less oppressive.

Women moved around the hold with mops, brooms, and buckets. They cleaned the hold and tossed the waste out the openings to the sea.

"What?" Teah said, looking to Galena.

"The men dropped down buckets and mops this morning at dawn." Galena nodded.

Teah smiled. Her suggestion must have made sense to Redrick.

Teah stood, brushing the dirt from her pants. She grimaced as she looked down at the soiled cloth. Blood from the battle with Caldora's troops mixed with the dirt of Ter Chadain and the filth of the ship's hold. A few blood spots showed brighter than the rest and she turned her head away, knowing they more than likely belonged to Lizzy.

Tears filled her eyes again and she turned and strode to an open porthole before the others could see. The sea breeze hit her face and brushed the tears to the sides of her cheeks as she took a deep breath.

Death seemed to follow her wherever she went.

Exactly, Falcone began, but Teah sensed the scorn from the other protectors and he went silent.

Teah stared out over the sea, nothing but water stretched out and disappeared in the distance. She turned, but then stopped and spun back to the porthole. She leaned out as far as possible, straining her eyes to make out what she thought she saw.

In the distant, sticking out of the clouds in the distance, a peak stretched for the sky. She held her gaze upon it for a moment to be sure and then gave a nod.

"Land," she shouted and the activity behind her paused for a moment followed by a rush of feet as bodies pressed up behind her and to every porthole along this side of the ship.

The entire hold burst into excited conversations as the end of their torturous journey loomed before them.

Teah gazed with a smile on her face, but the smile faded as the reality set in. I am the property of the empress herself. How will I ever be free of that servitude?

I have faith in you, Bastion reassured. Tera, your ancestor, the first queen of Ter Chadain did, and I know you will also.

But Tera possessed great power and I am...

You are the first female Protector of Ter Chadain and also the Queen of Ter Chadain, Stalwart encouraged.

You will prevail, Galiven agreed.

Teah smiled as, for once, the protectors lifted her spirits. She turned from the port, pushed past the pressing mass of women, and walked over to the stairs.

A hand stopped her before she began her climb. Teah looked down as Rachel held her firm.

"Rachel, I'm so happy you're all right," Teah said as she embraced the girl.

Rachel didn't return the embrace, but stood with her arms hanging at her sides.

"Try not to get the rest of us killed with any of your ill-planned heroics," Rachel said.

Teah stepped back, shocked as Rachel met her gaze with a flat, accusing stare.

"I, I..." Teah stammered.

"Every time you act rashly, one of us is killed or injured. Please don't include me anymore in your plans. I lost my friend because of your vanity so don't make them kill me to punish you for trying something stupid." Rachel held Teah's gaze for an awkward moment and then turned, walked back to the mast, and sat down without looking back.

Teah stood stunned as Rachel's words drilled into her mind, echoing their truth as they cut like a knife.

Silly girl doesn't realize you are the only one who can save them.

Teah's eyes shot wide in shock at the statement. . . no, not the statement, but who said it. . . Falcone.

Even though I distrust you and despise you, I do understand the truth that you are the only hope for Ter Chadain and these prisoners, Falcone clarified.

Teah stepped onto the first stair. Galena and Caldora each grabbed an arm and hauled her back to the floor of the hold.

"Where do you think you're going?" Galena asked.

"To tell Redrick we know our time on this ship is limited now that we have seen the mountain peak and I will hold him responsible for any harm that befalls anyone on this ship."

"That is just foolish," Caldora whispered." You can't go around acting like a queen when you're trying to hide that you are the queen."

"She's right," Galena nodded." You will do no such thing. And what mountain are you talking about?"

"But they are afraid of me. I can use that to our advantage," Teah argued.

"The only reason they fear you is that you belong to the empress. If they thought they could kill you without reprisal from her, they would have done so," Caldora explained.

Teah hadn't thought of it that way. She nodded and frowned." The mountain I refer to is the one rising above the clouds as plain as day."

Galena frowned and Caldora groaned.

"That is no mountain," Caldora said." That is the Spire of Ramashka, built by the first emperor to commemorate his victory over the magicals and remind us that we will always be slaves to the Caltorians."

Teah stared at her in disbelief.

"There is a jewel at the top of the Spire that is said to have the ability to concentrate the power from the slaves of Caltoria and focus it as one. That is Caltoria's ultimate weapon," Galena explained.

Teah walked to the port again, staring out at the Spire, now easier to discern as man-made. She gave a shudder.

It will assure a ship carrying magicals will not escape from Caltoria as we did, Bastion said.

And will stop Logan from coming to our aid, Teah added.

Chapter 14

Logan hurried the next morning to be on deck with Talesaur early. They wanted to do a head count to determine the crew member missing after the mysterious activities surrounding Morgan last night.

Logan scanned the crew as they went about their duties in the early dawn hours.

"Nope, don't see him," Talesaur said turning to Logan.

"Benton," Logan said sadly." Why would Morgan kill his First Mate?"

"A mystery to me," Talesaur said shaking his head." Do you think the crew will start something when they find he's missing?"

Logan looked at Talesaur with a raised eyebrow as he contemplated his question.

"I don't know. They all liked him from what I could tell. I don't know how they will take to him being missing," Logan said with a shrug.

Talesaur watched as a crew member walked by carrying a coil of rope over his shoulder.

"Let's find out," he said and took a step into the sailor's path.

The man stopped abruptly in front of Talesaur and looked to Logan with an uncomfortable smile.

"What can I do for ye, Master Logan?" the man asked.

"Have you seen Benton today?" Logan asked and waited for a reaction from the man.

The man turned pasty white and began to sweat as he hefted the rope back onto his shoulder and avoided Logan's stare. "Nope, no one has," the man said quietly and then looked around to assure no one overheard.

"Where do you think he has gotten to?" Talesaur added.

The man looked to Talesaur, hesitated, and then turned back to Logan.

"Quinty says he went overboard or else this one killed him and threw him overboard," the man said gesturing to Talesaur with a nod of his head.

"I never. . ." Talesaur began, but stopped when Logan flashed him a look.

"Do you believe Quinty?" Logan asked.

"About the overboard part, not so much who he says did it," the man said and gave Talesaur a nod.

"Thank you," Talesaur said.

"Ain't anyone believing the protector would befriend a killer," the man replied." I best get at it before Quinty catches me talking to you. Watch your back, gents; something isn't right on the Morning Breeze."

Logan and Talesaur nodded in thanks at the man as he strode off across the deck.

Morgan and Quinty emerged from below deck to climb up to the wheel and stare down at them suspiciously. They whispered back and forth, never taking their eyes from Logan and Talesaur. Sasha and Saliday appeared top side as well. Saliday went to the wheel near Morgan and Sasha walked over to Logan and Talesaur against the rail.

"So Morgan and Quinty are trying to pin Benton on me," Talesaur said.

Sasha stopped and looked from Talesaur to Logan trying to get caught up with what she missed.

"Looks that way. Glad the boys don't buy it," Logan said." Maybe we should have a word with them." Logan took a step towards the wheel when a cry rose up above deck.

"Ship ho," the man cried and pointed from the crow's nest at the peak of the mast.

All heads on deck swiveled, first to the man above, and then across the sea searching for the ship in the direction the man indicated.

Logan raced to the rail, staring out across the sea, his eyes picking up a small spot in the distance.

Morgan stood with a spy glass to his eye and nodded." That's her," Morgan said, "the Caltoria Star."

"Land ho," the man from the crow's nest shouted.

Logan peered past the Caltoria Star. Sure enough, he could see a mountain's peak reaching above some low lying clouds.

The ship began to veer to one side, away from the Caltoria Star and Logan leaned heavily against the rail as the ship bucked the sudden change of direction.

He spun and glared back at Morgan, spinning the wheel frantically, steering them away.

Logan rushed past Sasha and Talesaur standing against the rail and stormed up to Morgan as he straightened his course. Saliday stood shocked next to her fellow Tarken.

"What are you doing?" Logan shouted coming to a stop before the man.

"Keeping us alive," Morgan stated.

"But the Star is going that way," Logan said, pointing towards the land mass.

"But we cannot," Morgan argued." That is no mere mountain you see rising from Caltoria. That is the Spire of Ramashka and it is a lethal weapon against any unwanted guests."

"What are you talking about?" Saliday asked and glanced at Sasha and Talesaur joining them.

"There is a crystal upon the Spire that the empress can concentrate all of her slaves' power into and destroy any ship approaching. We must stay clear of their sight and the reach of the crystal. I watched it destroy a ship as it ventured too close in pursuit of a Caltorian frigate. It left nothing but the burned timbers behind."

They turned and stared at the Spire as Morgan steered the ship away.

"What about Teah?" Logan asked as hope slipped from him.

"I hoped we'd catch them out at sea, but since we didn't, we need a plan to get into Caltoria without drawing the attention of the Spire," Morgan explained.

"Why can't we pose as a merchant ship dropping off goods? Your holds are full," Talesaur suggested and then clamped his mouth shut at the mention of the holds.

Morgan gave Talesaur a wary look and shook his head." They know this ship and me too well for that, I'm afraid. I didn't leave Bellatora on good terms last time. I need to do some diplomacy before returning and we don't have time for that. We need to head to a port close by and see if we can find another way."

Logan hung his head as he walked to the rail, watching the Caltoria Star vanish from view again.

"Take the wheel," Morgan addressed Quinty and stepped away. He smiled at Saliday as she turned to him." I need to take care of some things below before we reach port."

"And where is port?" Saliday asked.

"Scalded Island," Morgan said. When Saliday didn't appear to fathom his explanation, he nodded." An island off the western coast of Caltoria. The Caltorians stripped it clean of anything usable to build or eat. Pretty much a dry, barren, rock, but we found a way to put it to good use."

"We?" Saliday said and raised an eyebrow.

"Pirates. . . who did you think you were dealing with?"

"A fellow Tarken," Saliday growled, placing her hands on her hips.

"Oh, but I've had to be much more resourceful than that, my dear." Morgan gave her a wink and ducked below.

"Scalded Island?" Logan said.

"Aye, 'tis said the emperor used it to test out the Spire of Ramashka," Quinty grinned, showing off his many missing teeth.

"Then why would we choose to go there?" Sasha asked.

"The far side of the island is safe enough," Quinty explained.

Sasha exchanged a shrug with Logan and turned back to stare at the sea.

****

Morgan entered his cabin and closed the door after him, securing the latch. He moved over to his desk and pulled out a drawer and withdrew a rag. He laid the rag on the desk and carefully unfolded it to expose the contents. The glow from the stone lit up Morgan's face as he leaned over it, studying it. Taking the stone in his hand, he held it on his flattened, open palm. The stone twisted and turned on his palm similar to a compass needle searching out north, until it stopped, pointing towards the deck.

"Well, well, our good captain has plans of his own, it would seem," a voice said from the dark corner of the office.

Morgan jumped, nearly dropping the stone, but clasped it before it fell. He pulled his short sword free with his other hand, but far too slowly as his adversary covered the distance to the desk in an instant and held a dagger to his gut.

Morgan gently set his sword on his desk, raising his hands up, one still clasping the stone. He glanced down at the hand holding the dagger and gasped as the crooked blade caught the lamp light and reflected it back to him.

"Senji?" He said breathless.

"Yes, Captain, and I have come to collect a debt and settle a contract."

"But, I, I, I didn't realize I had a contract on me," Morgan stammered.

"We seek the same person."

"Who?" Morgan frowned.

"The boy."

"Logan? I'm not interested in him," Morgan argued.

The Senji reached out and grasped Morgan's wrist of the hand which held the stone. He forced it open and the glow filled the space.

"The boy is also a Viri Magus."

Morgan gasped." How can that be? The protector and a Viri Magus?"

"That is why I am here to finish him," the Senji chuckled.

"But I thought Englewood put out the contract on the boy," Morgan reasoned.

"He did, but he wasn't alone. Another put a price on his head if he were to ever leave Ter Chadain. His power in Caltorian hands is not an option. Besides, he killed a Senji. That in itself is a lifelong contract."

The knife eased a bit and the Senji stepped back from Morgan to look him in the face. One of Banderkin's soldiers smiled down at the captain.

"Why are you exposing yourself to me and why now?" Morgan asked.

"You know where we're heading and can give me valuable information as to when will be the best time to strike."

"And if I don't help you?" Morgan frowned.

"Your choice, but I think you're a smart man." The Senji pushed the tip of the knife a little harder against Morgan's stomach.

A circle of blood showed on Morgan's shirt as sweat ran down his face. He froze for a moment and then nodded.

"All right, I'll help you. The island will not be a good place since it is heavily guarded and you will never escape once the deed is done," Morgan told him.

"Then onboard is best?" the man smiled, "Just as I planned."

****

Talesaur turned from side to side, scanning the deck. Logan looked at him and frowned." What are you doing?"

"Where are the guards?" Talesaur asked.

"I haven't seen them. They didn't come on deck when we spotted the Caltoria Star."

"With all that commotion, they should have."

The men exchanged shocked looks and raced for the cabin entrance. Logan slammed the door open and raced down the narrow hallway, turning at the end and bursting into the soldiers' cabin with Talesaur right behind.

Logan and Talesaur pulled up short as the stench and gore overwhelmed their senses. Blood and dismembered bodies covered the cabin. The walls and ceiling soaked red with blood. Talesaur bent down and touched the blood, bringing it to his nose.

Logan clasped a hand over his mouth, trying to keep the smell out and the contents of his stomach in as he looked down at the men.

"No more than an hour dead. The blood releases a copper odor for the first hour or so," Talesaur explained.

"Everyone is on deck except. . . Morgan," Logan shouted and ran past Talesaur out the door.

"Logan, wait," Talesaur said, trying to catch hold of the boy as he rushed past.

Logan hurried down the hall to the captain's cabin and tried the latch. Locked. He reached for his swords on his back, but only then realized they sat in his cabin against his bunk. Being on the ship gave him a false sense of security and now he only wore the small sheath holding the piece of silver rod. He shook off his hesitation and shouldered the door as Talesaur slid to a stop beside him.

The door creaked under Logan's weight and force, bursting off the hinges and collapsing on the cabin floor. A figure dressed in black stood with a knife to Morgan's mid- section. Both men's eyes stared at him in surprise and the figure lunged at him.

Logan stepped to the side, letting the glancing blow of his attacker bounce off him and then propelled the man into the cabin wall.

The man bounced off the wall, shaking his head from the impact, but continuing to advance on Logan, the crooked blade shining in the lamp light.

"Senji," Logan whispered at the sight of the dagger.

"For my brother, die," the Senji shouted and leapt at Logan.

Talesaur threw himself between them, taking the man down as they rolled upon the cabin floor. The assassin regained his feet and raced towards Logan, leaving Talesaur lying on the floor.

Logan caught the man's arm holding the dagger, blood dripping off the blade, and flung him against the far wall of the cabin. The man slid down the wall and pulled himself to his feet again, but slammed back into the wall, his eyes coming up to Logan as he stood holding his silver bow, the string still vibrating.

The Senji looked down at the arrow protruding from his chest and impaling him to the wall. Blood began to seep from the man's lips and he smiled.

"This isn't over. . . it has only begun," the Senji said and then his head slumped and his body went limp, the arrow holding him upright against the wall.

Logan lowered his bow and it became the silver rod again. He sheathed it as he realized Talesaur still lay on the floor, a circle of blood spreading out from beneath him.

Logan dropped to a knee next to the Captain of the Queen's Guard as Talesaur raised his hand. Logan clasped Talesaur's hand between both of his and squeezed. Talesaur looked up at Logan, a slight smile curling his lips.

"I guess you will need to tell Teah I won't be making it," Talesaur said and then began to cough, blood spraying from his mouth and dropping on his lips.

"You are a hero of Ter Chadain," Logan told him, holding back tears.

"It is no longer my journey, Protector. I go a different path now."

"Teah will know your valor."

"Tell her I lov. . ." Talesaur's words trailed off and his hand relaxed in Logan's grasp.

Logan reached over and slid Talesaur's eyelids over his staring eyes, fighting back his tears." I will, my friend. I will."

A shuffling of footsteps stopped outside the cabin door and Logan looked up to see Sasha and Saliday standing in the doorway. The women shared the same shocked expression on their faces.

Saliday moved towards Logan, but then saw Morgan, dabbing the blood off his stomach with his shirt open. Saliday rushed past Logan and embraced Morgan.

Logan's eyes, filled with tears, hardened as his gaze moved from Morgan and Saliday back to Talesaur.

Sasha knelt next to Logan, placing a comforting hand on the boy's shoulder as he turned to her and nodded. She stood and moved to the Senji stuck against the wall.

"One of Banderkin's men," Sasha said.

Logan nodded." What's left of the rest are in their cabin."

"But why here and why now?" Sasha asked.

Logan frowned at the Betra in thought and stood slowly. He turned to Morgan being tended to by Saliday." What did the Senji want with you?"

"Wanted me to tell him the best place to kill you," Morgan said. He pulled the scarf away from the wound on his stomach, looking at the fabric to see if the bleeding stopped.

"What would make him think you'd cooperate?" Sasha said. She moved over beside Logan.

"A knife to a man's gut is very persuasive," Morgan pointed out.

"Logan, what are you doing?" Saliday asked an edge to her voice.

"He is hiding something," Logan said.

"What can he possibly be hiding?" Saliday exclaimed throwing her hands up in the air.

"He put something in his pocket," Logan answered.

Morgan's eyes went from Saliday to Logan in a heartbeat, his expression turning angry.

"Get out, all of you, out of my cabin." Morgan strode from behind his desk, brushing off the comforting hands of Saliday and stopping at the door." Quinty."

The deckhand appeared in the doorway with a couple more crew behind him, all carrying swords.

"Escort Sasha and Logan to the protector's cabin and see that they stay there until I can sort things out," Morgan said.

Quinty nodded with a grunt and motioned to Logan and Sasha.

Logan let Sasha lead. She pressed through the doorway and the crew members and down the hall to the cabin.

Logan walked to the door, stopping when he reached Morgan and stared him down." I know you're hiding something. . . I can feel it."

Saliday hurried over and forced herself between the men, facing Logan." Please, don't cause any trouble," she asked him.

Logan hesitated as he stared down at her.

"For me," she added. He held her gaze for a moment longer and then gave a curt nod and stepped through the doorway and strode down the hall to his cabin.

The door slammed behind Logan and he heard the bolt slide across the latch.

Sasha stood in the room, waiting." What now?" she asked.

"Morgan's up to something, but I can't put my finger on it."

"It looks like it's just you and me now," Sasha sighed.

"I think we need to start using those odds to our favor," Logan said with a nod.

Chapter 15

Teah stood before Redrick, her long golden hair washed and pulled back from her face with a piece of lace. A tight-fitted black dress covered most of her as she continued to tug at the low neckline and the hem just above her knees.

She liked pants and shirts, not dresses, if this fell into that category. It fit so tightly, her ribs showed through the fabric. But it wasn't her ribs making her feel self-conscious. Wrapping her arms across her chest felt feeble, but she did what she could to hide her curves.

The men on deck panted like wolves as she walked to Redrick's cabin for his inspection. She now frowned at the man as he smiled and stroked his ample chin with his hand.

"Nice, very nice," he said." What is the matter, little witch? Don't you enjoy your new wardrobe?"

"Why don't you leave me naked, it has the same effect on them," she said, nodding to two guards standing on either side of the doorway. The men's eyes scanned her body lustily.

"Ha, ha, ha," Redrick leaned back and laughed." Not to worry, little witch, they know better than to touch you. It would cost them their lives. Nothing wrong with looking."

Teah reached for her magic, grasped it and sent a pulse towards the men at the door. The protectors cried out in warning as she released the magic.

The men lunged awkwardly towards each other, banging heads and falling unconscious across each other in front of the door.

Redrick stood in alarm." Guards," he shouted.

A group of men rushed in, stepping over the bodies of the incapacitated guards. They searched the room, looking for an assailant, but turned to Redrick in confusion when none could be found.

Pain exploded in Teah's head, catching her off-guard for an instant, dropping her to her knee before she stood back up. She took a step towards Redrick and then flew back against the far wall with her arms pressed tightly to her sides.

The petite magical girl crept from her hiding place in the shadows of a corner, her eyes gleaming with anger and fear, more like panic, but they held Teah's stare and Teah knew she possessed great power.

The girl moved below Teah and eased her down the wall with her magic. Teah's feet touched the floor again beside the girl and then the magic released her.

The girl leaned closer, her lips brushing Teah's ear as she spoke.

"Zeva," the girl whispered. Teah turned her head to look at the girl, confused." I am Zeva. Don't use your magic without permission. . . until the time is right," she explained softly.

"What are you saying to her?" Redrick shouted.

Zeva dropped to the floor writhing in pain. She went still and lay panting for a moment before getting back to her feet." I said I was sorry for making you hurt her for something I did," Zeva said, bowing to Redrick.

"And why would you do that to my guards?" Redrick asked, not convinced.

"The way they look at her is. . . appalling," Zeva said. Zeva fell to the floor again, gasping and wailing in pain for a long moment and then went still.

"I have given you too much latitude, it seems," Redrick said, staring flatly at her." I will give you no second chance. The next time you use magic without my permission you will be punished instantly."

Teah's eyes widened. He can do that?

Tera said the one who holds the matching soul stone can set limits with their will, Bastion said.

Don't give him a reason to set more limits on you, Galiven told her. The pain is hard to tolerate now.

Teah watched as Zeva stood with great effort and then straightened her clothes. She bowed to Redrick and shuffled back to her shadowed corner.

"Two of you stay here and the rest carry them out of here," Redrick directed the guards, waving a bothersome hand at the unconscious men.

Two guards took up positions on either side of the doorway while the others dragged the incapacitated men out.

"Enough excitement for one day," Redrick said shaking his head." Come," he motioned to pillows positioned around a small table to one side of him." Eat with me, little witch."

"I have a name," Teah said, wrapping her arms around her chest again.

"And what would that be? Not that it will matter. The empress will call you what she chooses."

"Teah."

"Sit, Teah, and eat while I tell you how your life will be."

Teah stepped over to the pillow and waited while Redrick slid around on his fat bottom until he faced the table. Redrick looked up at her, confused.

"I prefer to eat in the hold," she said.

"With the powers you have, I'm surprised you associate with any of the others at all."

"They're my friends."

"Be sure to say goodbye to them before we reach port. You likely won't see any of them again."

"What?"

"The empress keeps her slaves in the palace. You may find one or two of those in the hold chosen by the empress, but most will be auctioned off to the nobles and royals."

Teah sank down on the pillow, her head hanging low. We will be with you, to guide you, Stalwart comforted. The other protectors said nothing. Their silence only exacerbated Teah's anguish.

How will we ever find them all and escape once Logan arrives?

Chapter 16

Logan strapped his swords across his shoulders and pulled them tight as he strode to the window.

"What are you thinking?" Sasha asked." Time to make it on our own. . . can you swim?"

"On our own, you mean out there?" Sasha pointed to the sea. "Can you swim?"

"Yeah, I can swim, but. . ."

Before Sasha finished, Logan took hold of the porthole in the cabin with both hands and then planted his feet firmly against the cabin wall. He pulled with all his strength calling upon the protector's abilities. The porthole groaned in protest as it pulled free of the ship taking some of the surrounding planking with it. He dropped to the floor with a thud still holding the porthole. He stood leaving the porthole on the floor, stepped to the hole, and leaned out looking up at the deck to see if anyone above had noticed. He pulled back inside the cabin with a satisfied nod.

Logan looked over his shoulder at the door and waited. When no one came to investigate, he stepped through the opening with one leg, pausing to look up at Sasha as she stared at him in shock.

"You coming?"

"Where?" she asked.

"There, Scalded Island," he pointed out the opening.

Sasha looked out and saw the island in the distance." I'm not sure I can make it that far," she admitted.

"I'll get you there. Trust me," he smiled, extending a hand to her.

She stared at his extended hand. If she couldn't trust Logan, who could she trust? She gave a curt nod and grasped his hand.

He dove through the opening carrying her with him and splashed into the water below.

They came up sputtering and gasping as the ship slipped past them and continued on without them. They exchanged confident grins and began to swim towards the island as the ship veered away from them.

****

"Why would you do that?" Saliday said spinning on Morgan as the door closed on Logan and Sasha.

"He just killed a Senji. I need to evaluate what to do next," Morgan reasoned.

"He is the Protector of Ter Chadain. He will need to kill people in order to do what he must."

"But he has put me and this ship at risk. When word gets back that a Senji was killed on this ship, they will be out to get us as well."

Saliday turned away, her eyes falling on Morgan's desk where a stone lay glowing brightly.

"What is that?" She asked, not taking her eyes from the stone.

"Nothing, just a trinket," Morgan said as he walked over, snatched the stone from the desk, and plunged it into his pocket.

"No... I think I've heard of those before," Saliday said, her mind processing." That's a finding stone. . . like the ones the magicals use to find those with the gift. . . but what are you doing with it?" Her eyes shot up to his filled with confusion.

"I have need for many things, it doesn't concern you," Morgan said and moved past her for the door.

Saliday grasped his arm, stopping him beside her, her accusing eyes peering at him, fire burning below the surface." What are you doing with it?"

Morgan looked down, his expression a mixture of panic and anger that turned indifferent and he shrugged.

"Guess it doesn't matter," he said.

"What doesn't matter?" she pressed.

"The Viri Magus pay me to find those with the gift and I found one onboard." He left out the rest.

"Who on board has the gift? One of your men?"

Morgan looked at her flatly.

"Logan," she gasped.

Morgan pulled the stone from his pocket and extended it in his hand before them.

The stone glowed weakly, spun to face Logan's cabin, and then went dark.

"What?" Morgan frowned and then his eyebrows shot up and his eyes went wide in realization.

He pulled free of Saliday's hand on his arm, raced into the hallway, and down to the room guarded by two of his men. He pulled the bolt back and burst through the door.

The sea breeze greeted him as he stared out the gaping hole Logan left behind.

Saliday slid to a stop behind Morgan, bumping into his back as she peered around his shoulder at the empty room. Her mouth dropped open, stunned.

Morgan hurried to the hole and stuck his head out, scanning the water. He straightened and turned to his men as they stood in the doorway, confused.

"Come about, we need to head them off before they reach Scalded Island," Morgan ordered.

The men flew into activity at his command.

"What aren't you telling me?" Saliday said.

"Nothing."

"Morgan, you need to tell me the truth."

"I'm the captain and I will decide what you need." Morgan glared down at her and then strode from the room.

Saliday stared after him. She turned, moved to the hole in the wall, and looked out. In the distance, two small spots continued to shrink as Logan and Sasha raced to Scalded Island." What have I done?"

****

Morgan reached the wheel as the men raced around the deck, struggling to change course and pursue Logan and Sasha.

Morgan grabbed a spyglass and spun searching for the swimmers. He moved from side to side and finally found them. He lowered the spyglass, amazement on his face. He lifted the spyglass again.

"Quinty, get this thing turned around," Morgan ordered, still watching Logan and Sasha extend their distance.

"We're trying, Captain, but we seem to be caught in some sort of current. No matter what wind is at our sails, we can't seem to turn her." Quinty stepped to the wheel and cranked it all the way to one side, but they continued to go straight ahead.

"That's crazy," Morgan shouted, pushing Quinty away and taking hold of the wheel and turning it the other way with no effect. He ran to the side of the ship and stared down at the water. He stumbled backwards, stammering." Red Tide," Morgan shouted.

The crew scurried to the rails and peered over the edge.

Saliday stepped on deck as Morgan backed from the rail. She rushed to the rail and stared down at the sea. What she saw amazed her.

The ship sailed in the midst of water as red as blood. The water churned and gurgled as bubbles percolated to the surface.

"What is it?" she said turning to Morgan.

"A current that rolls through the sea and takes any ship that happens into it for a ride," Morgan said in frustration.

"How do we get free of it?" Saliday shouted over the noise of the crew pulling out the long oars.

"We row free of it, but that will take some time," Morgan said and then looked through his spyglass again at Logan and Sasha." Time we don't have. Quinty, get us out of this, now."

The First Mate scrambled around the deck shouting orders as the crew dropped oars into the dark red water and began to ease the ship towards the edge of the strange water.

****

"I'm not sure I'm going to make it," Sasha gasped as they swam.

The island still lay far ahead and it wouldn't be long before Morgan realized they escaped.

Logan slowed letting her catch up to him and then swam next to her.

"Climb on my back until you get your strength back."

"No, I can do this." Sasha shook her head.

"Don't be stubborn. You're not used to this. Let me help you."

Before Sasha could answer the water beneath them began to rumble, churn, and froth. Logan reached for a sword, but his body lifted out of the water and then flew through the air more than ten feet from Sasha. He plunged beneath the water. Opening his eyes, Logan let out a muffled cry as enormous fish swam around Sasha.

Logan burst to the surface with a gasp and scrambled towards Sasha in a panic. A dozen fins circled the Betra as she treaded water, having no way to escape the circling predators. Logan reached the outer fins of the circle when a large body lurched above him and then drove him beneath the surface again. Rage filled the protector as he drew a sword. His powerful legs propelled him beneath the circling fish and up beside Sasha. He burst to the surface as Sasha jumped in fright next to him, her dagger gripped in her white-knuckled hand.

"What are they?" he shouted over the splash of churning water, his sword held at the ready in front of him as his legs scissored to keep him above water.

"Megalodon," she gasped as fear and fatigue gripped her. One of the Megalodon charged straight for Sasha.

Logan surged between the predator and its prey, driving a sword through the skull as it lifted for a bite.

"No, don't," Sasha shouted, but her warning came too late.

Blood sprayed everywhere as Logan ripped his blade through the skull like soft bread. He turned to Sasha, confused, as a feeding frenzy erupted around them.

A Megalodon clamped down on Sasha's arm, its enormous head lurching out of the water. The Betra slashed at the giant head, her dagger glancing off the hard skull underneath.

Logan dove and severed the head as the teeth loosed from Sasha's arm and her blood added to the crimson cloud of Megalodon blood surrounding them.

Another beast struck Logan from beneath, lifting him in the air and clamping down across his midsection. The teeth shattered against the protector's invisible chain mail and the Megalodon recoiled and released Logan, disappearing into the murky water.

Sasha looked to Logan and her eyes opened wide with shock as her body jerked down a moment and came back up, but then she screamed and went under.

Logan dove after, unable to see anything in the dark, bloodied water, he closed his eyes and "felt" for her. He didn't know why, but he reached his thoughts outward. When they brushed against her feeling her presence, he dove deeper after her.

He grasped the tail of the Megalodon with his free hand and slashed with his sword, severing the tail. The beast released Sasha as it spun over and over, trying to rid itself of the pain. Sasha continued to sink deeper and Logan kicked hard, reaching her. He turned and swam towards the surface away from the rolling water above them where the Megalodon fed upon their injured.

Logan splashed to the surface with a gasp, pulling Sasha's head above water. Her skin looked pale and her breathing came in long rasps as blood pulsed from the teeth marks in her arm. Not wasting time, Logan slid his sword back in the scabbard and swam for shore with all his strength, Sasha leaning against his side, the blood trailing behind them.

Logan looked back at the trail, noticing a large gash in Sasha's leg, so deep the white of bone showed as the water flapped the skin back while he swam.

As the shoreline loomed closer, Logan gave one last glance back as several fins surfaced behind them, following the blood trail they left. His feet hit sandy bottom and he leapt up, cradling Sasha in his arms, and raced to the shore.

The fins trailed in closer, hesitated for a moment, and then sank beneath the surface, leaving a swirl of the water as the only evidence of their presence.

Logan laid Sasha on the sandy beach. He frantically ran his hands over her wounds, not knowing what to do, possibly hoping something would happen. Some magic would come to him and heal her. But she lay unconscious before him, bleeding to death as he stared at her helplessly.

"Fool, get out of the way," a voice hissed.

A firm hand grasped his shoulder and pulled him back. He stumbled over, as a figure wearing a long black cloak with a hood hiding any features slipped between him and Sasha to kneel before the Betra.

Logan scrambled beside the figure now deep in concentration running its hands over Sasha's body. Logan watched as the wounds slid together and the skin melded together leaving a thin scar behind. As the last open wound closed, Sasha drew in a long gasp of air, rising up at the waist and arching her back.

Seeing Logan, she wrapped her arms around his neck and sobbed against his shoulder. Leaning back and wiping her tears, she gathered her composure.

Logan turned to the cloaked figure standing above them. "Thank you," he said. Getting to his feet, he helped Sasha up. He let go and the Betra began to crumble to the ground. He spun back to her and caught her in his arms.

"Fool," the figure said." Her wounds may be healed, but their damage beneath is still there. Help her."

"That's the second time you've called me a fool. It will be your last time as well." Logan glared.

"Prove to me you are not. Let us move," the figure said motioning them to follow as it headed down the beach.

"We need to wait until she regains some strength," Logan called after the figure.

"We cannot unless you want to be called a fool again," the figure said shaking its head.

"And why not?" Logan asked.

The figure motioned with its hand behind Logan.

"Stay where you are," a voice shouted from up the beach.

Logan and Sasha looked down the beach as a dozen men in golden body armor rushed towards them.

Chapter 17

Teah sat through the meal, not eating, but staring in disgust as Redrick filled his face with food. It felt like a dream as the room took on a hazy appearance. She never considered how this would play out. Never thought Logan wouldn't save her or she could save herself. But as they inched closer to the end of the journey, she felt panicked.

Being separated from her friends didn't scare her, it terrified her. If Logan arrived to save them and the others were sold to different nobles around the country like cattle, they may be forced to leave them behind. She knew this, but fought the need to accept it.

After Redrick got tired of her watching him in disgust as he ate, he sent Teah back to the hold. She descended the stairs, walking over to Galena, Caldora, and Rachel. The women were bathed and wearing identical dresses, all in black and very tight fitting. Teah stopped before them, still stunned by the revelations Redrick shared with her.

"What?" Galena said as she came closer." What is the matter?"

"I, I..." Teah stammered.

"Speak up girl," Caldora urged.

"I'm to go to the empress," Teah said still staring off at nothing in the distance.

"We knew that, "Galena said confusion heavy in her tone.

"But you are to be auctioned off to the nobles," Teah finished, her eyes snapping to catch Galena's shocked look.

"But that means. . ." Galena gasped.

"We will be left behind if Logan saves you and we are too far away to retrieve," Rachel said. Teah, Galena, and Caldora spun on Rachel, shocked by her statement more for her speaking at all than what she said. Rachel had spoken very little since her whipping and now she stood with her arms crossing her chest and a matter-of-fact expression on her face.

"We will never do that," Teah began, but Rachel silenced her with a raised hand.

"You are the one who needs to escape. The rest of us are expendable," Rachel stated.

"Rachel," Teah gasped.

"It's true. Ter Chadain can survive without us, but it will perish beneath the Caltorian oppression if you do not return."

Teah turned away from Rachel's hard look, not wanting her to see the pain of the truth in her eyes.

As Teah turned, she saw the looming mountains of the Caltorian coast along with the deadly Spire. She walked to the porthole and stared out as the ship eased into the harbor. The city sprawled across the hillside, dotting the slope with buildings and roads. Large structures stretched skyward, dwarfing the other buildings.

Caldora joined Teah gazing at the amazing city.

"Emperor and empress alike build temples to themselves. There are a total of forty temples across Caltoria, each ruler building a larger monument than the last. Bellatora has fifteen," Caldora said.

A place I hoped never to return, Bastion moaned. Many magicals died here. That haunts me. I left so many magicals behind keeping the cycle of slavery and death going.

You had no choice, Stalwart said.

I should have done something, anything. . ., Bastion's thought trailed off.

Galena and Rachel came closer as they took in the enormous city with awe.

Galena stretched her arms across the two girls' shoulders and pulled them closer while Caldora shuffled awkwardly.

"No matter what happens to us, we need to do everything in our power to get Teah out of here and back to Ter Chadain."

Teah spun on the Zele Magus, her mouth open to protest, but Galena silenced her with a hard look." You know it to be true, Rachel is right. Ter Chadain will go on without us, but it will surely perish without your return."

Teah's head bowed in acceptance.

Galena reached out, placing a hand on Teah's chin, raising it so they made eye contact.

"You have come a long way from that terrified girl at the Protector's Fortress. You will get through this and will make a powerful queen."

They held each other's gaze for a moment longer and Teah nodded with confidence.

"I will make you all proud of me," she said.

"You already have," Galena said.

Caldora nodded as Rachel stared indifferently out at the coast line.

A loud clank came from above as the hold's gate flew open and slammed against the deck. Men raced down the stairs, motioning the slaves, all cleaned and groomed for their arrival in Bellatora, into groups of ten.

Mr. Gentry gathered Teah and her friends, ushering them up the stairs to the main cabin where Redrick waited.

"My prized group of witches," Redrick sneered, rubbing his hands together." The empress will reward me for such a collection."

Teah clenched her teeth as she fought back a response.

Good, learn to control that tongue of yours, Falcone chided.

Falcone! Galiven reprimanded.

Quiet. I need to concentrate. Leave me be. Teah blasted back.

"So we're all going to the empress?" Teah asked.

"For now," Redrick smiled." But where you go from there is up to her." He motioned to Gentry and the man spread his arms and ushered them out the door onto the deck.

The ship's deck ran over with chaos as the other magical slaves congregated in huddled groupings, some women not seeing the open sky above them since the start of the trip.

Teah turned to Galena and realized she stared at the blue sky dotted with white fluffy clouds like a child seeing something for the first time. Teah slid next to her and placed a comforting arm around her shoulders.

Galena jumped at first and then softened as she stared, watery-eyed, at Teah.

"I don't think I've seen anything so beautiful in my life," she took a deep breath, "or smelled so good."

Teah nodded but couldn't respond as Gentry motioned them to the side of the ship and down a gangplank to the docks below.

Soldiers in light body armor shining gold in the sunlight met them as they stepped upon land for the first time since leaving Ter Chadain. They crowded around, pressing close to the women and moved away from the ship at a fast pace.

This is bad, very bad, Bastion moaned. These are the empress's Elite Guard. They don't escort slaves unless. . . they know.

Know what? Stalwart asked.

The empress must know you are the Queen of Ter Chadain, Bastion groaned.

How could she? Galiven argued.

Then what? Why would she send the Elite Guard? Bastion wouldn't relent.

Teah listened to the protectors argue the point, but didn't add to the discussion. She turned her thoughts to Falcone who remained silent. She reached her senses towards him and finally found him, curled up and small, keeping to himself. When she touched him with her mind, his spirit flinched.

What are you doing? Falcone gasped.

What is wrong? What do you think is happening?

Nothing good, Falcone spouted. You must prepare for the worst and be ready to strike when the time warrants it.

What's with the sudden concern for my safety?

If you go down, Ter Chadain, Logan, and the rest of us go down with you. . . that's all. Falcone said.

Teah pushed the protector's thoughts aside and turned back to her world, unconvinced by his feigned sense of the greater good. He cared, even if he didn't want to, he didn't hate her as much as he claimed.

Teah stumbled over Caldora's feet as they scurried along, sending them tumbling forward onto their faces. They landed on the hard paver stone road and the party staggered and stumbled around them. Rachel and Galena kept going, unaffected by the collisions as they moved along ahead. The guards behind Teah and Caldora stumbled and yelled over the slaves. Teah's head slammed into the pavement as the mass stumbled upon her and everything went black.

****

Galena stopped and spun to watch Caldora tumble over Teah and then a number of guards fall on top of them. Teah slammed hard to the road and her head made a loud thud sound as it hit and reverberated along the road to Galena's feet.

"Oh no," Galena cried out.

Rachel turned and gasped watching the pile of bodies finally stop piling up.

Guards gathered around the fallen bodies, pulling them free one by one until they reached Caldora.

The Zele Magus straightened with a hand against her back, wincing in pain. She turned and looked to Teah who laid motionless at the bottom the pile. Caldora crouched to Teah's side while guards restrained Galena and Rachel from getting closer.

Caldora looked for any sign of life, searching for a pulse on the girl's neck. Fear tore at her features as she turned to Galena. Then, Caldora's eyes spread wide and she looked back to the unconscious girl and hope crossed the sorceress's face. She turned to Galena and gave a nod.

Teah lived. But she lay bleeding from a large gash in her head on the road to the empress's palace. Caldora held Galena's gaze as they exchanged looks of uncertainty.

Chapter 18

Lifting Sasha into his arms, Logan raced after the figure with the patrol close behind. They reached the cover of the trees at the edge of the beach and then pushed off the path ahead into a stand of trees before a cliff.

Logan began protesting the poor choice of hiding place when the figure pressed a boulder on the wall and the cliff opened to expose a black tunnel.

Without looking back, the figure disappeared into the darkness.

Logan looked to Sasha in his arms as she shrugged.

They stepped into the passage and the rock door slid closed with a thud plunging them into darkness.

A torch burst into flames and the figure glanced back at them and then headed deeper into the rock.

Logan and Sasha followed, the walls crowded them. Sasha banged her head a few times and finally leaned against Logan's shoulder for cover. Logan slid along the thin corridor, his shoulders rubbing against the stone as they went.

When he thought he couldn't take the scraping against his shoulders and arms any longer, the passage opened into a large cave.

The cave shone bright with torches lining the wall and the high ceiling. The stone shone white in the light.

Sasha and Logan stared in awe at the expanse.

"Who are you?" a man said as he approached. His long white hair hung past his waist and his black robe hung over a frail frame. Even though he stood as tall as Logan, the man seemed to be dwarfed by the Protector's size. His face bore many scars running through it, leaving deep voids of flesh and muscle behind.

Logan set Sasha down as she leaned heavily against him, supporting her weight against his shoulders with her arms wrapped around his neck.

"Logan and Sasha," Logan said, still looking around. The man spun on the figure that helped them on the beach.

"How many times must I tell you not to bring in strays?" The man shouted.

The smaller figure straightened and pulled back its hood to reveal a girl with short black hair, dark eyes, and a scowl to match the man's.

"You forget your place," she shot back." I decide who enters our inner sanctum."

"But your foolishness imperils us all," the man said not backing down." Maybe the rest will realize you are not fit to lead, making decisions like this."

"They needed my help and I sensed kinship in them," the girl said, waving an arm in the newcomers' direction.

"They are obviously warriors," the man argued." They might be spies for the empress."

"Are you?" the girl asked striding over in front of them. She stopped and stared at Logan and Sasha as they stood looming over her smaller frame.

"No," Logan answered." We're here to recover those the empress has taken as slaves."

"He's lying," the man said, tipping his head back and letting out a laugh.

Logan's muscles flexed and his free hand went for his sword, but Sasha put a calming hand on his chest. He glanced down at her and she shook her head. Logan relaxed and let his hand slip down to his side again.

"We tell the truth," Sasha said.

"The two of you against the empress and her troops is suicide," the man said walking up beside the girl, sizing them up. His eyes scanned over Logan and as they reached the handles of the swords, he gasped and stepped back.

The girl turned as the man stepped back, confusion on her face.

"What is it?"

She looked from the man to Logan and then back to the man, still unable to determine the source of the man's reaction.

"He's the one," the man stepped close and whispered in her ear.

Her eyes shot to Logan as the man spoke, narrowing as she forced herself to see him differently.

"How do you. . .?"

"His swords," the man said." It is he."

Logan and Sasha tensed as they discussed the protector's swords on his back.

The girl looked to the pommels protruding over Logan's shoulders. Her eyes widened and she drew her sword as the man drew his and stepped to her side.

Logan raised his hands while Sasha still stood with her arms around his neck.

"We are not here to harm you," Logan said.

"You do not have that choice. It is preordained. You are here to change our world forever," the man said, stepping closer so the tip of his sword touched Logan's chest.

"I don't understand," Logan said.

"Guards," the man shouted and half dozen men ran into the chamber from passages just off the main room.

The men leveled spears at Logan and Sasha as the girl and man stepped away.

"Drop the swords," a guard ordered." This isn't necessary," Logan said.

"He's right," the man said." Our doom is upon us no matter if he has his swords or not."

"Why would you think Logan is your doom?" Sasha spoke up.

"Come," the man said motioning for them to follow as he made for a passageway across the chamber.

The men around Logan and Sasha hesitated for a moment, then let the two prisoners follow the man and girl and then trailed behind them. Logan helped Sasha, supporting her weight. They entered the stone passage lined with burning torches and moved down the curving trail until it opened into another chamber about half the size of the chamber they just left. The room glowed more from the walls than the torches as they curved upward to stop at the top of the opposite wall Logan gazed in disbelief as he stared at the gold lining the walls and ceiling. Ornate carvings of people adorned the gold everywhere he looked. A large red tapestry hung on the far wall, the only flat wall in the chamber.

The man stopped before the smooth wall covered in the lush piece of fabric. When the others gathered behind him, he gave a questioning look to the girl and she nodded.

The man pulled the fabric to one side and painted on the wall before them stood a rendition of Logan with his swords crossed before him. Written below the image the words, "Beware the Harbinger of the End of This World".

Logan and Sasha exchanged shocked looks.

"Can't take you anywhere, can I?" Sasha said shaking her head.

Chapter 19

She opened her eyes, her head pounding so hard, she pressed her hands to her temples to keep it from exploding. Wrong thing to do, she cringed as her hand pressed into her wound, causing her to cry out and lose consciousness again.

She woke again, the room pitch-black. She lifted her hand to her temple, but then thought better of it as she recalled her last encounter. She gingerly touched the swollen bump on her head and grimaced. Sitting up, she couldn't tell if the injury or the darkness made her dizzy.

Where am I? In the empress's dungeon, Bastion told her.

She jumped at the sound of his voice in her head. What the. . .? What's the matter? Stalwart asked.

What are you doing in my head?

What are you talking about, Teah? Galiven said.

Who's Teah? Get out of my head. What are you doing in my head?

Ha, ha, ha, Falcone laughed. I guess one more won't make you any crazier.

Four? Four voices in my head?

The voices went silent.

Stay quiet until she figures this out, Bastion ordered. Understood?

Their silence marked their assent.

Am I going crazy? Where am I?

No response came. Instead, she had a strange feeling of emptiness in her mind. Like she had pieces missing where there should be something. . . anything.

"Where am I?" she shouted.

A light shone in a thin line on the other side of the dark room. She concentrated on it and tried to stand, but fell back. She looked at the line of light again and shadows crossed in front of it, dancing across the floor. A click of a lock and the door opened outward and light flooded the room.

Teah lifted her hand to shield her eyes from the sudden brightness and stared at the figure standing outlined in light in the doorway. The figure held a candle that lit a man's, no, a boy's face from below, giving him a sinister appearance. He moved closer and his features changed from evil to concerned and soft.

He stopped in front of her and stared at her, his large pupils encircled by a thin blue iris filled with compassion.

"How are you feeling?" he asked.

"Uh, sore, confused."

"You took a nasty fall on your way here." He held the candle closer to her face and reached for the wound on her forehead.

Teah pulled back raising a hand to the egg on her head and cringed as she brushed it.

"I won't hurt you," he assured.

"Where am I?" "The empress's palace." Teah sat, staring at the boy as he brushed his shaggy brown hair away from his face. His answer meant nothing to her." Why am I here?"

The boy laughed, but stopped when he saw she wasn't joking." You're a magical slave to the Empress of Caltoria."

"How'd I get here?"

"You were on your way to the palace with the rest of the slaves to be presented to the empress when you became injured on the road. We brought you to this room to recover."

"Who are you?"

"Nobody you need to be concerned with." He lifted the candle closer to her again, studying her." You seem to be well enough to join the others," he said nodding. He extended a hand to her and she looked at him curiously. He waited until she placed her hand in his and he helped her to her feet. She stumbled and fell against him, but his solid body supported her and kept her from falling as his arm wrapped around her waist.

A large man stepped into the doorway, his arms crossed across his chest and his shadowed face frowning.

"Are you coming?" he asked gruffly.

"Yes, in a second," the boy answered.

"The empress wants to see them all right now," the man explained.

"Here, you better take her then, I won't be coming up," the boy said handing off Teah to the man who roughly pulled her out of the room and into the hallway.

Teah stumbled to her knees with a gasp as her little black dress hiked up and her knees scraped the stone floor.

"Idiot," the boy shouted, striking the man across the back of his head.

The man recoiled and brought his fist up in anger, but then dropped it with a sigh of resignation.

The boy helped Teah to her feet and looked compassionately into her blue eyes.

Teah wrapped her arms around him as he supported her weight and she regained her balance. She held his gaze for a long moment, with their faces close together.

The boy cleared his throat and leaned back, but didn't let go of his hold on her.

"You all right?"

"Yeah, I guess."

The boy stepped back assuring Teah wasn't going to fall again, then turned and backhanded the man, sending him sprawling against the open door. He stood over the man pointing a threatening finger at him." Don't you see her soul stone?" the boy chided." I wouldn't want to be the one who damages her. Understand?"

The man came to his feet, his anger wafting away as he stared at Teah's forehead. He nodded.

"Good, now bring her up. It appears the others are already taken," the boy said looking at the open cell doors next to the one they stood by.

The man nodded again and took hold of Teah's arm, firmly, but not roughly. He led her away as she turned back and stared at the boy over her shoulder as she went.

The boy watched her go, the sadness in his eyes deepening as she left.

The man led Teah up several levels of stairs hewn into rock until they reached a level where the stone gave way to stone block, brick, and wood. The hallway they entered towered over them twenty feet and sprawled out as far as Teah could see.

The floors shone back at them, polished to a high gloss, and their footsteps echoed as they walked along. The man didn't slow as Teah pivoted her head to take in the beauty and extravagance all around her. Pillars reached for the sky as windows at the peak of the roof shone light everywhere.

They marched up another two staircases and stood before a golden door adorned with jewels of every color imaginable. A large bird of prey etched in the door greeted them with spread wings and talons bared to take a victim.

Teah felt the victim to those talons, uncertain what she would find on the other side of the door. The great doors opened inward to a large chamber with golden accents everywhere.

A line of women in identical black dresses knelt before a dais where a woman wearing a long, flowing, silken blue dress sat on a throne depicting the same bird as the door hovering over her, the talons digging into the back of her golden chair.

Teah's eyes met the woman's upon the throne and for a second, fear stirred in those eyes, but fear soon became rage as she stood and pointed at Teah.

"She looked at me, right at me, teach her respect," the woman cried.

The man shoved Teah down to her knees in the doorway, not stopping until his hand forced her face to touch the floor, smashing her nose into the shiny surface.

Teah's head pounded as the blood surged to her head and filled her throbbing lump. The man held her down, not letting her move.

Teah listened to the panicked breathing of the woman slow and calm. The man's hand released from the back of Teah's neck and she lifted off the floor just a bit. She waited to hear what to do next, not wanting to be shoved into the floor again.

The man's breathing brushed her ear and she jumped at his closeness." Keep your eyes down and never make eye contact with the empress. Understand?"

Teah nodded and the man lifted her to her feet by an arm. He ushered her over to stand in line with the other women. Teah stood with her eyes to the floor and listened as the man stepped behind her. She turned slightly and noted a man behind each woman in line. She snuck a glance at the three women in line with her.

The nearest woman stood tall and lean, a dark red gem in her forehead. Her long blond hair hung over her shoulders. She hid a slight smile as she looked at Teah.

The next woman's red jewel shone a little darker than the first, and her blond hair showed a tinge of brown to it. She stood about a hand shorter than the first woman and lacked the shape of the other woman. Her eyes held Teah's as if searching for something. Her features turned fearful when she didn't find what she expected.

The third woman looked more a girl than a woman. Her short brown hair matched her sad brown eyes and her red jewel shone lighter than the other two. She glanced to Teah, but the fear in her eyes soon had her staring at the floor once more.

Teah turned her gaze to the floor again, wondering what connected her to these women. The way they looked at her, they had history, but why couldn't she remember? Her hand reflexively went to the lump on her head and she froze.
Who am I?

The magical prisoner of the Empress of Caltoria, right now, Bastion broke his silence.

Teah clenched her eyes shut, trying to control the terror ripping through her from hearing that voice again.

We are here to help. Give us time to explain, Galiven said softly.

Wait for a better time and we will explain everything, Stalwart added. The empress must not suspect who you are.

Not a problem, since I have no idea.

Chapter 20

"Kill them, kill them now," one of the guards shouted and lunged his spear at Logan.

Logan shoved Sasha out of the way and rolled the other direction, the spear stabbing harmlessly in the air. The ring of steel filled the chamber as Logan came up holding the swords before him, his back to the wall.

"I'm not here to end the world," Logan shouted.

"It is you," the man cried. He turned and ran into the passage pulling the girl behind him.

"Wait, let him explain. . ." the girl protested, fighting against the man as he yanked her into the tunnel." There's something about him. . ." Her voice trailed off as the man dragged her away.

Sasha got to her feet shaking her head as Logan stood exactly as the picture behind him.

"That's not helping," she shouted.

Logan looked over his shoulder at his image and groaned, rolling his eyes.

The guards advanced on him as the man and girl inched out of the chamber back through the passage.

The six men attacked with spears leveled at Logan. He jumped above the spears, spinning as he did and slashed the spears in half. He landed next to Sasha as the men stared in shock at the remnants of their useless weapons. They turned and ran down the passage.

"We better get out of here before they block us in," Sasha suggested.

The last man slapped a spot at the entrance of the tunnel sending a stone door sliding shut, trapping them in the chamber. Sasha and Logan exchanged worried looks as the door slammed shut, trapping them.

Logan ran to the door, slamming his hand against it in anger over and over again.

"Let us out," he shouted. His fist pounded against the golden overlay on the stone sending shudders through the stone as rock dust fell around them.

He pounded until blood ran down his arms and dripped off his elbows with each blow.

Sasha limped up behind him and placed a hand on his shoulder. Logan's blood splashed across her face, but she didn't wipe it away, waiting patiently.

Logan banged the door a few more times before he realized Sasha stood behind him with her hand on his shoulder. He stopped without looking back at her, leaning his head against the door in resignation.

Sasha shifted her weight onto her uninjured leg and took Logan by the shoulders and turned him to face her.

Logan's face shone wet with tears and blood as his red, watery eyes stared back at her, beseeching her for hope.

Sasha pulled Logan into a hug, placing a hand behind his head and easing his forehead to her shoulder.

Logan wrapped his arms around her and sobbed like a child.

Sasha stared at the stone door, Logan's blood dripping down the surface through the indentations from his anger and the remnants of his skin. Her eyes grew wide, not because of the door, but because for first time, she thought of Logan as his true age, a teenager without a parent and at this moment, without his sister.

"I'm sorry," Logan said taking a deep breath and straightening from the Betra's shoulder.

"No need to be," Sasha said, looking at him hard.

"I can't believe it ends here, in this cave. I have failed my sister. . . and my country." Logan began to turn away, but Sasha stopped him with a hand on his shoulder.

"You have not failed anyone."

"Teah will be a slave for the rest of her life, and soon the Caltorians will invade Ter Chadain."

"But it is not your fault. Ter Chadain's fate has come to this over many years, no centuries, and you have done your best."

Logan bit his lower lip and ran a hand through his hair leaving a streak of red blood. He nodded, knowing she spoke the truth, but it didn't make it any easier or remove the burning in his belly.

Logan leaned his back heavily against the bloodied door and slid down to the floor, hanging his head between his bent knees. Sasha sat down next to him with a groan as her injuries pulled at her insides.

"We are quite the pair," Logan moaned.

"That we are," Sasha forced a smile and slid against him.

****

Raven Gassler sat at the table with the men, staring down Massa Blane with her black eyes until he could stand it no longer.

"It is what must be done," Massa said coming to his feet and slamming his glass of ale on the table.

The other men stared at the seer in shock.

"It is what you say, must be done. . . but I think you see what you wish, not what you can," Raven said in a whisper. The effect proved rewarding as the man burst into one of his rants and Raven's lips pressed tight, trying to conceal the upturn of a smile.

"You are a foolish child holding out hope for legends to come and set us free. There is no Protector of Ter Chadain, only a boy who is a poser hoping to trick us into following him into a battle we cannot win," Massa said, striding from the table and then rushing back and slamming his hands down, sending echoes through the chamber." You will not cross me on this, Raven. You cannot. This is my call and I say, let them die in the chamber that bears his likeness. He is nothing more than a false hope."
Massa held Raven's gaze, staring right into her soul.

Raven deflected the weave the old man tried to place around her, sending it instead into the man next to her. The man's eyes glazed over and he nodded his obedience to Massa.

Massa turned to the man realizing what just happened. He threw up his hands in disgust, shooting Raven an angry look. He turned and stormed from the chamber.

Raven watched Massa leave, her mind working her plan the entire time. She couldn't let the boy die no matter what Massa said, but if he discovered she went against his wishes, it wouldn't matter if she led them or not; Massa would win out on this point.

She needed to act now, before the elders convened that night. She needed to free the two strangers, but without letting Massa discover it until too late.

But how?

Her eyes went wide and she grinned. Of course, the tunnel behind the waterfall. She hadn't been there for years, but it might still be passable. If she could get to the passage, perhaps the boy could open the doorway.

Raven got to her feet; the men gave her a passing nod, but continued enjoying their ale without any more notice. She raced away, hoping her idea had merit.

****

Sasha watched Logan out of the corner of her eyes, the concern carving deep lines in her face as the wrinkles showed in her forehead.

Logan hadn't moved since his attacks on the door proved fruitless and bloody. The blood on his arms congealed and hardened as the bleeding stopped. He kept his eyes closed, searching for some strength inside his mind.

How could I let this happen? Without me, Teah is a slave forever and the empress invades Ter Chadain.

He leaned his head back against the wall and opened his eyes. The gold shone in the dim torch light giving the chamber a warm glow. Logan frowned as he looked around and then his face turned curious as he spotted something sitting on a raised stand off to one side.

He pushed to his feet and walked over to the stand as Sasha followed his movements with her eyes. He reached down and lifted a length of rope from the stand with one hand and then a piece of parchment in his other and read the inscription.

"The rope used to bind the hands of the family of Tera Lassain, First Queen of Ter Chadain." His eyebrow lifted in surprise looking down at the other two pieces of rope.

Sasha moved over next to him and touched the rope." Your ancestor's parents and sister were hanged by the Emperor during the 'Magical Uprising' to punish Tera and the other magicals from forgetting their place."

Logan nodded, the loss of his own family, the Lassains and his adoptive family, the Saltos ringing sharply in his memory.

Sasha moved to a stand next to the one holding the rope and lifted a clear jewel in her hand. She stared at it, turning it in her fingers, examining it.

"What's that?" Logan asked moving next to her.

Sasha handed the jewel to him and lifted the card sitting on the stand.

Logan gazed at the gem in his hand, lifting it to his eye level.

"Tera Lassain's soul stone," Sasha said, her voice a whisper.

Logan held his breath, easing the stone back to the stand and rolling it from his palm and stepping away. Sasha watched with a curious smile on her face. Logan stopped backing away and exhaled a long breath. He looked over at Sasha as she stared at him, amused.

"What?"

"You act as if it will bite you," she grinned.

He didn't want to get into the protector spirits being ripped from his mind, but the thought of the stone's power made him shudder.

"I don't know it won't," he shrugged.

"Come on, it's a jewel, there is nothing special about it," Sasha laughed.

"Shush," Logan said, placing a raised finger to his lips.

Sasha began to protest being shushed when she heard the light tapping and she turned with a raised eyebrow to Logan.

Logan moved over to the wall bearing his likeness and placed his ear against the stone. He listened for a moment and then moved a step one way and pressed his ear to the wall again. He repeated this several times until he zeroed in on the tapping behind the wall. He stepped back, looked to Sasha who gave him a shrug.

A strange expression crossed Logan's face and his eyes glazed over. As if in a trance, he drew one of his swords, the grinding sound of metal against metal filled the space and then the sword rang musically as it pulled free of the sheath. Logan stepped to the wall and pressed the blade against a thin groove in the wall which happened to be directly over the heart of the rendition of the protector.

He pressed his weight behind the blade and it slid into the stone up to the hilt. A loud click echoed through the chamber like the releasing of a lock. Logan turned the handle of the sword and a crack appeared alongside the image on the wall.

The rock swung inward as Logan pulled his sword free and before them in the opening of a tunnel, stood Raven.

Raven looked first to Logan and snapped her fingers.

Logan blinked several times and then shook his head to clear his mind." What was that?" Logan asked as his eyes narrowed with suspicion.

"A little weave to instruct you, nothing more. Quite harmless," Raven assured him. She looked to Sasha and gasped at the sight of the gemstone in the Betra's hand." Place the stone back onto the dais," Raven said in a reverent whisper.

"You two act as if this is dangerous. It's just a stone," Sasha said, placing the jewel down.

"You are so wrong," Raven said." It is very powerful magic. Best to leave it alone."

"You're setting us free?" Sasha asked, changing the subject and turning the unwanted attention to Raven.

"I am, but no one else must know about it," Raven told them.

Logan nodded and walked towards Raven as the girl turned and led the way into the tunnel. Logan looked back at Sasha.

"Coming?" he asked, but entered the tunnel without waiting for an answer.

Sasha snatched up the soul stone and shoved it into her pocket with a shrug.

"Might come in handy," she said and limped after Raven and Logan into the tunnel.

Chapter 21

Teah Lassain, Queen of Ter Chadain, stood in front of Shakata, Empress of Caltoria, with her head bowed and eyes concentrating on the floor and feet around her. The smell of burning incense filled Teah's nose and light chimes rang in random cadence as the wind blew through the room.

Teah's calmness came as a gift of her amnesia. If she realized how close she stood to the end of Ter Chadain's existence, she may have panicked. But instead, she possessed no memory of her home country, its plight, or that she held the key to its freedom from Caltorian control. So Teah Lassain stood before her nemesis with no recollection of the past and thus no sense of her future.

For at this moment, Teah stood before Empress Shakata as a magical slave "retrieved" from Ter Chadain. Retrieved. That's what the Caltorians called it since all the magicals living in Ter Chadain were direct descendants from those who escaped from Caltoria long ago.

Only the women standing by Teah's side knew her true identity and they weren't sharing that information.

A large muscled man stepped up beside Teah. He stood tall and proud next to her and she flicked her eyes to catch sight of his golden military uniform and muscular arms. She chanced a glance to the man's face and caught her breath.

His chiseled chin set with confidence along with his golden hair hanging to his shoulders posed a striking image. But his hazel eyes concentrating on the empress before him held a smoldering fire beneath their surface threatening to expose the passion burning within his soul.

Teah pulled her eyes away to stare at her feet again as she blushed with the feeling she saw something not meant for her. "My Empress, Governor Redrick has returned from his retrieval to Ter Chadain," General Anthony announced.

"Governor Redrick, what have you brought me?" Empress Shakata said, her voice light and musical, yet driven from a place of authority and control.

"Humph," Redrick cleared his throat and stepped in front of the line of women. He bowed low, struggling to keep his balance as he held it for a moment before standing upright again." My Empress, I bring you the prize selection from our latest retrieval. A fine group of magicals for you to have first pick."

The empress stepped down from her dais shadowed by two people robed in black. The hoods on the robes hung back away from their faces revealing one man who stood about a hand taller than Teah and a woman much shorter. The man's short black hair parted on his forehead to expose a dark blue stone. His brown eyes constantly scanned the room. The woman's dark hair hung past her shoulders and a deep red stone shone above green eyes. She also watched the occupants of the room closely. The empress and the two magicals walked in front of the women. Teah and her friends kept their eyes lowered, fighting the urge to look upon the empress, but stared at her golden slippers on tiny feet as they shuffled in front of them along with the two magicals' feet flanking her.

They stopped in front of Teah and the empress placed her hand on Teah's chin. Teah allowed the empress to raise her face and Teah's eye flickered to meet the empress's dark orbs.

Teah let out a gasp as the woman's beauty took her breath away. The empress's black eyes were actually very large pupils with only the slightest sliver of a golden iris circling them. Her skin shone with light as the pale coloration reflected all the light from the room. The skin looked silky to the touch as it flowed over high cheekbones and a perfect nose and chin. The empress's black hair hung long and straight past her shoulders, a braid of hair pulled back from the middle encircling her head and tying off in the back.

Empress Shakata stared at Teah's eyes, pushing past the surface and delving deeper, trying to catch a glimpse of the girl's soul. She paused for a moment, a curious look on her face as she took in this strange magical before her.

She let her eyes wander to the soul stone and her breathing stopped. Not a gasp, not an exhale, but nothing. Her eyes widened as they flicked from one side of their sockets to the other, her brain trying to digest what she saw. She looked to the magical on either side as they exchanged shocked stares.

Empress Shakata turned to Redrick as he stood watching with anticipation. He answered her gaze of amazement with a nod. "Is she a . . .?" Shakata started, but couldn't finish as her breath ran out.

"She is a caster," Redrick said nodding.

"Dear gods," Shakata gasped along with the two magicals beside her." Her name?"

"Teah," Redrick answered.

Teah still stared at the empress as she turned to address Redrick. Teah gazed at the earrings dangling from the empress's ears, the gold and jewels beyond anything Teah could imagine. *Keep your focus on what's going on,* Falcone chided. Teah jumped at the voice in her head. Empress Shakata still held Teah's chin in her hand and turned back to her when she jumped.

"What did you say?" Shakata asked.

"Nothing Empress," Teah answered.

"I heard a voice. Say something again," Shakata ordered.

"I said nothing Empress."

"No, it was deeper, like a man's voice," the empress insisted.

She turned to the woman and then the man at her side, but both gave her an unknowing shrug and shake of their head.

How could she. . . Falcone began, but stopped when the empress's eyes widened and her mouth dropped open.

Silence, she hears you, Stalwart shouted.

The empress dropped her hand from Teah's chin and took a step back, her face filled with horror. The two magicals stepped between Teah and the empress, pressing the empress away from the girl. The guards, sensing their empress's fear, stepped between her and Teah, looking at Teah for any sign of aggression. They found none, but maintained their position between them.

"What is it, my Empress?" General Anthony asked.

"I heard men's voices, she is possessed," Shakata whispered, moving back to her dais, her eyes flicking from side to side nervously." Berza, Tanlor, didn't you hear them?"

The magicals shook their heads." We heard nothing, our Empress," they said in unison.

General Anthony's face went pale as he moved closer staring at Teah and then back to the empress.

"What?" he said in a hush.

"I..." the empress began and then stopped as she saw her General's face.

"That would be magical ability," he continued to whisper." That is not possible." He held the woman's attention for a moment longer and gave a curt nod as she nodded slowly.

"Of course it would," she agreed. She sat down upon her thrown, the scared look on her face passing as she watched General Anthony straighten from her and nodded again.

"I will take them all for now, until I have the opportunity to decide who I shall keep permanently," she told Redrick.

The governor motioned to the guards and they ushered the slaves out of the room in single file one after another. They shuffled out without a glance back.

****

The empress stared after Teah as she left, her fear not washing away totally, but lingering in her mind as the implications of what she had experienced hovered over her.

General Anthony ushered the guards, Governor Redrick, Berza, and Tanlor out of the room closing the door behind them. He then turned to his empress.

Her eyes met his and then flicked away. She stood as he approached, moving away from him to the window. She gazed out at the city and the ocean beyond. Everything she beheld belonged to her and she held complete command over it.

Her usual confidence wavered as she fought to quell her uncertainty. She couldn't possibly hear another's thoughts. . . could she? That would mean she was a magical. None of her bloodline before her possessed magical abilities, yet she heard what she heard. Men's voices coming from that girl.

Empress Shakata glanced over her shoulder as General Rowan Anthony approached. He set a comforting hand on the woman's shoulder but she didn't turn to him.

"You mustn't speak of this to anyone," Rowan instructed." I wondered when the gift would manifest. . ."

Shakata spun on the man, sending him staggering backwards. Rage boiled in her eyes.

"You knew of this, yet kept it from me?"

"I didn't think you would react this way, announce it to all," Anthony explained.

"How did you expect me to react when I discovered I possessed magic? The same magic we claim needs to be controlled and enslaved."

"No," Anthony shouted.

This only brought more fury to Shakata's face as her stare cut into him.

"I mean, your magic is given by the gods to rule," Anthony blurted out, trying to cool the fire inside his empress.

"So my parents knew of this and chose not to tell me?" she said, her words betraying her hurt.

"They feared the knowledge would scar you, hinder your development. They decided to wait and see if you possessed the magic before they put you through that pain. You were too young when your parents died." Anthony took a comforting step forward, but Shakata put a hand up to stop him.

"And when they died suddenly in the earthquake they didn't have time to tell me," Shakata nodded.

"Yes," Anthony said.

"So my bloodline is that of a magical?" Shakata said, the words disgusting her.

"No, never that," Anthony said, his hands coming up before him as if being stricken.

"Then what?"

"The royal bloodline doesn't possess magic that is woven, but ability, a gift bestowed upon you from the gods."

"To hear voices that aren't there?" Shakata said, unconvinced.

"No, the gift to read another's mind. This gift has allowed the royal bloodline to stay in power and foresee any coup attempts on the throne. It is what made your ancestors the powerful rulers they were and... what will take you to the next level of rule." Anthony dropped to a knee and bowed his head as he finished.

She reached down, placed a hand on his chin and raised his face as their eyes met." Rowan Anthony, I am not pleased you kept this from me," Shakata scolded at the look in the general's eyes.

"I couldn't stand the thought of causing you more pain after. . ."

"We shouldn't speak of the past." "I can't rid myself of the feelings and fond memories of our time as lovers." "I moved on, I assumed you had as well. It is sometimes uncomfortable due to your position, but I value you as a general."

"We will always be connected through our son," Anthony shrugged. Empress Shakata's eyes shot wide and her mouth moved without any words coming out. She stared at Rowan with her thoughts displayed plainly on her face.

He nodded as if he could read minds as well." Our son may also have your ability someday."

The empress moved back to her chair and dropped down in despair, the weight of this gift feeling too heavy for her to bear. And the thought of magic coursing through her son's veins as well felt unbearable.

Chapter 22

Logan and Sasha followed Raven through the tunnel that ended in a large chamber behind a wall of water created by a huge waterfall. Raven picked up a canvas bag leaning against one of the many stalagmites jutting towards the ceiling, pulled some meat and bread from it, and handed some to Logan and Sasha.

"You must be hungry, but we need to eat and be on our way before Massa discovers me missing," Raven said.

Logan and Sasha took the offered food and tore large bites from the bread and then the meat, chewing ravenously.

"I'm Logan and this is Sasha," Logan introduced through a mouthful of food nodding at Sasha.

"Raven," the girl said." Leader of the resistance. . . at least until Massa finds out about me setting you free. He will have the elders toss me out and take my place."

"We are very grateful to you for setting us free," Logan said, motioning with his arms caked in his dried blood.

Raven grimaced at Logan's arms, but didn't mention them.

Logan glanced down at his arms, realizing the spectacle he must seem. He walked over to the waterfall and stuck his arms in the flow of water, washing the blood away.

"Is Massa that old guy who locked us in?" Sasha asked and then took a large bite of meat.

"Yes, he is our seer," Raven said." He is the one who drew your image on the wall of the temple."

"That was a temple?" Logan asked, shaking the excess water off his arms and wiping them off on his shirt as he walked back.

"The temple is there to hold the precious artifacts from the first magical rebellion. It is a place to give us hope for our future."

"And then he traps the chance of a future in the temple to starve to death?" Sasha said, unconvinced.

"I think Massa truly believed you were coming to save us. . . at first. . ." Raven explained.

"And now?" Logan asked.

"He feels you are here to lead the rebellion to destruction."

"But you don't," Logan said.

"I feel he is interpreting the prophecy wrongly. It says you are here to destroy the world as we know it. . . but isn't that what we are hoping for? To change this world of slavery and cruelty over magicals?"

Logan glanced to Sasha who gave a shrug and a nod.

"We are here to rescue someone who was taken to Caltoria as a slave," Logan said.

"You are not here to lead our rebellion against the empress?" Raven asked disappointment heavy in her voice.

"My goal is simple, put my sister on the throne of Ter Chadain," Logan said." That has never changed."

"If your sister is the queen and you carry the Protector's Swords. . . that makes you. . ." Raven didn't finish the thought.

"The Protector of Ter Chadain," Logan stated." And not a pretender as Massa suggests?"

"No, Raven. I am the true Protector of Ter Chadain."

Raven staggered a bit, her hopes becoming a reality too overwhelming for her to comprehend. She put her hand against the stalagmite for support and slid to a sitting position.

"Are you all right?" Sasha asked, dropping to a knee beside the girl.

"Yeah," Raven said nodding." I never thought I would live to see this day. The day the protector came to Caltoria."

"I know the feeling," Sasha said grinning up at Logan.

Raven looked long and hard at Sasha, the Betra's black clothing shredded in places where the Megalodon's teeth made contact.

"Of course, you are one of the Forbidden," Raven said pointing at Sasha." Massa said the protector might have a traitor   blood v

"She is no traitor and the Betra are well on their way to becoming part of Ter Chadain again. Their army fights the Caltorian occupation of Ter Chadain as we speak," Logan explained.

Sasha smiled and puffed up with pride as Logan spoke in her defense.

"We must be moving," Raven said coming to her feet." Take what food you wish and hurry. We need to get to the passages before the next patrol or risk entering the tunnel at the worst time possible." She turned and hurried off, leaving them behind to stuff food into their pockets.

"What time is the worst time?" Logan shouted after her.

"Mashlad feeding time," Raven shouted back over her shoulder.

"That doesn't sound pleasant," Sasha said shoving the remainder of the food quickly into a pocket.

"Not at all," Logan agreed. He stuffed the last piece of bread into his mouth and hurried after Raven with Sasha close behind.

****

Saliday's eyes threw daggers at Morgan as he piloted the ship into the port on the far side of Scalded Island. She fumed over leaving Logan and Sasha in the water while they struggled to free the ship from the Red Tide.

Morgan insisted that until his men freed the ship, Logan and Sasha were on their own.

Once free of the Red Tide, they hurried after Logan and Sasha only to find a trace of blood diffusing into the water after the feeding frenzy ended.

Saliday refused to cry, fighting back the tears and pulling her Tarken upbringing of grit and strength from her reserves. She now saw one clear path before her and that path did not include saving Ter Chadain, but maintaining her bloodline, rebuilding her people's population.

At least she needn't feel guilty about hurting Logan, but she hated that it ended like this.

The ship eased into port and then settled into a slip where a large armed contingent of men boarded as soon as the gang plank lowered.

The soldiers, all wearing gold uniforms with an eye, pupil large and black with a thin golden iris surrounding it embroidered on the chest, marched onto the deck.

Morgan met them and spoke to a man with several black stripes on his left sleeve.

"Captain, we come to trade and fill our holds to take supplies back to the troops in Ter Chadain," Morgan said.

The man nodded and then motioned for his men to search the ship. The guards scattered, disappearing into every doorway and hold entrance.

"What news do you bring of the war in Ter Chadain?" the man asked.

"King Englewood is dead, but the occupation expands as planned and soon all the magicals will be rounded up and controlled as they should be," Morgan said.

The captain nodded his approval of the information and smiled.

The men began to file back one at a time, speaking to the captain quietly. The captain's expression didn't change as each man reported back and soon the entire boarding party stood at attention behind their captain.

"All is as you say, except for the large hole in one of your cabin walls. What happened?"

"Mishap when we got too close to a ship in Stalwart," Morgan lied." We didn't have time to wait for repairs. We will have them done here, if there is a shipwright close by?"

"One right down the dock," the captain pointed to a sign displaying a large ship over a door on a nearby building.

"Thank you," Morgan said.

"I'll send the dock manager down to supervise the unloading," the captain said.

"I do need to meet with the governor," Morgan added as the captain began to turn and leave. The man froze and turned back cautiously to Morgan, his hand coming to rest on the hilt of his sword.

"That is very unusual for a mere merchant ship captain. Who might I say is requesting his audience?" the captain asked.

"Morgan Task."

The man's eyes shot wide and his men began to draw steel, but a raised hand from their captain stopped them.

"It has been some time since Scalded Island has been host to your presence," the captain said, choosing his words carefully.

"Yes, yes it has, but you can assure the governor that seeing me will be quite fruitful." Morgan grinned so wide, his face nearly split in two.

The captain nodded and hurried down the gangplank followed closely by his men and then along the dock until he and his men were out of sight.

Saliday moved over next to Morgan as he watched the guards disappear." What was that about?"

"The governor and I go way back. Kind of a give and take relationship," Morgan said, nodding nonchalantly.

"How do you mean?"

"I give him something so he doesn't take my life," Morgan sighed.

"And coming here was a good idea, why?"

"Because I have something to give him that will make him let me take anything I want," Morgan said grinning and tossing the magical stone into the air and catching it again.

"Why would you give him a seeking stone?" Saliday asked.

"Because, my dear Saliday, there is only so much sniffers can do, and this will allow the governor to search out and destroy the last magical rebellion here in Caltoria." He turned and snatched the stone from the air one last time before striding away humming proudly.

Saliday stared after him, her face awash with horror at the man who held the key to the future of her people.

Chapter 23

The newest slaves of the empress marched down the hallway and into a room filled with wooden tables, chairs, and cots. The furniture lined either wall of the room that stretched to a window with only a narrow path in the center of the room for movement. The guards ushered the women in and one stopped in the doorway after they entered.

"You may change into the undergarments and robes on the hooks. Put the display dresses on the hooks when you are finished." He motioned to the row of dark robes and white linens lining the wall and closed the door behind them.

Teah turned back to face the others as the door closed. Galena, Caldora, and Rachel pounced at once, bombarding the girl with questions.

"Where did they take you?" Galena asked.

"What did they do to you? Caldora pressed.

"What's the matter with you," Rachel asked, the only one of the three who noticed Teah's blank stare at them.

"Who are you and what am I doing here?"

The room echoed with Teah's question making it that much more poignant. The women exchanged worried looks and then turned back to

Teah who stared at them without expression. Galena gathered Caldora and Rachel, ushering them to one side. She crouched lower as the other women huddled nearer.

"She has amnesia," Galena said.

"She hit her head on the road pretty hard," Caldora agreed.

"What do we do now?" Rachel asked, the wavering in her voice betraying her fear.

"We must tell her everything, get her memory back," Caldora said.

"We need her to know who she is to protect herself against the empress," Rachel agreed.

The two women straightened and began to move away, but Galena took hold of their clothing and pulled them back." No," Galena said shaking her head.

"No?" Caldora echoed, incredulous.

"Why not?" Rachel frowned." Why should we make her hide her true identity if she doesn't have to? If she doesn't know she's the Queen of Ter Chadain, she couldn't possibly betray that information to the empress. The less she remembers the better for her. . . for us all."

Rachel and Caldora looked to each other sharing the moment of revelation to Galena's plan and then turned back nodding their agreement.

"Good," Galena grinned." Now we can fill her in on her magical abilities and that her name is Teah Glasson from Ter Chadain, a student at the Zele Magus Citadel, now the magical slave of the Empress of Caltoria."

Rachel looked over her shoulder at Teah staring out the window at the city and harbor below." I think she might have that last bit of knowledge already." Rachel tilted her head towards Teah so Galena and Caldora looked over at their queen.

Teah stood staring out at the city, tracing the outline of the soul stone on her forehead as tears ran down her cheeks.

Rachel started to go to Teah, but hesitated.
Galena edged by the girl and hurried to Teah, placing a comforting arm around her shoulders. Teah bristled at the contact at first, but then relaxed as her eyes met Galena's and she set her head on the woman's shoulder.

"Humph," Caldora grunted." To think this is what we have come to. The Mistress of Power reduced to a nursemaid.

The Zele Magus lifted her chin high and strode elegantly to the window and leaned against the sill. Teah lifted her teary eyes from Galena's shoulder and stared at the tall Zele Magus.

"Time you realize what kind of power you possess and why you are now a slave to someone with no power but in control of that stone on your forehead," Caldora said flatly.

Teah wiped her eyes and looked to Rachel as she walked up behind Galena.

"Yes, I guess it is," Teah said with a curt nod.

"Then you better sit down," Galena told her." This is going to take some time."

****

Empress Shakata sat on the window seat of her throne room gazing out at her city. Her city. How that thought gave her an empty feeling. Her entire life to this point in time felt like a complete facade. She now realized she wasn't who she pretended to be. She shook her head at the thought. She never pretended. She lacked important information to realize she held a closer relationship to her slaves than most of her faithful royal subjects.

She possessed magic, even if it truly was a divine magic, it still was magic. She pressed her lips together and furrowed her brow. Rowan Anthony. He knew this entire time and failed to warn her. Even during their love tryst, he never felt obligated to tell her of the possibility of her having the magic passed down through generations of her bloodline to read minds. Why not?

A tap came at the door and she pulled her attention from her thoughts.

"Come," she ordered.

General Anthony stuck his head in the door and looked for her first on the throne and then noticed her behind the throne at the window.

Her demeanor turned stormy in an instant.

"Haven't you done enough damage today?" Empress Shakata growled.

"I think this may lift your spirits." He took a tentative step inside carrying a bundle in his arms, eased the door closed behind him and waited.

"Very well," she sighed.

He hurried across the room to stand next to her as she sat by the window.

She looked up at him without any emotion." Well?"

"Yes, right, these were obtained from the group of magicals brought to you earlier today." He laid the bundle on the wide window sill and unfolded the cloth.

Empress Shakata gasped.

On the sill lay two swords in black sheaths, long black handles with gold woven throughout, the pommels consisted of large round crystals embedded with the images of a crown and two swords crossed above it.

Shakata tentatively reached out and touched the crystal pommel and grinned. She knew these blades. She read books and prophesies containing descriptions as well as drawings of these blades. She knew these blades to be the weapons of the Ter Chadain warrior, the Protector. She knew that only one with Lassain blood can claim the blades and she doubted anything but death could separate the blades from their master. Certainly they wouldn't be in Caltoria if the protector still survived in Ter Chadain. The thought flickered in her mind and her eyes shot to General Anthony, busy ogling the weapons.

"Did they take male captives this trip?" she asked.

"Uh, no, no, my Empress, only female."

"Then the owner of these blades is dead?" she pressed.

"Redrick said the late Captain Ordestan took them without much effort," he assured.

She smiled at the knowledge of being one step closer to claiming Ter Chadain as part of her kingdom. She turned back to the window, but something reflected the setting sun, shining in her eyes. She looked down at the cloth holding the sword and reached over to take a small leather sheath holding a smooth silver rod. She pulled the rod from the sheath and curled her hand around it. The smooth, cool metal felt natural in her hand, like it belonged there.

"What is that?" the General asked, reaching out and accepting the metal rod as she handed it to him. He examined it, turning it over and over again in his hand and lifting it to gaze at it in the light.

"I'm not sure, but I think I'll keep it as a trinket from the journey that captured a black stone," she said smiling up at him. He gave a slight bow and turned to leave, but Shakata caught hold of his wrist as he moved and pulled him to a stop. He looked down as her features softened and she looked longingly up at him.

"You are displeased with me for not telling you what your parents did not," he said, looking away.

"This is true, but you have been gone for so long... I missed you and your warmth in my bed while you traveled in the north," she said.

He turned back to her and she met his gaze without embarrassment." It does not feel right," he said softly.

"I am your empress and the mother of your child. I will tell you what feels right and what doesn't." She reached up and took a handful of his shirt, pulling him down to her longing lips. He resisted at first, but gave into her demands and lowered his lips to hers, kissing her deep and long. An amulet dropped from his shirt and hung down between them. Their kiss broke and he lifted a few inches from her face, their eyes holding the other's passionate stare.

Shakata took the amulet in her hand and studied it with a frown. The gold jewelry displayed an eye partially covered with a hand. She frowned." I've never seen this before."

"Something I picked up on my travels," he said and quickly moved in for another passionate kiss.

She leaned her head back as their lips eased apart." Stay with me," she whispered.

"Your wish is my command, my empress," he said as she pulled him down to her hungry lips once more.

Chapter 24

Raven, Logan, and Sasha crouched in the tunnel as they peered into the larger cavern. Raven frowned as Logan and Sasha looked on in shock as a large contingent of golden-clad soldiers ushered a small group of people consisting of men, women, and children, most of them dirty, wearing torn and tattered clothing, towards a gated tunnel on the far side of the cavern.

The cries of the people being pushed along rose in frenzy as they edged closer to the gate. A guard pulled down on a large chain next to the gate and it began to rise from the floor. This only escalated the panic to a higher level as the people began to shuffle away from the gate, picking the children up and pushing to the rear. The few men in the group stepped forward allowing all the women and children to move behind them as the guards continued to edge them to the gate.

"What's happening?" Logan whispered.

"We got here too late," Raven answered." Now we will have to wait until the Mashlad has finished feeding and the guards are gone, in order to proceed. Might as well sit tight."

Logan frowned and turned to Sasha who shrugged." What's a Mashlad?" Sasha asked.

"An ill attempt of the last emperor to create a magical of his own making," Raven said without looking back.

"It didn't go so well?" Sasha asked.

"It created something uncontrollable and horrible. The Mashlad are vile creatures who feed on the magic from natural magicals. They roam the tunnels leading from Scalded Island to Caltoria."

"So they will take the magic from these people the guards are pushing towards the tunnel?" Logan asked.

"They will suck the magic from them after removing their heads," Raven said.

"We can't let that happen," Logan protested.

"It is the way it is. All the captured rebel magicals are tried and then sentenced to death. This has been going on for centuries," Raven explained.

"We have to stop it," Logan argued.

"I can't do anything to stop it. Even if we can get past the guards, the Mashlad are unaffected by our magic weaves and will prevail."

"Then don't use your weaves, use your physical strength," Sasha reasoned.

"The Mashlad emit some magical spell that drains the magic from us before we can do anything. Kind of like a spider injecting its prey with venom, incapacitating it before killing it. You will see, once the Mashlad appear, the magicals will be entranced and unable to flee."

As if on cue, the people ushered into the opening of the tunnel became still and the gate lowered behind them.

"No," Logan said shaking his head." This isn't going to happen."

He leapt from the tunnel and rushed the guards as he drew his swords. The sound pinged off the walls and ceiling of the cave and the guards spun around looking for the origin.

Sasha pulled her blade and hurried after Logan, limping slightly.

Logan burst through the guards before they realized, reaching the guard by the gate before any of them reacted to his presence. Logan shoved the guard aside and began raising the gate. The guards turned to rush him when Sasha attacked from the rear, scattering any attempt at a consolidated assault on Logan. Logan raised the gate and pulled one stunned magical back into the cavern after another. He reached for the last woman standing inside the tunnel when a cry came from one of the men. Logan looked up in time to see the man lifted off the ground by an enormous, hairy hand jutting out from the shadows.

Logan threw the woman out of the tunnel and turned to save the other men when the Mashlad stepped forward into the light with the man raised to its hideous jaws. Dagger-sharp teeth protruded from the large maw, drooling profusely. Small, beady eyes stared at Logan as the long snout holding the deadly jaws sniffed and then spat out snot. The black-haired Mashlad then clamped down on the man and the teeth cut through the man's skin, bone, and skull with a sickening crunch.

The Mashlad tore the head from the rest of the body and spat it towards Logan. The decapitated head bounced and rolled to Logan's feet, spinning on the hard stone until the staring dead eyes of the man stared up at the protector.

Logan shoved the rest of the magicals out of the tunnel where Sasha battled the guard, holding her own. Logan stepped out of the tunnel and turned to drop the gate when a furry arm darted out from the tunnel and a clawed hand grasped his leg.

Logan held the gate rope in his hands as the Mashlad pulled him off his feet. Logan suddenly yanked free of the rope and vanished into the tunnel as the gate slammed closed behind him. Sasha saw Logan disappear into the tunnel and the gate bounce shut after him.

"No," she cried and then ducked to avoid a sword slashing at her head.

Many of the guards lay either dead or injured, but Sasha still remained outnumbered and now needed to get to Logan.

The guards regrouped and began to advance on Sasha and the magicals as they backed up to the gated tunnel.

Without warning, the guards slammed together and lifted off the ground. They hovered tight to the ceiling of the cave as Raven walked casually beneath them, a wry smile on her face.

"Go, escape and hide," Raven told the magicals who scattered into the tunnels at her command.

"Why didn't you do that sooner?" Sasha said, turning to lift the gate.

"I couldn't risk Logan and you setting the Mashlad free in the tunnels. They would track every magical down here and kill them."

"What changed?" Sasha asked, grunting as she pulled on the chain raising the heavy gate.

"The Mashlad has taken Logan and is gone, I can sense it. We need to find a way to save him if we are to fulfill the prophecy." Raven grabbed hold of the chain and helped Sasha lift the gate.

Sasha fastened the chain on a peg in the wall next to the tunnel and looked into the pitch black passage. She took a torch from the wall and stepped inside, holding it above her head.

Sasha shuddered as she looked down the corridor.

Raven glanced down at the recent victim's head at their feet and then further down the passage as the light illuminated the floor and the walls, piled high with bodies and bones in different points of decomposition. Raven placed a hand over her mouth and nose to block some of the stench.

Sasha held her arm across her face as she kept the torch high and stepped over the head of the dead magical. Flies took to flight in large swarms from the decaying matter on the floor and Sasha ducked to keep from getting a face full of insects.

Raven hesitated a moment and then turned back to the gate. Sasha looked back, certain the girl changed her mind about going after Logan.

But Raven stopped at the doorway and flicked her hand, sending a weave of magic at the chain holding the gate. The gate slammed shut with ground shuddering force sending some of the bones and bodies tumbling from their resting place.

Sasha stared at the gate and then at Raven in disbelief.

"We can't let the Mashlad escape this tunnel," Raven replied to Sasha's look.

"You do realize that was our only escape as well," Sasha said.

"Actually, we needed to go through here and out the other side anyway. Now we will just have to retrieve the protector first." Raven walked up to Sasha, took the torch from her hand, and headed down the passage through the mountains of carnage the Mashlad left behind.

Chapter 25

Saliday sat in the common room of The Emperor's Inn drinking ale and waiting for Morgan to finish his business. They planned to meet with the governor and work a deal for the searching stone over the evening meal.

She stared off at nothing, remembering Logan and Sasha and the trip to the Forbidden. In a stone-heated fur tent in the Betra camp, she first discovered the amazing qualities Logan possessed, not only as a protector, but as a person as well. Sure, it was easy to get caught up with all his power and skill as the protector, but his kindness and insight is what makes him so special.

She flicked her eyes to her mug of ale. It made him so special, she corrected, putting thoughts of him in the past tense.

How could it all go so badly so quickly? The thought of Logan and Sasha perishing in the jaws of sea creatures felt grotesque and absurd, but. . .

Now her journey changed to a different direction. No longer saving the Queen of Ter Chadain, but saving the Tarken race. She hesitated as the thought swept through her mind. What will happen to her homeland, Ter Chadain, if the queen does not return?

Could she brush Logan's quest aside without considering the greater good? After all, if Ter Chadain fell under Caltorian control, her race would end up nothing more than servants. Trackers forced to find anything the Caltorians wished. Could she live with that?

"Ready to go?" Morgan asked, standing across the table from her.

Saliday jumped, spilling her ale. She awkwardly got to her feet brushing the liquid from her clothing and gave him a halfhearted nod.

"What's wrong? You seem preoccupied."

Saliday gave him a blank stare and he shrugged pressing his lips tightly together.

"Thinking about them again?" Morgan sighed.

"It's only been a day and we shared a lot of time together over the last few months," Saliday said." I'm going to need a little more time to deal with this."

"Fine, no problem," Morgan said, but his voice lacked sincerity.

"We might have to wait a while before starting that family," she said searching his face for a reaction.

His cheek fluttered as his muscles clenched across his jaw, but he maintained his control." Whatever you need," he said, not making eye contact, but looking at the spilt mug of ale on the table.

"Where are we going?" she asked stepping over the stool and leaving the mess behind.

"Governor Stone is waiting for our arrival at his castle," Morgan said and motioned for her to go ahead of him.

"Why do you need me to come?" she asked, not wanting to leave her state of contemplation yet to deal with the real world.

"With you there, he might be more amiable to my deal," he said with a smirk.

"Always playing the angles, aren't you?" she said, stopping and facing him.

"What's wrong with using what we have to our advantage? It's called survival and I've gotten pretty good at it."

"I guess," she said with a shrug.

"You guess? While you've been skirting around Ter Chadain avoiding detection, I've been hitting the Caltorians where it hurts at sea, making their trade routes a bit less comfortable."

"And yet here you are openly trading with them without fear of repercussions," she said raising an eyebrow.

He glanced around the room nervously and then took her by the arm and pulled her to one side. He hunched close to her and whispered.

"It is this that hides me from their prying eyes and suspicious glances," he said, pulling a large medallion hanging around his neck by a cord from under his shirt. It depicted a golden eye, much like the ones on the soldier's uniforms with a hand across it as if to blind it.

Saliday frowned, not understanding what he told her.

"This is a medallion that keeps us from being seen when I wish it," he sighed." Whenever we are a pirate ship, they never remember what the other ship looked like, because they never see it."

"That's some powerful magic. Where'd you get it?" Saliday asked, reaching a hand to touch the talisman.

Morgan pulled it away and tucked it back into his shirt.

"Never mind, just know that I use all the tools available to me and I use them well."

Saliday's eyes grew as the pieces to the puzzle fell into place. "At the inn in Stalwart, when you sat in the room and I didn't detect you at first. . ."

"I didn't want to be noticed, so I wasn't until I felt I needed to be."

"So it makes you or your ship invisible?" Saliday asked.

"Not invisible, something we're not. Call it camouflage. Shall we go?" He motioned her out the door and then followed after.

That explains a lot, Saliday thought as they moved through the streets. What else has he camouflaged from me?

Morgan stopped before a large metal gate guarded by a contingent of men. One stepped forward and eyed Morgan up and down for a moment, but then settled his eyes on Saliday.

The man took no care in hiding his lust as he ran his eyes up and down her frame." What have we here, Captain Morgan? Have you been whoring again?" the man sneered.

Morgan laughed with the man as he turned to Saliday, but she strode past Morgan and kicked the man square in the groin.

The man exhaled, dropping to his knees for a moment before his eyes rolled into his head leaving only the whites showing and fell forward onto his face.

The other guards drew their weapons and surrounded Morgan and Saliday giving the woman a wide berth.

"What are you doing?" Morgan hissed.

"Being the man. . . since you weren't," Saliday spat.

"He didn't mean anything by it," Morgan protested.

"Oh, in that case, neither did I," Saliday said with a nod.

The men surrounded them. Two men stepped forward and dragged the man who now lay curled up in a fetal position, out of the circle.

"Just a misunderstanding," Morgan said raising his hands in front of him, trying to calm the situation.

"He got what was coming to him," a guard spoke up and the others nodded in agreement." The governor is expecting you and your guest, Captain Morgan," the man said with a crooked smile. He gave a nod and they all sheathed their swords.

They stepped aside and motioned Saliday and Morgan inside the courtyard where a young boy dressed in a golden silk tunic and black pants motioned for them to follow. His cropped black hair bobbed as he led them into the governor's residence.

They passed row upon row of artwork displayed on the walls and across the marble flooring until they reached a bronze door. The door opened before they reached it and they continued their pace into a great dining hall as a servant closed the door behind them. The table appeared to be as long as Morgan's ship with chair upon chair pushed up to it.

Morgan and Saliday hesitated for a moment to take in the incredible sight as the boy continued walking. He moved to one end of the table where a solitary figure sat, his attention on a large tray of food before him. He poked and picked at the food, finding what he looked for and then plucked it from the platter and tossed it into his mouth.

The man looked up as the boy stopped and gave a bow. He motioned to Saliday and Morgan to come closer as they walked up and stopped before him. Morgan bowed and Saliday dipped her head.

Morgan rolled his eyes, trying to get Saliday's attention, but her focus remained squarely on Governor Stone.

The governor also ignored Morgan, looking at Saliday, not like the guard at the gate whom she needed to put in his place, but like an artisan discovering a new piece of rare art. He absently wiped the grease from the food off his chin with a napkin and stared in awe.

He rose from his chair extending to his considerable height, brushed his long black hair from his face as he moved next to the table and extended a hand to Saliday." Governor Albright Stone, at your service." He smiled, his teeth sparkled and his cheek dimpled.

"Saliday Talis," she said placing her hand in his with a nod, taken aback. She never expected the Governor of Scalded Island to be so handsome.

He brought her hand to his lips and brushed them against the back of her hand.

Saliday felt her face flush with heat as she stared at his bent head.

"Humph," Morgan cleared his throat.

This didn't speed up the governor's pace as he eased Saliday's hand from his lips, holding her gaze for a moment longer, and then casually looking to Morgan.

"Hello, Morgan, I hear you think you have a trinket I will be interested in," he said releasing Saliday's hand and moving back to his seat. He sat, looking at Morgan with a bored expression.

"Not likely."

"Oh, you won't say that once I show you," Morgan groped in his pocket for the stone.

"Please sit," Governor Stone said to Saliday, motioning to the seat on the other side of him, away from Morgan.

Saliday walked around and sat, staring back at Morgan in amazement. He seemed flustered, something so unlike him. At least 'the him' she knew, or thought she knew.

The boy who escorted them appeared at Stone's side, funny, Saliday never saw him leave or return. He leaned in and whispered in the governor's ear.

Stone nodded as the boy spoke, but brushed him aside until the last words escaped his lips loud enough for Saliday to hear. "Magical."

Stone sat straighter in his chair and then looked to the boy who nodded that the governor heard him right. The governor leaned his head towards Morgan with a hopeful look on his face, but the boy shook his head. The governor frowned and then leaned towards Saliday, regret heavy in his eyes. The boy nodded.

The governor gave the boy a quick gesture with his hand and he scurried from the room needing no further instruction. Saliday felt the strange urge to leave. She stood and stared across the table at Morgan.

"I think we need to leave," she said, putting a sense of urgency in her voice.

"We haven't finished our business," Morgan said glaring at her.

"Yes, come, come, eat, there is plenty of food and I don't get many visitors such as yourselves," the governor said motioning to the food covering the table before them.

"But I really feel it is time to leave," Saliday insisted.

Even as she spoke, the boy returned with a group of soldiers and two women with a red jewel on each of their foreheads. They spread out around the three at the table, the two women standing on either side of Saliday.

"What is this?" Morgan asked, his head swiveling to take in their predicament.

"I thought you were smarter than this, Morgan," Governor Stone said." Bringing a magical to my table no matter how beautiful is inconceivable."

Morgan looked from the governor to Saliday in shock." She is not a magical," he argued.

"My serving boy is a sniffer, one of my best, and he says she's a magical."

"Sniffer?" Saliday said." I'm no magical, so I think his nose is off a bit."

"Is not," the boy protested stepping forward and pulling his bangs back from his forehead to reveal a dark blue stone.

Governor Stone stopped the boy's outburst with a raised hand.

"Then explain yourself and realize all magicals deny they are magicals when we catch them."

Saliday looked to Morgan for help, but he stared back blankly. Tarken."

With a sigh, Saliday turned to the governor and said, "I am

Chapter 26

Teah stretched her back leaning to one side. Galena and Caldora explained to her why she now found herself a prisoner to the Empress of Caltoria. The sun set long ago and the moon now shone through the window of the otherwise dark room giving it an eerie glow. Rachel sat off in the shadows. Teah couldn't see her, but she sensed her there watching and listening.

Why did Teah have an urge to tell the girl she was sorry? What happened in their past to make Teah feel this incredible sense of guilt?

Teah stared at the darkness as Galena spoke, her voice droning on and on as all the information piled up and then washed away like writing in the sand swept clean with the splash of the waves.

"Teah, Teah, have you heard a word I've said?" Galena fumed.

Teah pulled herself from staring in the general vicinity of Rachel back to the Zele Magus.

"Yes," Teah sighed." We are Zele Magus taken by the Caltorians as magical slaves. I happen to have the most power between us and have no way of knowing how to use it now that I can't remember anything since waking up in the dungeon earlier today." She recited as if memorized over months of study.

"I'm tired of all this talk," Caldora said standing." Time for sleep." She walked over and stripped off the clinging dress and slipped on the light linen undergarments left for them. She went to a bed and crawled in without another word.

"She's right. We can take this up again in the morning," Galena said and stood to walk over and change into the other clothes and climb into a bed, pulling the blanket up against the chill of the night.

Teah turned to look out the window and the city below alive with torch lights flickering from the street lamps and windows of the buildings. It reminded her of standing on a hill overlooking a village. She recalled a tall lean woman and a man with her, someone she knew well, but she couldn't remember why.

Your brother, Logan, Bastion told her.

Teah tensed at the voice.

"Why must you always put everyone around in peril?" Rachel said standing over Teah.

Teah jumped at Rachel's voice." What?"

"You bring destruction wherever you go," Rachel said. She pulled the blanket wrapped around her shoulders tighter against the chill coming through the window.

"I'm sorry, but I don't remember what I've done."

"It's not so much what you've done, but what people do to protect you. They give up their lives to protect yours."

"And why would they do that?"

"Because you're the. . ." "Rachel," Galena cried out, standing behind the girl.

"No, I want to hear her," Teah shouted." People die protecting me because I'm what?"

"Because you are the most powerful Zele Magus in Ter Chadain history," Galena explained.

"No, that wasn't what she wanted to say," Teah argued looking from Galena back to Rachel." What were you going to say?"

"It doesn't matter. All that matters is you let my friend Lizzy die for you and I'm done trying to protect you," Rachel said, her anger boiling under the surface. She turned and returned to her bed in the shadows. Galena and Teah watched Rachel disappear into the shadows again.

"It's time for you to sleep as well," Galena said, putting an arm around Teah and ushering her to a bed. The Zele Magus waited for Teah to change out of her dress and climb into bed, pulling the covers up over Teah's shoulders and then returning to her own bed.

Teah laid staring at the ceiling as she pressed to remember, to try and make sense out of what the Zele Magus told her and why Rachel would hate her so much.

All right, who is in here and tell me what you know. She waited, hoping the response wouldn't come, but knowing it eventually would.

Bastion, my lady, the first Protector of Ter Chadain. Stalwart, second Protector of Ter Chadain. Galiven, fourth Protector of Ter Chadain.

She sensed another, but after a long pause, he didn't reveal himself, so she continued.

What is a protector and what can you tell me?

We can tell you that in spite of the Zele Magus, who refuses to tell you everything they know, it is our consensus that you should know everything, without the missing details that may cost you your life, Bastion said.

Teah hesitated, trying to decide if these voices of men in her mind actually existed or were a manifestation of her imagination. I can assure you we truly exist, Stalwart answered her contemplation.

Galiven then began to lay out Teah's history as the protectors knew it sharing everything they knew dealing with Logan and her as well as when the soul stone transported all of them to her mind.

From the time Captain Ordestan captured you until the soul stone sucked us into your mind we have no memory of what took place, Galiven finished.

Teah lay in stunned silence staring at the ceiling now beginning to glow with the rising sun. She didn't know how to feel, but had an uneasy feeling the protectors spoke the truth. The Queen of Ter Chadain and Protector of Ter Chadain, both titles and positions overwhelming to her. Granted, the protectors needed to explain the significance of each position, but the responsibility and power of each threatened to drown her in a flood of destiny.

No. Teah said after they finished.

No? Bastion said confused.

I don't believe you. I don't believe you are true and I certainly don't believe that I am a queen and a protector. You are a creation of my mind caused by my head injury.

Falcone laughed. This may be exactly what we need. . . a Zele Magus with no thought to control anyone else. As a matter of fact, no thoughts at all.

You're wrong. I still can think, but it doesn't mean I believe everything I'm told. Especially by voices in my head.

The protectors began to speak all at once, the noise reverberating in Teah's head. She wished they would go silent and without warning they did.

She turned her thoughts to them, trying to discover what happened. She pushed her consciousness deep into her thoughts and then brushed up against something rigid. She touched it tentatively with her mind and pulled back. The energy radiated from the barrier as she studied it. She heard a soft sound, like from a great distance or through a wall or possibly from beneath a body of water, the muffled voices of the protectors cried out to her.

She smiled; relieved to have her thoughts back to herself. Stay there until I can speak with the Zele Magus and question if your stories are true.

Still, frustration ached in her like a tooth with an infection. She had no knowledge of how to control any of the powers the protectors claimed she possessed and no memory of ever having a brother, being named a queen, and changing into a protector. But what if the voices did speak the truth?

As the sun rose on her new life as Queen of Ter Chadain and Protector of Ter Chadain, Teah Lassain stared at a future being pulled in two directions. One by her reality and one by her mind. She needed to speak with the Zele Magus again and see if the voices in her head spoke the truth.

The sound of the bolt sliding open at the door brought her attention to the here and now as she sat up and looked at the door. She expected to see more guards, but found the boy from the dungeon instead.

He stepped into the room leaving the door ajar behind him and peered around the dimly lit room as the dawn's light failed to illuminate the space adequately. He searched the room with his eyes, falling upon her as she sat up in her bed, studying him. When their eyes met, he flinched in surprise at her attention. He motioned her to come with him looking at the other women to be sure they still slept.

Teah stood, pulled a robe from the wall, and crept to the door, not wanting to wake the others if he didn't wish it. She slipped the robe on as she reached him and he ushered her from the room closing the door and bolting it as she waited in the hall.
When he turned, she stood inches from him and he jumped." You have to stop looking at me like that," he told her." Why does it bother you so much?" she asked.

"Magical slaves need to know their place and I can see you don't. I'm glad I got to you before you went before the empress again."

"And why is that?"

The boy's eyes widened with amazement." That very reason. You must not question anyone without the stone for any reason," the boy sputtered.

"That's ridiculous, I'm a person, you're a person, we can all talk," Teah argued.

"No, no, no, you must not speak to anyone without a stone except when ordered to," the boy said throwing his hands up in frustration." You're a slave here in Caltoria. It isn't like it was in Ter Chadain. You're not allowed to run around hurling your magic willy-nilly everywhere. Here there are rules."
Teah frowned at him as he went on.

"Why all this interest in me?" Teah asked leaning closer to the boy.

"Because you're the first spell caster since Tera Lassain, the magical who escaped to Ter Chadain and became their first queen."

Teah stared at this boy, not much older than her, and wondered if he spoke truthfully.

"You need to learn restraint and control. . . and above all else, you mustn't use your magic without being ordered to first."

"No problem with that one," Teah said shaking her head and giving a shrug.

"And why is that?" the boy questioned.

"Because I can't remember how to use my magic," Teah said flatly.

The boy rocked back on his heels and leaned against the door. His face turned pale and his eyes opened wide as they reeled in their sockets." Oh, by the spirits, I mean, that changes everything," he exhaled.

"How?"

"If you can't use your magic, you're of no use to the empress or any other noble for that matter. This is bad, very bad."

"Why, what happens if I'm not useful?"

"They feed you to the Mashlad or let the Monks of the Spire suck the magic from you until you are nothing more than a husk of yourself," he said.

Teah stared blankly at him.

"You don't know about the Mashlad or the monks? No, I suppose you don't, they're uniquely Caltorian," he rambled on before catching himself and turning his attention back to Teah.

"The Mashlad are disgusting creatures created by a past emperor who tried to instill magic in normal people to grow the magical gene pool. Unfortunately, it went horribly wrong and he created uncontrollable monsters that need to feed on the magic in magicals in order to survive."

Teah stared at him with a disgusted expression." Then why don't they let them die?"

"I agree, that would be a wise choice, but they seem to serve a vital service of patrolling the underground tunnels between Caltoria and Scalded Island to our south. They keep the magicals from escaping Caltoria while keeping the resistance on the island from doing too much damage here."

"Surely the resistance can find other ways of attacking and creating problems," Teah said.

Her mind erupted with muffled cries from the protectors for caution.

The boy tilted his head as he studied Teah after her statement." You mustn't think like that. If I didn't know better, I would say you are plotting to join the resistance."

Teah raised an eyebrow as her lips curled in a slight smile.

"Thoughts like that can get you killed," the boy growled.

"That seems like a common theme around here," Teah replied." I have no intention of getting myself killed."

"No one ever does," the boy snapped.

"Who are you?" Teah asked.

"Caslor."

"What do we do now, Caslor?"

"We find a way to keep you from the empress and to teach you how to use your magic before she finds out."

"All this interest in me because of the color of the stone on my forehead?" Teah questioned.

"Uh, let's just say I'm curious how powerful you are," Caslor stammered and turned red.

"Well, then you better be sure to keep me away from these Mash. . . what did you call them?"

"Mashlad." "Right, Mashlad and the monks," Teah said with a nod.

"Come on, we need to get you to someone I think can help," Caslor said, taking her by the hand and moving down the hall, pulling her with him.

"And who is that?" Teah asked.

"My father," Caslor said and hurried down the hall with Teah in tow.

Chapter 27

Logan slashed and hewed at the Mashlad as it dragged him deeper and deeper into the tunnel system. He tossed and turned, bouncing along, taking a swipe at the Mashlad every time he rolled over onto his back.

The debris of bones and clothing scattered about, banging into Logan, forcing the air from this lungs as he struggled to right himself.

They took a sharp turn in the tunnel and Logan grasped the corner and pulled with all his might. The claw around his ankle held for a moment as the force pulled him parallel with the tunnel floor and then let go.

Logan fell onto the floor, but didn't waste time to catch his breath. He leapt to his feet and turned in the blackness towards the heavy breathing mixed with growls coming from the Mashlad.

Logan relied on his ears as the darkness consumed him and his adversary. His swords crossed before him, but he only knew this out of memory as the weapons remained invisible to his sight.

The Mashlad's breathing slowed and calmed, the urgency filling the tunnel pulling back to a more cautious feeling.

The sound of air moving around something heavy swinging in the air came to Logan's ears just before he realized the Mashlad could see in the blackness. The swinging object hit Logan's left side, propelling him into the wall of the tunnel and knocking him senseless. He slid down the damp wall, his feet scrambling to catch underneath him, but failing to keep him from falling to his knees.

Logan knew if he didn't do something, and do it quickly, he would soon become another victim of the Mashlad. The image of the man, his head torn from his shoulders, in the grasp of the Mashlad as its fangs dug deeply into the exposed wound, jolted Logan and he willed there be light for him to see.

The reaction started slowly, but built in intensity as his swords, still in his hands pressed against the floor, began to glow. Logan stared at them in shock for only a second and then pushed himself to his feet, bringing the weapons before him in time to see the beady green eyes of the Mashlad a step away.

The swords burst with light, sending the Mashlad retreating, howling in pain at the sudden brightness. Logan squinted at the intensity, trying to see where the beast retreated, but the Mashlad was gone.

Logan peered at the lit tunnel where the Mashlad vanished, but saw nothing. He retraced his steps back to the turn and then headed in the direction he believed they came from. Every once in a while he felt as if something crept up behind him, but when he spun to face it, he found nothing there.

After walking for some time, he realized how quickly the Mashlad covered the distance into the tunnels. He expected it to be only a short walk back to the gate, but the tunnel showed no end in sight.

He stopped to rest when a soft glow lit the tunnel ahead. He lowered his glowing swords as Raven came into view with Sasha close behind.

They stopped in front of him, staring at him and his swords.

"You're quite the sight," Raven grinned. Logan held his swords higher to see the filth covering him from head to toe.

"I guess I didn't realize what that thing dragged me through," Logan laughed.

"And you couldn't smell it?" Raven said placing a hand to her nose in disgust." Never mind that, when did your swords start glowing?" Sasha said.

"I needed light and they gave me light," Logan said with a shrug.

"That isn't protector magic," Sasha said.

"That's . . ."

"Viri Magus Magic," Logan said and it all flooded back to him. The time Teah spoke to him, before he knew it to be her, telling him he wasn't only the protector, but a Viri Magus also. Things became crazy after that, everything moving too rapidly to take time and make sense of it. But now it made perfect sense. Why the Mashlad tried to take him in order to feed on him.

"Of course he has magic," Raven said flatly." I felt it when I met you on the beach. I was confused why you didn't heal Sasha yourself, but she didn't have time for us to figure that out."

"Why now?" Logan asked." Why did the magic wait until now to become known?"

"Magic doesn't usually work the way we want it to," Raven explained." Magic inside people tends to emerge when it is needed most. Showing up when the danger is greatest."

"The Mashlad was going to kill me and feed on my magic. I guess that's a great need," Logan agreed.

"Enough talk, we need to get moving before that thing comes back looking for its snack and finds Raven for a bonus."
Logan and Raven turned to Sasha as she stood with her hands on her hips.

"Well?"

"She's right," Raven said with a nod." Besides, that is only one Mashlad. There are supposed to be many more down here. We better keep moving."

Logan exchanged a worried look with Sasha as the Betra's eyes widened with concern.

Raven brushed between them and walked ahead, taking the torch and the light with her so only the swords dull glow lit the tunnel. They turned and followed her deeper into the tunnel, away from the metal bars and the chamber.

"Why aren't we going back?" Sasha called to Raven.

"We need to reach Caltoria and these tunnels will lead us there," she said without turning back.

"But we run the risk of running into more Mashlad," Logan pointed out.

"There is that, but that is a risk we need to take, unless you want to fight your way through an army protecting the harbor," Raven said, stopping and turning to them.

Logan stopped suddenly and Sasha bumped into his back. He glanced over his shoulder and Sasha gave him a curt nod.

"No, time is crucial and we are running out of it," Sasha said.

"What is so time sensitive?" Raven asked.

"My sister is prisoner of the empress and we need to get her back," Logan said without thinking.

Sasha gasped at his lapse of restraint.

"The Queen of Ter Chadain is the prisoner of the empress?" Raven exclaimed in shock." We must hurry." Raven turned and strode off, quickening her pace.

"What's wrong, what will the empress do to my sister?" Logan asked.

"If the empress finds out your sister is the queen, she will put her to death and crush the hopes of the rebellion. If she doesn't discover her identity, she may sell her to any noble from one side of Caltoria to the other, which will make it nearly impossible to find her. We need to get to her now."

Raven rushed ahead, forcing Logan and Sasha to scramble after her.

"At least she knows our need now," Logan said over his shoulder to Sasha.

"True, but I prefer a better place to choose allies than a tunnel under the sea," Sasha countered.

"Like an inn's common room?" Logan said, the hurt and sarcasm heavy in his voice.

"I guess that didn't turn out very well. Maybe this will end up better," Sasha added as they hurried deeper into the bowels of the Mashlad's home.

****

Governor Stone stared at Saliday as if she possessed a second head." Tarkens are extinct. Even the ones we captured and brought back refused to cooperate and were put to death." The governor turned to Morgan." This is a foolish ploy to bring a magical in and assassinate me."

"No, I would never do that," Morgan defended.

"I am a Tarken," Saliday said." I'm the last of my people." She glared across the table at Morgan whose features contorted as he tried to mask his fear." I kept my identity a secret from the good captain. He had no idea."

"That I find hard to believe. Morgan is never unawares," the governor said. He turned to Morgan who showed feigned shock at Saliday's statement." I'm not buying it. He's as much a part of this as you are. Guards, take them to the dungeon until I can decide what I want to do with them."

"Wait," Morgan sprang to his feet and the guards drew their weapons." No, really, wait. You haven't seen what I've brought you." Morgan dug into his pocket and pulled out the seeking stone. He held it out to the governor in his open palm.

The governor waved his hand at the guards who backed away and sheathed their swords. He leaned in and stared down at the stone as it glowed in his palm and pointed in the direction of the boy and the two women sniffers.

The governor frowned." All sniffers move over by the door," he said.

The three magicals walked behind him and stood in the doorway.

As they moved, the stone pivoted in Morgan's hand, following the three magicals.

"What about her?" The governor asked.

"Her magic as a Tarken is different than that of a magical. Tarkens' magic is who they are. It is nothing they can command, but flows through them like their blood," Morgan said.

"You know a lot about Tarkens," the governor said, raising a suspicious eyebrow.

"I make it my business to know a lot about a variety of things," Morgan said, his composure and confidence back. He extended his hand closer to Saliday and the stone still homed in on the magicals by the door.

"Very well, I'm not certain I believe you, but I'll let you go," Stone said.

Morgan nodded as he handed the seeking stone to the governor." We will be going then," he said and motioned to Saliday with a jerk of his head.

"Oh, she won't be joining you," the governor smiled.

"She isn't a magical," Morgan protested before Saliday spoke.

"That may be true, but she is a Tarken and the last of her kind," the governor said." She is that much more valuable than a magical."

"It's either that, or you both join me as permanent house guests and I tire of house guests who are of no value to me. I fear she will remain more valuable to me than you," the governor said, proud of his maneuver.

"Fine, I'll leave, but remember, I resent this kind of tactic," Morgan said. He turned, giving Saliday a hopeless glance over his shoulder, and hurried out the door.

Saliday stared after Morgan in shock.

He left me. . . bastard. He left me to be a slave. But why didn't the boy. . .?

She stopped in mid thought as it came to her. Why the boy and other sniffers didn't sense Morgan's magic but smelled hers. The amulet.

"Now, my dear, what value are you to me?" Saliday looked at the governor in a daze. What do I do now? Before Saliday could respond, the door flew open and a man rushed in. His torn uniform hung bloody and dirty as he panted, trying to catch his breath.

"What is it?" the governor asked.

"The magicals. . . the feeding. . . the Mashlad. . .," the man stammered between gasps for air.

"What about the Mashlad?"

"We were attacked by a man and two women. They freed the magicals. The two women chased after the Mashlad when it took the man, but the magicals escaped," the man said.

"Forget the magicals," the governor said shaking his head." I have a new way to track them, even more efficient than the sniffers. What did this man and these women look like?"

Saliday listened as the man explained the confrontation and even as she did, she felt a strange urge to move. To track this man and these women and reach them before the governor did. She frowned at the strange drive to track at the mere mention of this group.

"The man, well, more a boy, but he had curved silver swords, two of them, and he moved with the speed of a great warrior. The woman dressed in a black skin-tight wrap followed right behind him and held the rest of us off by herself until the warrior released all but one of the magicals. Only when the Mashlad took the warrior did the other woman appear and use magic to hold us against the cavern's ceiling until the two of them followed the Mashlad and warrior into the tunnels."

When Saliday heard the mention of the two swords and the garb of the Betra, her head snapped up with recognition as she listened closer to the soldier.

The governor didn't notice Saliday's reaction, but the boy sniffer did. He stepped up to the governor and whispered in his ear.

The governor turned to Saliday with a knowing smile." So, you know these people who attacked my men and allowed convicted criminals to escape their executions?"

"No, I don't think so," Saliday said with a shake of her head.

"Maybe, maybe not, but I now have a use for you after all. You are a tracker, so you will track down these criminals through the Mashlad tunnels," he said rubbing his hands together, very proud of his plan.

"As you wish," Saliday conceded, knowing she planned to do just that no matter if he ordered it or not. Deep in her soul she felt the tug of the need in her blood to find them. She needed to unite with them once more and tell Logan she would never hurt him again. The need pulsed through her and pressed her to follow her blood and find what she needed. She needed Logan and nothing could keep her from filling that need.

Chapter 28

Caslor pulled Teah after him into a large outer chamber lavishly decorated in plush chairs and couches. Tapestries and paintings lined the walls showing images of men in armor facing down evil looking creatures and armies of vile looking foes.

"Sit here and wait for me," he told her, motioning for her to sit on one of the burgundy colored couches.

"Where are you going?" she asked as she sat down, staring around at all the opulence and grandeur.

"I'm going to tell my father what is going on and he will know how to get your magic back before you are put to death for being useless."

Teah opened her mouth to object about being referred to as useless, but Caslor disappeared into the next room before she had the chance. She snapped her mouth closed in disgust and scanned the massive room. The contents of the room overwhelmed her as objects of wealth were strewn everywhere.

A diamond ring lay on a table nearby. A golden bracelet sat on a chair across from her. Everywhere jewelry and clothing lay about. She thought about touching a ring sitting on the couch next to her, but pulled her hand back at the possibility of Caslor returning and seeing her reaching for it. She stopped, remembering something from her past that might come in handy here.

She concentrated on the interior of the next room, wishing herself in that room. She began to feel light, airy, and lifted her hand to her face, finding it translucent and fluffy. Her spirit separated from her body, floated above it and stared down at herself.

How do you like that? She boasted at the protectors.

They didn't answer. She reached for their thoughts, for the barrier muzzling the protectors, but they weren't there. Her spirit grinned and she rejoiced at the separation between her body and her spirit. She finally had refuge from the protector's spirits when they proved too much.

Realizing that time slipped away from her, she sped to the room Caslor entered. She stood beside the boy as he slumped in a chair with disappointment. She looked across a huge desk to the back of a chair, its occupant facing the window and looking away from Caslor at the rising sun.

"But, Father, she is a black stone," he pleaded." We mustn't let her enormous powers be used as feed for the Mashlad or fodder for the monks."

"She is not ours to meddle with. She is the property of the empress and we must not risk jeopardizing our entire goal for one magical slave who can't remember how to use her magic."

"But if you meet her, you would see there is something special about her. Let me bring her in and you will see."

The man spun in his chair, the high back no longer blocking the sun as it rose over the wall of the palace, blinding Teah from seeing anything more than the outline of a very large man. He slammed his fist upon the table.

"What are you thinking? Have you gone mad? If she finds out about me it could ruin everything. I spent years getting close enough to the empress to be above suspicion, but you may have undone that in a single stupid act."

Teah lifted off the floor, trying to get a look at the man's face.

"Get out of here and take her back before the empress realizes she is gone," the man shouted." Now!"

Caslor leapt to his feet and raced for the door without looking back. Teah hesitated for a moment longer as she tilted her wispy head trying to see the man's face, but she gave up with a groan and shot back to her body.

Her corporeal body still bounced on the springs of the couch from her spirit bursting back into it when Caslor stepped up before her.

She looked up at his extended hand in a daze and placed her hand in his.

He pulled her from the couch with a jerk and out the door of the chamber. They raced down the hall stopping before the door to the magicals' bed chambers again panting from their exertion.

Caslor stood staring at the floor not making eye contact with Teah.

"Sorry, that didn't turn out the way I hoped," he mumbled.

"That's okay, it isn't your fault he didn't want to put himself at risk," Teah said, putting a hand to her lips realizing she shouldn't have known that information.

Caslor's head shot up and he stared into her eyes. His eyes clouded with confusion.

"How did you know that?"

"Uh, well, why else would we rush back here without a word? I just guessed he didn't want anything to do with a magical that couldn't control her powers."

"Yeah," Caslor nodded." I guess you might figure that out. . . but I doubt it." He finished and crossed his arms over his chest." You aren't telling me everything."

Teah leaned forward and kissed him hard and deep on the lips. She held the kiss for a long moment and then stepped away from the stunned boy.

She opened the door to the bed chambers and stepped in leaning against it, partway in and partway out." Where would the fun be in that?" she said and slipped into the room and closed the door behind her.

****

Caslor stood in the hall, confusion on his face. He frowned and reached for the door knob, but paused with his hand clasping it. His determination drained from his face as he grinned and brought a hand to his lips. His brows furrowed and he shook his head in frustration." Ah," he groaned, flailing his arms and marched off down the hall.

****

Teah leaned with her back against the door with a wry smile across her face.

"Where have you been and why are you so pleased with yourself?" Galena asked as she and the others gathered around Teah.

"Nowhere," Teah grinned.

"It doesn't seem like she wants to tell us," Caldora said with a chuckle.

"That reminds me," Teah said looking at Galena." Who is the Queen of Ter Chadain?"

Galena's body stiffened as her mind searched for an answer." Ter Chadain has no queen at this moment."

"Then who is ruling Ter Chadain?" Teah asked.

"King Englewood was killed not too long ago, or so I've heard, and the Protector of Ter Chadain now is in control," Galena explained.

"For now," Caldora added. Galena turned and glared at the Zele Magus. Teah looked at Caldora." The protector?"

The voices of the protectors shouted against the barrier.

"Has there ever been a female protector?"

Rachel, Caldora, and Galena exchanged worried glances." No, no there hasn't been a female protector," Galena said.

"So the protector is in control of Ter Chadain for now," Teah repeated slowly, letting the information sink in." What is he waiting for?"

"The true queen of Ter Chadain to claim the throne," Rachel said.

"And who is that?" Teah said, spinning on the girl.

"Uh, uh, I, I..." Rachel stammered looking to the others for help.

"No one really knows," Galena said, taking Teah by the arm and pulling her away from Rachel and Caldora towards the far window." You see, the rebellion has divided many allies and brought together many enemies. It is very hard to discern who is working with you and who is against you."

"I see, so the protector is a man in Ter Chadain waiting for a queen to come and claim the throne, yet no one knows who she really is. And there has never been a female protector," Teah concluded.

"That is correct," Galena said with a smile." Why so many questions? Are you getting your memories back?"

"Not really, I guess more like false memories. I seem to be getting misleading information," Teah said, referring to the protectors in her mind.

"Anything you remember may come to you in bits and pieces that will be confusing if not seen in context. If you have any questions, you need to come to us and make sure you get the entire picture," Galena insisted.

"I will," Teah said nodding. She sat next to the window and stared out at the city. The people bustled around below in their morning routine.

Galena stood next to her for a moment longer and then went back to have whispered conversations with the other two women.

Teah reached into her mind and slid the magical barrier aside. She expected the voices to burst out immediately, but they remained silent.

Nothing to say now that I know the truth and your lies are revealed?

There is nothing to say that will make you believe us over them, Bastion said.

You will stop bothering me now about being a queen and a protector?

If that is what you wish, to ignore who you really are and believe the lies of the Zele Magus, Falcone spoke up.

They are not lying, they speak more truth than you and I must hold onto the truth, she shouted in her mind.

But they tell you partial truths. They may have good intentions for doing so, but that does not stop you from being the Queen of Ter Chadain and the first female protector, Galiven insisted.

Stop, you must stop this, I cannot believe such outlandish claims. Unless you want me to keep you bottled up in my mind, you mustn't speak of me being the queen or a protector. Do you understand? Teah told them leaving no room for discussion on the matter.

The protectors went silent but she felt their reluctant acceptance to her terms.

Good, now speak to me only when you can help me.

She is much firmer than the boy, Stalwart said. What did I just say?

Sorry, Stalwart moaned and went silent.

Teah nodded curtly. She needed to concentrate on one thing now, learning how to use her magic to keep her alive. Something she intended to do.

Chapter 29

Logan looked back at Sasha behind him, the soft glow of his swords illuminating her weary face as she pressed on. Her face contorted with pain and fatigue as she placed one foot in front of the other with great effort.

"Raven," Logan called to the girl leading the way holding the burning torch." We need to rest."

Raven didn't slow, but glanced back at him over her shoulder." We can't. There are more than one Mashlad down here and any one of them will pick up our scent and hunt us down."

"We need to stop and rest," Logan said." Sasha's injuries are still painful for her. She needs to rest."

"I can continue, Master," Sasha said in a tired voice.

Raven stopped and turned holding her torch high to look back at the Betra. She nodded.

"Okay, we can stop for a moment or two. Logan, take up a post behind her and I'll watch this side after I see if I can ease her pain a bit," Raven said, motioning for Logan to move behind Sasha.

The large tunnels allowed ample room for Logan to step around Sasha and stand behind her in the passageway. He placed a comforting hand on her shoulder as he passed, giving her a smile as she pressed her lips together with resignation.
Logan never saw Sasha complain or give up, but her strength appeared drained.

Raven stepped close to Sasha and placed a hand on the side of her exposed neck. When their skin made contact, Sasha stiffened and her eyes went wide. Then her muscles relaxed and her eyes closed with relief.

Logan watched anxiously and stepped close in time to catch the Betra as she went limp. He eased her to the tunnel floor and looked up at Raven who stood over them.

"Did you mean to do that?" he asked." I didn't realize she was so spent," Raven admitted." So much for a short rest."

"She will be much stronger when she wakes. We can pick up our pace."

"How much farther?" Logan asked.

"A day, maybe two," Raven answered.

Logan shook his head." That's too long. The odds the Mashlad will find us increase the longer we are in the tunnels."

"I'm afraid the Mashlad may already be following us," Raven said.

"What?" Logan straightened, pulling his other sword. The blade glowing as it cleared the sheath.

"They seem to be keeping their distance, for now. But I can feel they are gaining in numbers."

"How many?"

"From the magic I feel, three, maybe four."

"What are they waiting for? Why haven't they attacked?"

"I think they're afraid of you."

"Good, but as their numbers grow, that fear will wane. We need to get going," Logan said. He sheathed his swords and lifted the unconscious Sasha in his arms." Lead on, we need to get out of here."

Raven turned without a word and headed down the tunnel. She set a fast pace, a light jog, glancing back to see if Logan kept pace. Seeing the protector right behind her, she nodded and picked up the pace even more. Soon they jogged quickly along the tunnel, the torch flickering as they ran.

They stopped in a cavern at an intersection of several branches of tunnels for Raven to choose the one giving them the most direct line to Caltoria.

She stood before the opening of one tunnel, closed her eyes and concentrated.

"What are you doing?" Logan asked as he scanned the dark tunnel entrances, still holding Sasha in his arms.

"Shush." Raven waved her hand at him without opening her eyes.

"We need to keep moving," he urged.

"I have to find the right passage. I'm trying to sense the strongest magic at the end of the tunnel. That should be the one leading to Caltoria."

"Should be?"

"If there is something down here with strong magic, it may lead us down the wrong tunnel." She opened her eyes in surprise like something struck her." This one," she pointed at the tunnel in front of her.

"You hope," Logan said.

"Would you like to choose?" Raven said placing her hands on her hips.

"No, no, that one is fine," Logan said, motioning with his head to get going.

Raven took a step into the tunnel and then catapulted past Logan. She collided with the far wall of the cavern sending the torch she held flying and slid down the wet, slippery wall unconscious.

Logan looked over his shoulder as Raven came to rest at the base of the wall and then slowly turned to peer into red glowing eyes, the flickering torch on the floor across the cavern giving him glimpses of a huge Mashlad filling the tunnel.

Logan eased back, the beast moving forward at the same pace, keeping the distance between them the same. It straightened as it left the tunnel's entrance, extending to its full height which towered over Logan. Logan never took his eyes from the Mashlad and the beast never glanced from Logan's eyes.

Logan moved towards the torch away from Raven, hoping to keep the Mashlad concentrating on him instead of the helpless girl. He felt the wall press against his back, pushing the sheaths of his swords into his shoulders. He and the Mashlad still held each other's gaze.

With Sasha unconscious in his arms he had no chance to draw his swords. He feared if he attempted to set the Betra down, the Mashlad would attack. He searched for a solution and came up with only one.

Setting his jaw, he drew a deep breath and heaved Sasha into the air towards Raven and in the same motion dove in the opposite direction. Tucking into a roll, he came to his feet as the sound of the swords sliding from their sheath echoed in the chamber.

The Mashlad rushed after him as he dove, but stopped short as Logan faced it with his swords glowing crossed in front of him. Black hair covered the Mashlad, its bulging muscles showing as white patches pushing through the matted hair. The red eyes locked on Logan, but then flickered to the side.

Logan looked away from the large teeth following the penetrating eyes to the side where another Mashlad appeared. Logan turned his attention back to the beast in front of him, but it slid back away, increasing the distance between them. Logan looked at the Mashlad, confused, but then realized it waited for more Mashlad to emerge from the other tunnels. Logan felt that this outcome would happen no matter what tunnel Raven chose.

The Mashlad had outmaneuvered them and now Logan stood before a cavern full of Mashlad. They varied in sizes with the largest Mashlad the one in front of him now.

Logan glanced towards Raven and Sasha, the Betra strewn across the unconscious girl. He looked back to the Mashlad, all standing stone still.

"Why are you here?" a voice said.

Logan looked at the Mashlad before him, confused by something so hideous speaking so plainly.

"Why are you here?" the voice said again and this time Logan knew it wasn't the Mashlad in front of him speaking, but someone behind the mass of Mashlad filling the cavern.

"We're trying to reach Caltoria," Logan said.

"Why are you not in Ter Chadain?" the voice asked.

Logan frowned. How did they know this? "Who are you?"

"Someone who is wondering why the Protector of Ter Chadain is not in Ter Rchadain protecting the queen?"

"Who are you?"

"Someone who gave up everything so you could have a chance at living and freeing Ter Chadain," the voice said.

Logan noticed movement out of one of the tunnels to his right and a small cloaked figure eased between the motionless Mashlad. It stepped up between Logan and the largest Mashlad, the flickering torch on the floor giving Logan glimpses of the face beneath the hood. Logan frowned as the face seemed to draw images from his past. The figure reached two weathered hands to the edges of the hood and pulled the fabric back.

Logan's mouth dropped open and his eyes shot wide as he stared at the frail man in front of him. He searched for words, but found none to fit what he now felt.

"You never were at a shortage for words when I knew you," the man said smiling and gave a chuckle that turned into a snort." Say something boy, or have you gone daft?"

"Grinwald?"

Chapter 30

The empress sat on her throne flanked by Berza and Tanlor as the magical slaves shuffled in before her. Her eyes flitted over each of the women to settle on the girl with the black stone shining on her forehead. Her hand fiddled with the silver rod taken from the protector's weapons stash now fastened with a clasp on a chain around her neck. This girl did something no other magical ever did to the empress. . . made her uncomfortable. She frowned as she concentrated on why the girl caused her to feel this way, but she couldn't put her finger on it. Something about her, the way she carried herself, the confidence she possessed even while being a slave made the empress uneasy.

Standing to one side of the new slaves, Governor Redrick and his slave Zeva observed in silence.

The empress stood and moved closer to the slaves, all with their eyes to the floor and heads bowed obediently. She paced, staring at the four women, taking in the color of their stones placed on their foreheads.

She stopped before the taller woman whose stone shone a dark red. Very strong, the empress thought with a nod. She moved over to the shorter, older woman, her stone nearly identical to the first. Also, very strong. She then moved to the youngest of the four, her face showing fear. The girl's stone shone red, but not nearly as dark as the older women. But this one could possess the ability to grow stronger as she aged.

The empress stared at the girl a moment and reached her hand to the girl's chin and raised her face until their eyes met. The girl's eyes met hers for a second and then flickered to the floor.

"Very good," Shakata said nodding her head." You have brought me a fine group of slaves." She looked over to Redrick who beamed with pride.

"I'm pleased you are happy," Redrick said.

"I said you brought me a fine sampling of slaves, I didn't say I was pleased with you," she corrected.

Redrick's smile washed from his face." I understand you lost Captain Ordestan on this trip."

"Yes, Empress, regretfully one of the slaves before you killed him," Redrick said, his voice wavering.

"And you killed a potentially valuable slave to offset the loss of the captain." Again the empress stated this as fact, not a question.

"One of the slaves captured with this very group paid with her life for the life of Captain Ordestan," Redrick answered.

The empress walked over to the governor and slapped him hard across his face." You are a fool," she spat." The captain was already dead, why waste magic on a dead man?"

"But we needed to set an example, to regain control of the ship," the governor explained.

"Who?" The empress asked.

Redrick stared at her blankly.

"Who killed the captain?" she sighed.

"The one with the black stone, Teah," Redrick said.

The empress's eyes went wide. She turned and walked back to stand before Teah. She stopped and stared at the girl standing with her head lowered.

"Look at me, slave," the empress ordered.

Teah tilted her head and her eyes lifted to the empress's.

"Do you feel guilt over killing my captain?" Shakata asked.

Teah stared without expression at her, having no memory of the action." I killed a man?" Teah asked.

"Yes, you killed a man, a very good man. A man who served me well for many years," the empress answered.

Teah's eyes went wide at the thought of it." You also are responsible for the death of. . ."

She turned to Redrick to provide more information.

"Uh, I believe her name was. . ." Redrick paused, realizing he

didn't recall the dead slave's name.

"Lizzy," Rachel whispered keeping her head down.

"Ah, Lizzy," the empress nodded, ignoring that Rachel spoke without permission.

"I don't remember," Teah said.

"You don't remember?" the empress repeated. She looked to Zeva, standing beside Redrick with her eyes locked on the floor." Zeva, please remind her."

"Empress?" Zeva said, not sure what Shakata meant.

"Place the images as you remember them back into her mind," the empress ordered.

Zeva looked to Redrick who nodded and motioned her to do as she was told. Zeva bowed to Redrick and then moved over next to the empress standing before Teah. Zeva bowed to the empress and closed her eyes.

As soon as Zeva's eyes closed, images burst into Teah's mind.

Teah's body went rigid as the magic played the scene of Lizzy being dragged on deck and knelt down before Teah. How Lizzy looked to Teah, begging for her help and then realizing Teah could offer none and her face went slack with realization of her imminent death. Lizzy gave one last look to Teah, bowed her head, and then a sailor decapitated her.

Zeva opened her eyes now filled with tears and stared at Teah.

Teah stared back at her, horror and shock consuming her face, tears rolling downs her cheeks.

"That is enough," the empress ordered.

Zeva bowed to the empress and took her place next to Redrick again.

"Why?" Teah whispered.

"What was that?" the empress asked, putting a hand to her ear and leaning closer.

"Why would you show me that?"

"A lesson isn't a lesson if it is forgotten, now is it?" Empress Shakata said." If you cross me or anyone in authority, this lesson will be repeated. Do you understand?"

Teah nodded.

"Good, now you will show me something you can do that I will approve of," the empress told her.

Teah looked to the empress.

"I am giving you permission to kill Governor Redrick," the empress stated.

"What?" Redrick cried." Why would you kill me?"

"Your incompetence to control the slaves cost me not only a great captain, but a strong magical slave. This is the last time you will fail me."

Redrick headed for the door, but the guards barred his way. He turned, panicking, searching for an escape.

"Now, Teah, kill Governor Redrick. Any way you wish."

Teah reached for her magic, but it fumbled in her grasp like a slippery fish. She looked frantically to the empress, pleading with her eyes as she sought to use her magic which remained elusive to her.

"Really?" the empress said in disgust." Tanlor, restrain the governor."

The black-cloaked slave stepped forward and with a wave of his hands the governor stopped rushing around and stood still with his arms tight to his sides and his legs clamped tightly together.

Teah saw the red weaves wrapping Redrick's body.

"Berza, the controlling stone for Zeva, take it from him," the empress ordered.

A pendant on a chain with a red stone in the center floated away from Redrick's chest. It lifted off over his head and crossed the room with the chain hanging below it as it eased into the empress's outstretched hand. The empress smiled with approval and then nodded to Tanlor to release Redrick.

Redrick stumbled forward a step and then caught his balance. He stared with horror at the empress and then in terror at Zeva.

"Zeva," the empress ordered.

The word hadn't finished escaping the empress's lips when Redrick's head exploded in a gory mess of blood and grey matter. The man's body fell to the floor twitching and flopping about for a moment before going still.

"I should have known you wouldn't be kind. . . or neat," the empress said with a hint of amusement in her voice." Men, take him away and get someone in here to clean up the mess."

The men walked to the body and picked him up, heading for the door, slipping in the mess on the floor, struggling to maintain their balance.

"Wait," the empress stopped them in mid-stride. She looked to Zeva and motioned with her head to Redrick's body.

Zeva walked over and pulled all the rings from the dead man's hands. She looked to the guards and gave them a nod. The men carried Redrick out of the room, blood dripping after them. Zeva walked to the empress and extended her open hands containing the recovered rings.

The empress looked at the rings with a nod from Zeva." And Teah's?" Shakata instructed.

Zeva took a silver ring from the pile and handed it to the empress.

The empress took the ring and held it up closer to her eyes, staring at the black stone.

"And the others who are here," Shakata ordered. Zeva took a gold ring and handed it to the empress." Whose is this?" Shakata asked." Galena's," Zeva stated and pointed to Galena. The empress nodded.

"And this is Rachel's," Zeva said handing a silver ring with a red stone to the empress and pointing to Rachel.

"And this one is Caldora's" Zeva said extending the ring to the empress.

The empress froze before she took the ring from Zeva and her eyes flicked to Caldora standing with her head lowered and eyes down.

"Caldora?" The empress said, surprise and excitement in her voice." King Englewood's precious Zele Magus?"

"Yes, Empress," Zeva said.

The empress took the ring and held it up to gaze at the dark red stone. She slipped the ring on her finger letting the too large ring dangle there. She then glared at Caldora as she concentrated on sending her wishes into the ring.

"Ahh," Caldora cried out and fell to the floor in pain.

The empress walked around Zeva as she stood with the remaining rings of Redrick's slaves in her upturned hand.

The empress stood over Caldora as she writhed in pain at her feet." I told Englewood I would make you pay for all the plans you interfered with. Now you will know the true meaning of obedience, witch." The empress glared down at Caldora, the hatred visible in her eyes.

Caldora screamed again as the empress sent another wave of pain shooting into the magical with her will.

"You will wish you died with your precious king," the empress told her." But now you won't be allowed to escape from my hell so easily. Berza, Tanlor, have some fun with her."

The two magicals grinned as they turned to each other in excitement.

Chapter 31

Saliday sat in her room by herself staring out the window. She followed the same obnoxious magical, the one who showed them into Governor Stone's dining hall and then betrayed her to the governor for possessing magic, to her quarters." Sniffer" is what the governor called him. The boy and the two other women with stones on their foreheads the governor used to find magicals.

She felt the bile rise in her throat at the thought of magicals hunting magicals, but realized the governor planned to use her in the same fashion.

As her mind moved from the sniffers to magicals back to her kind, the bile didn't hold back, but burst forth as she released her last meal's contents out the window down the side of the building.

She finished and leaned back, wiping her lips with the back of her hand in disgust.

Morgan, she thought and even in her thoughts his name came out bitter. Morgan betrayed her. He saved himself and offered her up to guarantee his freedom. She should have known better than to trust a man who hid his real identity. Logan was twice the man Morgan ever could be.

Her hopes lifted at the thought of Logan still being alive. The tug at her insides urging her to head towards Caltoria increased. Thinking he was dead, her Tarken sense of need didn't work like it usually did. Her grief over his loss clouded the pull of her instincts.

But hearing of the attacks in the tunnels erased her doubts and now her Tarken skills tingled like drinking cold river water stings as it finds its way to your stomach. She knew he still lived and she wouldn't stop looking until she found him and begged for forgiveness. She needed to tell him she loved him and not Morgan. And even though it meant the end of her people, she chose him, not Morgan.

A knock tapped on the door and Saliday walked over and opened it to find Governor Stone standing patiently out in the hallway.

"I was wondering if I may have a word with you?" he asked.

"Uh, I guess," Saliday said, walking back into the room without waiting. She returned to her seat next to the window and looked back at the governor as he closed the door behind him and came farther into the room.

"I want you to know that I don't see you and the magicals as the same thing," he stated and hesitated." But you're still considered someone with magic abilities, even though your magical capabilities cannot be projected onto others or put others in harm's way."

"That's good to know. Kind of like, you're a criminal, but not as bad a criminal as a murderer, but still a criminal," Saliday said raising a doubtful eyebrow.

"Yeah, sort of like that, but being the last of your kind, you're more like a priceless piece of art."

Saliday glared at him, causing him to take a step back." That is really rich. So you're not a slave owner, but a collector. That is much better. You still collect slaves."

"It is our way and will always be our way," Stone defended.

"But should it be your way? Only you can decide that. Society doesn't make that choice for you. Society says it's acceptable, but only you can accept it for yourself." She turned back to the window.

"I'm sorry Morgan brought you here, really. If we never met I wouldn't have you here in this situation now," Stone sighed.

"What is that supposed to mean?"

"I don't buy new magicals. All the magicals I have I inherited over the years or saved from the Mashlad, but the empress only allows so many magicals per noble. I'm forced to send the rest to the mainland or to the Mashlad."

"The same Mashlad who are in the tunnels you want me to go into?"

"No matter how soft I am on the magical rebellion, I must do as the empress orders. And she orders me to send all magical prisoners to the Mashlad. You need to help us find the people who attacked my troops."

"If these Mashlad feed on magic, won't they want to feed on me as well?"

"I hope your magic is different enough that the Mashlad won't want you. It will be a pity to lose you before I've had a chance to get to know you better." He gave a smile.
Saliday glared him down and turned away again." How about your troops, won't the Mashlad want them?"

"They feed on magic. My troops are relatively safe unless they threaten to take food from the Mashlad. They get very angry when you try to take their food."

"Wonderful. Isn't that exactly what you're asking me to do?" Saliday moaned.

"Technically, yes, but hopefully you can get to them before the Mashlad. However, if the Mashlad get them first, I guess our problems are solved."

Saliday stared at the governor for a moment and then turned back to the window, worry creasing her forehead. She couldn't lose Logan again. He had to be okay.

Saliday stood and walked for the door.

"Where are you going?" the governor asked.

"The sooner I do this the sooner it is over."

"I'll gather some troops. I'll have my boy take you to your things so you can get prepared." Governor Stone strode past her to the door and opened it, waiting for her to exit." After you," he said, motioning her from the room with his hand.

Saliday nodded and walked from the room.

****

Within an hour Saliday stood with the young errand boy as a dozen well-armed, golden uniformed soldiers filed into the cavern leading to the tunnels of the Mashlad. The gate stood closed to keep the Mashlad from wandering into the city.

A man with extra emblems on his sleeve approached and motioned the boy to leave. The boy, obviously nervous from

188

being so close to creatures that would love to have him for dinner, scurried away without a glance back.

"Captain Tan," the man said staring at Saliday's forehead. He frowned at her.

"Saliday Talis," Saliday nodded." Is there something wrong?"

"Stone told me a magical scout would accompany us, but you have no soul stone."

"He neglected to tell you that I am not a magical, but a Tarken."

At the mention of a Tarken, the other soldiers murmured to each other. The captain looked back and they went silent.

"I thought Tarken were extinct?" "All but little ole me," Saliday said with a shrug.

"We shall see. Stone also said the Mashlad wouldn't be coming after you?"

"I think it's his theory, but I'm not certain about anything. I've never encountered a Mashlad before."

"Fair enough," the captain nodded." If the Mashlad do come after you, we will try and protect you, but they are very strong and hard to kill."

"Thanks for the warning," she said as she pulled her short sword from its sheath and then a throwing knife from the straps of knives across her chest." Shall we get going?" The desire to find Logan pulled at her and she needed to close the gap between them. Just by coming into the cavern by the tunnel increased the sense of urgency she felt.

The captain raised a surprised eyebrow and gave her a smirk and a nod." Raise the gate," he ordered his men.

Two soldiers pulled on the heavy chain, lifting the gate inch by inch.

"You two stay here until we return. The governor said he would send down replacements in twelve hours. Remember, there must always be someone manning the gates if we are to get out again."

The men nodded their understanding and snapped to attention as the captain returned to the remaining soldiers.

"Are we ready?" Saliday asked.

"Whenever you are," Captain Tan said.

Saliday nodded, took a torch from a nearby support, and headed into the dark tunnel. She moved ahead confidently, not slowing as the gate came down with a thud and a shaking of the ground under her feet.

Saliday put her arm up to cover her mouth as the piled bodies filled the tunnel with the smell of death and rot. As they moved further into the catacombs, the body parts lessened allowing the air to go from rotten to simply damp and musty.

They walked on at a steady pace, not turning off the main tunnel even when branches offered a directional choice. This happened several times until they reached a tunnel heading to their right and Saliday stopped. Her sense of direction threw mixed signals at her, not showing a definite heading. She took a few steps down the branch and stopped.

"What is it?" Captain Tan said from behind her.

"They went down here for a ways, but now the trail is gone. They went back to the main tunnel again."

"Back out," the captain ordered and the men turned and gathered in the main tunnel until Saliday and Captain Tan emerged. He turned to her, holding his torch close so he could see her face." I've been given orders to kill you if you try to escape."

"Why would I try to escape?" Saliday said looking right into his eyes." I need you to defend me against the Mashlad, if we encounter any."

"Fair enough," the captain said with a satisfied smile.

"After I'm out of the tunnels I'll kill any of you who try to stop me and be on my way," she said, her own smile matching the captain's smile, which now faded.

Saliday turned and continued ahead, closing the gap between her and Logan.

Chapter 32

Logan pulled the man into a bear hug, lifting him off his feet.

"Set me down, we don't have time for this," Grinwald sputtered.

Logan set him down, sheathed his swords, and stepped back, looking to the Viri Magus expectantly.

The man looked the same as he remembered except for being thinner, if that were possible. His glasses hung on the end of his nose, hovering precariously on the verge of falling off. His salt and pepper colored hair looked longer than Logan remembered, but he figured this place offered little in the way of common comfort.

Grinwald walked over to the two women unconscious on the floor and knelt beside them. He sent his magic into Raven and the girl began to stir. He then put a hand on Sasha and shook his head in disgust.

"That girl has a lot to learn about healing. She loves to cover up the wound, but refuses to heal the deeper injury," Grinwald muttered half to himself and half loud enough for Logan to hear.

As Grinwald healed the women, Logan stood in amazed shock as he saw colors float above the women and then dive into them. Grinwald's hands glowed with magic that Logan could see.

The Viri Magus stood and noticed the look on Logan's face. He hesitated, glancing down at the women and then back at Logan. He shook his head and gave a sigh." You can see it now, can't you?"

"Uh, I don't know," Logan said with a shrug.

"Your sister saw magic weaves; now you can too. Don't deny it."

"Okay, so I can see them," Logan said." I'm even more of a freak now." He threw his arms up in disgust.

"No, my boy, it just means you must take more care in controlling what has been given to you."

Logan stopped and stared at Grinwald. Here stood the man he thought he abandoned to his death months ago at the hands of the evil Zele Magus Caldora. Hope surged in him as now with Grinwald's help, saving Teah felt much more real.

"We need to get out of here," Grinwald said as a Mashlad moaned behind them." I can only freeze them for a short time. They are learning how to unweave my ties much quicker."

"Then let's get out of here, old man," Sasha said, sitting up and rubbing her head with a hand.

"I see a bump on your head didn't quiet that disrespectful mouth much," Grinwald said.

"Grinwald?" Raven said her voice weak.

"Raven," Grinwald said helping the girl to her feet." What are you doing here?" "They told me you vanished along with our new guests and after they described Logan and Sasha, I knew you intended to bring them through the tunnels to Caltoria. I followed right after, and a good thing I did."

"We had it under control," Raven said as she brushed her clothing off and felt the lump on her head already starting to subside thanks to Grinwald's magic.

"Unconscious on the ground is not under control," Grinwald corrected." But enough, we need to leave before they. . ." Grinwald motioned to the Mashlad just as one let out a roar that shook the cave and caused them to cover their ears in pain." Too late, the weave is gone," Grinwald said as he began to weave again.

The Mashlad nearest them swung an arm and knocked them into the tunnel wall, breaking Grinwald's concentration and the forming weave.

Logan saw the magic dissipate like a wisp of smoke. He got to his feet and drew his blades, their eerie glow filling the cavern.
The Mashlad roared one after another again and again, their anger released in their savage cries.

Logan blinked the tears from his eyes as the pain of the roars blurred his vision. He pulled a deep breath into his lungs and held it for a moment forcing the pain from his mind. He sent his energy into the swords and let them spin and twirl before him.

A Mashlad hit him across the head sending him sprawling again. He sprang to his feet and moved closer, hacking at a nearby arm and dropped it to the floor with a smooth stroke. Another arm shot in and struck him in the midsection causing the wind to rush from his lungs. He crumpled to the floor gasping for air.

The largest Mashlad picked Logan up in his massive hands and lifted the boy to his jaws, open and drooling for the expectant meal of magical energy.

A burst of red energy hit the Mashlad in the face and sent Logan flying into a tunnel entrance. He slid down the passage a ways and rolled to a stop. He lay gasping for air, trying to get to his feet as the battle cries of Sasha and cries of surprise from Raven reached his ears. He gathered himself and stepped back into the cavern.

His companions battled for their lives. Raven dodged the grasp of the Mashlad as several converged on her and her tempting magic. Grinwald held his own as blasts of red energy kept the Mashlad around him at bay. Sasha battled to reach the magicals, her presence a mere irritation to the Mashlad as their attention focused on the irresistible calling of Grinwald's and Raven's magic.

As he hesitated at the entrance to the cavern, the Mashlad nearest turned their attention on him. He rushed past the first Mashlad ducking below a furry arm swinging for his head. He now stood in their midst and spun, letting the swords swirl into the dark mass of fur and muscle, teeth and sinew, cutting through anything they touched. His strength surged through him and he let his fury go, unleashing it upon the Mashlad who now stood between him and his sister. The glow of the blades dulled as the blood of the beasts clung to them. But the onslaught didn't slow, didn't lessen, until Logan stood in the middle of the madness and destruction that only the Protector of Ter Chadain could incur.

Not a single Mashlad survived the attack. Logan's wrath proved final and complete for these adversaries. He turned to his companions, their shock and disgust hung on their faces.

Logan stared at his swords covered in gory remains, steaming with the still warm blood of his victims. Blood caked his arms as well as nearly every inch of his body from head to toe.

Upon seeing the totality of his devastation, Logan leaned over and vomited, sickened by this display of savagery and madness. Grinwald picked his way through the gore to Logan. Pulling the cloak from his shoulders, he handed it to the boy." Clean yourself up and let's get out of here. There may be more around."

Logan took the cloth, wiping away the evidence of his uncontrolled fury and tossed it into the entrails on the floor. He lowered his eyes from Raven's and Sasha's eyes not wanting to see their judgment of his loss of control upon their faces. Logan slid the cleaned blades into their sheaths and the cave went dark.

Grinwald produced a ball of light hovering over his upturned palm that illuminated the gory scene again." Follow me; we need to get out of these tunnels before the rest of the Mashlad show up."

"There are more of these things?" Sasha asked.

"The Mashlad are many," Grinwald said with a glance back and then disappeared into a tunnel.

Raven followed after and Sasha gave Logan a comforting look before vanishing into the last glimmer of Grinwald's light in the tunnel.

Logan paused in the darkness for a moment trying to remember the times before death and destruction became the norm, but those times seemed so distant, like dreams of another person. The wizard's light vanished from the tunnel and Logan hurried after not wanting to slow their exit from these hideous tunnels.

The party moved quickly through the weaving catacombs. With Sasha healed by Grinwald's magic, she no longer lagged behind, but pushed the ones ahead to quicken the pace.

Logan felt fine, but fatigue pulled at him after his exertion in the cavern. His arms ached and his legs burned as he pressed on. He refused to let on to the others his need to stop and rest, denying his body the right to recover from his brutal display of savagery. He needed to keep the discomfort as a reminder of his lack of control. The battle with the Mashlad proved imminent, but what scared Logan was his inability to manage his power once it manifested. He became a berserker without any reason and that horrified him. If Grinwald, Raven, or Sasha stepped too close to his attack. . . he didn't want to think of the consequences.

They passed by some side tunnels as the roars of the Mashlad trumpeted.

"Hurry, they're onto us," Grinwald shouted and began to run. The others burst into a run as they drew their weapons.

Logan's swords glowed in the back of the party and Grinwald's glowing orb lit up the front as they rushed through the tunnels, weaving left and right.

When Logan felt he could run no further, Grinwald cried out." The exit is up ahead."

Sure enough, a light at the end of the tunnel signaled an end to their nightmare underground. The party picked up speed as the light beckoned them, giving them the last surge of strength. Grinwald sent a weave of air ahead of them, lifting the iron gate, the grating sound of metal on metal echoing back into the tunnel. The old, weathered gate pulled from the ground begrudgingly, lifting up until the spiked bottom separated from the earth. The gate eased high enough for them to exit and Grinwald tied off the weave.

Only twenty feet from the exit something clipped Logan's feet from under him and he tumbled forward, his momentum rolling him to a stop in the light of the exit.

The others burst into a bright valley with blue skies overhead, but Logan lay a few feet from the valley's floor, dazed and stunned.

Sasha turned first, hearing Logan's gasp as he tumbled to a stop. He lay on his stomach, the swords strewn before him, out of reach at the mouth of the tunnel. Looming over Logan stood something more than a Mashlad. Its body filled the tunnel completely, leaving no space as it pressed against the walls, ceiling and floor of the tunnel. The head, if you could call it that, looked like the combination of several Mashlad with multiple eyes and gaping mouths. A dozen arms stretched out towards Logan lying helpless on the ground.

Sasha rushed in, scooping up one of Logan's swords and tossing it to him as she put herself between the creature and Logan. The Betra stood dwarfed by the massive beast, her sword held high as it loomed over them.

A burst of red energy struck the creature in one of its heads, forcing it to retreat into the tunnel for a moment, but then it surged back.

Sasha didn't wait, but took the creature's hesitation as a chance to spin and grab Logan under the arms and pull him out of the tunnel as he leaned down and recovered his other sword.

The beast swung and struck them with a massive arm catapulting them out into the valley rolling and tumbling until coming to rest in a tangle of arms and legs.

The beast began to follow, but Grinwald unleashed another bolt of red energy into it from his raised hands and released the air weave from the gate. The gate rattled and slammed to the earth, breaking off one of the spiked bars when it hit. The bar dropped to the ground, rattling on the rocky soil and then went still. The Mashlad leaned against the gate, still much too large to fit through the slender opening made by the missing bar and then slid back into the tunnel. The glowing red eyes soon blinked into blackness and the beast was gone.

Chapter 33

Caslor hurried along the corridor deep in the bowels of the palace. The news of Redrick's death concerned him. If the empress lashed out so easily at a faithful governor, what might she do to a magical slave who couldn't use her powers?

He passed the open doors of the magical holding cells until he came to the closed door he sought. He looked around for guards and then slid aside the small door covering a barred opening. He stared inside the dark cell, searching for the occupant.

Caldora's face suddenly pressed up against the small bars startling Caslor and causing him to stumble backwards into the hallway wall.

"Help me," Caldora pleaded." Get me out of here."

Caslor pushed himself away from the wall and stepped closer to the door again." What happened in the throne room today?"

"Get me out of here and I'll tell you," Caldora said.

"Sorry, but I can't do that. The empress has given strict orders you are to stay in there until she releases you herself." Caslor stepped nearer, his face so close to Caldora's he felt her staggered breath against his face.

"Then leave me be," Caldora spat and her face disappeared from the grate.

"Wait, I need to know if Teah is all right," Caslor blurted and then snapped his mouth shut.

"Oh, does our Teah have an admirer?" Caldora said, her face coming close again, but not pressing against the bars with need.

"No," Caslor said with a forced chuckle." I just don't want any needless harm to befall her, that's all."

"You needn't fear, Teah remained unharmed when I was removed from the throne room and brought down here. What happened after I left, I have no idea."

"Oh, good, I would hate to see a magical with her potential destroyed for not being able to use her powers," Caslor sighed.

"You're the boy who was at our quarters. You have feelings for her," Caldora said.

"That's absurd. If you won't tell me more, we are done."

"The empress was disappointed Teah couldn't kill Redrick for her, but she seemed understanding enough to give Zeva the responsibility to teach Teah how to tap into her magic," Caldora said.

"Zeva?" Caslor said. He grinned.

"Is there a reason Zeva training Teah pleases you?" Caldora said, picking up on his reaction.

"Uh, no, no reason. I'm happy the empress chose to train Teah instead of disposing of her."

"As am I, but the empress hasn't shown me the same mercy," Caldora said, her voice bitter.

"What do you expect? Englewood did everything in his power to derail Caltoria's infiltration of Ter Chadain and you were usually at the heart of his plans."

"But I only followed Englewood's orders," Caldora protested.

"But you were a thorn in the empress's side nonetheless."

"When does she plan to put me to death?" Caldora cut to the chase.

"I doubt that is her plan at all," Caslor said.

"Then what?" Caldora moaned.

"She needs to teach you a lesson and get some satisfaction from all your hindrances in the past. Once she feels she has enough retribution, she will either keep you as her slave or sell you to a noble. This treatment will not be permanent."

"So there is some hope?" Caldora asked.

"If being treated as a normal magical slave can be considered hope," Caslor said, his voice betraying his compassion.

"Why is a Caltorian in the palace so kind to magical slaves?" Caldora questioned.

"I'm not," Caslor said.

"Okay, okay, you're not. So what is your name, boy?"

"You have no need for that information," Caslor said sliding the small door closed and walking away.

Caldora stood by the door in darkness smiling. She may be a slave being punished right now, but this boy held the key to her escape and possibly the escape of Teah and the others as well. He held far too much compassion for slaves to follow the

Caltorian philosophy of controlling magicals for the good of society. No, this boy thought differently and his beliefs led him on a different path.

****

The vase hung in the air in front of Teah, hovering above a pile of smashed vases scattered across the floor.

Teah stared at the vase, her forehead wrinkled in concentration, her lips pressed tightly together with determination.

The vase dropped an inch and then hesitated a moment before joining the other rubble with a crash to the floor sending shards of pottery everywhere.

Teah threw her arm up to protect her face as she turned away and cringed. She turned back sighing with frustration and then looked to Zeva standing with her arms crossed over her chest and disgust on her face.

"I'm trying," Teah cried.

"Not hard enough," Zeva said shaking her head.

"What am I supposed to do? It is there, but I can't take hold of it. It's as if it's blocked from me, somehow."

"I've never heard of amnesia blocking access to someone's magic, but I've never encountered someone with amnesia before," Zeva conceded.

"I know I can use it," Teah said and then wished she hadn't from the look on Zeva's face.

"You used your magic without the empress's permission?" Zeva asked.

Teah nodded.

"When?"

"This morning."

"What did you do?" Zeva questioned.

"I..." Teah hesitated not sure she wanted Zeva to know.

"What did you do?" Zeva said forcefully.

"I left my body and traveled as a spirit," Teah admitted.

Zeva's eyes opened wide as she stared at Teah." And where did you do this?"

"In an outer chamber to an office," Teah said." I went into an office so I could hear what was being said and with whom."

"You went as a spirit into an office to eavesdrop on a conversation?" Zeva repeated.

Teah nodded.

"Who were you with?" Zeva continued.

"A boy named Caslor. He took me to see his father," Teah said.

Panic filled Zeva's eyes. She rushed to the door and opened it, looking both ways down the hallway. She closed the door and hurried back to Teah. She grasped Teah's arm and pulled her over to a couch set in front of a large fireplace.

She leaned close to Teah and whispered, "Did you see Caslor's father and what did they say?"

Teah stared at Zeva, confused by her behavior." They spoke of my inability to use my magic and Caslor's father sent us away in fear of jeopardizing something they have worked towards for many years."

"Did you see who Caslor spoke to?" Zeva said grasping Teah's arms between her shoulder and elbow shaking them.

"No, no, he ordered Caslor out before I saw his face," Teah said." Ouch, you're hurting me."

Zeva released Teah and stood, pacing in front of the couch as Teah rubbed her arms where Zeva grabbed her.

"The person who Caslor spoke with must never be revealed or even mentioned. Do you understand?" Zeva turned to Teah, the intensity in her eyes so strong, Teah cringed from her.

Teah nodded.

"Good."

Teah stared at Zeva as she turned away and walked to the window to stare out." Why so much interest in me?"

Zeva looked over her shoulder at Teah still sitting on the couch and then back out the window when she answered." You mean besides the fact you are the first black stone since Tera Lassain, the first Queen of Ter Chadain?"

"Yeah, besides that."

"You create disruption wherever you go," Zeva said." We've heard you created quite a stir at the Zele Citadel before you left. Then Caldora chased you until you all were captured by Captain Ordestan who you subsequently killed on the ship over to Caltoria causing Redrick to execute your friend which drew the wrath of the empress who then killed him. Caldora, once your enemy is now your ally and a prisoner to the empress being punished for her behavior in Ter Chadain. Many might say also getting justice for her crimes against you." She turned from the window and walked over to stand before Teah." You see, death and destruction follow you around. Foe and friend alike perish in your company and we are interested in using that destruction to aid our cause."

Teah sat staring blankly at her. Could it be true? Could the life she didn't remember bringing so much pain and destruction to those around her, that someone wanted to tap into that carnage for their own purposes?

Sorry to say, she speaks the truth, Bastion said.

Teah closed her eyes, trying to remember even a glimmer of what Zeva spoke of, but only Redrick's demise and the empress's wrath on Caldora formed in her mind. Zeva said Redrick executed her friend because she killed a man? She caught a glimpse of the vision Zeva showed her about that execution, but the clarity faded the longer time passed.

Is that true?

I'm sorry, but we weren't with you when that occurred, Bastion answered.

Weren't with me? Then where were you before you were with me?

Bastion hesitated, uncertain, but then responded, with your brother.

Teah lost her control. We spoke of this; you were never to speak those lies again. I warned you I would block you off again if you spoke of such things.

I speak the truth. It is the Zele Magus who wishes to keep the truth from you, not us, Bastion pleaded.

No, it is you who speak lies to me, to try and tell me I'm someone I'm not.

If we lie about who you are, then how do you possess such powers as to do the things Zeva speaks of? Galiven spoke up.

No! No! No!

She slammed the magic up blocking the protectors behind it. They didn't cry out in protest, but accepted their fate in silence.

"No, no, no, no..." Teah shouted with her hands to her head rocking back and forth on the couch.

"Teah, what is it? Teah, are you all right? Teah," Zeva said as she held Teah in her arms trying to comfort the girl.

Teah leaned her head against the woman's chest and sobbed uncontrollably, the truth of her life she no longer remembered swirling in contradicting explanations through her mind.

"It will work out," Zeva whispered." You need to believe it will work out."

But how? Who told her the truth? The women who claimed to be her friends or the voices in her head telling her she was more than what they said?

"A little more practice will occupy your mind so you don't dwell on it," Zeva told her.

"I need to know my past. That is the only way to get my powers back. I need to remember."

"Let us hope not," the empress said standing in the doorway." You are of little use to me without your powers unless I keep you merely as an oddity."

"She will learn to use her powers again, Empress," Zeva said as she bowed.

Teah looked to the floor as she stood and wiped the tears from her cheeks.

"Let me show you how we display oddities," the empress said with an evil grin.

Teah lifted her eyes to the woman afraid of raising her anger for doing so.

"Come on then," the empress motioned to Teah.

Zeva took a step to follow, but the empress raised a hand, stopping her." That will be all, Zeva."

Zeva nodded and hurried from the room.

Teah followed the empress out the door and into a room off the other side. She hurried into the other room, stopping just inside the doorway.

Many glass covered displays filled the room with candles hanging over each and mirrors reflecting light on the valued item each contained.

The empress stood before one staring at Teah expectantly. Teah hurried to her side and looked at the item beneath the glass. A golden crown set with multiple jewels shone under the directed candlelight.

"This is the crown of the first Queen of Ter Chadain. We acquired it when Englewood eliminated the Lassain line, or so we all thought, but in due time we will accomplish that feat, we al- ways do," she told her and then moved to the next display.

"This is the stone which controlled the first Queen of Ter Chadain when she wore the matching soul stone," the empress stated before Teah came to a stop and gazed at the large golden ring with a clear jewel set in it.

"This over here," the empress said as she strode to the next stand, "is the crown of the first Emperor of Caltoria.

"And the newest additions to our collection are these one-of-a-kind weapons taken from the dead Protector of Ter Chadain," the empress said waving her hand over a much larger glass container proudly.

Teah walked close, the partitioned off protector's shouts rumbled muffled in her mind as she stared down at two swords laying unsheathed across their black sheaths, their silver blades shining brightly and the black pommels with the emblem of the crossed swords over a crown.

As she stared at the swords, her hand drifted across her left breast and she pushed her mind to remember why she felt tied to these swords.

"You must remember the legend of your own country?" the empress said.

"No, no, I don't," Teah said shaking her head.

"No matter. The legend is now ended."

"What of the stone from the first Queen of Ter Chadain's forehead?" Teah asked, not certain why she thought of that, only it confused her as to why the matched set wasn't under glass.

"Tera Lassain removed the stone and it hasn't been seen since. We assume it is now in Ter Chadain as inspiration to deny the true destiny of all magicals," the empress said bitterly.

"So it is not being used?" Teah asked.

"No, if it were, the stone would take on the color of the power the soul stone emits. No, that soul stone is not placed and hasn't been used for hundreds of years. I would know if it were."

"Why are you showing me all this?" Teah asked.

"I'm showing you the futility of believing that you or any other magical will ever be free of our mastery again. It is a clear example that we will always be your masters and in the end, nothing will change that. Black stone or not, you will always be my property and Ter Chadain rightfully Caltoria's."

Teah turned back to the swords under glass as the protectors in her mind shouted their muffled plea to be heard and to be believed. But for Teah, it only confused her more.

Chapter 34

Saliday rushed ahead of the Caltorian troops through the tunnels of the Mashlad as her need grew with each step closer to Logan. It didn't matter the Mashlad might mistake her for magical lunch, as long as she felt drawn to Logan somewhere in these tunnels. She pressed on even as the troops fell so far behind, their torches couldn't be seen any longer.

Remembering the threat of trying to escape, Saliday stopped and stood leaning against the tunnel wall waiting for them to catch up.

The glow of the soldier's torches soon shone brightly as they marched closer. Captain Tan strode up to her and backhanded her across the face.

Saliday went flying, her torch skittering across the stone floor. She lifted herself off the floor and wiped the blood from her lip as she glared the captain down.

"You outdistance us like that again and we will slit your throat and return to the governor with the terrible news that the Mashlad actually did have a taste for Tarken. Do we understand each other?" Tan stood with his hands clenched at his sides. A vein on his temple bulged and pulsed with his heartbeat.

"Sure," Saliday said, spitting blood from her mouth." But you should know that Tarkens have good memories and I will not forget you."

"Oh," the soldiers jeered from behind the captain.

Tan turned and glared at his men and they went silent. He then turned back to Saliday.

"Caltorians never forget as well, little Tarken. That is why we are in the process of conquering Ter Chadain to pay that bitch Tera back for forgetting her place. Now get going." He gave Saliday a shove towards her torch.

Saliday stumbled off balance for a moment and then scooped up the torch and headed out again at a noticeably slower pace. She wiped the blood from her lip one last time and then fingered her blades under her cloak.

"One of these has Tan on it now. . . that's for sure," she mumbled and pressed on.

The tunnel they followed opened without warning into a large cavern. As soon as Saliday set foot into the cavern, she felt strange. She lifted the torch above her head and stared in shock as Captain Tan and his men entered the chamber and froze at the sight before them.

Body parts and blood filled the cavern from wall to wall. Blood clung to every surface including the ceiling some twenty feet above. The stench filled her nostrils and she lifted her arm to cover her nose trying to stave off the nausea pressing at the back of her throat.

"By the spirits, what happened here?" Captain Tan said from behind his hand pressed to his nose.

"Looks like the Mashlad met Logan," Saliday mumbled.

"What did you say?" Tan asked.

"The Mashlad met something that tore them apart," she said.

"What could do this?" Tan shook his head.

Saliday picked her way across the slick cavern floor and searched for signs at each tunnel entrance. She moved from one tunnel to the next and then tracked back to the first again to start over.

"What are you looking for?" Tan asked.

"I will know it when I see it. . . there," she said pointing at the floor of one tunnel entrance.

Tan hurried across the cavern, slipping and sliding, trying to keep his footing. His men rushed after, several falling into the slimy entrails and blood, followed by curses against any spirit they might think of.

Tan made it to the other side without falling and stood beside Saliday with his arms folded across his chest. He stared down at the dark tunnel floor and then looked up to Saliday with a raised eyebrow.

"You don't see it?" Saliday said.

"See what?"

She stepped into the tunnel further and dropped to a knee

pointing to footprints of blood. The dark floor nearly made them invisible, but Saliday's training and keen eyesight picked them out plainly.

"Impressive," Tan said with a nod." Men, let's go."

Saliday headed down the tunnel with Tan close behind. His men followed after, several trying to wipe the blood from their bottoms.

Saliday grinned as she pressed onward. The mess in the cavern possessed the signs of the protector in action. The sheer madness of the battle scene screamed of Logan.

She rounded a corner and her head began to spin causing her to stumble. She caught herself on the wall of the tunnel shaking her head. *That's odd*, she thought. She righted herself and peered into the darkness ahead as she lifted her torch. Red circles flickered on and above in front of her. She squinted at the red dots as they began to move closer.

Tan and his men stepped up behind her as she stared at the approaching red lights.

"What's wrong, Tarken?" Tan asked.

"Something isn't right about those," she said pointing ahead of them in the tunnel and looked back at him.

Tan tilted his head and searched the tunnel ahead. He stared for a moment and then looked down at Saliday again." Nothing there," he said with a shrug.

Saliday frowned at him and turned back to the tunnel. Nothing but blackness filled the tunnel. But even though she couldn't see it, she could feel something. And that something wasn't right.

"We should go back and find a different way," she said taking a step past Tan heading back towards the cavern.

Tan caught her arm in his hand and stopped her. He leaned down so his face nearly brushed hers." Is this the way they went?"

"Yes but. . ."

"Then we go this way too," Tan said holding her attention.

"It doesn't feel right. We should go a different way," Saliday argued.

"By the spirits, you are a coward. There is nothing down here except Mashlad and they don't like the taste of non-magicals. I'll lead," Tan said pulling the torch from her hand, giving her a shove back towards the men, and taking a confident stride forward.

"Captain, don't," Saliday said as some of the men began to step past her, but her warning came too late.

Captain Tan stepped forward and slammed into something black and hard, mistaking it for the darkness of the tunnel. He fell backward onto the floor as the torch lay before him flickering where he dropped it.

All at once, red eyes opened from every height and angle in the tunnel as the mouths of multiple heads opened and roared. The nearest head of the creature reached out and snapped shut on Captain Tan's head, taking it clean off with one bite leaving his shaking body spewing blood on the tunnel floor.

The closest man cried out in horror only to have his cry cut short as another head of the creature took half the man's face off. He twisted sideways from the impact of the attack rolling into the group of men directly behind him.

The men up front hacked at the beast with their swords, slashing and stabbing, but the creature took armed limbs off one by one without the slightest sign of slowing from the men's attack.

Saliday ran down the tunnel away from the assault, snatching a torch from the last man as he stood staring at the carnage ahead of him. Saliday grabbed at him, trying to pull him with her, but he stood frozen with fear as the cries of his comrades echoed in the tunnel. She gave up trying to help him and rushed back to the cavern. She slid into the mess and then scurried back to the wall nearest the tunnel she had just exited trying to catch her breath. Saliday took deep breaths trying to calm and focus her mind. She closed her eyes and reached out with her Tarken need. The need now fell upon a direct and safe path to Logan. She held her breath and waited for need to grip her, to take her ahead to the tunnel leading her to the protector. Her eyes flew open and a smile split her face as the Tarken blood didn't let her down. She stepped away from the wall and shot across the room to a tunnel three openings away from where she stood and disappeared into the opening, the fading flickering torchlight the only evidence of the path she chose.

Chapter 35

Logan, Raven, Sasha, and Grinwald made camp in the valley a safe distance from the tunnel entrance. The blue skies gave way to a dark and starry heaven above them as they sat around a small fire, trying to stay warm.

Despite the warmth that engulfed Caltoria during the day, the nights proved to possess cold that struck a body to the bone. The feeble fire gave some relief from the night's chill.

They ate rations Grinwald carried in a small pack hidden under his black cloak, dried fruits and nuts mainly, but no one complained, eating quietly watching the fire. Grinwald stood and walked to each, offering a few more nuts. He paused as he came to Logan, staring down at him as the boy gazed into the fire.

Logan shook his head to the offer of nuts and Grinwald took a step to return to his seat around the fire when Logan spoke for the first time since the Mashlad massacre in the cave.

"We thought you were dead," Logan said, not turning his gaze from the fire.

Grinwald hesitated for a moment and then sat down nodding." As did I," Grinwald agreed.

"What happened after Caldora hit you with her magic?"

"Everything went black. I woke in a slave ship to Caltoria. Drugged up and powerless, it was the most horrible experience in my life." Grinwald gave a visible shudder.

"I'm sorry," Logan said. He glanced over at the man and then turned back to the fire.

"Why should you be sorry? You didn't hand me over to the slavers," Grinwald said, a confused expression on his face.

"I should have stayed and fought with you," Logan said, the pain of reliving those memories showing in his eyes.

Sasha and Raven looked from Grinwald to Logan in silence.

"You did the right thing," Grinwald said.

"Sasha and Galena forced me; otherwise I would have stayed and fought by your side."

"Then they were right. That battle could not be won. By running, you assured that Teah reached the Citadel safely and trained to be the Zele Magus Queen."

"But it was all for nothing," Logan said standing and turning his back to the fire.

"What are you talking about?" Grinwald frowned and looked to Sasha and Raven's blank faces for explanation before staring at Logan's back again.

"In the cave you asked why I was here," Logan said looking back at Grinwald." I'm here to save Teah."

"What?" Grinwald leapt to his feet.

"Teah is a slave and we came to get her back."

"This is horrible," Grinwald ranted.

"Tell me about it. After I killed King Englewood I thought the danger was over, but. . ."

"But what?" Grinwald shouted flailing his hands above his head." How do you lose a queen?"

"A queen?" Raven interjected.

"Your sister is a queen?"

Logan nodded to Raven and hung his head at Grinwald's words." I tried to reach her, but the fighting around the palace in Cordlain kept us in the castle for days after I killed Englewood."

"How did she get taken prisoner?" Grinwald asked.

"As far as I can tell, a party dressed in Ter Chadain army uniforms approached them while they ran from Caldora. That party was actually a Caltorian regiment and they captured Teah and her group." Logan's shoulders slumped.

"Do you know who else was taken?" Grinwald asked.

"Teah. . . got word to me," Logan began, not wishing to give away that he and Teah were connected mentally, at least when she didn't have a soul stone on her forehead." She traveled with Galena, Zele Students Rachel and Lizzy, and the Queen's Guard."

"So the Queen's Guard is captive as well?" Grinwald pressed. Logan's eyes watered as he recalled Talesaur's tale of how his men fought valiantly, but perished to the man in the battle.

Talesaur escaped without his right arm and survived by sheer will to reach Logan.

"All gone," Sasha spoke up as Logan couldn't get the words out.

Grinwald stared at her, his face frozen with shock.

"What is our next move?" Raven asked bringing the men out of their stupor.

"Uh, well, yes, what now. . . we need to find out where they've taken Teah," Grinwald grumbled.

"That's easy," Raven smiled." The empress's palace. If she is as strong as Logan is with the magic, she will certainly be the empress's choice."

Grinwald frowned at Raven and then turned nervously to Logan." Magical powers?"

Something snapped in Logan like nothing since the death of his family. Anger surged to the surface and he closed the gap between him and Grinwald in a second, grabbing the man by the front of his shirt and lifting him off the ground so their faces hovered only inches apart.

"Do not lie to me that you were unaware I possess the powers of the Viri Magus," he said in a low and threatening voice.

"Logan, stop it, what are you doing?" Sasha cried out as she rushed over to the men.

"Teah warned me that you and Galena knew of this and kept this from us." Logan glared hard into the man's eyes.

"Stop it, we need to stay unified if we are to get Teah back," Sasha pleaded pulling at Logan's arm.

"I, uh, we didn't want to burden you with that knowledge until you grew into your skin as a protector. I planned to train you myself until Caldora disrupted our plans." Grinwald's eyes stared back, wide with fear.

Logan held Grinwald's stare for a moment longer and set him down, but didn't relax." I'm too tired for this right now, but I promise you, if you withhold vital information again, I will not be so forgiving."

Sasha stepped cautiously back to her place next to Raven, watching the men as she went, ready for another outburst from Logan.

Grinwald nodded and then he smiled." You have grown into a fine leader."

Logan laughed in spite of himself." Ha, no thanks to you. You missed most of it."

"Not by choice."

Raven looked back and forth at the men as she frowned." Let me get this straight. . . Grinwald is a Viri Magus and you are the Protector and a Viri Magus?"

"Viri Magus of the Highest Order," Grinwald corrected.

"And we all thought you were some kind of eccentric old fool who wandered the caves of the Mashlad," Raven laughed.

"I think the 'old fool' still fits, but now you know him as an old fool who holds a title," Sasha said, leaning closer to Raven with a raised hand in front of her mouth.

"I heard that," Grinwald protested.

"So, we head to the empress's palace?" Logan said as all their attention turned to him.

"Not that simple," Raven said." Magicals can't get close without the sniffers finding them out. Our only way in is through the help of the Rebellion."

"How are magical slaves going to get us into the palace?" Grinwald asked.

"Not slaves, but magicals who are able to mask their magic and get close to the empress. . . very close." Raven crossed her arms and smiled confidently.

"So tomorrow we enter the empress's palace and look for Teah," Logan said with a nod.

The others nodded with a bit less confidence, but they nodded, nonetheless.

****

At daybreak, Logan and his party followed the road leading out of the valley and towards the port city of Bellatora. The road they traveled remained empty as they approached a small town with a few gray earthen homes circling a well. The heat of the day beat down on them and they shed layers of clothes to lessen the effects of the unforgiving sun.

Raven led them to the well and pulled the bucket from the water below, sitting on the edge and scooping mouthfuls of water with her hand.

As the others drank, Logan stared at the well, remembering his sister laying over the edge of their well back home in Treebridge. He recalled the blood running down her legs onto the ground and dripping from her head and neck into the water below. He shook himself from the memory and looked around the small center square. To one side stood an old tree, the trunk showing bare spots where the bark dropped off over the years, but yet it still stood tall without any signs of life. From the lowest branch swung three tattered ropes whitened by the years in the sun with nooses tied into the ends.

"That is where Tera Lassain's parents and sister were hanged. The emperor ordered the ropes to remain as a reminder to all magicals what will happen when they are defied," Raven explained.

"So my ancestors perished at the end of those ropes?" Logan asked his voice hardening.

"Don't do anything rash," Grinwald said.

"Logan, you aren't thinking what I think you're thinking?" Sasha said as she stepped between Logan and the tree, placing a hand on his chest.

Logan looked down at her, his eyes swirling with turmoil. He reached over his right shoulder and sidestepped Sasha so quickly that he strode to the tree before she reacted. The blade rang in the courtyard as he raised the sword above his head and severed all three ropes with a single swipe.

"What have you done?" A woman cried running from a house.

The other houses emptied as men, women, and children ran out to see why the woman shouted in distress. When they reached the well area they stopped and gaped at the tree, now with strands of ropes without any nooses.

The men drew their swords and circled Logan cautiously.

Grinwald rushed into the circle raising his hands in a calming gesture." Now, now, gentlemen, we don't want any trouble."

"A little too late for that, don't you think?" A tall, dark-haired man shot back with his sword held at the ready.

Grinwald spun to Logan, his eyes locking on to the boy's eyes." We don't want to draw attention to us and you do this?"

"Please, everyone calm down," Raven said in a raised voice.

The men surrounding Logan glanced at her, but didn't lower their swords.

"He is a foreigner and did not understand the significance of his action," Raven explained.

"Then he can tell that to the soldiers when we hand him over to them," the tall man said.

"I will not have a reminder of the decimation of my ancestors hanging from a tree like they were common criminals," Logan said through clenched teeth." I have witnessed enough death in my family and will not allow anyone to flaunt the killings of a Lassain as long as I am alive to do something about it."

A collective gasp rose from the villagers.

"You're a Lassain?" the woman who first discovered them said as she walked forward towards the men surrounding Logan and Grinwald.

Logan stared at Grinwald's resigned face and then sheathed his sword before looking past the men to the woman.

"Yes, I'm Logan Lassain, son of the last Queen of Ter Chadain."

"Lassain or not, he has destroyed the nooses, something the emperor decreed is punishable by death," one of the men said.

"What are we going to tell the soldiers when they come?" a woman cried out.

"They are due to pass through today," another woman shouted.

"They won't believe us if we tell them a Lassain did it," a man said." Not without proof."

Logan watched as the people panicked. What was he thinking? He wasn't thinking. He just reacted again and stepped into another pile of horse shit. Now his mission stood in jeopardy and the entire village might be punished for his actions. He wished the protectors were still inside him, keeping him from being so rash.

"We need to leave," Grinwald said standing by his side." Now."

Logan shook his head." No. I can't let them be punished for something I did."

"Then what?" Grinwald asked.

Logan looked down at the nooses lying on the ground at his feet and then back to Grinwald with a raised eyebrow and a light in his eye.

"What?" Grinwald said uncomfortably." Use your magic and mend the rope," Logan said.

"It doesn't work that way," Grinwald explained.

"What do you mean?"

"Teah said you weave magic. Weave the rope together with your magic."

"My boy, you have a lot to learn about magic. First, magic can't be woven and tied to anything but itself. For me to mend the rope, I would need to attach a magic weave to each end of rope and use the magic as a splice. . ." Grinwald's voice trailed off as he stared into space and a smile curled his lips." You know, you might be onto something."

"You are a magical?" the tall man said upon hearing Logan's and Grinwald's discussion of magic.

The men in the circle bristled at this new information about the strangers.

"Great, now we might as well shout and wave a red flag when the soldiers come and take us away," Raven groaned. She waved her hands before her and the men in the circle rose above the ground about ten feet kicking and shouting. She then walked calmly to where Logan and Grinwald stood with Sasha close behind.

"What are you doing?" Logan said staring up at the men as they struggled and cried out above him.

"Getting us out of here," she said.

"Will they be punished for the cut nooses?" Logan asked.

"Probably, but that isn't our problem," Raven said flatly.

"You don't know Logan very well," Sasha sighed." It seems that everyone's problem is his problem."

"Can you do it?" Logan said spinning to Grinwald as he stood staring up at the dangling rope.

"I think so. . ." he said trailing off.

One of the nooses rose from the ground and up to the cut end of the rope hanging from the tree. When the ends touched the strands of the rope seemed to wrap back around each other and become whole again.

Logan watched as green weaves of magic bound the rope back together. He studied it carefully, hoping to learn how Grinwald controlled the magic.

After fastening the last noose, Grinwald sighed and let his shoulders slump." There, that should hold, at least until we're long gone from here."

"It isn't permanent?" Logan said.

"I can't say," Grinwald said with a shrug.

Logan looked at Raven and motioned to the men suspended in the air above them.

She nodded and the men floated lightly to the ground. They stood listening to Logan.

"What will happen if the soldiers come and find the nooses cut?" Logan asked.

"The entire village will be punished down to the last man, woman, and child," Raven said without emotion.

"No, I can't make them take the punishment for something I did foolishly." Logan ran a hand through his hair.

"We can't stay here and protect them forever, even if we could hope to repel the patrol," Raven argued.

The woman who first spotted Logan and his party walked over hesitantly." We are here because we have nowhere else to go. Through the centuries, the emperors and empresses have held us to the punishment of our past. Maybe it is time we stood up for ourselves or left."

Logan stared down at the woman. The determination in her eyes burned strong.

"How long do you think the weave will hold?" Logan asked Grinwald without looking at him but still holding the woman's gaze.

"A week, maybe more," The Viri Magus told him.

"I promise in a week's time, the empress will have far more important things to worry about than some reminder of the wrongdoings done to my family." Logan's gaze burned fierce.

The woman nodded and then turned to the others gathered around." We speak of none of this, even amongst ourselves, understood?"

The villagers all nodded.

"Why would you protect us?" Raven asked.

"Many of us have lost relatives, even children, to the empress's collection and control of magicals," the woman said.

"We did not see any strangers today, agreed," the tall man said.

Again, the villagers nodded their agreement.

Logan leaned close to the woman and whispered something in her ear and her eyes grew wide and a smile curled her lips. She looked at Logan as he straightened and nodded her understanding.

Logan turned to leave and the woman took hold of his arm at the wrist and pulled him down to her, kissing him on the cheek. Logan smiled, turned, and walked away leaving the rest of his party to gather themselves and hurry after.

Sasha caught up with him first striding beside him on the dirt road as Grinwald and Raven scurried after.

"What did you say to her?" Sasha asked.

"I told her the Protector of Ter Chadain has come to Caltoria to end magical slavery."

"What?" Grinwald said as he got closer, huffing to catch his breath." When did we decide to do that?"

"Just now," Logan said and walked on ahead as Grinwald, Sasha, and Raven stopped and stared after him in shock.

"This rescue just got a lot more complicated," Sasha sighed.

"And decidedly more dangerous," Grinwald agreed.

"Exactly what the prophecies said would happen," Raven said smiling.

Grinwald and Sasha turned to Raven in surprise. She gave them a nod and hurried after Logan. They shared a distressed stare and then rushed to catch up.

Chapter 36

Empress Shakata sat in on her throne staring at the floor. She hated waiting, but lately, General Anthony repeatedly kept her waiting and her patience grew thin. She ordered him to meet her in her throne room to discuss the newest magical slave, the black stone, Teah. She needed to discuss the options of what to do with her if she never regained the control of her magic.

The door swung open and General Rowan Anthony strode in, confidence exuding from his tall, muscular frame. His hair hung loosely around his shoulders and his eyes searched her out, finding her on the throne.

Shakata gave an involuntary shudder as his eyes met hers. The passion between them dug deep at her control trying to break her command over the man. She loved him, but she was still his empress and he needed to heed that relationship better.

"You're late," she said as he entered and bowed to her.

"My apology, Empress, but I was detained by certain matters of importance."

"What matters come before me?" she asked, her voice escalating in pitch as her anger grew.

"Nothing comes before you," he said bowing lower." It won't happen again."

"Good," she said and waited for him to rise from his bow before she continued." I haven't heard any more voices since the day I first saw the black stone."

Rowan looked at her and raised an eyebrow in concern, stroking his chin in thought." And you said the voices you heard coming from the black stone were male?"

"Yes," she said nodding.

"It makes no sense." He frowned." I've tried reading others' thoughts and nothing comes to me."

"Then perhaps you were mistaken?"

"I know what I heard. The girl had male voices coming from her mind. Not just one, but several."

"And you tried hearing them again from her?"

"Of course I did, but all I heard were mumblings and nothing more."

"The skill came to your father slowly. You have to give it time to develop. If you heard it once, you will hear it again."

Shakata stared at him. His confidence infuriated her. How did he know what would happen? He always held such certainty when she seemed to falter.

"I hear you killed Redrick?"

"He was a fool. Letting my best collector get killed by some helpless girl and then killing a valuable slave to double the loss. He deserved to die."

"Are you sure this girl is helpless?" Rowan pressed.

"She has posed no threat here and seems more than manageable."

"I urge you not to take her lightly. We all know what happened with the last black stone."

Shakata jumped to her feet, strode over, and slapped him full across the face. The man staggered back a few paces before steadying himself and rubbing the side of his reddening face.

"Who are you to remind me of my family's failings? We lost many trusted and loved people in the rebellion that ensued after the Lassain witch escaped with the ship full of slaves. That rebellion is still smoldering and I will not allow it to ignite again with this black stone. I will kill her first."

"I'm sorry, Empress," he said, bowing again.

"Double the guards around the girl and report any suspicious activity surrounding her or her friends."

"Yes, Empress," Rowan said and turned for the door.

"One other thing," Shakata said.

Rowan stopped at the door and turned back expectantly.

"Increase the magical search patrols around the tunnels of the Mashlad."

"You have news of activity?" Rowan asked with a frown.

"Governor Stone says he sent a patrol after a group that stopped a Mashlad feeding and then fled into the tunnels. He has not heard back from that patrol and suspects the worst."

"You don't think the rebels made it through the tunnels?" Rowan said, incredulous.

"I won't take any chances. The coincidence of this happening when a black stone arrives here is disturbing. We need to be sure the rebel group did not make it to Caltoria."

"I will see to it," he said with a nod and left the room.

Empress Shakata turned from the door and stared out the window as the sun lowered in the sky. Who would be so daring as to enter the Mashlad tunnels in the hopes of reaching Caltoria? Whoever it was, their need drove them to desperate acts and acts of desperation posed the greatest danger to her rule.

****

Teah sat on the edge of her cot, watching the sun travel across the sky. She wished she could put a finger on the strange feeling she held that something greater than her played out before her. Her hopes of gaining control over her magic in order to save her life seemed to slide back into her mind as irrelevant to what she

must do now, but no matter how hard she tried to remember what she must do, it wouldn't come to her.

The voices continued to scream non-stop from behind her magical barrier since seeing the protector's swords. She refused to drop that barrier, afraid that once down the voices would take control of her mind and her free will. She couldn't risk losing herself forever.

"What troubles you?" Galena said, causing Teah to jump with a start.

"Uh, I'm just trying to remember. I still can't remember why I need to get away from here."

"Because we are slaves and any in slavery must always strive for freedom else lose one's self forever," Galena said.

"I agree, but there is more, I can feel it." Teah turned back to the sun and the sea.

"You don't remember anything from your past yet?" Galena asked.

"No, but the empress took me to a room today and showed me all the treasures of Caltoria's conquests over the years."

"And what did she possess?"

"The controlling jewel of the first black stone, Tera Lassain, and the crown of the last Queen of Ter Chadain," Teah stated.

"And this distressed you?" Galena questioned.

"I was confused as to where the soul stone from Tera Lassain's forehead was, but the empress said that stone remained lost since Tera's escape."

"That is perplexing, since we know that stone is not in Ter Chadain," Galena said frowning.

"But the things that made me uneasy were the weapons of the Protector of Ter Chadain. I don't know why, but when I saw them I felt they meant something to me."

Galena gasped and lifted a hand to her mouth, trying to hide her reaction, but Teah spun from the window to the Zele Magus.

"What? Do the weapons hold a connection to me?" Teah asked.

"I... No, they belonged to a legendary hero who is no longer alive," Galena said, but her voice lacked conviction.

Teah stood and walked up to the Zele Magus. She stared into the woman's eyes and pressed past them into her mind.

"Is there a meaning those weapons hold for me?" Teah said her voice strong and demanding leaving no room for deception.

"They belong to you," Galena said and then flung both hands over her mouth, horror and outrage on her face.

Galena swung and struck Teah sending her sprawling over the cot into the wall. Teah lay dazed against the wall as the woman stormed up and loomed over her.

"I warned you against using magic on me ever again," Galena ranted.

Teah looked back in confusion." I did magic?"

Galena's anger washed away as she looked down at the confused girl.

"Oh dear spirits, you don't even know when you're using your magic. This is bad, very bad. If the empress sees you using your magic without permission, you will be put to death."

Teah righted herself as Galena stepped back staring off at nothing as she thought.

"What am I to do now?" Teah asked.

"I don't know, child," Galena admitted.

"How about you explain why the protector's weapons belong to me and then we can figure out how to control my magical outburst," Teah said as the confidence began to return to her.

"This is very hard to explain," Galena said, her face turning pale." You are not going to like this, but you must remember we did it for your own protection."

Teah sat down on the cot, crossed her arms over her chest, and looked up at Galena.

"Go on."

"How do I start?" Galena said as fear filled her eyes. This girl sitting before her held enough power to end her existence with a simple thought and right now, the thought might come by accident.

"You are not merely a Zele Magus student," Galena began." You are the last female of the Lassain line."

"Lassain. . .?" Teah said without comprehension and then her eyebrows shot upward as her eyes opened wide." The Queen of Ter Chadain?"

"The very same, but that is not all," Galena whispered.

"That seems quite enough," Teah gasped.

"Those weapons the empress showed you. . ." Galena continued.

"Yes, the Protector of Ter Chadain's weapons," Teah urged her on.

"Belong to you because you are the first female Protector of Ter Chadain," Galena said so softly that Teah barely heard.

Teah's breath caught in her throat. This can't be.

The protectors behind her barrier cheered in unison as their existence inside her mind finally became validated. They shouted with joy as Teah, the first female protector of Ter Chadain finally knew the truth.

Teah felt the protectors' exhilaration in her mind and acknowledged their truthfulness.

Now what?

The barrier between her and the protectors lessoned enough for a unified voice of the protectors to break through.

We take the fight to the empress, resounded in her mind.

****

Caslor hurried down the hall to his father's chambers and rushed in. He tapped at the door leading to the inner office and waited.

"Enter," the voice commanded.

Caslor shuffled into the dark room lit only by the late sun shining and stood in front of the desk. The large office chair was turned so the occupant could stare out the large window over the harbor as the sun was just touching the horizon.

"You summoned me, father?"

"Take a party out and search near the valley of the Mashlad for any in the rebellion," the man said.

"Who in the rebellion would be in the valley of the Mashlad unless. . ." the boy hesitated at the unthinkable." They came through the tunnels?" he said in shock.

"The empress believes a party entered at the island and traveled here. Governor Stone alerted her of the possibility," the man explained.

"Raven," the boy gasped.

"She is the only one foolish enough to try," the man agreed.

"What do I do if I find them?" Caslor asked.

"Take them somewhere safe if they haven't been discovered by the patrol party yet," the man instructed.

"And if they are known to the patrol, what then, do we help them escape?"

A long silence followed as the man contemplated." No, if they are discovered, we mustn't risk exposing ourselves by aiding them."

The boy nodded, turned to leave, and then stopped at the door." Raven knows of us here."

"True," the man sighed." If they are in danger of being captured, be sure she cannot divulge our existence."

The boy's eyes opened wide at the implication." You want me to kill her?"

"She is a liability to our cause if she is captured." Caslor nodded as his head drooped and he left his father in silence.

Chapter 37

Saliday ran until she reached the rusty gate. She pressed her face against the bars, breathing in the fresh air with a smile of relief. She tried to lift the gate, but the heavy metal bars wouldn't budge. She was ready to give up when she spotted a bar from the gate laying on the ground. She stared at it curiously for a moment and then slid down the gate until she found the spot the bar had vacated. She pressed her head into the opening. Her temples touched a bar on either side, and then she leaned back studying the gate again. She nodded and pressed her head into the opening and then continued to push until her head eased through, scraping her cheeks as she forced her head completely through. She turned to her side and slipped a shoulder through and then her chest and then fell to the ground on the other side of the gate, her feet still on the tunnel side of the gate. She lifted her feet through and rolled onto her back, taking in a deep breath of fresh air and exhaled with a sigh of relief. She lay panting as her muscles gave out and refused to work any longer. How long had she run? It seemed like forever. Like she might never feel the breeze on her face again or smell the fresh, musty-free air in her nose again.

She lay hoping no one spotted her lying on the valley floor since she couldn't move from the spot. For what felt like forever, she lay helpless. Even the strength to keep her eyes opened failed her and she fell into a deep sleep.

When she woke, darkness filled the valley and she shivered on the sandy ground. She pushed herself to her knees and looked around for any signs of Logan, but saw nothing. Urging her stiff and protesting muscles on, she stood and staggered in the direction her need instructed. She grew stronger as she walked, but she knew her strength would not hold out if she didn't find food and soon.

Coming over a slight rise she found the remnants of a camp. She moved to the matted down grass where someone slept the night before. She scanned with the help of the moonlight above to find three more such spots. Four, Sasha and Logan have allies.

She smiled at the thought. Of course they found allies. That's what Logan did. He inspired hopeless, desperate people to follow him. He gave them hope and a chance at change.
She pressed on following the path they took. As she walked she scanned the landscape searching. A rustling in the brush brought her to a stop and she drew a throwing knife from under her cloak easing it with familiarity between her thumb and first finger. The brush moved again and she flicked the knife with deadly accuracy as a squeal rose from the bush along with the thrashing of the animal in the throes of death. It didn't last long and the movement stopped. She walked over and pulled a rabbit from the bush by its ears, her dagger sunk deeply into the animal's neck.

She used the full moon to skin the rabbit. She lifted the steaming carcass to her lips, hesitating only for a split second and took a big bite. The blood ran down her chin as she tore a piece of flesh free and chewed a few times and swallowed. She shuddered with repulsion, but dug her teeth into the animal again, tore another piece free chewing quickly, and swallowed.

She paused, putting a hand over her mouth, holding back the gag reflex urging her to vomit.

"Keep it down. . . keep it down," she urged." It won't do you any good to throw it up. If you want to find Logan, you have to get your strength back." She took a deep calming breath and then sank her teeth into the rabbit again. The blood dripped from her chin and she wiped it away with the back of her hand. When there was nothing left of the rabbit but the head and bones she tossed it to the side and continued on her way. Logan and his group were at least a day ahead of her and she needed to pick up her pace, but she continued to walk, not sure the meal would stay down if she ran right then.

She walked for a long time and then began to jog, gaining speed and confidence as she went. She needed to reach Logan before he came to a town or city where she might lose his trail. She could find him by only her sense of need, but a trail made it much simpler.

Saliday ran through the night finally coming to the first signs of the Caltoria population at a small settlement surrounding a

well and large tree. She stopped by the well in the deserted square. Pulling up the bucket she took a deep drink of cold water and then dumped the rest of the bucket over her head, washing the blood from her face and hands.

A foot crunched on gravel behind her and she spun pulling a knife. Her arm swung to find a head and pulled it into the crook of her elbow as she brought the knife to the throat.

"Wait, please, please, I mean you no harm," a woman's voice whispered.

"All I want is water and I'll be on my way," Saliday said.

"You are like the others, from Ter Chadain?" the woman gasped.

"You saw them?" Saliday said loosening her grasp a bit.

"Yes, they went that way, towards Bellatora," the woman said pointing the way.

"How long ago?"

"This morning," the woman said.

"Then I will be gone and trouble you no further," Saliday said letting the woman go.

The woman turned and stared at Saliday knowingly." You are a friend of the Protector of Ter Chadain?"

Saliday's eyes shot wide and her mouth dropped open.

"Don't worry. No one else here knows and I'm not telling anyone."

"You just told a stranger," Saliday said pointing her knife at the woman.

"But I felt your need to find him," the woman said holding her hands up defensively in front of herself.

"How could you. . ." Saliday began, but stopped." You're a magical?"

"Not really, nothing they can sense or the sniffers can smell," the woman shrugged." I can feel connections between people when they are particularly strong."

"I hate those sniffers," Saliday said as she tucked her knife away.

"They do pose a problem, but most have no choice in the matter. Sniff or die."

"Still, I might choose to die," Saliday said, but she knew Governor Stone used her in the same way by sending her into the tunnels with the patrol party to find Logan.

"Do you need something to eat?" the woman said offering a bundle she held in her hand.

"Thanks," Saliday said taking the food." What is it?"

"Rabbit," the woman said and Saliday cringed.

"Uh, not sure I can stomach that right now," she extended the rabbit towards the woman.

"I roasted it over the fire last night. It will make a good breakfast," the woman said waving off the food.

"Thank you," Saliday said tucking the rabbit under her cloak into an inside pocket.

"If you hurry you might catch them by sunrise," the woman said.

Saliday nodded and took off at a run in the direction the woman instructed. She needed to catch them before they reached Bellatora.

****

Raven leaned against the tall stone, staring around it at the town below. She looked back at her party waiting along the path expecting her report. She shook her head as she slid down the steep slope to the path.

"What is it?" Logan asked upon seeing her disheartened face.

"Stone Town, we need to keep moving," she said and took the path at the fork where they stood leading away from the town.

"Stone Town?" Sasha questioned.

"A town of slaves," she answered.

"What?" Logan said confused by the idea.

"We are close enough to Bellatora that the slaves are allowed to have homes and families here. You can't expect all the slaves to reside in the city."

"So they live normal lives here?" Sasha said, amazed.

"If you think being at the beck and call, day or night, for your master normal," Raven said sarcastically.

"You know what I meant," Sasha said.

"I lived here with my family until I was old enough to be stoned. They sent me to the island to keep that from happening. It cost them their lives," Raven said, the bitterness heavy on each word.

"I'm sorry," Logan told her.

"Save your sympathy for those who need it," Raven said." I don't." She continued to walk along the path and then froze." Get down," she whispered.

The others ducked down behind the rise in the path, watching as a large group of soldiers on horseback came into view on the path up ahead.

"We can't let them catch us out here in the open," Grinwald said.

Raven turned to the Viri Magus, staring at him in thought. She gave a curt nod." Okay then, it's into the town for us then."

"That should help us blend in, keep the sniffers off our path," Grinwald agreed.

"Not really," Raven said frowning." Magicals who have the stone smell different from those who don't, or so I've been told."

"But with all the stoned people around us, it should mask us somewhat," Logan reasoned.

Raven stretched up to look over the rise at the approaching patrol. She sank back down with a scowl on her face." And they have at least one sniffer," she said with distaste.

"If we go into the town they may punish the slaves if they find us there," Logan said.

"So what do you suggest we do?" Sasha asked.

"Give the sniffer a strong scent to follow," Raven said as she stood up in plain sight of the patrol.

"What are you doing?" Logan said.

"Giving them a target to zero in on. Head for the town and stay there until I come for you," she said as she stepped out onto the path and began to run.

A cry came from the patrol in the distance upon seeing Raven.

"I'll go with her, she may need some help," Grinwald said." Besides, this makes the scent stronger than yours." He ran after Raven without looking back.

Logan and Sasha stayed low and scurried onto the path over the hill leading to the town. They crawled from the path into the brush against the hillside and waited for the patrol to pass. Once the sound of the patrol faded in the distance, they headed across the open field towards the town.

They entered the town as people bustled around carrying foods and goods to and from a market set up in the middle of the town square. People of every age and size crowded the square, some with stones on their foreheads and some without. The stones on the women varied in colors from a light pink to a dark red while the men's stones went from a light blue to a deep blue color.

Children ran through the square as laughter and sounds of play filled the air.

Logan paused as these sounds felt so strange and foreign to him. Had it been so long ago that we felt happy and carefree? It seemed ages ago. The days of happiness and joy going up in smoke with their home that horrifying day his family died and the farmstead burnt to the ground. He may have killed Englewood, the man behind it all, but he still needed to make Caldora, the king's evil Zele Magus, pay for her part in carrying out Englewood's orders.

Logan snapped back to reality as a tingle ran up the back of his neck and he spun to find a woman with a dark red stone staring at him from across the square. He knew immediately she was a sniffer. He didn't know how he knew, she was the first sniffer he ever came face to face with, but he knew.

He went rigid as she stared at him, with curiosity at first, and then shock as she saw him for what he was.

Sasha felt Logan go stiff at her side and turned in time to see a woman push through the crowd towards them, her eyes firmly locked on Logan. Sasha grabbed Logan by the arm and pulled

him behind her as she shouldered her way through the thick crowd. They reached an opening in the buildings and ran into an alley heading away from the square.

Steps away from the end of the alley something hit them from behind sending them sprawling face-first into woven baskets lining the alley. They tumbled to a stop as they struggled to right themselves.

The sniffer raced to them, not giving them a chance to recover before she lifted Logan with a weave of air. He struggled to get free, but his arms pressed tightly against his sides. His feet kicked futilely as he hung in midair.

Logan clenched a fist and a bolt of red energy shot out at the woman. The energy missed the mark, but the impact sent the woman sprawling.

Sasha drew her sword and rushed the woman, but was thrown backward by a swipe of the woman's hand sending magic into the Betra.

Logan unleashed another blast of magic which the woman deflected to one side. She extended her arms towards Logan and he slammed into the wall with such force the stones crumpled under the impact. Logan's head slumped forward as he lost consciousness.

The woman concentrated too long on Logan allowing Sasha to recover. She threw herself on the sniffer, driving her to the ground. With her sword in one hand and a dagger in the other, Sasha overpowered the woman before she regained her senses. Sasha drove the dagger through the woman's chest as a last burst of magic sent Sasha hurtling against the wall.

Sasha slid down the wall to the ground, stunned and disoriented. Her vision blurred as her head throbbed with pain. She raised her sword in defense as the sound of footsteps rushed down the alley.

"Who are they?" a woman's voice asked.

"I don't know," a man answered.

"This one's a sniffer, or should I say was a sniffer. . . she's dead," another man said.

"Get rid of her body," the first man instructed." We'll take these two to the hall. Send my boy here to help us and hurry there when you're done."

"We won't hurt you," the man said by Sasha's side and she felt a hand set gently on her hand holding the sword.

She stiffened at first, but realized she didn't have much choice in her current condition. He could slay her easily if he wished. She nodded and released the sword. He helped her to her feet and she felt the sword slide softly into the sheath on her back. He placed her arm around his shoulders and supported her as they moved down the alley, the different colors passing before her blurry eyes.

"Logan," she said worried about the Protector.

"My boy and wife are right behind us with him," the man assured.

Sasha fought to stay conscious and managed until they entered a building and the man set her down. Once she sat down, the blurry surroundings dimmed and everything went black.

****

Raven ran a ways and then glanced back, shocked to see Grinwald close behind.

"What are you doing?" she said.

"Helping lead them away," he said.

"I can do this myself, get back there and protect Logan," she insisted. She looked back to see the patrol moving their way." Forget it, it's too late now." She motioned with a nod of her head at the approaching patrol.

Grinwald turned back and nodded as Raven spun and started running again. Grinwald kept pace as they raced along the path.

They reached a manor house with several out buildings and slipped behind the barn, watching the road for any sign of the patrol.

The patrol soon came over a rise not far off and Raven slid along the wall of the barn to the door. Just as she eased the door

open a hand shot out from the barn, wrapped around her mouth and yanked her inside.

Grinwald ran to the door and two hands reached out and jerked the Viri Magus inside.

The patrol entered the manor and stopped in front of the large house with a covered porch. A tall, heavy set man sporting a long black beard and neatly trimmed hair dismounted and stepped onto the porch.

An average size man, his head bald and his face clean-shaven sat in a chair on the porch and watched without reaction as the man stopped in front of him.

"Afternoon, Governor," the soldier said stepping forward and bowing.

"Captain," the governor said giving a nod.

"We're on the trail of some magicals and their scent led us here," the captain said.

The governor glanced over at the woman with a light red stone on her forehead and gave another nod.

"I see. You must have picked up a scent of some of my slaves. They went to the market for me today in the village and just returned." The governor stared hard at the sniffer.

"She says these smell like un-stoned magicals, Governor," the captain replied.

"They do smell a lot alike, don't they?" the governor said still staring at the sniffer.

The woman's face softened as she looked at the governor and she began to nod.

"Really?" the captain said, his anger rising.

"Yes master, I'm sorry, but I must have been mistaken as the governor suggests."

The woman cried out and dropped to her knees, her hands shot to her temples and she clenched her eyes shut battling the pain sent into the stone on her forehead.

"You had us chasing after stoned slaves in the heat of the day out here in the middle of nowhere?" the captain said, his anger unleashed.

"Captain," the governor shouted.

The sniffer fell over gasping for air as the captain released her from the pain of the stone.

"Sorry you needed to witness me disciplining my sniffer, Governor," the captain said and bowed." We will be on our way."

"They need to be kept in line constantly," the governor said, trying to exude understanding in his voice, but failing miserably.

"You disagree with my treatment of my slave?" the captain said as he straightened and stared at the governor with defiance.

"Excuse me?" the governor said his voice filled with anger.

"You live a long way out and are surrounded by magicals. One might say you like being around them if you live so close to their town," the captain said not backing down.

"Where I live is not your concern," the governor shot back.

"But you are very isolated, you are somewhat vulnerable outside the protection of the empress and her troops," the captain said.

The patrol bristled behind the captain, familiar with his demeanor.

"Oh, Captain, you misread your surroundings here at my manor," the governor said with a grin. He whistled and archers appeared on the building's rooftops with arrows trained on the patrol. A dozen men with drawn swords stepped from various buildings and formed a loose circle around the patrol.

The captain took a step back, his hand dropping to the hilt of his sword.

"Now, Captain, this is not the time for you and I to discuss our philosophies of the treatment of magical slaves. Your sniffer caught the scent of my slaves returning from market and that is that. Now I believe it is time for you to leave."

"The empress shall hear about this," the captain threatened.

"Yes, please, explain to my cousin how I frowned when you punished your sniffer for doing what she is supposed to do. . . sniff magicals."

The captain's face went pale and he stiffened." Thank you for your assistance, Governor," he said with a bow." We shall return to the town and see if perhaps the un-stoned scent leads there."

He turned, mounted, and rode from the manor with his men following after.

The sniffer hesitated, giving a thankful look to the governor. She scrambled to her feet, mounted her horse, and hurried after the captain already disappearing with the patrol behind the buildings.

The governor watched them leave and when an archer waved to signal the patrol was gone, he turned to the nearest swordsman.

"Bring our guests into the main house and feed them. I'll join them in the parlor shortly," he said and went inside.

The governor closed the door behind him, proceeded upstairs, and entered a bedroom facing the courtyard. He walked to the window where Caslor sat in a chair.

"You enjoy the show?" the governor asked.

"Very much," Caslor said with a smile." Thank you."

"For what?"

"If they didn't leave, Raven would be dead right now."

"You would have killed her?" the governor said looking at the boy in shock.

"She knows too much. We couldn't risk that knowledge reaching the empress."

"These are sad times," the governor said looking out the window as his men ushered Raven and Grinwald across the courtyard to the main house." Who is the old man?"

"I have no idea," Caslor said standing." Shall we go find out?"

Chapter 38

Remember, remember, remember, remember, Teah urged over and over. She stopped and concentrated on what she remembered before reaching Caltoria, but found nothing.

Don't try so hard, Galiven said.

But I need to remember so I can control my magic.

She has a point, Bastion agreed.

She is no good to us dead, Falcone added, finally coming out of his silent phase and trying to help.

If it isn't there it isn't there, Stalwart stated the obvious.

Her brother was never this difficult, Falcone complained.

I have a brother?

Oh, great, way to go, now she has one more thing to worry about, Galiven scolded.

She should know. Besides, who forgets their twin brother? Falcone shot back.

I have a twin brother?

You are a fool, Falcone, Bastion roared and all four protectors exploded into argument.

Teah slammed her barrier up and let them argue in muffled shouts. They drove her crazy when they got like this which seemed to happen more and more the longer her memory refused to come back. She racked her brain all day long trying to pull something, anything, back from the void in her mind, but she found nothing.

She glanced up to see Rachel sitting on her cot a few rows away staring at her. Teah stood, walked over to Rachel, and sat on the edge of her bed.

"You don't like me much, do you?" Teah asked.

Rachel held her gaze and shook her head.

"Why? What did I do to deserve your hate?"

"It didn't start that way," Rachel admitted." I liked you as well as anyone at the Citadel at first, but. . ."

"But what?"

"When Lizzy and I discovered you were the Queen of Ter Chadain, the choice of being a part of the madness around you

was past. And when you exposed your identity as a Protector of Ter Chadain as well, we found ourselves tied to a monster." Rachel stared hard at Teah.

"What made me a monster?"

"Do you know what a protector is. . . or does?" Rachel asked.

Teah shook her head.

"A protector is a killer. Everywhere around a protector is death and destruction. I feared it was only a matter of time before your violence would engulf Lizzy and me," Rachel paused as her eyes filled with tears at the mention of her friend.

"I wish I could remember, truly remember, not the visions Zeva put in my head. Was her death truly my fault?" Teah asked.

Rachel took in a slow jagged breath." She loved you, you know. She would do anything for you and that is what got her too close to you to save her. She disobeyed the captain's orders on the ship and took extra food for you. When they confronted you and asked who was responsible, I said I did it in order to protect Lizzy." Rachel stopped and wiped the tears from her eyes
and off her cheeks.

Teah stared at Rachel, horrified by the story." So you and I were taken on deck to be whipped for our disobedience."

Rachel's demeanor went from sorrow to anger in a breath." You attacked the captain, killing him and then were restrained by Zeva and were stoned yourself. Governor Redrick ordered the one responsible be punished for your action and they first grabbed me, but Redrick knew Lizzy took the food and they brought Lizzy onto the deck."

Rachel's body started to shake as she cried uncontrollably and the rest of the story came out between sobs and raspy breaths." They beheaded Lizzy. Right there in front of you with her staring up at you, pleading for you to save her." Rachel leaned over and cried into her lap.

Teah placed a comforting hand on Rachel's shoulder and the girl recoiled as if bitten by a viper." No, no sympathy for me

from you," she cried." You killed the best friend I ever had and you can't even remember it. Damn you. Damn you and everything about you." Rachel stood and ran from the room.

Teah felt sorrow for her, but she couldn't recall any of it. Not even Lizzy.

Why can't I even remember her?

Zeva stepped into the room cutting short Teah's thoughts." The empress wants you to have use of your magic by the end of the day so we better see if we can accomplish something to appease her," Zeva said.

Teah stood and followed Zeva out of the room and down the hall to the room adjacent to the trophy room they used for their lessons. Two guards stood at attention by the door and gave them only a cursory look. Once inside, Zeva closed the door behind them and then turned to Teah.

"We need to do this and we need to do it now," Zeva explained." The empress is out of patience."

"How am I supposed to do that," Teah spun on Zeva, her anger boiling over.

Zeva lifted off the ground and flew across the room, slamming into the wall. She exhaled when she hit the wall, the air driven from her lungs, and slid down to the floor. She rolled onto her hands and knees and gasped for air.

Teah ran over and knelt beside her in shock." I'm so sorry, I didn't mean to," Teah said in a panic.

"How did you do that?" Zeva said still trying to catch her breath.

"I don't know," Teah shouted.

"I didn't see your magic at all, it just hit me," Zeva said straining for air.

"Are you going to be okay?" Teah asked.

"Yes, I think so," Zeva said sliding over onto her butt.

"I still can't figure out what is happening," Teah said.

"What were you thinking right before I went flying into the wall?" Zeva asked. Her eyes searched Teah's face for an answer.

"I guess I was thinking how I wish you would stop pressuring me, just get away from me," Teah said and her eyes grew wide.

"You don't suppose my magic happens when I think about something?"

"You are a caster, you don't need to build a weave, but even Tera Lassain, the last caster to be in Caltoria, never had such easy access to her powers."

Teah stared at Zeva, intrigued.

A smile curled Zeva's lips and her eyes twinkled." See that vase over there?" Zeva pointed at an old elaborate vase sitting on a table filled with an arrangement of flowers." Destroy it," she ordered.

Before the words finished exiting Zeva's mouth, the vase exploded into thousands of tiny pieces and the water and flowers sloshed across the table.

Zeva stared at the remnants of the vase and then turned back to Teah who looked giddily back.

"I did that?"

"You did that," Zeva said with a nod. She held her breath and listened, raising a finger to silence Teah when she opened her mouth to speak." The empress can feel when we do magic without her consent," she whispered." She should be rushing in anytime now."

They waited for the empress's arrival, but she didn't come.

"Are you sure that's how it works?" Teah questioned.

Zeva nodded again and unleashed a colorful display as Teah watched her weave a vase to lift the flowers and water off the table. She released the weave and everything fell back to the table again.

"You see, the empress can't. . ." Teah began but was interrupted by the empress along with Berza and Tanlor rushing into the room.

"Zeva, what is going on here? I felt you use your magic. I thought I told you to instruct, not demonstrate?" the empress ranted.

Berza and Tanlor eyed the two women suspiciously.

"I'm sorry, Empress," Zeva said getting to her feet and then bowing.

Teah followed Zeva's lead and stood to bow before the woman.

"I needed to show Teah how to weave in order for her to understand."

"Any success?" The empress asked." I'm sorry. She still cannot weave," Zeva said.

"Not much of a teacher," Berza said.

"Humph," the empress grunted.

"Remember what I said. By the end of today or else we find other uses for her or kill her." She didn't wait for a response, but stormed out of the room.

Berza followed right behind, but Tanlor stopped at the door with his hand upon the knob.

"There is something going on with you two," he said as his eyes narrowed." I'll be keeping an eye on you." He walked out and slammed the door.

"He gives me the creeps, him and Berza," Teah said.

"They've been with the empress since their magic developed, ten, maybe twelve years old. She trusts them almost as much as non-magicals and they are loyal to her."

"The empress talks about me as if I wasn't here," Teah said.

"In her mind, we are nothing but possessions. The only thing she cares about is how she will use you."

"But she couldn't tell I used magic?" Teah said raising an eyebrow.

"Apparently not."

"What now?"

"We use that to our advantage," Zeva said with a sparkle in her eye." I need to contact someone; wait here and I'll be right back." She walked from the room.

****

Zeva hurried down the hall as the possibilities swirled in her mind. A stoned magical who can use her powers without the control stone registering it. . . amazing.

She stopped before a large door and hesitated a moment before going in. Once inside, she went to the inner chamber doors and knocked.

"Enter," a man's voice from inside ordered.

Zeva entered and strode in front of the desk where a man sat going over papers and writing on them. The shadows hid his face from Zeva, but she knew him well. He led the magical rebellion inside these walls.

"We have a development with the black stone," Zeva said.

The man set his pen down and looked up at the woman, the shadow falling away revealing his face to her. General Rowan Anthony leaned back in his chair and fiddled with the medallion hanging around his neck. The medallion depiction of an eye covered by a hand, and stared up at her curiously.

****

The minute Zeva left, the protectors burst into discussion.

If the empress can't tell you are using magic, we should be able to escape, Galiven said.

We still need to get past the guards, Stalwart pointed out.

But this is an amazing development, Falcone weighed in. With the empress in the dark about your magic, you can kill her and end this now.

You all seem to be forgetting one thing, Bastion said.

What's that? The empress still possesses the controlling stone. Even though she can't sense when you do magic, it doesn't mean she can't control you with it just the same. Remember the pain Redrick gave us when Teah displeased him on the ship?

Teah didn't remember the pain from the ship because she didn't even remember being on a ship, but the feelings she sensed from the protectors told her she didn't want to feel that pain.

She needed to remember in order to escape. With so much still a mystery to her, how could she hope to free herself from the stone's power?

That's it. The thought reverberated off the inside of her skull. Bastion, you were Tera's Protector, right?

Yes, Bastion replied.

How did Tera remove the stone from her forehead? Teah surged with excitement, exhilarated by the prospect of being free.

I'm sorry Teah, I don't know. Tera already removed the stone before we made our escape. She never shared her means of taking the stone from her forehead.

Teah's hopes tumbled down around her. She moved over in front of a mirror hanging on the wall. Her blue eyes stared back at her, like a stranger's eyes. She leaned in close and brought her hand to the stone. Carefully she took a fingernail and slid it under the edge of the stone. Taking a deep breath and holding it, she lifted on the stone. Immediately white-hot searing pain erupted inside her head. The protectors cried out in pain as she fell backwards on the floor screaming and thrashing uncontrollably.

The two guards stationed outside the door rushed into the room and stood laughing at her as they saw the trickle of blood running across her forehead from the stone. They understood what that meant. Every magical tried it at least once, but usually only once. They shook their heads in amused disbelief at her ignorance and went out to their posts again leaving her lying on the floor panting for air.

Teah lay there for a long time, her eyes closed and her heart racing. She waited until her heart didn't feel as if it would burst from her chest and then sat up.

I hope we don't try that again, Falcone said.

I won't, Teah confirmed.

****

"So you've discovered our little black stone does have use of her powers?" General Anthony said leaning back in his chair and crossing his arms over his chest.

"More than that, General, the empress cannot detect when she is using her magic," Zeva said fighting to contain her excitement.

Rowan's eyes shot wide at the statement.

"Don't you see what this means? We have a magical in the palace that can use her powers without recourse."

"Now hold on, let's not get ahead of ourselves," he said lifting his hands in front of him to calm her." You said that Redrick inflicted pain on her while you were still on the ship."

"Yes, but he couldn't tell that she used her magic. He accepted my confession that I did it."

"You're missing my point," the General said shaking his head." She can still be controlled by the stones. This changes nothing."

Zeva's shoulders slumped and her head dropped at the point. She nodded.

"And the empress will discover this anomaly when the black stone performs magic tonight to save herself," he added.

"I didn't think of that," Zeva said disheartened.

"At that point, the empress may choose to kill her and eliminate any threat she may pose."

"What are we to do? We can't let that happen."

"It will happen. Either the black stone performs magic and exposes the anomaly, or she doesn't and thus is deemed useless. Either way, she may die tonight," he said flatly.

Chapter 39

Saliday ran all night and into the next day. She stopped as the sun came up in the distance and took a few tentative bites of the cooked rabbit. Surprisingly the cooked rabbit tasted nothing like the raw one and she devoured it.

She felt Logan somewhere up ahead, not too far ahead, but still a ways off. She tossed the bones of the rabbit to the side of the trail and folded the cloth it was wrapped in, tucking it into one of the many pockets of her cloak.

She adjusted her cloak and assured her knives rested safely in their sheaths across her chest and then double checked her short sword at her side. With a confident nod, she took off at a run again. She wanted to close the gap quickly and be within view of them before they reached the city.

The morning dragged on, but she continued her pace without issue. This is what a Tarken did. They tracked tirelessly for days when they felt the need grip them. Everything else came second. Rest, food, water, they fell behind the drive of the need urging her on.

She came up a hill and spotted a group a long ways ahead. The group crested a hill where the path split. The group paused and crouched down. What were they doing?

Saliday scanned the horizon and found the source of the party's reaction. A scouting patrol of soldiers in golden uniforms rode directly for them. She turned her attention back to the party and saw one figure head along the path leading away from the patrol towards a small gathering of buildings in the distance. Another member of the party ran after the first figure while the other two crept out of sight over the rise.

The patrol came to the fork in the road and paused for a moment.

Saliday saw the second figure catch up to the first. They hesitated looking back at the patrol. By this time the patrol kicked their mounts after the two on the road causing them to quicken their pace together.

Saliday waited, not sure where the other two of the party went, but then they appeared past the hill heading for a town beyond. She closed her eyes, waiting for her need to direct her. Her eyes flicked open and she nodded confidently. She jumped into a run and reached the fork in short order. She slowed for a moment, looking first to the side where the patrol now pursued the two members of the party and then straight ahead at the distant figures nearing the town. She took off at a run again, heading after the two going towards the town.

Her heart raced as her goal lay within her reach. Logan meant everything to her and she pressed on, refusing to be apart a second longer than necessary.

She arrived at the outskirts of the town and slowed to a walk. She had lost sight of the two travelers ahead of her a while ago and now she frowned as the search, although not impossible, became more difficult. She strode into the town square and people pressed in on all sides. She tried following her senses, but they seemed confused by all the people.

Looking at the people around her for the first time since entering the town, she realized nearly all of them had a stone on their forehead. An occasional man, woman, or child passed without a stone, but the vast majority bore a soul stone imbedded in their skin.

She pushed through the crowd, reaching for any sense of Logan as magic essence swirled around her. She finally sat down on the edge of a small fountain in the middle of the square to catch her breath and get her bearings.

That's when everything around her went terribly wrong. A golden uniform loomed over her and a gloved hand struck her across the face sending her backwards into the fountain. She came up stunned and sputtering as the water filled her lungs as she gasped with the unexpected dunking. Two powerful hands took hold of the front of her cloak and lifted her clear of the fountain. She hung dripping water in midair blinking the water clear of her blurry eyes.

The man wore the unmistakable golden uniform of a soldier, his black beard and hair hung long and tangled. He smiled as his

crooked teeth protruded and jutted in unnatural directions from his mouth as if they fought to free themselves.

"Are you sure this is her?" He said turning and looking over his shoulder.

Another soldier nodded.

Saliday stared at the soldier, his face vaguely familiar. Then it came to her, in the tunnel as she tried to pull him back from the devastation in the tunnels, but he refused to come with her.

"Yes, Captain," the man said." She's the Tarken Governor Stone wants back."

"That was too easy," the captain said with a laugh. He turned and tossed the drenched woman into the mass of soldiers standing around the fountain." Take her and get her cleaned up for the trip back to Scalded Island."

The men caught Saliday, but the Tarken made her move while still in the air drawing a dagger in each hand. She drove each dagger into a man's chest as she landed in their midst.

The men cried out in pain and surprise falling back into the next row of soldiers causing a gap in the ranks.

Saliday's momentum brought her to the ground on top of the fallen men and she crouched scanning for escape routes. Staying low, she darted between the men and into the mass of people beyond. The crowd closed behind like the sea washing away a footprint in the sand and she wove deep into their midst before the soldiers could react.

"After her," the captain cried.

Saliday heard his command, but it already seemed so distant. She pressed through the crowd sliding through with surprising ease while the soldiers met with resistance, either real or perceived as the crowd refused to part for them.

Saliday hurried down an alleyway between two buildings and then stepped behind a building resting her back against the stone and wiping the blood from the dagger she still held in each hand. She slid them into their hiding place as she peered around the corner searching the far end of the alley for signs of pursuit. She turned back taking a deep breath of relief. Her eyes caught sight of a glimmer of gold down the street as she noticed two

soldiers standing at a doorway to a dwelling. She moved closer to the soldiers sliding into a recessed doorway and watched. Something inside her urged her to watch and to wait. So she waited and listened.

Soldiers suddenly burst from the dwelling followed by a woman with a jewel on her forehead and a tall strapping man shoving the woman from behind. They rushed down the street away from her.

"Find them," the man shouted at the woman and gave her another shove sending her sprawling before him. The man kicked the woman until she got to her feet and ran after the soldiers. The man stopped and turned back towards Saliday without warning.

Saliday jerked back into her hiding place in the doorway holding her breath.

The man paused for a moment, wiped a hand down the side of his cheek against a long purple scar as his eyes narrowed suspiciously and then turned with a shake of his head and followed after the others.

Saliday waited for a long time being sure they were gone before she crept to the door the party exited. She heard muffled cries from inside. She froze as the words "you have condemned him" reached her ears.

****

Sasha opened her eyes to find a thatched roof over her head and white earthen walls around her. She sat up and her head throbbed with pain. Panic gripped her as she turned her head to search for Logan. He lay a few feet from her on a bed identical to the one she lay on. She stared at him holding her breath until she saw his chest rise and fall. He still lived.

She looked away from Logan to survey their situation and jerked in her bed with surprise as a man sat at a table close by staring at her.

"Where are we?" Sasha asked.

"Somewhere safe. . . for now," the man replied.

"Who are you?"

"It is better we know as little about each other as possible in the chance that one of us is captured and tortured for information," the man said.

Sasha nodded at the logic and looked around again.

"I will ask one thing," the man said and Sasha turned her attention to him again." How has one so strong in magic avoided being stoned?" He motioned to Logan with a nod of his head.

"We aren't from Caltoria," Sasha said.

"Fair enough," the man said." I must warn you that the closer you get to Bellatora, the more sniffers there will be and the chances of him being discovered will increase."

"How can these, 'sniffers', tell the difference between him and those with the stones on their heads?"

"As far as we can tell, the un-stoned give off a different aura than the stoned. It is actually about the aura, not the smell. The non-magicals never understood that when they first discovered the magicals who had the gift to sense another's magic. It is the magical aura each magical possesses that the sniffer zeros in on. They learn to ignore the aura that is given off by a stoned person and concentrate on locating the aura given off by the un-stoned."

"There is no way to hide the aura or get away from the sniffer once they discover you?" Sasha asked.

"There are said to be artifacts that mask or cloak aura, but I know of no such trinket. Once the sniffer has a scent of an un-stoned, the only way to end their sense of you is by being stoned or being dead. And that defeats the whole purpose of escape now, doesn't it?"

Sasha nodded.

"Well then, you hungry?" the man asked.

"I am," Sasha said, realizing she was famished. She looked over at Logan.

"He can eat later, obviously he needs the rest right now," the man said.

"But he's going to be all right?" Sasha asked.

"He should be fine. Just hit his head pretty hard, but our healers said he will come out of it."

Sasha stood and walked over to the table and sat down. The man slid a platter of breads and fruits in front of her and she lifted an apple to her lips and took a loud bite. The juice dripped down her chin and she wiped it away with the back of her hand.

A woman burst through the doors, panic on her face. She raced to the table and stopped, trying to catch her breath.

"A patrol with a sniffer," she warned.

The man jumped to his feet as Sasha dropped the apple and stood.

"Quick, help me get him hidden," he told the women as he hurried to Logan and lifted him up from the bed.

Sasha ran to his side and lifted Logan with him, supporting his weight between them. They scurried to a wall with some decorative grates and the man reached up with his free hand and pulled a lever hidden in the stonework of the wall. The grates slid to one side and they shuffled in. The small space left little room for maneuvering, but they reached a cot set along the back wall and laid Logan down. Sasha sat down beside Logan and looked up at the man as he turned to her.

"Stay here and stay quiet. Hopefully, the sniffer will not sense you through the wall. Listen carefully and if they try to get in, be prepared to fight," he explained.

"There isn't another way out?" Sasha asked.

"Hurry, they are just outside," the woman warned from the opening.

The man stepped out and the grates slid closed leaving them in the spattering of light seeping through the tightly woven metal on the grated wall.

Sasha moved to the edge of the bed putting her head to the grate and listened as someone pounded on the house's door. She heard the door open as the outside noise burst into the house.

"What is it?" the man asked.

"Our sniffer thinks you have an un-stoned in here," a deep authoritative man's voice said.

"She must be mistaken. As you can see, my wife and I are not magicals and there is no one else here," the man said.

"Go check it out," the deep voice ordered.

Sasha listened as footsteps shuffled along the dirt floor of the house. She pictured in her mind where in the house the sniffer stood, drawing on her memory of the layout of the room. The shuffling stopped on the other side of the grate and she held her breath. The sniffer's breathing came slow and steady as she stood with only the grated wall separating her from Sasha and Logan's hiding place.

"Well," the deep voice sounded.

"I think they are here, perhaps behind this wall. . . perhaps just outside," a woman's voice said.

Sasha felt her panic rise. She couldn't let them capture the protector. All would be lost. She needed to do something. She slowly drew her blade, careful not to make any noise. She still heard the sniffer breathing on the other side of the grate. She could kill a few but she would never be able to escape with Logan in his unconscious state.

She looked back to Logan hoping to see some sign of him recovering. As she sat next to him something dug into her leg. She shifted her weight and looked down at the bed, but saw nothing there. She patted her leg and found a lump in her cloak's pocket. Frowning, she reached in and pulled out the soul stone she took from the sacred chambers back on the island. The stone placed on Tera Lassain's head all those years ago.

The only way to end their sense of you is by being stoned, Sasha repeated the man's words in her mind. She stared at the clear smooth stone in the palm of her hand. Do I have a choice?

The sound of men filling the room forced her to choose. She took the stone between her first finger and thumb, holding it before her eyes in the dim light. She leaned forward, brushed Logan's hair from his forehead and gently set the stone against his skin.

Logan's eyes flew open and his mouth gaped to scream, but Sasha covered his mouth, muffling any sound. His back arched as agony shot through him and then he dropped back to the cot and lay still.

Even in the dim light, Sasha watched the stone turn blue and then continue to a solid black color. She eased back to the grate and listened.

"What's the matter?" the deep male voice asked.

"The scent is. . . gone," the woman answered.

"How can that be?" the deep voice questioned.

"He must be on the other side of the wall in the street. Hurry before I lose him altogether." The sniffer shuffled away followed by the sounds of the soldiers.

Sasha waited a long time with her ear pressed to the grate before the sounds of footsteps came nearer and the grate slid to the side. She held her hand up to shade her eyes from the brighter light as she looked at the man who hid them.

"They're gone," the man said with relief." I'm not sure how. That woman had your scent and then it was gone."

As the man spoke, Sasha went back and lifted Logan from under an arm and eased him into the room.

The man saw Logan and he stared at him with horror, covering his mouth with a hand." What have you done?"

"The only thing I could to keep him from being captured," Sasha said pressing past him to set Logan down on the bed.

"Dear spirits, he's a black stone," the man said staring down at the stone on Logan's forehead." Where did you get the stone?"

"From a chamber in the tunnels on Scalded Island," Sasha told him.

"The only stone I know of there is. . ." the man stopped." No, not that stone. Tell me you didn't use the stone from Tera Lassain. Tell me you didn't put that stone on him." The man reached over and took Sasha by her shoulders and shook her.

Sasha twisted away the man's hands from her." It is done with and he is safe," she said.

"You foolish woman. You have condemned him. Don't you know where the controlling stone is for that soul stone?" the man shrieked.

Sasha looked blankly at the hysterical man.

"The empress has possession of the controlling stone. You have just made him the empress's slave."

"What have I done?" Sasha said as her eyes filled with horror and tears.

Chapter 40

Teah sat on the floor as the sun set and the room darkened.
The entire day she spent discussing the options with the
protectors and unfortunately, nothing positive came of it.

A serving girl entered the room, lit the candles not noticing Teah in the corner, and hurried out.

The empress came in and lifted a candle off a desk." You said she was still in here?" she said to the guards as she looked back over her shoulder.

"I am here," Teah said standing.

"What are you doing hiding in here?" the empress said startled.

"I wasn't hiding, just thinking. It is so hard to think with the others hovering around all the time," Teah admitted.

"You don't need to think anymore now that you're my slave."

"Sorry, Empress," Teah said bowing.

"Slaves and thinking don't mix. It usually ends in dead slaves."

"Yes, Empress," Teah said keeping her head down.

If she only knew what you could do to her in a blink of an eye, Falcone said.

Teah took a sharp breath and held it as her eyes flicked to the empress.

The empress's eyes stared wide at Teah and her mouth hung open in shock." What did you say?"

"Nothing Empress," Teah said with a curtsy.

"I heard a voice again, what was it? Who is in your head girl?" she shouted.

The guard rushed in, their eyes searching for the source of the empress's distress.

The empress raised a hand to stop them." I'm fine, but stay ready to come if I call."

The men nodded and left the room.

The empress walked closer to Teah with her head held high and her shoulders back, strutting her importance and power before her slave.

Teah felt the empress's fear as it radiated from her in an almost palpable form.

"You have demons, girl," the empress said as she circled Teah." These demons taunt me with their words and threaten me with their intent."

"No, Empress," Teah said shaking her head.

"Then why do I hear their voices as if they stand before me?"

Teah didn't have an answer for that as it remained a mystery to her as well.

How is she hearing us? Bastion blurted out in frustration.

"There," the empress cried out pointing at Teah accusingly. "There it is again, but different from the first voice."

Pain erupted in Teah's head and she dropped to the floor on a knee raising her hands to her temples fighting the excruciating pain.

The protectors cried out uncontrollably in pain.

"There, I hear them all," the empress said, keeping the pain burning into Teah with her will through the paired soul stones.

"One, two, three. . . four," she gasped in amazement." Four demons inside one girl."

The pain stopped as Teah panted to catch her breath. The protectors went silent.

Now that you know of us, what do you plan to do? Bastion asked.

The empress stared down at Teah taken aback by Bastion addressing her directly.

What he means to say is what are you planning on doing with Teah? Stalwart added.

"I, I, don't really know. I've never been able to hear demons before and need to decide what I shall do with that knowledge now that I possess it," the empress said pacing away from Teah as she turned her thoughts inward. She walked into the next room containing the trophies of Caltoria's conquests.

Teah stood gathering her balance and strength, and then followed the empress into the trophy room.

The empress stood in front of the stand containing the crown of the first Emperor of Caltoria.

Teah moved over and stood between the stands holding the weapons of the Protector of Ter Chadain and the ring containing the soul stone connected to the stone once set on Tera Lassain's forehead. Teah stared at the empress, waiting for the decision of her fate.

"How long have these demons been inside you?" the empress asked.

"I don't remember," Teah said truthfully.

We are not now, nor have we ever been, demons, Falcone spoke up. We do not possess Teah or control her. We are spirits here to guide her.

Teah and the other protectors cringed and tried to reach out and stop Falcone before he could finish his statement, but he brushed off their attempts to stop him and pushed on through. The reaction Teah and the others feared spread across the empress's face.

"Guide her? Why would a slave have need of guidance?" the empress looked hard at Teah and the girl turned away from the empress's intrusive stare." Who are you?"

The protectors went silent as Teah looked away; she saw the ring containing the controlling stone of Tera Lassain's soul stone. She frowned as the clear stone turned light blue and then slowly darkened until the color was no longer discernable. The stone now sat in the ring as black as night. Teah began to send her thought to the protectors, but then realized their reaction may give her discovery away to the empress. She looked back at the empress's studying look.

"I'm no one, a student from the Zele Magus Citadel of Ter Chadain," Teah said and glanced back at the stone in the ring. Another black stone? Teah thought. At that moment she didn't feel so alone in Caltoria.

"I command the spirits tell me why they are inside of you," the empress ordered.

Nothing, the protectors remained silent, refusing to speak and imperil Teah further.

"Speak, I say," the empress shouted.

Still, the protectors refused to obey the empress. She glowered at Teah, opening and closing her hands in frustration." Guards."

The men rushed in and snapped to attention before their ruler.

"Take her to the dungeons and keep her there without food or water until the spiri. . . she is ready to speak to me," Empress Shakata ordered.

The men nodded and each took hold of one of Teah's arms and lifted her off her feet, carrying her out of the room.

Teah gave the ring one last look and fought to control her knowing smile as the guards hauled her away.

What's going on? Galiven asked once they were out of the empress's presence.

The controlling stone to the soul stone of Tera Lassain turned black, she said.

That's impossible, Bastion argued. That would mean it has been placed on someone who is as strong in the magic as you are. Who could that be?

Only one that I can think of, Falcone said.

Really? You think it could be? Stalwart asked.

Did you see it take a color before it turned black? Bastion asked.

Blue. . . it turned blue and then darkened until it was black.

It has to be him, Falcone said confidently.

Who?

But who would, who could, place a stone on him? Galiven argued.

Him who?

I don't know, but there can't be anyone else, it has to be him. He is the only one who could possess such power, Stalwart concluded as the protectors spoke amongst each other, ignoring Teah.

Who are you talking about?

Your twin brother, Logan Lassain, the Protector of Ter Chadain, Bastion said.

Teah's eyes went wide and she gasped. He's come to save me.

But who is going to save him?

Chapter 41

Caslor sat in a high-backed chair flipping a pendant of an eye partially covered by a hand across the back of his knuckles staring at Raven and Grinwald sitting across from him as the governor paced nervously behind him.

"This is not good, not good at all. A Viri Magus from Ter Chadain will draw unwanted attention to our cause. His powers are too great to go unnoticed for long. Eventually a sniffer will zero in on him and we will be sunk. He needs to leave." The governor didn't look at anyone but ranted to himself as he paced.

Caslor feared the man had lost his mind since Grinwald introduced himself.

The governor leapt to his feet and erupted into his tirade which continued on for several minutes while the others watched.

"Calm down, we can figure this out," Caslor said.

"He is too powerful; he must leave now before the patrol returns." The governor ranted, beside himself with fear.

"We will be on our way and you needn't worry about us. We need to catch up to the others in the village," Grinwald said as he stood.

"You can't do that," Caslor said.

"And why not?" Raven asked." This is as much our fight as yours. Just because you do it in the luxury of the palace doesn't mean we bear any less danger in our actions."

Caslor turned to Raven, his hard eyes softening as he looked at her." You shouldn't have come through the tunnels. Now the empress is suspicious that this has something to do with the new black stone slave she has."

"Black stone?" Raven gasped." There is a black stone?" She fought to contain her excitement.

"Yes, but she has no knowledge of how to control her powers so the empress may put her to death or give her to the monks. So instead of wasting my time out here protecting you and our cause, I should be in the palace helping Teah remember how to use her powers," Caslor said.

"Teah?" Grinwald said with disbelief.

"You know her?" Caslor asked turning to the Viri Magus.

Grinwald looked with uncertainty at Caslor and then Raven. He stood, pulling Raven with him to the side of the room and whispered." How well do you know and trust Caslor?"

"He has been an ally to our cause since he was old enough to understand it. I met him when I lived in Stone Town as a child. We played together in the streets." Raven's eyes glazed over with nostalgia as she recalled those carefree days.

Grinwald nodded and walked over in front of Caslor as Raven stood entranced for a moment.

"Wait. . ." Raven tried to stop Grinwald, but the warning came too late.

"Teah is the Queen of Ter Chadain," Grinwald said.

Caslor stared up at the man, his face losing all expression and the color racing from his cheeks. A pale-faced Caslor looked at Raven as she stood with her hands over her mouth staring at him in fear.

"I thought you said he was trustworthy," Grinwald said to Raven as she stood transfixed, staring at Caslor.

"He is, when it comes to the cause of ending magical slavery, but. . ."

"But what?" Grinwald pressed.

"He is faithful to the empress when it comes to the sovereignty of Caltoria. Knowing the ruler of Ter Chadain is in Caltoria could end the war and give Caltoria the control over Ter Chadain it seeks."

"That makes no sense. You want to defeat the empress and end slavery, but support the empress in her drive to conquer Ter Chadain?" Grinwald asked turning to Caslor.

"Raven can make that statement because she knows something about me that very few people know," Caslor said.

"And what is that?" Grinwald asked, knowing he wasn't going to like the answer.

"I'm the empress's bastard son and have no desire to bring the end of Caltoria about in our time." Caslor turned away from

Grinwald's stunned expression and gave a nod to the governor, who didn't react to the information.

"Teah is the Queen of Ter Chadain?"

Grinwald simply nodded.

"This is definitely a dilemma," Caslor said shaking his head." Now the thought of killing the black stone is not as bad as I once thought. We need to tell my father immediately."

Caslor and the governor lifted off the floor and flew across the room crashing into the wall as Grinwald stood with his arms extended and his fingers stretched out from his palms. He lowered the two unconscious men to the floor and raced for the door with Raven close behind.

He swung the door open and ran into a large guard with his sword drawn. The man tried to look around Grinwald and Raven to see what happened in the room, but Raven extended her arm past Grinwald's shoulder sending the man slamming into the far wall and crumpling onto the floor.

They raced down the stairs scattering guards here and there as they went. They burst outside and were met by a hail of arrows raining down on them from the rooftops. Grinwald swung an arm over his head and the arrows turned to ash and floated harmlessly to the earth.

Raven plucked the archers from the roofs one by one sending them tumbling to the ground as they ran to the stables. They took two horses and raced from the barn and out of the compound back towards Stone Town.

"Did you kill them?" Raven asked as they rode.

"Don't know," Grinwald shouted." Didn't think we had the time to check."

"That may come back to bite us," Raven hollered.

"Yes, yes it may, but there was something about the way Caslor referred to Teah that makes me believe she is more than just a black stone to him," Grinwald said.

"Possibly, but not killing them is a huge risk. What if they reach her before we do?" Raven pointed out.

"Then we need to assure they don't," Grinwald said with a grunt and kicked his horse to run faster.

****

Saliday rushed into the dwelling, her sword in one hand and a throwing knife in the other. She slid to a stop on the floor and scanned for danger. A man stood over Sasha as she knelt on the floor holding an unconscious Logan in her arms.

Saliday sheathed her weapons and hurried to Sasha, kneeling down beside her. Her eyes locked on the dark, panic-filled eyes of the Betra. She looked down at Logan and gasped as the black stone on his forehead reflected the light coming in from a window high along the wall.

"What happened? Who stoned him?" Saliday asked, fighting to control the terror in her voice. Once a magical became stoned, they remained stoned until death.

Sasha lifted her chin, the tears rolling down her face.

Saliday drew back as if bitten. Sasha didn't cry. She didn't show emotion much less lose her control.

"I was trying to keep him hidden from the sniffer. It was all I could think of. I didn't mean too. . ." Sasha said, her voice trailing off.

"What do we do now?" Saliday said, spinning on the man.

"There is nothing. The control stone will change color as well and whoever has possession of it will have control of his magic," the man said.

Logan stirred in Sasha's arms and they all turned to him expectantly.

****

Logan opened his eyes willing himself to wake from his bad dream, a dream where pain surged through him and he had no control over his body. His eyes struggled to focus on the face above him, staring down at him, and then the features of Sasha took shape. He blinked rapidly to clear the last haziness from his vision and saw Saliday looking at him with worry.

He pressed against Sasha's restraint to sit up, never taking his eyes from the Tarken who once held his heart, but now. . . he didn't have time to think of that now.

"Where are we?" he asked, his voice hoarse and scratchy. He reached a hand to his forehead to rub his aching head and his hand froze in mid massage when it touched something smooth and cold." What the. . .?"

"I'm so sorry, Master," Sasha gripped Logan tightly in her arms, squeezing the air from his lungs.

"For what?" Logan said out of breath. He pushed against her embrace and she reluctantly eased away from him, allowing him to sit up on the floor next to her.

Sasha looked to the man and Saliday. Logan followed her uncertain gaze to them and then back to Sasha.

"What are you sorry for and what is on my head?" he said still touching the stone.

"Hey, I just got here, I'm as much in the dark as anyone," Saliday said raising her hands in front of her defensively.

"If I may?" the man stepped forward. Logan nodded." I am Brock and you are in my home. We brought you here when you were attacked close by in an alley by a sniffer. I'm part of the magical resistance in Stone Town and we saw your need."

"Thank you, Brock," Logan said with a nod." That explains where we are, but it doesn't explain this," he pointed to the stone on his head.

"Another sniffer tracked you here and I hid you and your friend in a secret room. But the sniffer had your scent and stood right outside your hiding place. I thought we all were doomed. . . but then the sniffer lost the scent and they rushed out into the street to try and find it again."

The man began to fidget as he searched for the words to tell Logan the rest. He flicked his eyes to Sasha, the pleading reaching out of them to her.

"I needed to keep you safe and I remembered how Raven said stoned magicals give off a different scent or aura than non-stoned magicals." Sasha struggled with each word of explanation as Logan stared at her in disbelief." I could see no other option so I . . ."

"You stoned me?" Logan said his words coming out filled with distaste.

"I, I..."

"Where did you get the stone?" Logan said as his eyes searched hers for answers, confusion filling his features.

"The chamber back at the rebel camp," Sasha said and then looked away.

"Tera Lassain's stone? You put Tera Lassain's soul stone on me? Are you crazy?" Logan didn't try to hide the horror and fear bursting from him." Who has the other part?" Logan looked at Sasha and she turned away, afraid to meet his condemning eyes. He turned to Saliday and she shrugged. He slid his gaze to Brock who cringed under his searching stare.

"The empress has the stone in the palace. It is said she keeps it in her trophy room," Brock said.

"Great, that's just great," Logan said as he rolled to his knees and pushed himself to his feet." What happens next?"

"Do you feel any overwhelming urge to go to the palace?" Brock asked.

Logan stopped moving and stared off at nothing in the distance as he searched for an answer. He shook his head." No, no driving urge."

"Maybe she hasn't noticed the stone has turned. She doesn't control you unless she wears the ring and puts her thoughts or commands into it. So for right now, it may be sitting in the trophy room with the change still undetected."

"So he can still be in control of his magic?" Saliday spoke up.

"As long as no one takes possession of the other part of the stone," Brock said.

"What if he takes possession of the stone?" Saliday asked.

"It is never done, but this situation has never come up." Brock put a thoughtful hand to his chin." I guess if he is in control of that stone he will retain control of his magic."

"Then we must go to the palace and retrieve the stone before the empress realizes it is placed once more," Logan said.

"That is good, because we need to go to the palace to get Teah," Grinwald said as he walked into the building with Raven and the woman from the alley right behind.

The woman walked over to Brock and wrapped an arm around his waist. She looked at Sasha, Saliday, and then Logan." Dear spirits save us, what have you done?" she cried when she saw the stone on Logan's forehead.

"Sasha was trying to save me from a sniffer," Logan explained.

Raven marched up to him and stared at the black stone. She nodded and pursed her lips." Black, very impressive. Where did you get the stone?" Raven said turning to Sasha.

"The chamber back on the island," Sasha said flatly.

Raven's face burst into anger and Sasha flew across the room and slammed into the wall.

Sasha gasped as the air rushed from her lungs. She fell to the floor when Raven's magic released her and flopped onto her stomach gulping for air.

"Stop it," Logan shouted and rushed to Sasha's side.

"She has taken a sacred artifact from our temple, doomed you to a lifetime of slavery, and ended our mission," Raven ranted." Don't you get it Logan? When a stone is placed, it remains there until your death."

"Then how did Tera free herself?" Logan asked as he knelt next to Sasha.

"She was special. . . one of a kind. She found a way to remove the stone, but she was the first black stone. . . ever."

"But Logan is a black stone also," Saliday pointed out.

"I can see that," Raven said rolling her eyes." But he has little control over his magic and Tera had much. He cannot be compared to her. And who are you?"

"Saliday Talis, Tarken and friend of Logan's," Saliday said with a nod.

"Raven, Grinwald, this is Saliday. Saliday, Raven from Scalded Island and Grinwald, High Viri Magus of Ter Chadain,"

Logan introduced hastily as they all gave a nod of acknowledgement." And this is Brock and his wife. . ."

"Dee," the woman spoke up.

"Then I guess we have no choice, but to retrieve the controlling stone for Logan's soul stone in order for him to stay free," Grinwald said breaking his long silence.

"And how do you suppose we get into the palace?" Raven said.

"Sniffers can pick you and me out, but now that Logan's stoned, he can enter the palace undetected by the sniffers," Grinwald explained.

"No, no way, he's not going in there alone," Saliday argued." I'd go, but those sniffers can sense me as well."

"What I do is not up to you," Logan said standing as Sasha sat up and started to get her bearings again. He locked eyes with Saliday and her eyes dropped from his.

"I don't intend him to go in alone. Sasha can go with him," Grinwald explained.

"She's done enough," Raven argued.

"Enough," Logan stopped the discussion as everyone turned to him." I forgive Sasha and I think Grinwald is right. Sasha can go with me to get the controlling stone and free Teah."

"Teah?" Brock interrupted." The empress's black stone?"

"Yes," Logan said nodding.

"You better hurry," Brock said." The empress plans to either accept her as her slave or hand her over to the Monks of the Spire of Ramashka tonight."

"The spirits help her," Raven gasped.

"Monks of the Spire Ramashka?" Logan questioned.

"There is a Spire which holds a crystal that concentrates the magic of slaves which the empress uses against her enemies. She has destroyed many ships trying to enter or flee Caltoria with that crystal and so have all the empresses and emperors before her," Brock explained.

"Maybe we should hope for the latter and then free her from these monks?" Grinwald suggested.

"No, bad idea," Raven said." The monks alter the minds of those slaves chosen for the Spire so they are nothing more than shells of magical energy. The crystal in the Spire pulls the magic from them until there is no magic left."

"How long is that?" Saliday asked.

"Some last many years while others last much less. Once their magic is gone, they are cast out to die or be taken in by family. A black stone may last a long time, but if the empress sends her there we don't have much time before her mind will be turned to mush and then what good will she be to us?"

"What are we standing around for?" Logan marched up to Grinwald." Let's get to it."

"Okay," Grinwald said.

"Hold on a minute," Raven said stopping them before they could begin making ready." First thing we need to do is hide that stone."

"I thought the entire idea of me going in is that the stone will aid in my disguise and let me move about unnoticed?" Logan said.

"Not a black stone. That is too rare not to draw attention. We need to change the color of your stone."

Logan looked surprised at Raven and then at Grinwald who shrugged." Okay, let's get to it," Logan agreed.

"You won't be so accepting when you discover how painful changing the stone color is," Raven said.

"You can't be serious," Brock said as Dee took his hand in hers and squeezed.

"You do realize that everyone has died trying to do what you suggest," Dee said, her face held all her doubt for them to see.

"We have no choice," Raven said flatly. She looked at Logan." Ready?"

"I'm ready to save my sister. How I get to that point matters little to me. Let's do this," Logan said mustering all the courage into his voice that he could.

Chapter 42

General Anthony stood behind Empress Shakata as she stared out at her city and harbor. The sunlight shimmered on the water as the sun touched the water at the horizon.

"This is my favorite spot and time," Shakata said.

"Yes, Empress."

"So you don't approve of my treatment of the black stone?"

"I feel you can get further with more persuasion and less force."

"Ha, that coming from my general known as 'heartless' by his own men."

"That is battle, this is different," he argued.

"This is a battle, it is always a battle. This black stone is giving rise to ideas of another revolt. I will not allow an uprising like in the days of Tera Lassain. Never again. The girl will be controlled or she will be dealt with."

"What do you mean. . . dealt with?"

"She will find the use of her magic which I will control or she will be given to the monks."

"You must be joking."

She spun on the general and glared at him." I most certainly am not."

"But the monks are animals. They have no business touching a black stone; they can barely keep pinks and sky blues in line without hollowing out their minds completely."

"Then she will be taught to do as she is told and control her powers." Shakata turned back to the window.

"There's more. You usually don't get so upset over slaves. What's going on?"

"I heard the voices again. . . from her. Men, four I think," she told him.

He stared with raised eyebrows at the back of her head.

"One of them stated they were in her mind to 'guide' her," she said with sarcasm." What does a girl need of guidance by spirits?"

"I couldn't tell you," Rowan said." Where is she now? Perhaps I should have a word with her, persuade her?"

"Not to worry, I have Signun dealing with her. He'll loosen her tongue."

"You want her alive, don't you? Signun is barbaric, even for me," Rowan protested.

"But he gets results and I trust him to get me answers," she said with a nod.

"Very well, but I'd like to speak with her before he kills her." She turned her head and looked up at him curiously." Do so, and be sure Signun keeps her alive. I need her alive to make an example of her at the very least. If the slaves see a black stone made to heel, they will be less likely to think they can rise up against me."

"As you wish," Rowan said and bowed to her, "Good night, my Empress."

Shakata turned back to the window giving him a wave of her hand to leave.

Rowan stopped outside the door glancing at the guards on either side, giving them a nod. He hurried down the hall on a mission. He needed to keep the girl alive in the hopes of keeping the resistance alive. If the spirits inside her head were there to guide her, then she must have a major role to play in Ter Chadain. He needed to figure out what it was.

****

Teah hung chained in nothing but her light undergarments in the dungeon cell, her legs and arms spread wide, stretched uncomfortably out to the walls. She had lost the feeling in her extremities hours ago and now her back and neck throbbed with each beat of her heart. She tried to use her magic, but the empress must have done something to prevent her from doing so.

The door opened and a guard stepped in as he did every few minutes since she arrived. He walked in front of her holding a cup of water.

Teah licked her lips at the sight of the water involuntarily and then snapped her mouth shut as she realized what she did.

"Thirsty?" the man said with a wry smile.

"No," Teah lied.

"The empress wants to know why you have voices in your head and you can eat and drink once you explain this to her," the man took a sip of the water letting some run down his chin. He didn't wipe it away but smiled with wet lips at her.

"I have no voices in my head," Teah said.

Rage erupted from the man and he strode to the wall and retrieved a bull whip. With a flick of his wrist, the metal-tipped strands tore into Teah's clothing and then shattered on her invisible mail.

"What kind of magic is this?" Signun shouted, his rage reaching a higher level. He walked around in front of Teah and slapped her full across the face

"Ahh," Teah cried her head snapping to one side and then she spit the blood from her mouth.

"So I can hurt you after all. Let us see how you like fire." He walked behind her and pulled a red hot poker from the pile of coals glowing in the corner.

The man moved close behind Teah so he breathed throatily in her ear." You calling the empress a liar?" He placed the poker against the back of her bare leg, a plume of smoke rose up behind her and the smell of skin burning filled the cell.

"Ahh," Teah bit her lip trying to control her outburst, but with little success.

"Now tell me why you have voices in your head, witch," the man said stepping close again.

"I don't know," Teah gasped, her tears rolling down her cheeks in steady streams.

"That's better, least you ain't telling me they ain't there anymore," the man said in her ear. He stepped back and struck her hard in the kidneys.

"Ahh," Teah cried when the blow caught her off-guard.

"But you ain't answering the question of the hour yet," the man said, amusement in his voice." I'll see you in a bit little witch. Don't miss me too much," he laughed and walked out slamming the door behind him.

Teah let her head drop as she sobbed.

Hold on, Galiven urged. Hold on, Teah.

Hold on for what?

Logan will come, Galiven told her.

He is already a slave to the empress. He will be no better off than me.

There you are wrong, Bastion corrected. Logan knows he is the Protector of Ter Chadain where you have yet to be convinced. He is something the empress and her people have never encountered before.

He is a slave. Even with powers, his powers belong to the empress now.

I believe that is false, Stalwart said. The magic the stones seem to control is that which is directed outward. It appears it has nothing to do with magic that is inner, flowing through your body to strengthen you personally.

And he has this power?

Indeed, Falcone piped up. So do you, if you only remembered. Your amnesia seems to have taken any control of that magic from you, just as it has wiped your Zele Magus powers from your memory as well.

So I have this inner power as well?

You should, Falcone said.

Should? You aren't too convincing. You need to believe in order for you to use it. Faith is a key component to controlling the powers of the protector, Bastion said.

Teah let the voices echo in her mind as they went silent. She searched for anything inside her mind that could give her a hint as to how to access the powers. After a few moments of deep concentration, she sighed with disappointment.

Nothing.

It is there, we can feel it, Stalwart told her.

The door swung open and the man strode in scooping up the hot poker again. He moved up so close his breath stirred her hair around her face as his stench filled her nostrils with the sweet sickening smell of his sweat.

Teah's eyes narrowed as she stared back at the man.

He leaned back from her gaze, his resolve softening ever so slightly.

"Tell me what the empress wants to know and I may only burn you a time or two more for good measure and send you back to her," he growled.

Teah motioned with her head for him to come nearer.

He raised a surprised eyebrow and leaned in close.

"You're right, I have voices, spirits in my head. . . and you know what they want me to tell you?"

The man shook his head hanging on Teah's next words.

"They want me to tell you that I'm going to free myself and then strangle you with that poker of yours until the very last twitch."

The guard's eyes shot wide in shock and rage. He recoiled, stepped behind her, and brought the poker against the back of her other leg.

Teah stared straight ahead as the hot steel burnt into her flesh. Her eyes stared flatly at the door of the cell as her mouth stayed closed and relaxed.

The man moved the poker to another spot on her skin without any reaction from Teah again. He lifted his arm to strike her in the kidneys again and Teah sprung into motion. As the blow bore down on her, Teah arched her back, pulling at the chains with such force that the stones holding them into the wall groaned as they ground against the neighboring stones.

The man stumbled forward as his strike missed its mark. The man roared in anger at her avoiding his punishment and drew back to strike again. Again, Teah maneuvered her body around the blow and once more the stones grated as their hold on the chains weakened.

The man howled with rage and stomped in front of Teah, his eyes glowering red as his anger surged out of control. He backhanded her across the face with such force his momentum turned his back to her.

Her head bounced to one side, but she met his gaze as he turned to her." My turn," Teah whispered.

"What?" the man said frowning at her.

"My turn," Teah whispered again.

"What? Speak up," he said grabbing her by the throat and pulling her face so their noses brushed.

"My. . . turn," Teah repeated and flexed her arms, pulling against the chains as the stones exploded into shards and her arms burst free. Her hands slammed into the man's head so hard blood oozed from his ears and he stumbled backwards.

Teah fell forward as her feet still hung by the chains above the floor. Her hands cushioned the fall and she gathered the discarded poker and pushed herself upright again, balancing for a moment and then falling forward and sliding the poker around the man's neck as he lay with his hands cupping his damaged ears. She deftly pulled the poker from both sides of the man's neck causing the light steel to bow and then let herself fall upon him as she flexed her muscles and arched her back.

The man tried to cry out and fought back, flailing at her in a panic, but she calmly tugged on the ends of the poker and his efforts soon went from defense to survival. His hands raked at the metal across his neck as his eyes bulged and his mouth gaped open for air that had nowhere to go. He stared back at her, realizing his end had come and then his eyes lost their focus and his legs twitched a while longer as she looked emotionlessly at him.

When the last muscle releases of his death throe ended, she rolled off him and searched his clothes. She pulled a collection of keys from his pocket and unlocked the shackles holding her wrists and ankles. Tossing the chains aside, she slid back against the cold stone walls and took a deep breath.

Is that what you meant when you said I needed to dig deep into my physical ability? She sensed stunned shock from the spirits inside her and she smiled. I'll take that as a yes.

She stood and wiped the blood from her hands onto the dead man's clothes. She stepped out into the hall and lifted the cup floating in a bucket of water to her lips, savoring the coolness of the liquid as it ran down her throat and seemingly spread across her chest.

She took a grey cloak hanging on a hook next to a table and chair and swung it over her. She lifted the hood up and let the shadows hide her features. She needed to find Galena and the others. They needed to know that Logan came for them and to be ready.

She hurried up the stairs recalling the path down. She slipped around corners avoiding guards moving around the palace and soon stepped into the bed chambers for the empress's slaves waiting to discover their fate.

She shut the door quietly behind her and let her eyes get accustomed to the darkness in the chamber. How long did they have her down in the dungeon?

She eased between the beds to Galena and shook the woman awake.

Galena opened her eyes and slid back away from Teah.

Teah pulled the hood back and Galena relaxed.

"What is it, child?"

"We need to prepare for escape," Teah whispered.

"There is no escape," Galena said.

"Logan is in Caltoria and we need to prepare for our escape when he reaches us," Teah explained.

"Logan is here? How do you know this?" Galena said and then put a hand over her mouth.

"I saw the ring to Tera Lassain's soul stone turn black in the trophy room. He is the one with the stone and he will be coming to free us soon."

"Teah, if Logan is stoned, he is the slave of the empress as well. There will be no escape but the end of Ter Chadain."

"Then we must assure he is freed so we can escape together," Teah said as her mind spun in search of a solution." We need to destroy the soul stones."

The protectors laughed at her thought.

"That is impossible," Galena said.

"Nothing is impossible, just not done yet," Teah argued." We need to discover a way."

"There is no way. . ." Galena began, but then hesitated." I've heard from some of the other slaves that the soul stones all come from the same giant gemstone far beneath the palace in the catacombs. If we knew more about where the stones come from, maybe we can figure out how to destroy them."

"Now you're onto something. I'll speak to Zeva and see what she knows," Teah said and straightened from the side of the bed.

"You can't just go wandering around the palace."

"They think I'm in chains in the dungeon, they won't notice until morning," Teah said.

"How'd you escape?" Galena asked.

"I tapped into the protector powers I have, that you neglected to tell me about," Teah said.

The look in Galena's eyes told her all she needed to know of the woman's deception.

Teah nodded and hurried out the door in search of Zeva and some answers.

****

Caslor rode all night, pushing his horse until it drenched his legs with sweat. He skirted Stone Town and took a quicker route around Bellatora to the far end of the palace. He entered the gate and ran past the guard and stable boy coming to collect his exhausted horse. He ran through the palace halls to his father's chambers. Rushing through the outer doors he then burst through the office doors to find the room empty.

He stood, stunned at finding the space empty. His father always retired here this time of night. Something important must have sent him out at this hour. He hurried from the room and nearly ran into a servant coming in with the general's dinner.

"Have you seen the general?" Caslor asked.

"He told me to bring his food by later this evening," the servant said bowing to Caslor.

"Did he say where he was going?"

"I heard him tell a guard he was going to speak to Signun."

Caslor didn't reply as he spun and ran out the door to the stairs leading into the dungeons. He raced down the steps taking two or three at a time. He came to the dungeon level and sprinted down the long hallway.

If Rowan needed to speak to Signun the interrogator, the man must be torturing someone of great importance, either to the kingdom or the rebellion. Either way, the information the empress wanted, Signun would get.

He ran until his legs burned and then ran farther. He felt confident he knew the cell Signun held his prisoner in. The one with all his pain inflicting toys nearby. He turned a corner and slid to a stop at the open cell door. Lanterns lit the room, but barely illuminated his father crouching over someone.

Caslor moved closer and General Anthony jumped, spinning with his sword drawn.

"Hey, it's me," Caslor said shuffling back.

"Sorry, a little spooked right now," Rowan confessed.

"Why are you spooked in the palace?" Caslor asked as his father stepped aside so he could see Signun's body in the dim light.

"How?"

"Don't know," Rowan said shaking his head." The chains were ripped out of the walls." He pointed to either side of them at the shattered stones that once held the ends of the chains now draped over Signun's body.

"Who'd he have down here?"

Rowan looked at Caslor with an expression he never saw before. A mix of hope, disbelief, and terror etched the creases in his face." The black stone."

Caslor staggered back against the wall to catch his breath as the air surged from his lungs. He gasped to draw more air in, but his lungs didn't want to cooperate as his muscles tensed." Where is she now?" Caslor's fear nearly cut the words down as he spoke.

"I have no idea. But we shall find her. She has nowhere to go."

"We have to find her. She is a danger to the kingdom," Caslor said in a panic.

"Easy, boy, she is a magical cut off from her powers. She must have had help to escape Signun like this."

"No, father, you don't understand. She is not just a magical who might aid us in ending the slavery in Caltoria. She is the Queen of Ter Chadain who can end the existence of Caltoria."

"You must be joking." Rowan laughed.

"Raven came through the tunnels like you suspected and she came with three travelers from Ter Chadain. A Viri Magus, a Betra, and the Protector of Ter Chadain himself. Teah is the protector's sister and Queen of Ter Chadain. He has come to save her."

General Anthony gawked at Caslor in disbelief.

"We have a hard choice then," Rowan said regaining his composure.

"Which is?"

"We try to stop the one person who can end the slavery in Caltoria or. . ."

"Or what? I don't like the first choice."

"Or we let events run their course and if the empress and Caltoria fall, we pick up the pieces the best we can."

"I don't like that choice either. Give me another."

"I have no other for you, son." Rowan pulled the amulet from his shirt and stared at it.

Caslor lifted an identical amulet from his shirt and glanced at it and then back at his father. The eye partially covered by a hand explained the powers of the magical talismans. They kept the magic inside the wearer hidden from all.

"Funny how this seemed heavier every time I sat by and watched one of our kind being punished for being a magical," Rowan said." What would it be like to be able to take it off and be who we really are?"

"You gave me mine when I was eight," Caslor said.

"Your powers started to show. The sniffers began to get suspicious when they were around you. I needed to keep you from that fate."

"Mother would never have stoned me," Caslor said defensively.

"She is quite rigid about magicals, Caslor. If she discovered you and I are one of them, she would see that as a betrayal, treason, and kill us both."

"She. . ."

"She would cry about it and regret it later, but she is the empress, she cannot afford to appear weak before her people." Rowan said, cutting off his defense of his mother.

"What now?"

"I will let you make the call. Gather the troops to find and stop the girl, or find her ourselves and help her free the slaves and start the revolution for Caltoria. You have much more to lose than I. What will it be?"

Caslor stared back at his father and the leader of their resistance against his mother, the empress. He shook his head and whispered, "I don't know."

Chapter 43

"Ahh, stop, stop, I can't stand it, please stop," Logan screamed and thrashed as Grinwald, Saliday, Sasha, and Brock struggled to hold him down. Blood ran down his face from the black stone on his forehead and his eyes stared back like a trapped, panicked animal at Raven standing over him.

"Hold on, I'm almost there," Raven said frowning as she concentrated on maintaining her focus.

"No, I can't. Ahh, please. . . please don't make me. . ." he shouted and pushed himself up sending everyone trying to hold him scattering around the room. He stood and glared down at Raven, his expression homicidal.

"Okay, okay, I'm done," Raven said placing a calming hand against his heaving chest.

Logan's eyes narrowed with suspicion.

"Really, done, finished," Raven assured.

Logan's tension evaporated and he flopped down on a chair, exhausted. Raven pulled a cloth from a hidden pocket in her cloak and leaned down to wipe away the blood on Logan's face. Logan flinched, pulling away. Raven put her hand behind his head and stared into his eyes.

"It is done. I'm cleaning the blood off." She held Logan's attention for a moment and then began wiping the blood again without waiting for his reaction.

Logan stared at her as she cleaned him, not sure he trusted her after the pain she caused. Since he became protector, he suffered several injuries that tested his pain tolerance, but nothing even came close to the pain her magic imposed during the changing of the stone.

The others inched closer to them as Raven ignored their encroachment and continued to wipe the dark red blood away.

Logan watched their reactions as they leaned in for a closer look and their eyes grew wide with amazement as they nodded their approval.

"Amazing," Brock said glancing down at his wife by his side.

She looked up at him with an impressed smile." You look like an average slave."

"We wouldn't want him to stand out one way or the other," Raven said still concentrating at getting the blood from around the stone.

"You accomplished that," Grinwald said with a smile.

"Are you okay?" Saliday asked Logan placing a sympathetic hand on his arm.

Logan looked down at Saliday's hand on his arm and pulled away. He turned to Sasha, ignoring the hurt expression on Saliday's face.

"Are you ready to go?" He asked.

"Whenever you are," she said with a curt nod.

"I'll get my things," Saliday said and took a step towards her belongings sitting on a bench nearby.

"Not you," Grinwald said stopping her.

Saliday turned, fighting to hold back her hurt expression. She opened her mouth to object, but Brock spoke up first.

"Even though you are not a typical magical, your essence will draw attention to you making it too dangerous for you to accompany Logan," he said.

"Who else will go with him?" Saliday argued." Two of them against the entire Palace Guard? We might as well hand them over to the empress."

"That being said, it is our only chance to free Teah," Raven said stepping back from Logan and nodding with satisfaction at her handiwork. She motioned for Sasha to come closer and placed a stone against her forehead.

Sasha flinched when the cold stone touched her skin, but then smiled when the pain she expected didn't come. She looked curiously to Raven.

"No magic in you," Raven said shrugging." I will bond it to your skin with a weave. It will be nothing more than decoration." Raven closed her eyes as she wove the spell and then opened them with an approving nod.

Grinwald pulled Logan to one side, but everyone focused on the two anyway." You know what you're here to do. Don't try and do anything other than get your sister and get out. That's all."

"What about Galena or other Zele Magus from Ter Chadain?" Logan looked concerned.

"We need you and Teah back in Ter Chadain. The rest of us. . . all of us are expendable."

"I don't believe that, not for a second. We need everyone to win this," Logan protested.

"But without us the fight goes on. Without you, the fight is over before it starts. . . understand?" Grinwald held Logan's attention with his intense gaze.

"Okay," Logan said as he looked down." I guess that's why you sacrificed yourself to Caldora in order for Teah and me to get away."

"Exactly." Grinwald grinned and patted him on the back.

"We better go, the first groups of slaves are leaving for town," Sasha said as she stood by the doorway looking out into the street.

Logan nodded, slipped on his swords, and covered them with a cloak. He turned to join Sasha when Saliday stepped in front of him and stopped him.

"I'm sorry," she said as she gazed up at him, her eyes watery and red.

"Nothing to be sorry for," Logan said and shrugged past her.

Saliday couldn't be brushed off so easily and scurried around him to step in his path again.

He looked down at her, exacerbated by her determination.

"I only chose to be with Morgan for the future of the Tarkens," she began, but stopped when she saw his stone-cold expression.

"You can choose who you like, but I need to continue moving forward towards my goal of putting Teah on the throne whether you are by my side or not."

"But I choose you, don't you see? I followed you here because I needed you to know I choose you." She stared up at him hard.

Logan shook his head." No, not this time, not right now. I need to keep focused on getting Teah back. You chose Morgan and now you have to deal with it. . . I don't. I'm going to get my sister now. Goodbye, Saliday." He stepped around the stunned Saliday and walked past Sasha and out the door.

Sasha glanced sympathetically at Saliday for a moment, looked at the others awkwardly, and then followed Logan out the door.

Sasha caught up to Logan only a few steps out of the house and fell in next to him, matching his stride. She didn't look at him, but stared straight ahead.

Logan didn't turn his head, but kept walking, his eyes narrowing as his determination to keep Saliday out of his head and focus on Teah boiled to the surface.

The plan they devised seemed vague to him, but they agreed vague had to do. They didn't know where they held Teah or if she would be able to help in her own escape. They knew little about the palace layout except where Brock or his wife had the opportunity to go while in the empress's employ, but that remained very limited.

The one thing they did know, and the driving force behind Logan placing his life in such peril. . . Teah lived. . . for now. The rumors rolled through the town about the black stone as the hopes of another uprising churned in the slave populace. Logan placed a hand to the stone on his forehead, the cool surface still giving him a queasy feeling. He glanced over at Sasha, but turned back before she noticed. He never discussed her placing the stone on him. He felt the remorse and regret radiating from her the minute he woke from his unconscious state. He needn't churn over things that couldn't be changed. He wondered if the protectors might give him such council if they still resided in his head. He grinned. He would like to think they would.

They followed a small party of slaves as they trudged up the hill leading to Bellatora ahead. The city rose high above them, dwarfing them with multi-level buildings that blocked out the early morning sun.

Most of the slaves wore similar cloaks as Sasha and Logan. Brock saw to that. The light grey cloaks sported a hood which Brock advised to keep up at all times except when forced to address a noble, guard, or the spirits forbid, the empress herself. Logan had no intention to meet the empress face-to-face. His goal, get Teah and get out. Simple as that. And, right, get the controlling stone for his soul stone. No problem, Logan thought as a wry smile curled his lips.

He flicked his eyes over to Sasha as the Betra scanned her surroundings relentlessly. Her mission never changed or deviated. Protect Logan at all costs. She would get him in and get him out.

Logan began taking note of the path they took so they might navigate their way back should they be lucky enough to exit the same way they entered. They'd be lucky to exit at all, he corrected chuckling to himself. He never held much hope of surviving long enough to finish his mission of putting Teah on the throne. He felt fairly certain his death would precede his success.

They took steep stairs that flattened onto a main road and followed the much wider path as it wound deliberately upward towards the palace ahead. Brock warned them that the palace covered a vast area, but Logan never imagined this. The building went on in either direction before him, disappearing into the distance.

He turned to Sasha and she leaned closer to him so she could hear him as he started to speak.

"How can we find her in there?" His eyes flicked back to the palace, their overwhelmed uncertainty pouring out.

"I say we stay away from the areas where slaves aren't allowed," she whispered." I'd bet that will narrow our search down considerably."

Logan looked back to her with pleasant surprise. He smiled.

"See, we can do this like we've done every other impossible thing before us in the past and will laugh at our fear at the time."

She flashed a rare smile, her teeth gleaming at him in all their whiteness.

Logan grinned and nodded." Let's do this."

Chapter 44

Teah headed for the long-time slave's quarters. Zeva became Redrick's property after the empress sold her to him, but Teah suspected Zeva always maintained a connection with the empress. Even though the slave treated her like a friend, Teah needed to use extreme caution when dealing with her.

The protectors reiterated that as she climbed the winding stairs to Zeva's quarters.

I know, I know, she told them and they quieted down as she reached up and knocked on Zeva's door.

Zeva answered the door." Teah, please come in."

Teah stepped into the room staring back at Zeva as her reaction, or lack of reaction made the hairs on the back of her neck stand up.

Zeva closed the door and turned to Teah. The woman's face looked drawn and tired.

"What's wrong?" Teah asked.

"Maybe we should ask you that?" General Anthony said from behind Teah.

Teah jumped and spun around to see the General and Caslor standing a few steps away from her.

"I, I..." Teah stammered.

Bad idea, I said, but no, none of you would listen, Falcone chided.

"What have you kept from me?" Zeva asked, her face showing her hurt.

"What are you talking about?" Teah looked back at the slave.

"We know who you are and why you are here," Caslor said as he took a step forward." Why couldn't you tell me the truth? I could have helped you."

"Helped me do what? I didn't even know who I was and I still can't remember anything past waking up in that cell with you," she said.

"The Queen of Ter Chadain?" Caslor exclaimed." You didn't think that information might have convinced some people to help you?"

"Or get me killed," Teah added.

"She's right, Caslor. She didn't have any reason to trust us. If the empress knew she was the Queen of Ter Chadain, she may have put her to death immediately," the General said and nodded.

"But why didn't you tell me you regained control of your magic?" Zeva asked.

"Because I haven't," Teah said with a sigh.

Nice, tell the enemy all your weaknesses, Falcone growled.

"The way you killed Signun, magic was involved," the general said.

"Not the kind you're thinking of. Not like Zeva's magic."

Teah, what are you doing? Bastion said.

"I possess a different kind of magic. . ." Teah continued.

Teah, don't, Stalwart cautioned.

"A very old magic that can't be controlled by the soul stone," Teah said, ignoring the protectors.

"You can't expose yourself like this, Galiven said, it may be our only chance to survive.

"What are you talking about?" Caslor asked and moved closer so he could look her in the eyes." I felt a connection to you the minute I saw you in that cell. I knew you held the key to my future and if given a chance, we might be able to make a future together."

"Caslor," his father shouted.

"It's true. I could never let any harm come to you no matter what. Even if you are the queen of the country my mother strives to destroy," Caslor said.

Zeva gasped and the general groaned as Caslor announced to Teah his connection to the empress.

"You're the empress's son?" Teah said, the protectors all shouting at once not to divulge she was a protector.

"Yes," he said stepping closer and taking her hands in his. He stared into her deep blue eyes, his green eyes flashing his feelings powerfully at her." And I want to get you out of here before something can happen to you."

Teah stared down at her hands cupped in Caslor's. She didn't know how she felt, but she knew she needed the protectors to be quiet until she sorted it out. She slammed her barrier up in her mind, muffling their voices and then turned her attention to Caslor. She looked at him as if for the first time. Yes, she did feel something for him, but she wasn't sure what that was. . . yet. She looked at the general who stared at them as if he were in pain.

Zeva smiled and nodded her approval at all the information shared with her this day.

Only one sure way to find out.

She gave his hands a squeeze and sighed, searching for the words." I'm not only Queen of Ter Chadain but . . ."

"You have a twin brother who is on his way to get you and he is the Protector of Ter Chadain," Caslor blurted out." I know and I don't care."

Teah stared at him curiously, still trying to sort out her feelings." No, well, yes, but. . ." she said shaking her head." That isn't what I wanted to tell you, there's more."

"I don't care what it is, we will get through this and get you safely back to Ter Chadain," Caslor said.

"I'm a protector, too," Teah whispered.

"See, you can tell me anything and... huh?" Caslor said and then stopped to look at her dumbfounded.

"You're a protector? Those weapons Ordestan recovered when he captured your party are yours?" the General asked.

"I guess so," Teah said with a shrug.

"So you physically did that to Signun?" the General continued.

Teah looked past the stunned Caslor to his father and nodded.

"Teah," Zeva said hesitantly.

Teah turned and looked at the slave.

"What do you need us to do?" Zeva asked.

"That is the problem," Teah said." I don't know what to do next. I hoped you could tell me what I should do?"

Zeva stared back in shock." I don't know."

****

Logan and Sasha marched up the stairs to the palace with the other slaves heading in for work that morning. The sun still struggled to rise above the tops of the buildings shadowing the city in darkness.

They entered the kitchens and moved into the dining hall. The enormous space dwarfed the hundreds of grey-cloaked magical slaves gathered there. The ceiling arched high above them. Logan and Sasha gave their surroundings a passing glance only to scope out threats and a return route. They kept their heads down climbing more stairs and continued to move with the group as slaves peeled off a few at a time on different levels of the palace. They walked with the others until the others were only them and the two slaves ahead. The slaves ahead of them stepped into a corridor and then stopped. They stuck their heads out of the doorway when Sasha and Logan continued past.

"I wouldn't do that if I were you," one of the male slaves said.

Logan and Sasha stopped but didn't turn around.

"They must be new here," the other man spoke up." Else they would know they can't go any farther."

"And why is that?" Sasha said as her hand eased towards the pommel of her sword.

"Only slaves housed here are allowed into those areas," the first man said.

"But you won't tell, will you friend?" Logan said turning just enough that his eyes fell into the light and the man locked on them.

"No, we won't, but the guards might if they catch you," the other man spoke up as the first man stood frozen in Logan's stare." Here," the man extended two black robes to them." This will let you get farther without detection."

Sasha took the cloaks and stared at the man in surprise.

"We have to stick together," the man said with a nod and then pulled the other man with him into the room.

Logan and Sasha exchanged pleased smiles and quickly changed into the black cloaks.

****

The empress moved through the hall of the palace as the sun splashed through the high windows with Berza and Tanlor close behind. She woke early this morning, anxious to hear what information Signun pulled from the black stone. She needed to know why spirits resided in the girl's mind. What made her so important?

She turned into the outer chamber leading to the trophy room as she did every morning. The guard held the door open as they entered and closed it quietly behind them. The empress valued the constant reminder of her country's triumphs and the lone symbol of its one failure. She rarely looked upon that failure sitting alone in the glass case. That clear stone in the golden ring haunted all the emperors and empresses before her as it haunted her to this day. If it weren't for Tera Lassain escaping the soul stone connected to that ring, Ter Chadain would be under Caltorian control.

She entered the trophy room while the two magicals waited at the door. She paused at the newest addition, the weapons of the legendary Protector of Ter Chadain. Her possession of these artifacts only solidified her control of this conflict and her dominance. She smiled as her eyes slid up the black scabbards and the dark pommels holding the insignia of the Protector. Silver swords crossed over a crown.

She smiled as she turned and moved past the case holding the ring containing Tera Lassain's controlling part of the soul stone. She glanced at it in passing as she did every morning, but then stopped as her eyes flew open wide and her chin dropped. She stepped back and crouched down to look at the stone closer. Her face reflected back at her from the pitch black surface of the stone.

"Guards," she shouted.

Berza and Tanlor and the men guarding the outer door rushed into the trophy room scanning for a threat to the empress.

"Smash that case so I can retrieve the ring," she ordered.

One of the guards drew his sword as the other motioned the empress back and stood between her and the case. The man lifted his sword and crashed it down onto the glass. The case exploded with shards of glass everywhere showering the floor with splintered glittering pieces.

The empress stepped around the guard and snatched the ring, holding it close to her face as her eyes studied it.

"Find General Anthony," she ordered and one of the guards ran off." Get Signun up here as well."

The other man nodded and hurried out of the room leaving the empress and her magicals to stare at the ring and imagine where this new black stone could be hiding.

****

"What do you mean, 'you don't know what to do'?" Zeva said.

"Galena heard that all the soul stones are chipped from one giant gemstone in the catacombs beneath the palace. If we could destroy that gemstone, maybe we can end this slavery." Teah said.

"No, I doubt that very much," General Anthony said shaking his head." The soul stone source is far too powerful to be destroyed. And it is heavily guarded in a secret location. Only a handful of elite guards even know of its location in the catacombs."

"But if we can get to it, maybe we will have a chance to end this," Teah reasoned.

"The catacombs are vast under the palace. There is no way to get to it," Zeva said.

"I know where it is," Caslor said bringing the attention of the others to him.

"How?" his father asked.

"I know the guards and they let me go with them to the stone. Being the empress's son, even a bastard son, has its benefits."

"Can you take me there?" Teah asked.

"Sure, but what good will it do?" Caslor said.

"The empress will soon find out about Signun and your escape," the general pointed out." And she will do more than just cut you off from your magic.

She will paralyze you with pain until they find you," Zeva said.

"But we need to try," Teah said.

"Have you remembered how to use your magic? Even if you manage to break free of the soul stone, without your magic, we don't stand a chance," Zeva said.

"No, I can't even remember my brother who is on his way to find me," Teah admitted.

"Do you know where he is?" the general asked.

"Stone Town," Caslor spoke up." The Viri Magus and Raven said they were going to meet up in Stone Town."

"There is something else," Teah said as they turned to her, exhausted by all the new information.

"What could possibly complicate things more?" the general said with a sigh.

"I think my brother has been stoned with the soul stone from Tera Lassain."

"What?" Zeva shouted." How would you know this?"

"The ring in the trophy room containing the controlling stone turned black yesterday," Teah explained.

"Could it be someone else?" Caslor reasoned.

"Not likely," the general said shaking his head. He put a hand to his chin in thought at the new developments flooding into his controlled uprising. Things spiraled out of control and he didn't like it, not one bit.

"We need to get to that ring before the empress does," Zeva said.

"Zeva and I will head to the trophy room and try to recover the ring before the empress notices it. You two head into the catacombs and see if you can find the source stone and destroy it," Rowan said as he strode to the door with Zeva close behind.

"What do we do if we can't destroy it?" Caslor asked.

"Pray we think of something, because our uprising is about to be blown wide open. We act or we die," the general said as he disappeared out the door and down the hall.

Zeva gave Caslor and Teah a supportive, but doubtful look and hurried after Rowan.

Caslor headed for the door with Teah close behind. They turned the opposite direction in the hallway heading for the stairs at the end. They started down the stairwell without a word, both trying to decide how to destroy the source stone when they reached it.

Chapter 45

Zeva shuffled a ways behind General Anthony as he rushed down the hall. She stopped short and stepped into a doorway when a guard approached the general and hailed him.

"General Anthony," the guard said coming up to the man.

"What is it?"

"The empress demands your presence in her throne room at once."

"I need to run an errand first, tell her. . ." the general began, but the guard stopped him in mid-sentence.

"My pardon, General, but she insisted you come at once. It seems the soul stone of Tera Lassain has been placed on another black stone yet unknown to the empress. She needs your presence at once," the guard said firmly, but respectfully.

Zeva listened in horror at the news. Now what?

The general nodded to the guard to lead the way and glanced back at Zeva with a helpless look as he strode after the guard.

Zeva stood in stunned shock as she processed the information and what it meant. The empress would use the ring to draw the one with the black stone to her much like she would do with Teah once she realized what happened to Signun.

Zeva headed towards the throne room, considering discussing options with Galena in the slave chambers.

As Zeva walked down the hall, two black robed slaves, a man and a woman, passed. She glanced at them and froze when the man made eye contact with her. Their color was different, but their intensity, the same. She spun and followed them down the hall.

"Are you the protector?" Zeva whispered.

Logan and Sasha whirled around with weapons drawn as Zeva retreated a few steps with her hands raised defensively.

"I'm here to help," Zeva said.

Logan and Sasha exchanged doubtful looks and turned back to Zeva.

"Help us do what?" Sasha asked.

"Save Teah," Zeva responded.

Logan moved up close to Zeva." Where is she? Is she all right?"

"She's fine," Zeva said glancing up at Logan's light blue stone and frowning." Teah said you were a black stone."

Logan glanced back at Sasha who nodded at him to tell her. "I am, we changed the color to throw everyone off track," Logan explained.

"I didn't think you could do that without killing the stoned person," Zeva said.

"It nearly did, but I'm here to get Teah back and get this stone off my head before the empress realizes I'm wearing it," Logan said.

"I'm afraid you're too late, the empress already knows someone wears the soul stone of Tera Lassain," Zeva said.

"Great, so much for our element of surprise," Logan groaned.

****

General Anthony entered the throne room as the empress paced back and forth behind the throne dais next to the window with her two magicals hovering nearby. She gripped the ring tightly between her fingers glowering at the shiny black stone. Seeing the general enter, she stopped pacing and hurried over to him.

"I've got someone on the other end of this and they're a black stone," she held the ring up before him to show him the black stone." I wanted you here when I send the command to the stone to come to me, just in case."

"Surely you can't think this black stone would be anywhere near the palace? They may be hundreds or thousands of miles from here. It could take weeks once you send the command before the black stone shows up."

"That may be, but I want you here for this," she said closing her eyes and slipping the ring on her finger. She concentrated as she sent the command to the soul stone of Tera Lassain to return to the control stone.

The general waited patiently, his mind racing as to the possibilities of where the protector was now.

"There, it is done," the empress said with a smile and a nod as she opened her eyes." Now we wait."

The general turned to a guard at the door." Send some men to watch for a black stone slave who is in a great deal of pain trying to get in here. If you discover one, bring the slave to us immediately."

The man nodded and left to see to his orders.

"If I didn't know better, I would say you are concerned that the black stone will be exposed to too much pain if detained too long," the empress said with a hint of accusation.

"I prefer the black stone get here with as little damage as possible. To have one black stone slave in your lifetime is incredible, but to have two is simply amazing."

The empress's eyes narrowed as she considered this. She grinned as she nodded her approval to the observation.

****

Logan finished uttering the words about their lost element of surprise when pain exploded inside his head and he toppled to the floor, his arms and legs flailing.

"Ahh, what's happening?" he gasped between strained breaths.

"The empress must have commanded the stone to return," Zeva said crouching over Logan with Sasha by her side.

"Do something," Sasha said in a desperate whisper.

"I can't, the spell is coming from the controlling stone. . . oh my," Zeva's thought drifted off as she stared at Logan's forehead.

The blue stone turned darker, turning black as night once more.

"What do we do now?" Sasha asked.

"I, can. . . take it. . . let's find. . . Teah," Logan said, forcing the words out between grimaces.

"No, it doesn't work that way," Zeva said." The longer you don't go to the controlling stone, the more pain is inflicted. If it is this bad now, it will kill you if we wait too long."

"Then what do we do?" Sasha asked.

"He needs to go to the controlling stone in order for the spell to end. He needs to go to the throne room," Zeva said.

"No... way. . . I... can. . . take. . . it. . . Ahh," Logan gasped from the floor.

"Right, I can see that," Sasha said and then looked at Zeva with concern.

The magical slave shook her head.

Sasha lifted Logan to his feet and slipped his arm around her shoulder.

"What are you doing?" Zeva asked.

"Taking him to the throne room. . . which way?" Sasha looked up and down the hallway and then back to Zeva.

"No, let me take him," Zeva said.

"I've got him. I have no plans of abandoning him."

"Trail us, but stay out of sight. They'll think nothing of me bringing him in. I'll tell them I found him unconscious in the hallway." Zeva said leaving no room for argument.

Sasha looked to Logan, his eyes clenched closed, fighting the pain. She took his arm and slid it across Zeva's slender shoulders and shifted his weight to her.

"Can you handle it?" Sasha asked watching the woman fight to support the much larger protector.

"I have him, now stay out of sight." Zeva said and then slowly trudged with Logan towards the throne room.

Sasha followed after them, being sure to keep enough distance to not appear with them if happened upon. She was about to throw caution to the wind and walk up to help them when two guards emerged from a side hallway and stopped Zeva and Logan. Sasha ducked into a doorway and peered around the corner.

"What have we here?" one of the guards asked.

"I found him writhing on the floor in one of the side halls," Zeva said.

The other guard reached over to Logan, took hold of his chin, and lifted his face to look at the stone on his forehead. His eyes flew wide and he stepped up to Zeva and pulled Logan from her. "This is the black stone the empress is seeking," he told the other guard who took hold of Logan's other arm. He pulled the black hood back to get a better look and Logan stared at them, his eyes rolling in their sockets and his head lolling to one side from the unbearable pain.

The men didn't waste any time but hurried down the hall with Zeva close behind.

Sasha moved cautiously after them slipping from one doorway to another.

The men and Logan turned and entered a room.

Zeva paused to look back towards Sasha and made eye contact with the Betra before entering the room after them. Sasha stared after her with panic.

Sasha moved to within a doorway of the throne room and waited, listening for any sound that may indicate she needed to aid Logan.

The men entered the room with Logan between them, his feet dragging helplessly behind him on the floor and his head hanging heavy to one side. He couldn't see or hear clearly and had no sense of where he was. He felt the strong hands on his arms and the power of the men dragging him along, but that was all.

The empress, the general, Berza, Tanlor, and the guards lining the room looked up as the men entered with Logan between them.

The general caught Zeva's eye when she entered and she shook her head with resignation. He turned back to Logan as the boy struggled to remain conscious.

The empress stepped forward and placed the stone in the ring against the stone on Logan's forehead.

The pain lifted from Logan's head immediately and his bearings came back to him in an instant. He shrugged his shoulders, surprised to feel his swords still strapped to his back. He fought the urge to pull them and end this now, realizing if the empress could impose such pain from that distance; she could render him helpless before his blades cleared their sheaths. Logan looked to the empress, his eyes catching the glimmer of light shining off a silver rod hanging by a chain between her breasts. He instinctively reached for the identical rod fastened in a sheath at his hip. The empress stared down at him in delight.

Her expression turned to disgust when their eyes met. A shot of pain surged through his mind and he dropped to a knee.

"That is much better," the empress said." Slaves do not look upon me, but kneel before me."

Logan didn't fight, but remained staring at the floor as she glowered over him.

"Where did you come from, slave?" she asked.

Logan clenched his teeth, refusing to answer.

"We can work on your obedience all day, if you wish," she said.

Logan flopped onto the floor as the pain ripped through him again. His back arched off the floor and his limbs went rigid. He dropped panting on the stone floor when the pain stopped. Just then, a guard rushed in and dropped to a knee before the empress.

"Yes, what is it? Where is Signun?" she asked.

"He is dead, my Empress," the guard said.

"And the girl, the black stone?"

"Nowhere to be found," the man replied bowing lower.

"We can fix that," she said and lifted her amulet containing the other black stone. She closed her eyes again and whispered, "Come before me." She opened her eyes and looked down at Logan who dared a glance up at her." That ought to do it. Soon she will be beside you."

She smiled a wicked smile that made Logan's blood run cold.

A burst of pain surged through him again and he cried out, fighting to stand the pain.

"You looked at me again, shame, shame," she said and began to laugh.

Chapter 46

A group of guards rushed past Sasha's hiding spot and she eased farther down the hallway as the men took up positions around the throne room's entrance. She slipped back into a doorway as another wave of guards rushed down the hall.

The men stopped close by and she found the knob of the door, turned it silently, and stepped into the room. She remained with her ear against the door after closing it, waiting for any sign that she needed to get to Logan.

"Betra?" a familiar voice came from behind her.

Sasha turned to see Galena and another woman standing behind her.

"Zele Magus," Sasha nodded, not truly happy to see the woman who wanted her dead or imprisoned when they first met at the Protectors Fortress.

"What are you doing here? What's going on?" Galena asked.

"Master Logan has come to free Teah, but now he is in the throne room under the empress's control." She pressed her ear against the door again.

"Logan has been stoned?" Galena gasped.

"Yes, but we're planning on making a break for it," Sasha said and nodded without looking back.

"Where is Teah?" Rachel asked.

"Don't know, but hopefully far from here," Sasha said.

"Does she have her weapons?" Galena asked.

"What weapons?" Sasha said turning to her.

"Teah is also a protector. They took her weapons when they captured us, thinking they belonged to Logan."

"Where are they now?" Sasha asked, hope rising in her voice.

"She said they are in the trophy room," Galena said.

"And where is that?" Sasha asked.

"I think a few doors down the hallway," Rachel said." Zeva and Teah trained in the outer chambers."

Sasha eased open the door and peered out.

"Where are you going?" Galena asked.

"We need to get those weapons," Sasha said glancing back and then disappearing into the hallway and closing the door behind her.

****

Teah and Caslor raced down the stairs flight after flight, their footfalls echoing off the stone walls and steps as they ran.

"How much farther?" Teah asked as they continued their downward spiral.

"Not far to the bottom and then a ways from there."

They finally came to level ground again and stopped to catch their breath.

"The source stone is that way a mile or so," Caslor said pointing down the long tunnel with torches on the wall every so many feet." What will you do once we get there?"

"I don't know, but if we can destroy that stone, we may be able to destroy the power of the other stones that came from it."

"That is a lot of ifs." Caslor said, not convinced.

"We need to . . . Ahh, no, not now, not yet," Teah screamed as the pain in her head sent the protectors into frenzy. They cried out so loudly, she wasn't sure if her screams reached the tunnels or their screams.

"The empress knows about Signun and has summoned you to her," Caslor reasoned.

"What. . . do I... do?"

"You have to go to her or die, simple as that," Caslor said, his voice shaking.

"I'm no good dead. If I go to her, I may live to win yet," Teah said through clenched teeth, fighting to maintain control.

Caslor stepped next to her and pulled her arm across his shoulders. She leaned on him and let him help her to the stairs and began to climb. They reached the first landing and Caslor stopped to catch his breath.

"I can't do this. You will die by the time I get you to the top at this rate."

"What choice do we have?" Teah asked, tears of pain blurring her vision.

He looked to her and then looked around, nervous someone would see even in this deserted stairwell." You mustn't speak of this to anyone. . . do you understand? No one."

"Speak of what?" Teah asked and then lifted off the landing to hover above the stone surface.

Caslor stood with his hands moving in front of him as he murmured to himself. He took hold of Teah's cloak and began to run up the stairs with her floating effortlessly behind him. He raced ahead taking two stairs at a time, his energy level seemingly endless.

They passed landing after landing so quickly that Teah lost track. They stopped before a doorway and Caslor unwove the spell and let Teah settle back to earth. He slipped under her arm and wrapped an arm around her waist.

Teah locked her teary, bloodshot eyes upon his and he looked back with empathy.

"Not a word," he whispered.

"About what?" she asked holding his attention.

He nodded and they hurried down the hallway.

A guard spotted them moving down the hallway and came to help." What have you found here, Cas?" the man asked.

"I think the empress is looking for this one," Caslor replied.

"I'll take her," the man offered, but Caslor placed a restraining hand on the man's shoulder." I found her, I got this," Caslor said.

The guard nodded and stepped to the other side and brought Teah's other arm around his neck. Caslor and the guard hurried down the hallway with Teah between them. She wasn't able to see what passed by or even the faces of Caslor or the guard anymore. Her pain threatened to blind her as she fought to keep control.

The protectors went silent some time ago, either blinking out of existence for a time or just losing touch with her mind.

They entered the throne room and Teah made out shapes around her, but none of the shapes had identity. They stopped and eased her to the floor. Her legs felt like jelly as she lowered to a half sitting, half kneeling position.

"What have you here, Caslor?" The empress asked.

"I found her lying in the hallway; she is one of yours, is she not?"

"Indeed. Thank you for bringing her to me."

Teah felt someone beside her and looked to see a motionless mass lying on the floor. The swish of silk told her the empress stepped up before her and then pressed something against her forehead. The pain washed from her in that instant and her vision rushed back to her. The man next to her lay in a black robe with his eyes closed and his breathing slow and steady as if he slept. She searched for any sign of his identity and bit her lip as her eyes fell on the black stone.

Logan! Galiven cried as the consciousness of the protectors surged back into her.

Who?

No! Bastion screamed and the protectors went rigidly silent.

Teah looked up to see the empress staring at her, the rage threatening to burst through the woman's eyes.

She heard Galiven, but did she know who Logan was? Teah suspected this was her brother, but the face and the name meant nothing to her.

"Teah and Logan. . .?" The empress said her words low and threatening.

"What, my Empress?" Rowan asked and moved closer, stepping between the empress and the teens.

"The last living descendants of the Lassain line here in my throne room?" Her words came out mixed with awe and disbelief.

"Who are they?" Rowan asked.

"The Queen of Ter Chadain and the Protector of Ter Chadain, my slaves," she said and beamed with pride of her conquest." I have vanquished my enemy without even realizing it."

"These are the Lassain twins we have been warned about?" Rowan said and forced a laugh. He glanced over at Caslor who looked very pale and like he might be sick all over.

"He must have come to save his sister and retrieve his weapons. How did he come to wear the stone of Tera Lassain?" she said looking to Rowan for an answer.

Logan opened his eyes and sat up. Seeing Teah next to him, he fought his urge to hug her and eased a hand to touch hers along the floor.

Teah looked back at him with a blank expression and no recollection of him at all.

He frowned at her reaction and turned his attention to the empress. He lifted his eyes to her as he felt his weapons still strapped to his back under the black cloak. He knew the pain the empress could inflict with a thought, but he still needed to try something in order to escape.

His eyes flicked up to the empress as he opened the black cloak and eased it off his shoulders letting it fall to the floor behind him. The handles of the swords stuck out over his shoulder and he eased his hands closer to them. His hand brushed the pommels when a surge of pain rushed through him. His body convulsed, but he still kept his hands hovering near the handles.

"No, no, no, you mustn't do that," the empress said.

Logan closed his eyes and gritted his teeth, forcing his hands onto the handles and wrapping his fingers around them. The pain ebbed and he pulled the swords free of their sheaths filling the throne room with the ring of their steel. The magic of the swords filled him with a flood of power and the control of the stone, still present and dominating, became bearable.

Logan eased himself to his feet and stood before the empress, his eyes locked on hers. The fear in her eyes rose to a panic and she turned to the black-robed magicals at her side.

Tanlor stepped between Logan and the empress, unleashing red bolts of energy from his fingertips.

Logan brought the swords before him, the rush of energy parted around him, and blinked out. Logan stared back at Tanlor as wisps of smoke and steam wafted from his blades.

Teah stared in shocked amazement at Logan standing before the fiery attack. She looked at the blades with longing, feeling like she missed a part of herself for not having her own.

Without warning, Logan lifted from the floor and sailed across the room impacting the wall with such force, the stone crumbled. Logan hung a few feet off the floor, stunned, but conscious, yet unable to move. He struggled to raise his arms, but they pressed firmly against the wall along with the sword in each hand.

Teah cried out in surprise at the sudden assault on Logan and crouched on her feet, uncertain of what to do.

Berza stood next to Tanlor on the dais before the empress, her hands before her, holding the weave of air tightly against Logan.

"You foolish boy," the empress said from behind the two magicals." You and your sister aren't worthy of kissing my feet and yet, you try to keep Ter Chadain from me. And both of you have enough power to conquer the world, but you have no idea how to use it. . . pathetic."

"Ahh," Teah cried out as the stone transmitted the pain from the empress into her mind. She held her crouch, but fought to stay aware of her surroundings.

Caslor took a step towards Teah, but then pulled himself back. His eyes watered at the pain Teah crumpled under. He bit his lip and eased back a step and flicked his eyes around to see who may have noticed.

Rowan made eye contact with Caslor and he too fought to keep from acting. He gave Caslor a slight shake of his head to discourage any rash actions.

Shouts came flooding into the throne room as the door opened and the sounds of guards in the hallway burst in. A lone black-robed figure strode in, head bowed and hands tucked into the sleeves. The hood hid the occupant to everyone in the throne room, but the person stood tall and broad under the concealing fabric.

"What is this?" The empress asked.

One guard stepped in behind the cloaked figure and looked to General Anthony who turned and stopped both the magical and the guard from entering farther.

"She insisted she had something for the empress she needed to see. Something belonging to the black stones," the guard said.

The general looked over his shoulder to the empress who nodded and motioned the magical through. He nodded to the guard who turned and left the room and then ushered the magical before the empress a step ahead of the crouched Teah.

The empress turned away from Logan and looked at the cloaked figure assuring Tanlor and Berza still focused on Logan pinned to the wall.

"Yes, what is it?" The empress asked impatiently." What do you need to show me?"

"These," the cloak flew back to reveal Sasha and the two protector's swords. She turned and tossed the swords to Teah, realizing as she released them from her hands, that Teah didn't see them coming.

Teah fought the pain in her head, trying to concentrate on the cloaked figure as it came in and stood a few feet away. She closed her eyes as a pulse of pain stung deep into her. She heard the figure say 'these' and then the protectors all shouted her name at once.

Teah looked up as the swords of the protector came at her as if time slowed down. She reached up and grasped a sword in each hand. Energy rushed through her. Every thought, feeling, face, memory, flooded her brain threatening to wash her away with vision after vision. All the past she fought so long to recall now shone clear as the sun in her mind. The death of her parents and sister, Logan saving her from the Shankan, her killing Zele Astoria with her bow, Ordestan capturing them and taking Talesaur's arm off, Lizzy looking into her eyes just before being beheaded, the stone placed on her head and the protectors entering her mind, all of it came back in that instant the swords touched her skin. Her eyes filled with the confidence of the Queen of Ter Chadain and a Protector of Ter Chadain as well.

She locked her attention on the empress as the woman scrambled further behind her magicals in fear.

"Tanlor," the empress shouted.

The magical stepped between Teah and his empress, sweeping a hand at Sasha sending her flying across the room. He bore down on Teah sending assault after of assault of red energy shooting from his hands.

Teah brushed them aside with her swords. She tried to advance, but his attacks kept her from moving forward.

"Guards, guards," the empress cried out.

The doors burst open and guards rushed in, but then stopped as if hitting a wall and were propelled back out of the room into the hallway in a jumbled heap. The doors slammed shut and the guards pounded on them, trying to break them down.

General Anthony stood with his hands before him facing the door, holding it tight against the guards' efforts with his magic.

"Rowan, what are you doing?" the empress said, not realizing the implications at first. Her eyes grew wide as the truth registered." You're a magical?" The words came out as condemnation instead of a question.

The guards in the room, after a confused hesitation, rushed the general, but they never reached him. They hurtled backwards against the bank of windows, some falling out and others crumbling to the floor under the sills.

Zeva took a step to aid Caslor, but the empress sent a thought of pain into her stone and she fell to the floor unconscious.

The empress then turned to Caslor as he stood before her." My son, why are you doing this? You need to remember who you are."

"I remember who I am every day of my life. . . the bastard son of the empress," Caslor said.

"But you're my son."

"I'm your son who is also a magical and who you would stone if you'd known."

"We would have thought of something. I could stone you and then set the controlling stone aside where no one could use it to control you," she insisted.

"And what about my father?" Caslor asked.

"He is a traitor. He lied to me about being a magical and he will die," she said.

Rowan didn't look back at her, but concentrated on his weaving to hold the door closed against the guards trying to break in.

Teah still struggled against Tanlor's stream of energy she deflected with her swords. She listened to Caslor and the empress as they argued.

We need to get out of here, Stalwart said.

"There is no escape for you," the empress said drawing Teah's eyes to hers." I still hear the voices in your mind."

"Caslor, get them out of here," Rowan shouted as he struggled to hold the door closed.

The empress turned to look at Rowan and a glint of silver caught Teah's eye. She knew at once what she needed to do.

Taking a step and diving to one side, she evaded Tanlor's attack for a second and then thought of the silver rod in her hand as she rolled to her feet again. The rod pulled from the empress's neck breaking the chain securing it. The rod flew the distance between Teah and the empress in an instant. The second it touched Teah's hand the silver rod expanded into a bow and she pulled back as the silver arrow appeared in the notch. She let the arrow fly, striking Tanlor in the chest, sending him plummeting backwards into the throne, toppling the chair over as he collided with it, falling dead on top of it.

Teah spun to Berza as the woman's eyes shot wide with terror and she released her spell on Logan, throwing a weave at Teah in time to send the arrow loosed at her deflecting to one side.

Sasha got to her feet and rushed over to help Logan up.

"See to her," Logan said motioning to Zeva on the floor.

Sasha went to Zeva easing her into a sitting position as she slowly regained consciousness.

Caslor ran to the far wall of the throne room and pressed a block in the wall. The wall swung open, revealing a hidden passage that disappeared downward into darkness.

"Hurry, this way," he shouted.

Teah turned her notched arrow at the empress and let fly a bolt to her heart, but Berza stepped in front of the shot and the arrow bounced off a barrier of air, clattering on the floor before disappearing.

"You have to get out of here, I can't hold them much longer," General Anthony said.

Logan went and stood beside Caslor as he motioned for the others to follow." Zeva, Sasha, get in here," he ordered.

Sasha helped Zeva over to the opening, but the magical stopped next to Caslor." I can't go, she still controls me and I will only slow you down, go." She looked from Caslor to Sasha." Destroy the stone and I will be beside you as a free magical. Go." She pushed Caslor into the tunnel.

Sasha stepped into the entrance and turned to wait for Logan and Teah.

Logan ran up beside Teah as she fired arrow after arrow at the air barrier protecting the empress and Berza.

"Come on, it's no use. We have to leave," he said.

"I can't let her win, she can't win," Teah said between volleys.

"She won't, but we can't defeat her if we are captured again."

"The pain, it's bearable, but still there. As long as she lives, we will have this pain," Teah said.

"We need to destroy the main stone," Caslor said from the entrance tunnel as he stuck his head out past Sasha.

Teah looked to Logan and then to Caslor and gave a nod." Let's go." She turned and the bow shrunk into the silver rod again and she tucked it in a pocket of her cloak. She hurried into the tunnel without looking back.

Logan raced after her and waited just inside the tunnel for Caslor and Sasha.

"Father, come on," Caslor shouted.

Rowan nodded and ran towards the tunnel. As he reached the opening, the door burst open and guards, along with loyal magicals, flooded the throne room. Seeing the overwhelming numbers, the General stopped and turned his back to the tunnel.

"Come on," Caslor called.

"You'll never make it out of the tunnel. I need to seal it from this side."

"No, you have to come."

He looked over his shoulder at his son, his eyes sad and a resigned smile on his face." This is what I need to do. I love you. I'm proud of you, son," Rowan said and swung the door shut.

"No, father, no, no, no," Caslor pounded against the stone door as it swung closed.

****

Rowan Anthony, High General of Caltoria, and magical, stood with his back to the door leading to the hope of freedom for all magicals in Caltoria, including his son, and faced the mass of guards and magicals hoping to deny that hope. He gathered his strength and his eyes eased to the dais where Empress Shakata stared down at him. The love she once held in her eyes when she gazed upon him, now gone, and disgust filled her black orbs circled by gold.

He didn't have anything to say. His son knew he loved him and he wanted him to remember him that way. General Anthony pulled in more power than he ever thought possible, building it up until he thought he would explode. The weave surged inside of him as it threatened to consume him.

The magicals saw it and turned back as the guards pushed forward, trying to gain distance from what they saw coming, but the mass pushed them forward ignorant of the devastation awaiting.

The throng drove towards the General and he loosed the magic in him that cried to escape. It tore through his flesh and bone from the inside out and consumed everything in its wake. Guards and magicals alike perished in an instant, turned to ash in an instant.

As the human cremation wafted to the floor, the empress and Berza stood stunned behind the magical's barrier unharmed.

Zeva crouched in the far corner away from the massacre, protected by a ball of air dusted with the human remnants.

Horror and tears filled her eyes as she looked at the destruction and the secret passage, collapsed so no one could follow the others. She smiled at the valiant display by General Rowan Anthony, a tear running down her cheek, her final tribute to the man.

Chapter 47

Caslor stood at the closed doorway unwilling to move, but Sasha pulled him away as the blast sent them hurtling down the passageway. They collided with the others waiting for them and rolled to a jumbled pile of arms and legs as dust filled the tunnel. Logan pulled himself out of the pile and helped everyone to their feet.

Caslor created a floating ball of light to illuminate the dark space.

"What next?" Logan asked.

"To the source stone," Teah said.

"We can't now, Empress Shakata will be expecting that," Caslor said.

"What is the source stone?" Logan said rubbing his hand on the soul stone. The pain still pounded in his head, but with the strength of the protector's magic in him, bearable.

"Where all the soul stones come from," Teah turned to him." If we destroy that, all the magic in the stones may be destroyed as well."

"May be?" Sasha said." Kind of risky for a 'may be'."

"It's our only chance. I'm not going to have this on my forehead the rest of my life," Logan said with a shrug." Lead on."

Caslor looked at them doubtfully, nodded, and headed out down the tunnel. The tunnel circled downward until Caslor slid a large hollowed-out block aside to reveal a hallway.

"This is the dungeon. If we connect with the stairs down the hall, we will be able to take them to the catacombs where they keep the source stone. But it is heavily guarded. I hoped to use my position to gain access, but now, that seems doubtful." He stepped into the hallway and stretched his back.

"If we hurry, they may not know we're coming," Logan said.

"Over here, over here," a voiced called from down the hall.

They hurried to a large door with a metal plate slid across the small window. Caslor slid the plate open and remembered he spoke to this prisoner once before.

Caldora wasn't at the door this time, but suspended with chains by her wrists and ankles. Her tattered clothes hung on her and a pool of blood collected beneath her. She faced the door struggling to hold her head up and look at the small window.

"Help me," she pleaded. Teah pushed Caslor aside and stared in.

"Caldora," she said.

"Caldora," Logan exclaimed and pushed his sister aside to peer at the woman who killed his family.

"Let her out," Teah said to Caslor.

He nodded and searched for some keys on a table nearby." Let her out?"

Logan spun on Teah." Why would we let her out? She is finally getting what's coming to her."

Sasha took the opportunity to look into the cell when Logan turned to his sister." No one deserves to be treated like that," Sasha said.

Logan snapped back to look at her, but she held his gaze without wavering." She is a slave just like me. Like you. We need to help her.

She only did what Englewood ordered because he threatened to turn her over to the empress if she didn't," Teah said.

Logan pulled his eyes from Sasha and turned them on Teah again, his jaw clenched as he fought the anger building inside him. The memory of his father, mother, and sister lying slaughtered playing with vivid color in his mind, he shook his head.

"No, she needs to pay for what she did," Logan said, not relenting.

Teah took a hold of Logan's hand and pulled him off to the side as Caslor found the keys and opened the cell door. Sasha and Caslor went inside to see to Caldora.

"Look at me," Teah said as she placed her hand on his chin and forced him to face her. He looked down at her, his eyes hard and cold. She recoiled slightly and then took a deep breath." We need to let her go, because she is one of us. She is a citizen of Ter Chadain and we are her leaders. We cannot leave her here even after what she has done in her past. She has been supportive and loyal since our capture and she didn't give me up to the empress when doing so may have saved her from this torture."

Logan stared at his sister, his mind racing as his emotions sought to overwhelm him. He listened as his pain throbbed in his head and he decided that his sister spoke wisely.

"How did you get so smart?" he smiled and nodded.

"Maybe because I have to deal with these idiot protectors bickering all the time in my head. How did you stand it without going crazy?" she said and gave him a shove.

"That's where they went," Logan said laughing.

"Yeah, they never shut up," she said and the protectors all protested, but went silent again.

"I kind of miss them," he admitted with a shrug.

"They are quiet now since the empress can hear them," Teah said.

"Really?" Logan said, amazed. He turned as Caslor and Sasha helped Caldora out of the cell.

"Thank you, thank you so much," Caldora said looking at Teah and then Logan.

"You have strength to walk?" Teah asked.

"Yes, I think so," Caldora said nodding.

"Sasha, give me your cloak," Teah asked extending a hand to the Betra.

Sasha pulled off the black cloak and handed it to her.

Teah gave it to Caldora who pulled it on." Find Rachel and Galena, get them out of here. Head to the harbor and wait for us there," Teah said." We will meet up and find a ship to escape when we get there. That is our only chance so we need to find a captain not loyal to the empress to take us back to Ter Chadain. "

Caldora nodded her understanding.

"Let's go," Logan said motioning to Caslor who nodded and strode off ahead with Logan and then Sasha right behind.

Teah smiled at Caldora and turned to follow the others, but the Zele Magus grabbed Teah's arm stopping her.

Teah looked up at Caldora and something passed between them.

"Thank you," Caldora whispered.

"It is who we are," Teah said with a smile and patted Caldora's hand resting on her arm. Teah looked at the others down the hall and strode after them.

Caldora watched them disappear around a bend in the hall, turned, and ran the other direction to find Galena and Rachel.

Chapter 48

Empress Shakata watched her future and the future of Caltoria slipping away. As the dust settled from the suicide of her lover which killed everyone in the room except herself, Berza who protected her, and Zeva cowering in the corner, she realized Caslor along with the Lassains might reach the source stone and destroy it.

Terror gripped her as the image of thousands of magicals, free of their soul stones, decimating her country and her rule, came to her. She couldn't let that happen. She needed to take measures so her army could still defend her rule and that vast numbers of magicals didn't roam free in Caltoria.

Guards from the hall cautiously eased into the room to survey the carnage General Anthony did in his last act of betrayal. The dust hung in the air and a few bodies lay against the wall opposite from the tunnel entrance, now caved in with debris.

"Get to the source stone and warn them to expect an attack," the empress shouted at the first man in the door. He snapped to attention when she spoke and then raced from the room.

"Where does that tunnel lead?" Berza asked.

"Directly to the dungeons."

"They will reach the stone before that guard can reach the chambers," Berza said.

"What will I do?" the empress said and began to pace. She stopped when she spotted Zeva cowering in the corner." What will happen if the source stone is destroyed?"

"You don't think they will succeed?" Berza said, incredulous." What could happen?"

"If the magic is destroyed from the source of the soul stones and controlling stones, it would be reasonable to suspect that the magic will be drained from all the stones coming from the source stone."

Berza stared out the window past the empress at the thought of it.

"Will you stay faithful to me?" the empress asked. Berza looked at the empress in a fog.

"I've been good to you, treated you well, will you be faithful to me if your stone is no more?" the empress pressed.

"You will need to rely on a magical advisor to work at controlling the magical threat," Berza rationalized.

"Of course, of course, you will have power, position, and wealth if you are loyal," the empress said.

"Very well, then I will remain faithful to you, Empress," Berza said bowing.

"You have family in Stone Town?" the empress asked.

"A father and sister," Berza said, confused by the question.

"You best get them out of there if you want them to stay alive."

"What are you going to do?"

"I can't have all those magicals walking around without being stoned. Guard."

A guard rushed in to stand at attention before the empress.

"Take Berza to Stone Town with some men and bring her family back here," the empress ordered. She looked at the stunned Berza and motioned with her head." Better get going. I'm not waiting."

Berza jumped from the dais and ran out of the room with the guard close behind.

The empress sent a pulse of pain into Zeva and the woman yelped in the corner and then hurried over to stand before her." Guard," she shouted.

A man rushed in, his golden uniform still clean and shiny. Three stripes across his arm showed him to be a captain.

"Good, Captain, I need you to take a contingent of men and go to the Spire. You are to instruct the monks to destroy Stone Town if the source stone is destroyed," the empress ordered.

Zeva gasped as she heard the captain's instructions, staring with horror at the empress.

The empress noticed Zeva's disapproving stare and smiled. "You think me too harsh? I will do whatever it takes to make sure Caltoria survives and in order for Caltoria to survive, my rule must continue."

"But all those innocent people. . ." Zeva said, but couldn't continue as she began to cry.

"Oh, that's right, don't you have family in Stone Town?" the empress said feigning concern.

"My mother, father, brothers, sisters, aunts and uncles, cousins, all reside in Stone Town."

"Pity your bloodline is tainted with magic, else they wouldn't be living there, now would they?" the empress said without expression.

"No, you can't do that," Zeva pleaded.

"Let us hope we won't need to take such drastic actions. It depends on Caslor and the Lassains. If they destroy the source stone, Stone Town will be destroyed."

She looked at the captain who pulled his sympathetic eyes from Zeva." Take her with you. If her soul stone is no more, then Stone Town is no more."

She turned back to Zeva." It is a shame that your freedom will come at the cost of your family's life."

"That is all," she told the captain.

The captain stepped over and took hold of Zeva's arm and ushered her out of the throne room.

Empress Shakata turned and stared out at Bellatora as the sun crept lower to the horizon. Soon her favorite time to be looking out over her city would be here again, and she intended the city to still be hers.

****

Caslor led them to the stairs and then proceeded to descend as they all followed. They walked in silence developing their own plans on how to destroy the source stone and escape. But only Caslor knew the enormity of the mission. Only he knew that the source stone was three times the size of Logan and possessed the magic to power all the shards chipped from it. Caslor visited the stone often, spending hours gazing at the glimmering surface, wondering if the magic came from within or was bestowed upon it centuries ago before slavery existed in Caltoria. He often tried looking deeper into the stone, to have some kind of insight, but the revelation never happened and now he led these foreigners to the stone in order to destroy it and release all the slaves from its control.

They reached the bottom of the stairs and Caslor stared down the long tunnel of the catacombs as the others dropped down the last step behind him.

"Here's where it can get a little bit sticky," Caslor said." Guards are continuously patrolling the catacombs and where they are at any given time is a mystery. We need to be alert."

"Okay, eyes and ears peeled," Sasha said pulling her sword.

"One other thing," Caslor said and everyone looked at him." If I die before we reach the stone, keep following the tunnels to the right, it will lead you out of here."

"What do we follow to get to the stone?" Logan asked.

"If you don't have me to guide you, you won't reach the source stone. Your only choice would be to follow the tunnels out of here," Caslor said.

"Then we better keep you alive," Teah stated." I have no intention of leaving here a slave."

Caslor nodded and led on.

Teah and Logan drew the blades filling the catacombs with a light metallic ring and followed after.

Sasha let them pass and took up her position in the back, covering the rear.

Caslor took them on a deliberate and direct path making sure he didn't waste any time in the tunnels.

He froze in place raising a hand to stop them. He listened intently and then motioned with two fingers that two guards approached from the tunnel on their right.

Logan stepped up to the passage entrance and waited while Teah crouched at his side.

The men stepped clear of the tunnel and Teah took the guard in front with a slash across his chest as Logan sliced through the second man with little effort.

They wiped their swords clean on the dead men's clothes and followed Caslor as he started off again.

Caslor stopped outside a chamber door and frowned as the others stopped behind him.

"What is it?" Teah asked.

"This door is never closed. They must know we're coming," Caslor said.

"Why wouldn't they attack us in the catacombs if they knew we were coming?" Logan asked.

"Because this chamber is designed for defending. Behind this door is a circular chamber that houses the source stone. The stone is tall and circular with a rounded top. The chamber is massive. Along the walls of the chamber are rows and rows of staggered balconies designed to house archers. I've never seen archers, but I've seen the balconies. There are quarters that lead to the chamber from six identical doors to this one. Each chamber is said to house six swordsmen."

Logan kept track of Caslor's accounting as he explained the layout of the chamber. He drew in all the information and then reached an arm around Teah and Sasha, pulling them closer.

"That is thirty-six swordsmen and countless archers. What we need to do is figure out how to eliminate the effect of the archers so we can concentrate on the swordsmen and destroy the stone."

"I can cover the stone with a barrier," Caslor spoke up.

"Do you have the strength for that?" Teah asked.

Caslor gave a nod.

"You need to hold it until we dispatch the swordsmen and destroy the stone," Teah added.

"I got it," Caslor said insistently.

"Okay, that's covered," Logan said.

"That leaves the thirty-six swordsmen for the three of us," Sasha said eagerly.

"Not really," Logan said to her." You need to protect Caslor so he keeps the archers off us. Teah and I will handle the swordsmen."

Sasha stuck out her lip, pouting at the thought of missing out on a fight.

Logan laughed and slapped her on the back." Don't worry, I'm sure one or two will slip by us and give you a little fun."

Sasha beamed at the prospect.

Caslor stared at the woman in amazement." Wanting to be in a fight, crazy," he said.

"You don't know the Betra," Teah said with a smirk.

"Are we set?" Logan said drawing their attention back to him.

The three nodded.

"Here we go," Logan said as he lowered his shoulder and banged into the door.

The door shuddered, but held and the loud collision echoed through the catacombs.

"Great, so much for sneaking up on them," Teah said with a sigh. She lifted her hand and the door burst into splinters as she sent a burst of magic through it. She waved her hand at the door motioning Logan to enter.

He laughed and ran into the chamber.

Caslor ran in right behind him and sent a barrier of air up over the top of the stone. Arrows immediately started to fall upon them, but bounced harmlessly against the air barrier and the walls coming to rest on the invisible wall of air. In a minute the cover of air held hundreds of arrows piled up so high the balconies became obscured to them on the floor.

Teah and Logan stared at the clear, glimmering, sparkling gemstone. The mother stone to all the stones placed on every magical slave in Caltoria. It shone with inner magic that lit the chamber in glowing light.

The six doors burst open and out rushed the guards. They filled the chamber pushing their backs against the crystal preventing Logan and Teah from getting close.

Six men rushed forward while the others stood close to the crystal.

Logan and Teah sprang into motion, the blades of the protectors slashing and hacking in smooth arcs as cries of pain and death filled the chamber.

Teah let loose blasts of energy when she slid one blade back in its sheath to give her a free hand to cast magic. Men flew everywhere she turned as her magic sent them sprawling.

Sasha stood watching the chaos as she kept her back to Caslor standing just inside the door. A guard rushed them and Sasha stepped up and met his strike to kill Caslor, deflecting it to the side. She spun, dipping the man's blade to his side and then turned to quickly impale him on her blade. She slid the blade free and met the blade of another guard attacking her. The smile on her face beamed as she felt at home for the first time in weeks.

Teah and Logan turned back wave after wave of attacks and soon the remnants of the stone's guard retreated back into their chambers and barred the doors.

The archers finally halted their relentless, but futile attack on Caslor's barrier and retreated back away from the balconies. Caslor held the barrier up just in case, but looked to the twins as the drain became evident on his face.

"Hurry, I'm getting weak," he told them.

Teah and Logan went to the stone and placed their hands upon it. The magic in it sent them flying back into the walls of the chamber where they crashed and slid down to the floor. They picked themselves up and moved closer again, cautious about touching the stone this time.

Teah sent a trickle of magic into the stone and it dimmed slightly. She looked to Logan who shrugged. She sent more magic into the stone and it dimmed again. Setting her chin, she surged as much magic into the stone as she could control. The stone went almost dark, but surged back in brightness the minute Teah stopped her attack.

"I don't have enough to do it," Teah said.

"I don't have any control of my powers," Logan said.

"Let me help you," Caslor said. He moved over next to Teah and they both sent magic into the stone.

The stone went black, all light gone inside it to the point it seemed to draw in light from the torches lit up by the balconies.

They maintained the assault as long as their energy lasted, but released it and stepped back panting for air.

The stone surged back to life again.

"Ahh," Teah groaned." We need to do more. The magic is working, but it rebounds once we stop. How can we stop it from coming back?"

Logan grinned as he held a protector's blade up.

It just might work, Bastion said.

"Get the stone's power low, and I will hit it with my swords," Logan said. His swords began to glow as if on cue. He stared at them and laughed.

Sasha stood and watched the balconies as they worked on destroying the stone. A slight movement came from the top tier of balconies as an archer; arrow already notched, stepped to the rail and loosed a shot. She dove for the arrow, knowing its mark before she intercepted it, the arrow driving through her back and into her organs, the broad head tearing and ripping as it went, leaving nothing to heal or be healed by any means. She crumpled against Logan's back as the impact staggered him a step or two.

Logan felt a person collide with him and he spun to defend himself only to find Sasha clinging to him. An arrow jutted from her back and he wrapped his arms around her, cradling her to his chest.

Teah hurried over, broke the arrow shaft and helped Logan lower to the floor with Sasha still in his arms.

Caslor lifted the air shield up again and a few more arrows bounced helplessly away.

Logan searched Sasha's face as Teah sent her magic into the Betra. She met Logan's hopeful stare and shook her head.

Sasha's eyes opened to look deeply into Logan's eyes and she fought to force a smile across her lips one last time.

"I now send you to my second for safe keeping, may she die protecting you as I did," Sasha said, her voice incredibly strong for her condition.

Logan leaned down and kissed her deeply on the lips. His eyes locked with hers as he pulled back from the kiss.

"I loved you," he whispered.

Her dark eyes sparkled one last time and went dim as the Seeker of the Protector of the Betra left this world.

Logan's body shook with rage, as this loss seemed to be too much for him. His mind churned at the thought of all the pain, the suffering, the sacrifice given freely from everyone around him, and for what, at what cost? Here his friend, companion, and protector died covering his back while he tried to free himself from the soul stone's slavery. He gently set Sasha's lifeless form on the floor and then stood as every muscle in his body went rigid with his fury. His eyes cried uncontrollably, but his anger fueled him as he retrieved his swords from the floor next to Sasha and stood facing the source stone. He gave her one last look and then turned to Teah.

"Let's end this," Logan said seething.

"I can't drop the barrier to help you," Caslor cried out.

"You won't need to," Logan said, his jaw clenched. He looked to Teah as she cried softly and gave a curt nod.

"Do it now." Teah hesitated for a moment, filled with doubt.

As their eyes met, that doubt vanished and she quickly gathered all her magic and sent it into the stone which dimmed and went black.

Logan pulled from down deep, everything he felt for his parents, his sisters, his friends, and now Sasha as he raised the swords of the protectors who came before him. The swords radiated with bright white energy as they hovered above his head. His anger surged to his will and he willed the stone to be destroyed.

Leaping at the stone, he drove his swords down into the crystal, slicing into the core and continuing downward as he raged them onward.

"For Ter Chadain!" he screamed. The tears streamed down his face as he pushed every ounce of his being into his swords.

The stone began to shudder and shake as it fell into itself where Logan sliced it apart. It shrank smaller and smaller and then expanded, blowing Teah and Logan backwards towards the walls with shards of crystal following them and imbedding into the walls.

Caslor saw the release of energy and ran between the twins, wrapping an arm around each and gathering them to him as he threw up a wall of air with as much strength as he still possessed. The three fell against the wall, the sheer force knocking them senseless.

Chapter 49

Grinwald, Raven, and Saliday hurried towards the palace as the day turned later and they still received no word or contact from Logan.

They knew they could do very little if something did happen, but Saliday posed that they look for an escape route from Caltoria, anything other than going back through the Mashlad tunnels to Scalded Island.

They stopped at the 'y' in the road with one path leading to the palace and the other to the town and harbor.

"I wish we could go to him," Saliday said, her separation from her current need pulling at her Tarken blood.

"The sniffers in the palace are much stronger and stand by the palace door to catch any magical who happens in. If the governor's sniffer detected you, the palace sniffers surely will as well," Raven said.

"It is a moot point; we are not going to the palace. Logan and Teah are on their own until they are clear of the palace. We need to secure passage on a ship to get us away from here as quickly as possible when they arrive," Grinwald said.

With great effort the three turned away from the path leading to the palace, each wanting to be of some assistance to Logan and Teah, and continued down the path to the harbor.

****

Zeva and the contingent of guards reached the peak of the Spire of Ramashka and waited for the end. The end of her slavery and the end of Stone Town and everyone in it, including her family.

The captain placed several guards around Zeva and then stationed the rest on the guard's floor of the Spire hundreds of feet above the ground. The Spire's normal garrison stationed at the base of the Spire assured no one would interfere with his mission.

The structure stood solid and tall, the base the size of a palace with the vast majority of the structure a long spiral staircase that seemed to rise to the clouds. A stone said to be of similar origin and composition as the source stone, but having the ability to channel magical power into a sustained flow of energy capable of destroying anything it came in contact with, was housed at the top.

The magic the stone channeled came from magicals sent to the monks by the empress. No other punishment, save death, held more terror in the minds of the magical population. The stone drew the magic from a person, draining it permanently from their bodies. The interwoven nature of the magic with the very being of the person left nothing but a burnt out husk of a person without magic. Few survived their time in the Spire, but those who did, were incoherent people without the ability to care for their own needs any longer.

Zeva sat chained in a chair used by the monks to extract the magic when the stone called for it. The high back and head rest contained thousands of tiny holes where the stone literally sucked the magic from the person. Just sitting in it gave Zeva the creeps.

Her head began to tingle and then her mind spun as if being turned upside down. She closed her eyes and bit her lip, trying not to cry out, but a cry escaped her lips. The captain and several grey-cloaked monks turned to watch as the deep red stone on Zeva's forehead turned into a powdery residue.

They moved in closer to inspect her forehead as she sat with her eyes closed, seemingly unconscious.

Zeva's eyes flew open unexpectedly. She lifted the men with magic, floating them out the window of the Spire and dropped them the thousand feet to their death. She looked around and smiled when no one ventured up the stairs. She concentrated on removing her chains noticing too late as a fist at the end of a grey sleeve smashed into her face and everything went dark.

****

Caldora found Rachel and Galena in their chambers moments after leaving Logan and Teah in the dungeon.

"Where are they?" Galena asked.

"They headed for the source stone in the catacombs," Caldora said as she ushered them to the door, glanced out into the hallway, and then pushed them out ahead of her.

"We need to help them," Galena argued.

"Logan told us to meet him at the docks in the harbor. If we can, we need to secure a ship back to Ter Chadain and wait for them," Caldora said.

Rachel shuffled between the women looking back and forth as they argued.

"I don't take orders from that boy," Galena said.

"That boy is saving our butts, so keep moving and do what he says," Rachel said, her anger getting the best of her.

Caldora and Galena looked at Rachel with surprise, but did as she said and hurried down the hallway.

Confusion gripped the palace as guards, nobles, and magicals scurried everywhere. Caldora, Galena, and Rachel shuffled out the door, blending in with the chaos.

Most of the people headed to a town to the north of Bellatora visible along the road in the distance, but the three women made their way towards the harbor as directed.

Caldora stopped as they came around a bend in the road and the Spire of Ramashka towered over the harbor.

Galena and Rachel walked a few more steps, paused, and turned back to the woman as she stared at the Spire rising high above them, spiraling into the sky. They followed her gaze to the Spire's peak and then looked at each other, realization coming to them.

"We can't get away with that thing still working," Caldora said not taking her eyes from the structure.

"Maybe if Logan and Teah succeed in destroying the source stone, the Spire's crystal will be destroyed as well," Galena said, but her tone exposed her doubt in her theory.

"I never wanted to grow old," Rachel said with a sigh." Let's go."

Caldora and Galena shared a look of admiration for the girl's courage and followed her towards the Spire.

When they reached the base of the Spire, guards barred the entrance. The women slowed as they neared the men measuring their state of alertness.

The men appeared nervous, snapping to attention as the three women approached.

Galena began to move closer when a sharp pain in her forehead staggered her and she paused as her vision blurred and then cleared. She put a hand to her forehead and instead of feeling the soul stone, she pulled her fingers down in front of her eyes to see a red powdery substance on them.

She turned to the other women as they felt their foreheads, smiling with the pleasure of freedom finding the stones gone, replaced by a powdery residue.

A man at the front of the formation pointed at the women. "The stones, they're gone. The magicals are free," the man shouted.

As if on cue, a dozen men or more fell to the earth between them, exploding into pieces as they hit the ground ending their plummet of death from the top of the Spire.

Without warning, a hail of arrows and spears shot out towards the women. The magicals released the weaves they started forming the moment they realized the stones were gone. The men didn't stand a chance as the three deadly weaves turned them to ash.

The women moved forward and entered the base of the Spire. They paused to stare at the spiral staircase curling skywards toward the peak of the Spire and the crystal.

Men lined the stairs and showered arrows down on the women, but the arrows bounced harmlessly off the barriers of air they now wove around them. They started to climb, pausing only to dislodge a man barring their way, sending him plummeting down to his death at the base of the Spire below.

Windows dotted the stairs every ten to twenty feet and as the women neared the top of the Spire, the crystal above them ignited, shaking the Spire, and sending a solid beam of energy inland past the palace.

Rachel gaped out the window as she saw Stone Town explode and turn to ash.

"Why would they do that?" she shouted over the sounds of more men careening off the sides of the Spire as Galena and Caldora sent them to their deaths.

"The empress doesn't want any freer magicals to deal with than she has to. Stone Town is the largest single concentration of magicals in Caltoria," Caldora explained.

"And magical supporters," Galena added.

Rachel growled, pushing past the older women and unleashing a weave of energy that incinerated men ahead of them for many levels of the steps. She marched ahead, eyes consumed with rage as she stirred the dusty remains of those who opposed her last.

Galena and Caldora smiled to each other and followed Rachel up the stairs.

****

Logan, Teah, and Caslor lay against the wall as the dust and smoke cleared in the source stone chambers.

Logan held his head in his hand as the pounding seemed worse. He ran his hand against his forehead and found a fine powder residue rubbed off onto his fingers. He looked at the black substance and realized this was all that remained of the soul stone once enslaving him.

He looked at Teah as she rubbed her head and stared back at him, ecstatic to be free of her captivity to the stone.

Caslor gazed at the burnt remnants of the stone that controlled all slaves and held such wonder for him as a child and young adult, feeling a loss deep within him. The cinders smoked as did the ash remains of Sasha.

Logan crawled over to Sasha's sword lying in her ashes and placed his hands into her cremated remains. He closed his eyes and his hand began to glow white as the ash turned to vapor and lifted off the floor and then scattered into the air.

"Let your soul be free," Logan said the Betra blessing.

Sounds of guards echoed into the chamber as a group charged through the door. Logan spun on them, his hands still glowing white and sent a pulse of white magic into them, vaporizing them instantly, not even leaving ash to fall to the floor. He then collapsed to his side, unable to keep himself upright.

Teah and Caslor helped Logan to his feet pulling him along as they raced out the door leading to the catacombs, now hanging tattered on its hinges. They pulled around a corner and waited until a group of guards hurried by.

"Are you able to support yourself?" Caslor asked Logan.

Logan shrugged Teah's and Caslor's supportive hands from him and stood up straight.

"I'm fine, lead on," Logan said, "I'm tired of tunnels and catacombs."

Caslor nodded and then led them into the catacombs away from the chamber. He stopped for a rest after running for a long time, distancing them from the chamber, and turned to them.

"I know these catacombs better than anyone. I played here as a child. We need to get to the harbor and the quickest way is following these passages, they lead right to the sea." He motioned into the darkness.

"What about Galena and Rachel? We need to make sure they escape," Teah said.

"You said you trusted Caldora. She'll get them and head to the harbor," Logan said.

Teah nodded at his logic and then looked to Caslor.

"Okay," Caslor said and took off at a jog deeper into the catacombs.

****

The empress stood by the window in her throne room as servants cleaned the mess around her. None cleaning were magicals, she saw to that. She didn't want any magical being freed in such close proximity to her.

As she watched the sun touch the distant sea along the horizon, the Spire crystal ignited and sent a steady beam of light past Bellatora and into Stone Town on the far side of the hill out of sight.

She knew it reached Stone Town as smoke billowed to the sky in thick pillars filling the sunset with dark haze. The Spire went silent as suddenly as it ignited, leaving nothing but destruction and memories in its path.

The war for her survival and the life of her empire hung in the balance. No longer did the war take place on distant shores, but now erupted on her very doorstep in her cherished city of Bellatora.

She stared out at the sunset as a tear ran down her cheek." It has begun," she said to the setting sun.

****

Caslor, Teah, and Logan emerged from the catacombs under a bridge in Bellatora as the sun reflected off the sea. They stepped into the fresh air and inhaled deeply getting the musty stench of the catacombs out of their lungs.

"The others should be here looking for a ship to take us to Ter Chadain if they haven't already done so," Logan said.

"There aren't many captains who will take such a journey," Caslor said.

"As long as I'm not in a hold for the entire trip back to Ter Chadain, I don't care if I'm in a dingy," Teah said with a laugh.

They took the stairs at the side of the bridge, climbing to the top and then crossed into the harbor area of Bellatora. They descended the hill leading from the bridge when the Spire erupted sending a burst of energy, not at enemy invaders from the sea, but back inland past the palace and over a large ridge.

Teah, Logan, and Caslor stared at the beam of light in disbelief.

"It's aimed at Stone Town," Caslor said, his voice shaking with overwhelming emotion.

"Why would she do that?" Teah asked.

"She doesn't want freed magicals turning on her. Is that the largest magical city in Caltoria?" Logan said.

"Yes," Caslor said, too broken up to elaborate.

"We need to get out of here before she decides to destroy every ship to keep us here," Teah said.

They ran down the street towards the harbor below.

Chapter 50

Caldora, Galena, and Rachel stood on the top level of the Spire as the crystal blinked out.

People strapped in chairs circling the crystal lay in a state of unconsciousness as rods rose from the backs of the chairs and ran to the crystal.

"That's where the crystal gets its magic," Galena whispered with distaste.

"Aren't you the smart magical," a grey-cloaked monk said stepping out from behind one of the chairs.

He spun the chair around and Zeva sat strapped in the chair with her mouth gagged. Her eyes opened slightly as she struggled to stay conscious.

"It doesn't matter where the magic came from now that its time is over," Caldora said.

The monk raised his hand and sent a burst of energy towards the women.

Caldora and Galena dove one way and Rachel the other as the strike erupted between them.

More monks appeared and sent volleys of red energy at the women.

Galena deflected the assaults and sent shots of her own into the grey sea of monks, sending them flying in all directions.

Using Galena's attack as a distraction, Caldora ran towards the crystal, sending bolts of energy into the gem floating in the middle of a metal ring attached to the tubes leading to the magicals in the chair. Her assault struck home as the crystal shook from the force of her strikes.

The monks split in two groups, one continuing to exchange fire with Galena and another turning their attention to Caldora and stopping her.

Rachel spotted Zeva and hurried to her chair and crouched beside it, trying to free her.

A bolt hit Caldora in the side, sending her sliding across the stone floor and crashing into Zeva's chair. The woman moaned from behind her gag as Caldora struggled to get to her feet.

Rachel sent a weave into Zeva's bonds snapping the straps. Zeva slipped from the chair onto the floor where she tried to gather her senses as she pulled the gag from her mouth.

"You need to strike at the center of the crystal, build up the energy so it overloads and destroys itself. I saw how they scrambled to release the energy with that lever," Zeva said pointing to a lever on the wall.

Caldora nodded and got to her feet sending a blast of magic into the advancing monks, sending them flying.

She reached out with her magic, destroying the lever on the wall and immediately began sending her energy into the crystal.

The gem began to glow brighter and brighter, filling the room with an eerie white glow as the energy built.

Seeing Caldora filling the crystal with energy, the monks ran to release the buildup, but found the lever too damaged to operate.

With the energy building to extreme levels and nowhere for the energy to go, the crystal released energy straight down into the Spire, shaking the building as the energy discharged into the earth beneath the structure.

The violent discharge of the crystal shook everyone from their feet as the Spire swayed from side to side.

Caldora regained her feet and renewed her attack, sending all the magic she had into the crystal.

The monks retreated and regrouped on one side of the Spire while Galena joined Caldora and sent her magic into the crystal as well.

Rachel and Zeva tried to help Caldora and Galena, but monks stepped between them, forcing them to retreat.

The building shook and stone pieces fell around them as they sought to overload the crystal and destroy it.

A blast of magic shook the women from their feet. They skidded along the floor banging into the chairs surrounding the crystal, the unconscious magicals in the chairs unaware of the battle raging around them.

The women scrambled to their feet. Zeva and Rachel sent bolt after bolt of red energy towards the approaching monks.

The men scattered, taking cover behind fallen ceiling stones. Caldora and Galena renewed their effort on the crystal as it glowed so brightly, they squinted against the light.

"Take Zeva and get out of here," Caldora shouted over the hum of the vibrating crystal.

"I won't leave you," Galena said.

"I'll be right behind you once I send a last pulse to destroy it," Caldora said.

Galena turned to leave, but when she pulled her energy from the crystal and Caldora increased her power into it, the crystal dimmed and it became apparent Caldora didn't possess enough magic to destroy the crystal on her own.

Galena turned back and sent her magic into the crystal again, building the intensity of the light to blinding again.

"Get out of here, I got it," Caldora shouted.

"No, you don't," Galena shouted back." Rachel, you and Zeva, get to the harbor and tell the others to set sail."

Rachel hesitated for a moment, turned grabbing Zeva by her robe, and ran down the Spire.

A blast from the regrouped monks sent Caldora and Galena flying again. They slid along the stone floor littered with building debris and collided with the wall.

"What are we doing here?" Caldora moaned as she pushed off the floor and got to her feet. Anger raged in her eyes and she sent a massive blast into the monks, decapitating many and removing others' limbs.

"This was your idea," Galena said as she stood and drove a wall of air into a smaller group of monks by the windows, sending them plummeting to their death.

They looked around for signs of any other resistance, but the monks' assault seemed to be over.

They walked to the crystal and stared at the large, clear, gemstone.

"This will probably kill us," Caldora said.

"More than likely," Galena agreed." Do you see another way?"

"No, you?"

"No."

They stared at each other finding the situation ironic considering their history. Friends growing up in the Zele Citadel, rivals searching for positions with the nobles, adversaries in the fight for control of Ter Chadain, and now comrades working together to assure the future of Ter Chadain. They smiled.

"Strange how things work out," Galena said.

"You call this working out?" Caldora replied with a chuckle. "You ready?"

"I was born ready," Caldora said lifting her hands above her head.

Galena lifted her hands above her head, focusing all her magic. She looked to Caldora who gave a nod.

****

Rachel and Zeva raced down the path to the harbor, wondering how they would find the others as they sped past the ships in their slips. As they ran, each searched the decks with her eyes, looking for any sign of the others.

Rachel and Zeva looked back at the Spire, colliding with someone, sending bodies sprawling. Strong hands lifted Rachel and Zeva to their feet. Zeva looked up to find Logan holding her in his arms, steadying her.

Caslor held Rachel in his arms as she looked at him strangely.

"We need to set sail. . . now," Zeva said her voice panicked.

Grinwald, Raven, and Saliday ran up the dock to them.

"Did you find a ship?" Logan asked as they came up to them.

"No, we just got here," Grinwald said.

"Your ship waits," a familiar voice said from above them.

"Oh no, not that ship," Saliday said looking up at the deck.

The Morning Breeze sat in the slip beside them, Captain Morgan Task stood at the rail with his arms folded across his chest and a large smile on his face.

"Hurry, mates, we are ready to set sail," Morgan shouted.

"No, we can't trust him," Saliday said turning to Logan and the others.

"We don't have any choice," Zeva said running to the ship.

"Caldora and Galena are destroying the Spire of Ramashka."

The others looked to each other in confusion as the words sunk in. They burst into motion, running after Zeva to the ship and then up the gangplank onto the deck.

"Get below until we clear harbor," Morgan ordered and ushered them below deck." We don't need anyone spotting you and trying to stop us."

Teah looked as if she would be sick as she took the steps into the hold, but Logan held her hand as her knuckles turned white gripping his.

Saliday glared at Morgan who gave her a warm smile in spite of her dagger looks and went about his duties.

They cleared the harbor in minutes and everyone climbed back on deck as they passed the Spire of Ramashka high on the ridge overlooking the harbor. The distance between the Spire and the ship grew and still the Spire stood.

Morgan paced the deck behind the wheel manned by his first mate, Quinty, looking up at the Spire every few steps, knowing what it meant if the Spire fired upon his ship.

****

Caldora and Galena hit the crystal over and over again, dimming the glow of the crystal, but not destroying it.

They paused a moment, catching their breath from the exertion and looked at the hollowed out shells of the magicals who sat in the chairs around the crystals.

The women exchanged looks of compassion and began releasing the confused magicals.

"Go, run from the Spire," Galena shouted as the last magicals hurried down the spiral staircase.

She turned to Caldora who dropped to a knee and breathed heavily.

"Give them a minute," Galena said.

Caldora nodded." I can use a minute."

After waiting for the magicals to be clear of the Spire, they gathered themselves and walked over to the crystal again. With only a slight nod of their heads and a determined look in their eyes, they unleashed their magic into the crystal in unison, so strong and so powerful, the magic of the Mistress of Power and the once Zele Magus to the King of Ter Chadain proved too much for the crystal of the Spire of Ramashka.

The stone shone bright as the magic entered it, but then inexplicably went black.

Galena and Caldora halted their assault and slowly lowered their arms, looking to each other with confusion. The low rumbling reached their ears as the crystal surged with magic inside.

Galena stretched out her hand to Caldora as she did the same. Their fingers touched in one last act of human emotion.

The crystal erupted, sending the pent up magic out as its structure ruptured from deep inside sending shards speeding in all directions.

The energy vaporized Galena and Caldora in an instant, their hands still touching, snuffing them out of existence as they destroyed the last powerful gemstone of Caltoria.

****

A strange, low vibration rumbled from deep inside the ground under the sea where Morgan, his passengers, and crew sailed on The Morning Breeze.

They looked to the Spire as the structure shook and began to break apart high above them. The vibration shook the ship and the sea, ripples from the sound energy scattered across the surface of the water. Then everything stopped and silence filled the air.

Logan looked to Grinwald who shared a curious look with him.

A bright burst of energy, brighter than the sun, exploded from the Spire, turning it to dust in an instant and shooting into the sky for miles. Dust filtered down over them as they sailed past the destroyed bluff where the Spire once stood, now nothing more than a gaping cliff.

"They did it," Zeva cried out.

Everyone erupted in cheers.

Everyone, that is, except Teah. She stood at the rail looking out over Bellatora as the dark cloud that once was the Spire of Ramashka hovered over the city. She lost her mentor and nemesis in one catastrophic explosion. She felt somewhat alone. How could all this loss of human life be worth it? How can so much death and destruction come from her and the world around her? Her parents, Talesaur and the Queen's Guard, Lizzy, Sasha, and now Galena and Caldora, all gone trying to put her on the throne, was the cost too great?

Logan walked up behind her and slipped an arm across her shoulders.

She reached an arm around his waist and gave a squeeze.

"Time to go home," Logan said as he stared out at Bellatora.

"Where is that?" Teah said leaning her head against his side.

Ter Chadain is always home, Stalwart said.

No place like it, Falcone agreed.

A place with memories, good and bad, Galiven admitted.

Teah noted Bastion's silence. Aren't you happy to return to Ter Chadain?

Ah, yes, but seeing my homeland has stirred up many memories for me I wished stayed dormant, Bastion.

But. . . Galiven prodded and an expected silence filled Teah's mind.

There is truly no place like Ter Chadain, Bastion said and the other protectors burst into cheers and laughter.

Teah laughed and Logan turned to her with a raised eyebrow.

"The protectors are with you. . . it's time to go home," she said with a smile.

****

340

Grinwald stepped back, pausing to look at the blades on Logan's back and then an identical set on Teah's back. He moved away from the others to the rail at the bow of the ship, his face grim as the dust settled around him.

Raven followed him and then eased closer and looked to him, uncertain.

"What is it?" Grinwald asked as he noticed her hesitation.

"They have done the impossible, destroying the sacred source stone," Raven said.

"Yes, it is hard to believe that could be done," Grinwald agreed.

"Are you a believer in prophecy, Viri Magus?" Raven asked.

Grinwald turned to her as if being slapped." Yes, of course, why do you ask?"

"The prophecy says that the Protector shall destroy the world as we know it. Do any of the prophecies speak of two Protectors of Ter Chadain existing at the same time?"

"No."

"Do you think our world can survive with two?"

"I don't know."

"That is no answer," Raven said, her voice a whispered hiss.

Grinwald shook his head as his eyes filled with tears and sadness.

"Only one protector shall return to Ter Chadain."

****

This ends Book 2 of the "Protector of Ter Chadain" Series.